DR. ZASTRO'S SANITARIUM-
For The Ailments of Women

by
Ludmilla Bollow

Behler
PUBLICATIONS

Behler Publications
California

Behler Publications
California

DR. ZASTRO'S SANITARIUM – For The Ailments of Women
A Behler Publications Book

This is a work of fiction. Names, characters, places, and incidents either are the product of the author's imagination or are used fictitiously. Any resemblance to actual persons, living or dead, events, or locales is entirely coincidental.

Copyright by Ludmilla Bollow 2004
Cover design by Cathy Scott – www.mbcdesign.com

Library of Congress Cataloging-in-Publication Data is available
Control Number: 2004094870

ISBN 1-933016-01-9
Published by Behler Publications, LLC
Lake Forest, California
www.behlerpublications.com
California
Manufactured in the United States of America

Acknowledgments

There are so many who helped me along the way in my literary journey. Writing is a lone pursuit, but intertwined and nourished with gifts from so many others...

– To Dr. Rober Gard, a dear friend – to all writers, and my prime mentor in many areas.

– To all my teachers, from the nuns in grade school, and all those that followed – many, after school.

– To my Byliners writing group, who listened and critiqued this novel, chapter by chapter, word by word.

– To my family, especially my husband, who always has faith in my writing ability, and cheers me on.

– To Karen Novak, my editor at Behler, who helped so much to finalize this manuscript into an enchanced novel worthy of publication.

– And for my sustaining Faith, that begins each day and closes each night.

AUTHOR'S NOTE

It was the 1880's-- One century was ending, another dawning. Science, inventions, avalanches of social changes, were transforming the whole mode of American life.

In medicine, each new discovery was quickly converted to specialized treatments by innovative doctors in diverse institutions. Spas, sanitariums, and invalid hotels sprang up everywhere. For those who could not avail themselves of such treatments, mail order medicine and the all-encompassing medical books became the healing bibles in many homes.

One such book, MEDICAL COMMON SENSE, by Edward B. Foote, M.D., published in 1857, boasted sales of 250,000 copies and 100 letters per day. This unprecedented success resulted in the 300 page book being enlarged to 900 pages, with 200 illustrations, and republished in 1877 by Murray Hill Publishing of New York as, PLAIN HOME TALK. Esteemed reviews and glowing testimonials established Dr. Foote as a prominent and meritorious physician. His office, medical laboratories, and residence, were located at 120 Lexington Avenue, New York City.

* * * * *

Upon my first reading of PLAIN HOME TALK, I found the contents so fascinating, so bizarre; yet so believable, there was a compelling force to communicate all these once-credible doctrines into a wonderful work of fiction. My primary mission was to recreate this special time in medical history, record the stultifying attitudes toward women, while in the same process reveal the even more spectacular marvels taking place in the hearts of two dissimilar personalities.

Much of the medical background of that era, especially the essence of Dr. Zastro's lectures, is gleaned from this treasured book.

Gypsy lore and customs from that period have been culled from a variety of sources.

CHAPTER 1

Yana gazed up at the brownstone building where she would be confined the next three weeks. No bars on any windows. Good. She detested restraints of any kind. Her heart was fluttering wildly now, a lone bird gone astray, cut off from the rest of the flock. She had landed in a remote foreign field, the heart of New York City, and she was standing at the WOMEN's entrance door of Dr. Zastro's Sanitarium, hesitant to press the garish brass doorbell.

Fly away, while there is still time. Grandmama's forewarnings vibrated. Gypsy forces were tugging even stronger now, urging her to flee this ensnarling metropolis and return to the open spaces.

A sign? Somewhere there must be a good luck sign. Nothing. Only huge black letters on the signboard above her: DR. ZASTRO'S SANITARIUM. All around her streetcars clanged and carriages rumbled. It sounded like distant thunder.

A chilling spring breeze gusted, billowing her skirts, jingling her earrings and gold coin necklace. She dismissed the disturbing winds as any kind of warning message. Whatever fates had brought her here by train and by carriage from her farmland in Virginia, she had reached her destination. She was certain she was fulfilling her *drukkerebama*.

Determined to follow her path to its end, she pressed the doorbell and while waiting, once more perused the wrinkled brochure she carried in her pocket with its summoning words, the words that had first inveigled her: DR. ZASTRO'S SANITARIUM FOR THE AILMENTS OF WOMEN – MENTAL, PHYSICAL, AND SEXUAL – CURES GUARANTEED! The brochure had fluttered to the floor one day while she at the post office gathering her mail. Some impulse—she could not imagine what else to call it—compelled her to pick it up, to read the contents, and write the connecting letter. She knew it was useless to fight the fates that moved the pen, her reluctant fingers. It had always proven best to give in, follow her inner directives.

Unknown forces had seemed to be directing her from the very beginning, overpowering her inborn resistance to being dictated to by someone else, human or mystical....

She had balked at the idea of going to a male doctor, any doctor. However, there were few female physicians, even in the advanced state of civilization of the 1880's, and she had tried all the Gypsy remedies. Still, the pain kept throbbing in her right arm.

Again she cursed her horse Drom, running as if possessed, causing that injurious fall. The broken bone had healed but not correctly, making it difficult to paint in her usual swirling fashion or even hold the brush. Next month she would be going to Paris, where her Gypsy campfire painting had been accepted for a first time exhibition. She would not let herself be viewed as a painter with a malfunctioning arm or any other physical impairment, knowing she would be on display as well as her painting. She was willing to do anything, even accept treatment from this unconventional physician, in order to attain her longed-for goal—an exhibit in Paris.

Finally, the heavy oak door squeaked open and a foreign looking young man—*possibly from India?*—wearing a knee length white tunic and loose white pants, bowed in solemn greeting. "Welcome to Dr. Zastro's Sanitarium."

"I am Yana Kejako," she announced. She handed him her letter of acceptance. "I am here, at Dr. Zastro's request, for Sanitarium treatment." She picked up her valises made of thick Persian carpeting, one stuffed with artist supplies, the other bulging with personal items. New pain shot through her arm.

"This way please, Miss Yana." He pronounced the two syllables of her name as though they were separate words: *Ya. Na.* The greeter then ushered her into a large entry hall overflowing with opulent furnishings, stained glass windows, and gigantic sweeping ferns. *This was no ordinary doctor.*

A portly woman in crisp white uniform bustled in. "Good morning, Miss Kejako. Welcome to Dr. Zastro's Sanitarium." The woman moved ahead briskly. "Please follow me."

They proceeded up a winding grand staircase. Yana would never get used to climbing stairs, or buildings with floors overhead. Gypsies preferred the open skies, and when confined to buildings, almost immediately painted the ceilings of their rooms cerulean blue.

With stout arms, the woman pushed open two huge sliding doors at the top, clanging both shut behind them. "You are now in the Sanitarium area, for the treatment of female patients only." The first door on the right was posted: LECTURE ROOM—DO NOT ENTER. They entered anyway. "Please take a seat. The doctor will be in shortly."

It was a small room, with rows of white painted bentwood chairs. Windowless. Stifling. Numerous framed degrees and diplomas covered one wall; the other was obscured by a parade of white gauze screens. At the front, a polished brass lectern was centered on a stage-like platform. Yana took a chair near the door, in case she wanted to bolt early.

A few women were already seated. Immobile, except for sideways glances, coughs, clearing of throats. In the front row, a woman, about thirty, was swishing an ostrich feather fan open and closed, head bobbing back and forth as if in search of someone. Her ringlets of curls were bouncing under the fluff of a straw bonnet festooned with scarlet ribbons.

Soft crying turned everyone's attention. The foreign manservant was guiding in a beauteous young woman, who could be hardly more than seventeen. She was wearing a long white lace dress, pinched in at her narrow waist. A distinct frailness hovered about her whole person. Pale waxen complexion. Long blond hair that fell in rivulets over soft blue eyes that never looked up. She was gasping now in audible intakes of breath.

The servant said, "Please, Miss Althea, there is nothing to be frightened of in Sanitarium. This is haven. We make all things well here." Taking her hand, he guided her to a seat in the front row. The girl gave out a desperate wail and crumpled to the floor. The other women remained stoic, as if not seeing what was happening. Yana was on her feet, however, her skirts a flurry of wild colors as she rushed to the front.

"Cut her laces. Unloose her tight garments," she commanded. "Can't you see she is unable to breathe?"

"Please, patients must not interfere. Ever." The look in the man's eyes conveyed he was in charge, and only he knew what to do. Yana thought it unusual for servants to be so authoritative.

Gently, he lifted the girl from the floor, fanning her as he loosened her tight collar, unclasped the binding waistband. "Young lady will be all right. Every one calm down now."

Yana backed away, her panic easing. Why had this first small crisis caused her rage to explode so? How could she contain herself these next three weeks existing in such confinement? How could she live under what already seemed an overwhelming number of rules and regulations? It had never worked before. She was determined to make it succeed this time. Three weeks was not a life sentence. Anything for Paris.

The room quieted as if a presence had overtaken the whole enclosure. Yana looked up and there he was—Dr. Zastro! Her skin rippled. Contact was immediate; those dark, deep-set eyes, penetrated the silence, spoke a language of their own.

His walk was brisk as he approached the lectern. He wore a long white lab coat over creased, dark pants. He was a handsome man in his early forties, with a heavy black beard and thick dark eyebrows, again accentuating those commanding eyes. For one moment Yana had to close her own eyes to remove herself from his circle of power, silently chanting her *armaya* for protection against unknown forces. *Putch Develesko, trash jaul avree,* as fast as she could.

Dr. Zastro paused, looked out over the women, projecting absolute authority with his intense stare, before he began speaking.

"Good morning ladies! Welcome to Dr. Zastro's Sanitarium for the treatment of women's ailments—mental, physical, and sexual." His voice was strong and forceful, yet neither loud nor harsh. He had a soothing melodic quality conveyed in every word.

"I am Dr. Phillipe Zastro. And this—" he gestured to the servant "—is Shyam, my noble assistant. Shyam will be studying my advanced medical techniques so he can put them into practice when he returns to his native India. Shyam was Hindoo, but he converted to Christianity."

Shyam stood, bowed, smiled, and sat down again next to the young girl.

So, he wasn't a servant. Everything about this place was unorthodox.

The doctor continued, "Now, you all know the female is made up of body, brain and reproductive organs. These in turn, interact upon each other. Here, at my Sanitarium, we aspire to treat all parts of the woman."

Why did he seem to be gazing only at her? What was this instant connection?

Good omen? Bad omen?

His pervading voice made it difficult to concentrate on any of her own thoughts.

"I have always boasted, in my advertisements, my books— 'I have yet to fail to cure any woman.' How can I make this boast? Because I employ methods no other doctor has even attempted.

"I specialize in the latest scientific apparatus, many imported from Europe. I am in continual contact with the government patent office and the very best of our inventors. In addition, I have conceived numerous inventions of my own. I have pioneered in the use of therapeutic electricity in curing ills of the female body.

"Electricity—electromagnetic currents control every function in our body, and once these currents are understood, all ills can be cured"

Had she read the brochure too fast, skipping over these strange methods of treatment?

"I studied magnetic healing and Mesmerism in Paris with the renowned Dr. Franklin DuCharme. You ladies shall benefit from this new painless healing technique, which only a few are qualified to employ, but when used properly could revolutionize the medical profession.

"Now, I know some of you have been to other practitioners, and numerous cures are being advertised today. Many claims by nefarious physicians. Let me assure each and every one of you—I do not do bloodletting. I do not purge with enemas, mercury enemetics. Nor do I put leeches in the uterus, to eat out the cancerous material. Many have been known to work their way up inside and continue to live within the woman's private regions."

Women were squirming in their chairs. Yana had never heard such frank talk before either, but she was not uneasy, only piqued further.

"I do not remove the clitoris for nymphomania, nor do I cauterize your vagina with a white-hot iron. None of you will leave here with mutilated sexual organs, your insides eaten up by poisons. No, you will go back to the outside world energized. New and wonderful electrical currents flowing throughout your bodies. All I ask is that you trust me, implicitly."

He gave them another long penetrating stare and then continued. "Since I use currents of electricity for my cures, I want nothing to impede these wonderful forces. So, the first thing I am going to ask you ladies to do—to affirm your complete trust in me—is to remove your clothing."

A noticeable nervous movement rippled among the six separated women. Suppressed utterances. Yana sprang from her chair, preparing to leave and then, as if commanded by his galvanizing eyes, sat back down.

"Now, now ladies, we don't want disease carrying garments entering our sterilized areas of the Sanitarium.

"I also want you to get rid of those tight corsets with metal stays that interfere with the flow of magnetic currents. Those layers of petticoats that trap stale dead air next to your gummed up pores.

"God made each and every one of you a lovely human being. Why are you so ashamed of your bodies? Why cover them up so? Shyam has a special robe for each of you." He motioned and Shyam went behind a curtained screen and came out with a pile of folded robes, placing them on the lectern. As if a magician flourishing silk scarves, Dr. Zastro held up one of the garments. The shimmering colors attracted both Yana's artistic and Gypsy spirit, luring her back into this strange sideshow.

"These are scientifically designed robes, made in my own workrooms. Metal threads run through them, to help conduct the electrical currents. This first week—hollyhock rose for the married women; peony pink for the virgin maidens."

What about those who were neither? Yana raised her hand.

"There will be no questions today." Dr. Zastro dismissed her intrusion. "You will each be given a set of printed rules. For those of you who cannot read, they will be read aloud each morning at breakfast.

"You will be issued a white chemise to wear under the robe. You are not to wear any other undergarments. Each Monday, for the three weeks you are here, Shyam will issue a fresh new color, as you progress in your healing. The garments you are now wearing will be washed in a special chemical acid to clear out any disease. Then, they are run through my patented electro-charging machine. This clothing, and anything else you brought with you, will be returned when you leave—all of it sanitized."

Her paints and brushes! She had to make sure they were not taken away, recharged, sanitized—altered in any manner. Paints reacted in peculiar ways.

"You will eat together, but sleep in separate soundproof rooms. Your private room does have a window, but for health reasons, they cannot be opened.

"Your beds, all facing north for polarity, are made of special alloy metals, and recharged once a week. White lambs' wool coverlets and linen bedding also help conduct the electro-atoms."

She slept on a pallet on the floor, or eiderdown quilts under the open sky. Recharged beds? Electro-atoms?

"All food is electrically charged also. So, all the while you are here, electrical forces will be working within and without, and your ailments will shrivel and vanish. And you may even forget you ever had them."

He paused and then in a more commanding voice, "Ladies, I want you to begin to remove your garments. Now." There was no movement, as if a new fear had immobilized each of them. "There is no shame in this Sanitarium, not for the beautiful body God has given you." His chiding was kindly.

Some of the women stood and began unbuttoning their outer coverings. The pale young woman just stood there, stiff and unmoving.

"And remember ladies, those of you who did not follow the instructions listed in my final letter, hair clips, jewelry—all must be removed. They will be safely stored and returned when you leave."

Remove her gold coin necklace? It was her Mama's, and her Mama's before. It was never removed, not until death.

"However, since most of you still retain the maidenly virtue of modesty, thank heavens women still do," the doctor continued, "when you get down to your undergarments, you may step behind one of the screens for final disrobing. Shyam will check you off, and make certain all garments and adornments are removed. Some ladies have been known to cheat. I myself will not begin your personal examination until tomorrow."

He began reading from a list. "As I call your names, please come forward to receive your robes." He held up a hollyhock rose garment, announcing, "Edwina Weber. Married."

A middle-aged woman in the high style of the day, purple velvet suit with gathered bustle, huge hat with magenta bird wings, walked forward, her posture stiff.

"Behind the curtain, Mrs. Weber. And try to remember, wearing animal items on your person can only bring animal diseases into our lives." She took off the bird hat as if on command, hiding it behind her back.

"Mavis Michalek. Maiden."

A guttural groan was heard as a large framed girl, in her mid-twenties, stood awkwardly, eyes darting suspicious nervous glances. Head bent, mouth scrunched, she scuffled forward. Her greasy brown hair was pulled back in an untidy knot. She wore a wrinkled homespun brown dress, a dirty, fringed plaid cape, and she carried a country basket covered with a raggedy cloth.

"Delphine Applewood. Married."

The bouncing curls sprang forward, as the already partially undressed woman began speaking in a rapid southern drawl.

"I am so glad, Dr. Zastro, you helped me get rid of those tight corsets, and—"

"Please, Mrs. Applewood remember the rules." He spoke to her as if to a disobedient child, trying to suppress whatever it was bubbling from her.

"Heavens, I forgot every one of them. But never you." She giggled as she flounced past him to slip behind the screen.

"Isobelle Schmidt. Maiden." A heavyset woman in her mid-forties, eyes downcast, graying hair wound in a tangled pug atop her head, lumbered up to the front. She never looked away from the floor and had not so much as removed the heavy blue shawl that covered her coarse gray dress.

"Yana Kejako. Maiden."

How dare he assume—Yana picked up her traveling bags, tossing her head as she passed by the doctor. Before he had a chance to call the next name, she retorted, "I am *not* married, but neither am I a maiden virgin. Will that mix up any of your healing colors?"

"Later, please, speak to me later about any of your concerns." He went on to the next name, "Althea Willoughby. Maiden." Althea didn't move.

"Come ladies, throw all your disease-laden clothing and other items into your wicker basket with your name on it, and place your traveling bags next to it. When you leave here, healthy women, you can wear everything once more with pride and good health. And, let's hope a few less burdensome undergarments."

It was true—about the awful restricting clothing women wore as fashion. Yana herself still preferred the freeing movement of Gypsy attire, even though it had been years since she had lived with her people. At home, she wore as little as possible, but for travel, she donned the comfortable traditional Gypsy dress.

The doctor repeated, in a louder voice, "Althea Willoughby. Maiden."

Althea continued standing, wavering as if in a trance.

"Please come forward, Miss Willoughby." He moved off the platform toward her, speaking gently, "I must ask you to remove your garments. It is for your own—"

There was a slight scream and Althea wilted in a slow faint the moment the doctor touched her. Dr. Zastro called for Shyam as he began unbuttoning the lace dress on the lifeless form.

Yana continued undressing behind the screen, not as concerned this time about what was happening to Althea, only what was happening to herself, anxious to get her garments off, assume whatever new role these magnetized gowns might impart. Her body felt unusually warm as she ran her hands over the smooth bareness and then stopped, clutching at the gold necklace she was determined not to remove. Earrings, rings, bracelets—even the lucky charm sewn into the hem of her skirt had been removed, but never the necklace.

Where was Shyam? She was ready to be checked off. More than ready. Restless, she poked her head out from behind the screen, calling out, "Does anyone wish to check me off, see that I am completely naked?"

"One moment, just one moment, please," Dr. Zastro seemed preoccupied as Yana saw him picking up Althea and settling the limp form in Shyam's arms. "Disrobe her and put her in the Rocking Machine. Begin it at low and stay with her. I will be with you after I complete duties here." Shyam cradled the body in his arms and left the room.

After what she felt was a proper interval, Yana again called out, "I'm waiting doctor, for someone to look at me." She had been told, by other men, how impatience flashed gold into her brown eyes. This was not mere impatience; her heart was pounding as she stood awaiting approval from this man who was going to command her life for the next three weeks.

Dr. Zastro walked over, evidently still disturbed about Althea. He gave a quick look behind the screen, and for one moment he was transfixed, as if seeing a vision and then just as quickly regained his composure, his doctorly air. "Yes, yes, you are disrobed," turning his gaze away and then looking back once more. "No, no you are not entirely naked. Your gold necklace, it must be removed."

He did not continue to gaze. She wanted him to. Her artist's instincts told her that her body was beautiful, her curves well formed. Male art colleagues had wanted to paint her figure many times, but she never wanted herself captured, in any form. She called after the disappearing doctor, "My necklace is my family inheritance. It is bad luck to remove it."

He returned, looking only at her eyes. "Either you will remove the necklace, or you will be dismissed. I cannot treat anyone who fights any portion of my treatment, or any of my rules." Before she had time to protest, he was already walking toward another screen.

"Next? Who is to be checked out next?"

She had a choice. Leave now, with the necklace, or make the decisive commitment. Dilemma. Well, hadn't she already committed when she penned the initial letter? So, it was already written. She must follow what the fates had already begun. Reluctantly Yana lifted the heavy chain of gold coins over her head, hair strands catching, as if not wanting to let go. Once her heirloom was removed, she felt more naked than ever before. Again, she repeated her chant for protection, *Putch Develcko trash jaul avree.*

She slid on the soft chemise and then the silky peony-pink robe. *Was there really magnetism in these robes? Could it alter things deep within her, things she might not even know about herself?* Electricity was a different kind of magic. She didn't believe in any of it. It made no sense at all. Still, electric lights worked, somehow.

She had come for a cure. That was all. She did not want anything about herself changed. She was in complete charge of her life and wasn't about to allow any one, or any electrical currents, disturb what she had worked so many years to achieve. Not unless there were forces at work here over which she had no control.

She plucked her lucky charm from the hem of her discarded skirt—a fossilized stone with the markings of a human face—and put it into the large cloth purse she tied around her waist, under the chemise. In swift movements, she retrieved paints, brushes and small pieces of canvas, stuffing them also into the bag. The flowing robe would conceal all these needed items. Traveling Gypsies were experienced in secreting objects on their person—sometimes even whole chickens, to keep private items from prying eyes.

Marching out boldly from behind the screen, Yana put her belongings in the wicker basket with her name on it and placed her traveling bags nearby. She strode past Dr. Zastro; she was aware that he had turned to watch, knowing his gaze followed as she passed.

"The necklace is removed, doctor," she said. "I have decided to abide by your rules." She was certain there was a look of relief on his face, and yet it was hard to discern. He seemed to be a man who had many years of practice in taking charge of his life, the same as Yana. They may have taken diverse roadways only to have the wheel of fortune spin, bringing them together, here, now, in this strange sequestered place.

CHAPTER 2

Dr. Zastro retreated to his private office and sat in silence for a moment, fingertips pressing against his throbbing temples. The first day was always arduous, but today seemed especially distressing. The soft gleam on the rosewood paneling beneath the warm incandescent lights made for a comforting refuge for him. It was also calming for the ladies when they came for consultation.

This office, along with the Lecture Room and the Treatment Room, were the only areas wired for electricity. The other Sanitarium sections were lit only by candles. He disapproved the use of oil lamps, deeming the released fumes unhealthy in enclosed areas. He clasped his hands behind his neck and relaxed his whole body into the soft leather-tufted chair behind the mahogany desk that had once belonged to his father.

He was now ready to begin concentrating on the ladies' backgrounds while they received orientation from his well-trained staff. The ladies were being instructed, then would be settled into their individual rooms, six similar rooms that lined one side of the hallway. Each room had a different flower design painted on their door, a concession for those who could not read.

He retrieved the leather-bound portfolio from the center desk drawer: HISTORIES—SANITARIUM PATIENTS—MAY 1884. Inside were folders for each, with application letters, primary notations, and possible future treatment. From this day forward, precise histories for each female patient would be noted, later researched, with final summations published in recognized journals, referring to each by case number.

Every year he tried to pick six diverse women with a variety of ills. He was determined to find the right cure for each. So far, he had met with great success. His downstairs office was piled high with newspaper clippings, publications, and testimonial letters, all confirming his numerous achievements.

Flipping through the file folders, he paused at ALTHEA WILLOUGHBY—the frail young girl who had needed immediate treatment following her fainting spell. Shyam had put her in the Rocking Machine, a circular wire cage that rocked patients back and forth, soothing them as though they were babes lying in a cradle. The cage was electrically wired so the rocking was constant and no one had to wind it up, or push it mechanically. It never failed to calm any patient.

Many of his newer machines were wired for electricity. Some plugged into the household circuit, others were attached to galvanic batteries. Electricity—what a magnificent and wonderful discovery. And he, Phillipe Zastro, was one of the foremost innovators in using it as a method for curing.

He guarded his inventions and kept the original patents locked in the downstairs safe. Yet, he never hesitated to publicize in his books and papers how the cures were processed, always wanting to share his knowledge, if not his inventions, but only because they needed trained experts to administer them.

Shyam was instructed to leave Althea in the Rocking Machine for one half hour and then bring her in for her initial consultation. As a rule, he would wait until Tuesday to begin consultations, after the women had calmed down some and adjusted to their surroundings. However, it was evident Althea needed treatment, and possibly medication, as soon as possible.

While waiting for her, he was trying to concentrate on the other women in his folders. Shyam's folder was separate.

SHYAM: Dr. Zastro already had some doubts about the young assistant's abilities, but Shyam had seemed the most intelligent of those he had interviewed during his travels to India, and that impoverished country certainly needed more medical knowledge channeled back into its provinces. Shyam still had trouble with the English language, and even though a professed Christian, the doctor suspected he might still retain some of his old Hindoo customs. Well, he would just have to keep a closer watch on this assistant than he had on the previous ones.

Get on with the files, he reminded himself.

ISOBELLE SCHMIDT: A poor immigrant woman he was having work part time in the Sanitarium kitchen to help pay her way. A back problem; he was sure he could cure her.

DELPHINE APPLEWOOD: Why had he allowed her to return? Maybe he thought that this time he could cure her special type of nymphomania. He reread the notations from Dr. Hooper that he kept in Delphine's folder. Hooper described nymphomania as "a species of madness, or a high degree of hysterics. It's presence known by the wanton behavior of the patient; she speaks and acts with unrestrained obscenity, and as the disorder increases, she scolds, cries and laughs by turns."

References from other medical experts attributed the disease to "local irritability of the procreative organs—too much nervous or electrical stimulus present in those organs—plus an inharmonious distribution of the nervous forces among the organs of the brain."

Dr. Zastro himself thought females laboring under nymphomania deserved sympathy rather than the condemnation of society. When the blood is diseased and nymphomania exists, inflammation, irritation, and sometimes ulcerations, located about the pudenda, vagina, and uterus, rendered the parts sore and extremely tender.

He had placed in the file a letter from another patient, a respected married woman afflicted with this malady. Her desire for coition was incessant. In detailing her symptoms, her letter stated, "In describing myself, I cannot think of any better way of expressing my affliction than to say it feels good to be hurt."

Yes, he was still experimenting with cures for nymphomania, administering electricity calculated to equalize the nervous circulation and draw off the excess from the organ of amativeness and the sexual parts. In complications growing out of blood impurities, he combined both electrical and blood-purifying remedies.

His theory of this disease was original, as was his mode of treatment, but success in its management convinced him that both were correct. Sometimes he believed Delphine did not want to be cured. Was it useless to keep trying? Her masturbation and amorous dreams were only another extension of nymphomania. Nevertheless, he had found previously, that when one was cured, it followed the other was also. Some women had these amorous dreams once a month. Others every

night, and this frequency was frightful. Once a week would be
sufficient to overcome and debilitate the strongest constitution in
a few years. Surely, he had to cure Delphine before it would be
too late.

For most nymphomania cures, he found electrical
applications ever efficient.

And for those at a distance, it was his practice to send by
post "electrical medication," medicines prepared in such a way
that they possessed *latent* electrical properties, which were
rendered active by coming in contact with the gastric fluids of
the stomach.

In many cases, electrical medication by mail proved far
more beneficial than personal applications of electricity,
especially if administered by inexperienced operators.
Removing the clitoris and devices that strapped the hands at
night and sometimes day, common practices by many
physicians, were not procedures he believed in for alleviating
nymphomania.

He was dedicated to curing Delphine, no matter how much
she sometimes disrupted his Sanitarium routines. There were so
few who admitted to their nymphomania in the same honest
manner as she did.

EDWINA WEBER: He always tried to accept one woman
who was in her changes, a fascinating period for study of the
female. Very easy remedies. Eight children—surely, her body
needed a rest. The husband, a prominent lawyer, had made all
the arrangements for her stay. No problems that he could
foresee.

MAVIS MICHALEK: This one was a puzzle. Her mother's
crude letter was so difficult to decipher. Mavis herself appeared
withdrawn, backward, from a very ignorant background. There
might be difficulty in dealing with her, making her understand
what would be taking place here.

That was when his mesmerism became such a wonderful
tool, relaxing his patients, so they were not afraid of revealing
anything to him. Still, he must not rely on it too much, only for
the opening session, and then, only if needed.

The last file—YANA KEJAKO—what an enigma right from the beginning. Her application letter was filled with artistic drawings and strange symbols. Yes, that Gypsy heritage might also present obstacles. Then too, she was educated, which caused numerous problems in women. He wanted to study more educated females, to find out if overuse of the brain really did cause them physical harm, debilitate them in certain ways.

For awhile, there in the Lecture Room, he had been afraid she was going to leave rather than remove her ancient coin necklace. The expression in her eyes; he'd never seen such blazing anger. Well, he had to establish right at the beginning that he was in charge.

Her naked body—again it flashed through his mind. Surely, he had seen his share of naked women so that none should be more memorable than the next. What was so impressive about hers? Had he been taken off guard by the bold way she had displayed it?

He got up and walked about his office. How he wished he might open a window right now, if only for a change of circulation. It was his decision that windows in the Sanitarium area be constructed so they could not be opened. He desired only purified, filtered air circulating here. The air was scientifically processed elsewhere and then sent by special fans through vent ducts.

He had designed this Sanitarium addition to be as sequestered as possible from the bad air and ill effects of the outside world. True, he might have preferred locating in a healthier area, such as the pristine mountain regions, where sunshine and unadulterated fresh air were so abundant, but practicality precluded this.

He needed this New York address, East 28th and Lexington Avenue. It was accessible for most of his patients, New York being a great center of transportation. He also had numerous daily patients, but during these three weeks, his regular appointment book was closed, and his secretary took care of answering any urgent letters. This was treasured time to devote to the ladies only.

Eagerness for knowledge had been part of his make-up since childhood. He could never get enough, as if his head were an endless vessel in which to pour all the known information in the world, distill it, siphon it all, and come up with his own alchemy of answers. It was an exciting way to live.

Shyam knocked, opened the door and led Althea to the high-backed patient's chair covered in soft lambs' wool. "Miss Althea to consult with you, honorable doctor."

"Thank you, Shyam. You may leave now."

"Miss Althea—she may need further assistance?"

"I will ring the bell if I need you." He pointed to the gold cord that rang a bell in the hall. He used this to signal what was needed by the number of rings.

Shyam left with hesitancy and Dr. Zastro focused his attention on the trembling form huddled in the patient chair, clutching her pink robe with slender white fingers. She was like a frightened fawn, waiting for the arrow to pierce her heart, almost welcoming it.

"Miss Willoughby, you are not feeling faint again, are you?"

"I—I don't know." Her voice was soft, inward.

"And, if I touch you?"

"Don't. Please don't." Panic ripped at her whisper.

"It's all right. No one will harm you here," he smiled, trying to reassure her. "Because of your—condition, I decided to see you this afternoon, so correct treatment can begin immediately. It is evident you have a nervous ailment, that was why we put in the Rocking Machine this morning. Did the machine soothe you?"

There was no answer. He tried again, insistent. "Did it?"

"I don't know—I fainted."

"Well, let's see if we can find out what causes these fainting spells. First of all, we'll put you on the lounge, in a reclining position, and then, if you feel faint you'll be lying down already."

She was trembling. "No. Don't come near. Let me sit."

"All right. For the time being."

He consulted his notepad. "Now then, your name is Althea Willoughby.   Guardian, Arthur Willoughby.   And you have fainting spells. Do you know what brings them on?"

"No. I've always had them."

"With what frequency?"

"Since marriage. Very frequently."

"Marriage? You have down on the initial questionnaire— 'Virgin'. Has the marriage been consummated?"

"I don't know what you mean."

"Has your husband penetrated you?"

"With what, doctor?"

"How old are you?"

"Seventeen."

She was but a child. "And married for how long?"

"Six months."

"Did your mother instruct you? Give you sexual information before marriage?"

"I—have no mother."

"Someone raised you—"

"My Auntie—Ursula. My mother's sister."

"I see. Well, perhaps we need to begin with illustrations." He went to the wall before her and pulled down one of his instructional charts. "Now, here is the physiology of a woman." He pulled down the other. "And here is that of a man."

"I can't look. I feel faint." She grasped the arms of the chair tighter.

Dr. Zastro pulled both shades back up and began lighting the large white beeswax candle on his desk. "I think we need to relax you.   I am going to put you in a state of complete relaxation. Then you will be able to answer all questions freely. You want to be helped, don't you?"

"Yes."

"Your husband wishes you helped?"

"Yes."

"Now then, I'm going to put you in a deep sleep. When you awake you will remember nothing." He reached out for her hand as she withdrew hers in a cry of fright.

"Do not be afraid of me. I'm here to help you."

"I—I—can't have a man touch me."

"Not even your husband?"

"No." Her voice was a faint whisper.

"Steady now." Then in a stronger voice. "You are not going to faint. Hang onto those padded arms of the chair. Breathe deeply and slowly...listen to my voice. Watch the candle's flame. Keep watching."

He passed his hands in front of her face as he continued speaking. "You are getting sleepy.... Sleepier.... Keep your eyes on the candle. You will not faint.... You will only sleep.... You are completely relaxed now."

Within a few minutes, he raised her limp arm. Her face was at peace.

"All fear is gone.... All pain is gone.... Do you hear me, Althea?"

Her eyes were still open, but fixed. Her voice was a steady monotone. "Yes."

"Now then, Althea, tell me about yourself. Take your time.... Begin back when you were a child."

A little girl quality seemed to take over. It was as if she was reliving and seeing at the same time. "Yes. I am a child. I am playing in the tiny room next to the parlor. The minister is visiting Auntie Ursula. I hear them speak my name. I listen at the closed doors—" She stopped.

He gave her a moment to compose herself and then prodded, "Go on. What do you hear?"

"Auntie Ursula, she's telling the minister—" There was a new voice, slow and deliberate. "Althea must never marry, never have children. The blood of her father would make her offspring insane. The blood of her mother would make her—" Her voice went back to Althea. "I couldn't hear the rest."

"Your mother. Tell me about her."

"I never knew Mama."

"Didn't your aunt speak of her?"

"Only to the minister, what a sinful woman she was. Yes—I remember now." Her voice became her aunt's again. "Althea's mother was a harlot! Her father an imbecile! Now you know why she can't have children."

"What happened to your mother?"

"I—don't know. She died."

Why had the aunt not mentioned any of this in her letter?

"Where? How?"

"In jail. Auntie Ursula is telling the minister—" Ursula's voice returned. "The town imbecile, he kidnapped her mother from that whore place—took her to an old granary to live with him. He chained her up. Did all kinds of terrible things to her. You could hear her screams across the river at night.

"No one in town would help her. Not a woman of that kind. When she found out she was carrying his child, she killed him— with a hammer. Then she tried to kill herself, by jumping in the river. They pulled her out and put her in jail—for murder." Althea's voice returned. "I was born in Mama's cell. She died....in jail....in childbirth." She began sobbing softly.

"Do not be sad. That part of your life is over. You needn't ever remember it again." He clapped his hands, telling her to awake and rest. After a reasonable interval, he once more put her into deep sleep.

"Do you remember Althea, when you first became aware that you were afraid of a man's touch? Take your time."

"Yes. It was my twelfth birthday. I have a new white lace dress on. Blood is coming out from between my legs. I faint. When I wake up, I'm in Auntie Ursula's room. She's talking to me. 'You are a woman now. And you must never let a boy touch you. Anywhere!' She—she tells me what boys do to girls. I'm frightened. I faint again...."

"What about, when you went to school?"

"I never went. I was too sickly. Auntie taught me. Kept the boys away from me.... If one even looked at me, I swooned. If they came too near, I fainted."

"Your husband—how did you meet him?"

"Arthur? He was a friend of Auntie's, an older man. He visited. I always left the room. One day—I was listening at the door. He told Auntie he loved me, wanted to marry me. I was his angel.

"Auntie said I couldn't ever marry. Could never have children. My system was too delicate. Arthur, he said—he could not have children either. Auntie said there was no way a man could prove that. Even if he swore on the Bible that he would not touch me—he still might be tempted someday.

"Arthur said he could prove he couldn't have children, because during the Civil War he was shot. Part of his body was missing. Auntie still did not believe him. 'I'll prove it to you,' he said, 'Look.' Auntie screamed, and I think she fainted."

"Have you ever seen the wound?"

"No. Arthur always wears a white bandage down there."

"Does he come near you at all?"

"Once a week. On Saturday night—" She stopped.

"Keep going. What happens then?"

"Arthur puts on—he puts on—" Althea was in great distress.

"It's all right," he soothed with his voice. "Just relax deeper and describe to me exactly what happens."

"Arthur puts on his white silk nightshirt. Then his white silk gloves—so his bare hands won't touch me. It is when his bare hands touch me that I faint. Then, he undresses me, slowly and carefully."

"What are you doing?"

"Standing there, with my eyes closed. He slips a white silk nightgown—he had made for me for our wedding—over my head. He lifts me onto the high, carved bed and spreads my gown out over the white silk sheets, arranges my hair over the silk pillow...."

"Then what?"

"He stands there and looks at me, saying over and over, how beautiful I am. Like an angel. His angel, Althea. He sits beside me and begins brushing my hair. He asks if he can kiss me— No, I say. I am too frightened, especially when he is so very near. He brushes harder and faster.

"Then he asks if he can kiss my feet. I let him, but I do not look. I can feel his wet mouth and I shiver all over. Arthur says I must be cold, and he's going to lie down beside me, to keep me warm."

"Continue—"

"He lies on the bed—not touching me and begins taking off his gloves, finger by finger. Then—then, he reaches out for me. I begin to tremble. My head starts spinning—and I faint. When I wake up—" She stopped again.

"Yes, what happens?"

"I—I have a cool cloth on my forehead.... My gown is all crumpled, and—I am always wet between my legs.... Arthur says it's the fright pouring out of me. People perspire. That is where I perspire most...."

"Anything else?"

"One time—one time, I woke up—and Arthur, he was licking at me—between my legs. Like a dog, he was licking at me—and rubbing his bandage with his other hand.... I screamed out. He jumped away.... I didn't know if I was dreaming or not. I didn't say anything...."

"Did it happen again?"

"A few other times. I could feel him there—his rough tongue licking at me. I wouldn't open my eyes to look. I'd be too weak, from fainting, to push him away— So, I'd lay there, not moving—and let him lick. My heart would pound. My head feel hot—then sometimes, I'd have spasms between my legs and I'd cry out and faint again."

She began breathing in short gasps as she continued. "I—I don't know what causes them—these spasms between my legs. I keep thinking I inherited some disease from Mama.... I don't know what to do when they happen. They shoot way up inside my body—and—and—" she screamed, "Ohhhh—It's happening—now—" There were rhythmic short gasps and then a long orgasmic sigh.

Dr. Zastro spoke up quickly, "Enough. I am going to wake you, Althea. We've learned enough for today. I will clap my hands, you will wake up and remember nothing you have told me."

He clapped his hands. "Wake up, Althea."

Althea stirred, blinking her eyes. "I—fell asleep."

"Yes. You had a deep relaxed sleep."

"I'm—I'm all perspired. There's perspiration running down between my legs." There was a frightened look as she put her pale hands over her eyes as if to shield herself from some surrounding horror.

"It's all right, Althea. A normal occurrence in women. We're going to help you, Althea. Help you so a man can touch you and you won't faint. Science can help women now. We know what causes certain reactions in their body."

He pulled the cord two times. Shyam appeared at the door.

"Please accompany Mrs. Willoughby to her room."

"Come, Miss Althea," Shyam extended his slender brown hand. Althea looked up and saw him. "Don't—touch me." She let out a slight scream and fainted right into Shyam's arms.

"Take her to her room. Stay with her. Have her breathe vapors."

Shyam lifted the limp body and proceeded toward the open door.

"And Shyam, any time you touch Althea from now on, I want you to wear a pair of white silk gloves." He took the silk scarf off a small side table, "Right now you may use this."

"Yes doctor," Shyam covered his hand with the silk scarf and exited with the lifeless doll.

Dr. Zastro rubbed his temples in a circular motion as he always did after mesmerism sessions to recharge his fatigued intellect. There was always an answer. A different way to treat each patient. He was grateful for his vast medical background, his intuitive healing powers, and his research into new curing methods. Althea could benefit from all of them. An unusual case, but not incurable.

He blew out the candle. This was enough consulting for the first day. He checked his desk calendar. Tomorrow, Tuesday, his first patient would be Yana Kejako. He must make sure to get a good night's rest.

CHAPTER 3

Yana found it difficult to sleep in beds. That night she tossed and turned until deciding to take the thin mattress and lambs' wool coverlet to make herself a pallet on the floor. At her country home in the hills of Virginia, she usually slept on the floor, windows wide open. Sometimes she slept outside on the ground, as traveling Gypsies did, between thick eiderdown feather comforters, her body floating on soft downy night clouds.

The tiny blue-tinted window that she couldn't even see through, it would not open no matter how hard she pushed and banged. Right now she was ready to smash the glass to let the outside fresh air rush in, pulse through her. Only then would she be able to liberate these troubling thoughts, let them spiral freely into the night sky, release them from circling in her head without any means of escape.

Eventually she did fall asleep, only to be awakened by a dream—or was it a dream—an old woman standing by her side. Grandmama—all withered and bony, repeating in that rasping voice of hers, *"Come with me. Come, do not stay here."*

Yana shook her head awake, grabbing for her gold coin necklace as she did every morning. It was not there. Brief panic, desperate searching all around the bedding as she whispered the words of her protection chant. Then she remembered—the scene in the Lecture Room when she had taken it off. Almost in the same instant as remembering, Dr. Zastro's vaporous presence loomed into the room, intruding into her one private refuge free from overseeing eyes. She banished him with thoughts of former lovers.

Now she was even more restless. What had Grandmama been trying to tell her? *Puridaia,* Grandmama, was known to every one, Gypsies and outsiders, as the wise one. The tribe always consulted her about the unknown, the future. Even though she was long dead, Yana still spoke to her, consulted with her. Or she came unbidden, especially in times of duress.

It was frustrating to lie there, knowing that somewhere outside, high in the midnight sky the bright moon was shining.

A faint light seeped through the tinted panes, casting a glow in that area, a glow that beckoned her to leave the room. That was not possible.

Only one solution. Yana rose, lit a candle, pulled her artist's supplies out from under the bed and hastily proceeded to paint a golden crescent moon at the top corner of the window, plus a few hazy gray clouds. Over it all, she splattered golden pinpoints of bright distant stars, aware that her arm still pained as she painted.

There, now she could lay on her pallet and gaze upward into an illusionary sky. It helped. Even in the dimness of the narrow room she could more easily perceive connections to another atmosphere, pass through these restrictive walls on the wings of her imagination. She fell into a deeper sleep than the first.

This time Mama came to her. Mama was dressed in rags, wandering the halls of the mansion, wailing. Suddenly—loud thunder, flashes of lightning, everything shook. Mama cried out, but Yana could not remember Mama's urgent words to her. The sound of a bell was breaking her out of her slumber.

Shyam was going up and down the hall, ringing a small hand bell and knocking on doors. "Six thirty, ladies. Breakfast is at seven. Please be prompt."

At home, first thing she did upon rising was to plunge herself into the cooling river. Then, in simple attire, barefoot and bareback, she would ride Drom to wherever the spirit took her. On returning home, she would prepare a hearty breakfast. The rest of the morning was spent painting. Sometimes she would be so engrossed in the work that she painted straight through until dinner.

Well, she wasn't riding horses these days and was unsure how much painting she could sneak in while confined here. She might also have to find another place to hide her art supplies. They were told they had to clean their own rooms, except for Monday mornings, when staff would come in to do general cleaning, polarize the beds, and all the other strange rituals that needed to be performed for health reasons.

The air vent. It was huge, high up, and probably never searched. She could store things there. The covering grill unlatched easily, swinging down, and she stuffed in all she could. *There!* Her art supplies were secured.

She also had to figure out some way to retrieve her necklace and other necessary personal items. Her *dukkering lil*—prophecy book—it was almost like part of her thinking, a friend she consulted daily. How would she endure three weeks without it?

Yana was the last one into the dining room, taking the remaining chair at the long single table. Everyone looked so different this morning, mostly because of their similar gowns and new hairdos. They had all been instructed to wear their long hair only in braids, and were shown how to weave gold and silver metallic ribbons into the hair strands. They could wear the braid loose or wound in a coil atop their head. Yana's braid was loose and felt as if a whip were striking her across her back as she walked.

They all had been helped in the dressing room by white clad assistants, plus given special instructions for bathing—their monthlies. Rules. Rules. Rules.

Yana looked around the table. She could see Althea's face now that her hair was pulled back into feathery braids, but her eyes were still downcast. She seemed to be forcing herself to eat. Edwina sat with hands folded in prayer, her lips moving in a monotone mumble before touching her food. Isobelle was already eating everything before her, pouring herself more milk, taking extra slices of the thick heavy bread that was piled on a platter in the center of the table.

Delphine was seated on one side of Yana and Mavis on the other. Delphine moved her chair a few inches away as soon as Yana sat down. She gave Yana a disdainful look, and tried to shake her curls that were no longer there. Mavis had started to lift the silver-rimmed bowl of gruel to her lips when Yana interrupted, pointing to a metal spoon. She demonstrated for her how to unfold her napkin and place it across her lap.

With her hair pulled back and face cleaned up, Mavis had many pretty features. Yana perceived power in her eyes, power that had never been used. They were both possibly close in age, but that seemed the only commonality, except for being female.

Breakfast was unappetizing with its strange gruel, a coarse bread, and pitchers of warm milk. They had been told that mealtime was for concentrating on food and digestion; recreation hour for conversing. There was silence among them, yet Yana detected a distinct awareness of each other as eyes moved back and forth in quick glances.

Shyam entered, greeted them, and then stood at the head of the table and read the basic rules once more. He followed this with a chapter from one of Dr. Zastro's books, which he said he would do each morning at breakfast time. "To acquaint you ladies with the doctor's renowned work."

"Dr. Zastro will not give his morning lecture today, in order to give you ladies time to familiarize yourselves with your new surroundings. The Sanitarium floor is yours to roam as you wish, but adhering to rules. The outdoor Roof Garden and Treatment Room will be used only during posted, scheduled times. No one is allowed in the Treatment Room without an assistant. Also, Dr. Zastro's Consultation Room is strictly by appointment only."

The words seemed endless. Yana's thoughts were rushing ahead to the consultation she would be having with Dr. Zastro. Scheduled for nine, she would be his first patient that morning. Was it anxiety or dread that was circulating, zigzagging under her thin robe, shooting through the soft lambs' wool slippers and tingling even her toes?

Shyam ushered Yana into the Consultation Room as the grandfather clock in the hallway chimed nine times.

Let these three weeks go quickly, she repeated to herself, her new mantra. *If I'm cured before then, I'll be on my way home, as fast as these healed legs will carry me.*

"Dr. Zastro be delayed. Please wait. Make person comfortable." Shyam bowed and left, leaving the door open.

Yana paced about, pulling down both chart shades, she gave them a quick look and then snapped them back up. She did not enjoy viewing garish insides of bodies. This was not how she looked within, and even if it were true, she didn't want to see it. She preferred her interiors remain a mystery. Gypsy women's bodies and their female functions were viewed as great mysteries. Men treated them as special because of this mystique, attributing many remarkable things to women because of their unusual bodily functions, the greatest being the miracle of giving birth. That was one miracle she might never experience. She had no plans for children, since that also meant marriage.

There were so many old customs regarding the monthlies and other handed-down body taboos. It had been a long time since she had been with the tribe, but early-learned customs and inherited rituals still lingered—still comforted—still frightened. The oldest of these was dance.

She did a few whirling steps. Even with her pained leg there was added impetus, possibly due to the free flowing silky garment. Was this electricity already generating changes? She broke into singing, a plaintive song, memories crying out.

Aye solea, solea, Solea, del elna mia,
 Yo no te vuelvo a ver mass! Ay solea, solea
Solea! tristo de mi!—

Dr. Zastro appeared in the doorway as if the song had conjured him up. "Miss Kejako?"

She stopped as if a small child caught in an embarrassing act. Why was this so? Generally nothing embarrassed her. Now even her cheeks began to burn. "Yes," she answered, retreating to the patient's chair in front of the baronial desk.

"I'm sorry for the delay. But that is a doctor's busy life." He made it sound as if she would not understand about such alien matters.

"Now, for our consultation." He sat down in his high backed chair and thumbed through files.

"Your Sanitarium—it's not what I thought it would be," she commented, "and, neither are you." Sometimes words just flew out of her mouth like fluttering birds needing release.

"We will get right on with the diagnosis." Again, he dismissed her comments, consulting his pad before him. "Yana Kejako. Age thirty-three. And, you've never been married."

"No. But that does not conclude I am a virgin."

"We can discuss that later."

"You keep evading my—"

"Miss Kejako, I have my own methods of dealing with my patients, proven over the years."

"It's just that—"

"I will need your entire cooperation. Cures can only work on a calm body, when the electro-magnetic forces are in harmony."

Her eyes searched his face for certain signs. "You do have powerfully magnetic eyes. Yet, no trace of the Evil Eye," she concluded, as if giving him absolution.

"Miss Kejako, I need your cooperation."

"I'll cooperate," she said, "if you promise not to put me in that wretched Rocking Machine." There had been a picture of the weird looking apparatus in a booklet about the Sanitarium, in the reading room, and the circular cage did not appeal to her at all.

"If I deem it necessary—"

"I'm warning you, I get seasick. Every time I crossed the Atlantic my stomach turned inside out."

"You've been abroad?"

"Several times. The water's not my way to travel. My people avoid water as much as possible."

"What countries? Sometimes patients pick up strange maladies in foreign lands."

"Spain—to visit ancestral grave sites. And Paris."

"Paris. I studied there. Magnificent city. Startling medical discoveries."

"I studied there too."

"Studied?" A frown wrinkled his forehead. "For how long?"

"About two years. At the art schools."

"I see," he said, hesitant, as though debating whether to speak his thoughts. "I'm sure you are aware of the medical problems that can result from too much study. Overworking the brain causes great physical strain upon a woman's constitution. Females are created for reproduction, and higher education causes their uteruses to atrophy."

"*Dinilo!* Silly fool—you don't believe that." She had been trying so hard to keep calm.

"It has been proven. Medically and scientifically."

"Proven by *moosh*—man. Right now it's my arm and leg that's bothering me, not my brain or uterus." She wanted to get this consultation over with as soon as possible.

"Forgive me for digressing. We will continue with the diagnosis. Any apparent cause for the afflictions?"

"I fell off my horse, two months ago. I wrote you of that. The pain interferes with my ability to paint."

"You paint as a hobby?"

"No, doctor, as an avocation."

"A woman artist?"

"Yes. And I don't even disguise myself in men's clothing as Rosa Bonheur feels she needs to do."

"It's just that—I've never met one, a woman artist, before."

"And I've never met a doctor quite like you before either." She knew she was giving him one of her intense absorbing stares, softening it with a warm enchanting smile.

He looked disturbed for a moment and then went on with professional detachment, "We will continue."

"I have an art show scheduled in two months. At the Salon in Paris. If possible, I'd like my limbs restored before I leave for Paris next month so I can paint while I am there. This exhibition is very important to me."

"Yes, of course." He appeared not quite sure of all he had heard: Painting—Shows—Paris— "First, I'll have to examine the area of pain."

"I must be honest with you, I've been to other doctors and tried many cures on my own. You are my last hope. And, you do advertise, 'cures guaranteed.'" She felt she needed to remind him of the prime reason why she came. Why she was staying and why she was putting up with his ridiculous restrictions.

"Yes. I can assure you complete cure, if you cooperate. However, if you had female problems or headaches from your— studying—that I could not cure unless you gave up that stress on your system."

"I could never give up being an artist." She was positive of that. Painting was like a liberating roadway coursing through her life—a predestined path that nothing could deter.

"Let me take a look." He rolled up her sleeve so very gently, and then began probing lightly with strong sure fingers. "The tendon is indeed still inflamed."

His touch traveled throughout her body. "It is alive with pain when you press."

"Pressure brings its own pain," he said, rolling the sleeve back down. "And, since you were thrown from a horse, I will examine the legs also."

She lifted her gown and extended her bare leg. He raised the limb, laying it across his knee and began probing up and down with a penetrating touch. He did the same with the other leg.

She watched him, felt him, studied him, trying to ignore what was happening deeper within her body. "That's the spot. It cries out now. Also when I dance."

He lowered the leg, covering it with her gown once more. "You dance too?"

"For my own pleasure." She reached out to touch his hand, wanting to read his palm, needing to. He withdrew his hand as if touched by a hot poker.

"Normally, I can diagnose these sorts of maladies with ease. Most of my female patients fall into certain categories. You—" he shook his head, "I don't know. Yana—even your name is different."

"I was named after my Great Grandmama."

"I see. That song you were singing—"

"Romany. Mama was a full blooded Romany Gypsy."

"I see."

"And Papa—an aristocratic southern gentleman, originally from Ireland. He owned a large plantation in the state of Virginia."

"I see. A very interesting combination."

"One that was doomed before it even began."

"How does one know?"

"It was in his hand. Mama saw it the first time she told his fortune. But, she married him anyway."

"Surely you don't believe in fortune telling?"

"Yes. And I believe in dreams and prophesying. Good luck and bad luck. And that somehow fate has brought me here."

He contemplated this statement and then continued, "Your mother taught you these superstitions?"

"Mama, Grandmama, Great Grandmama. What they passed on to me is woven into the fabric of my life—the basis of my beliefs."

"And, your father? Tell me about him."

"I don't remember Papa too well. A large man with reddish hair—odd sounding voice." She could hear him now, in the vague distance—that strange Irish brogue speaking with a lilt to her mother—"Persa, sure'n you must not be so sad all the time...."

"Mama married him in Europe, soon after they met. He brought his new bride to his huge mansion in Virginia, where I was born. We lived there until I was about five. Mama hated being a Southern lady, bossing servants around and wearing hoop skirts. She missed the carefree traveling Gypsy life.

"One day, she just left him. Packed a few things together and we rejoined the tribe, taking back the Kejako name. Only once you leave the tribe, you're always *pikie*—outcasts. So, we took our own wagon and traveled with them, but still separate, staying on the fringes. Mama told fortunes. I painted, as if it were an inborn talent awaiting release." She paused, not knowing how much she wanted to reveal, yet wanting to tell him everything about her life, a compelling need to.

"Mama was never the same after leaving Papa. She died of a broken heart."

"No one dies of a broken heart."

"Gypsies do," she said. "She loved my Papa, but she couldn't live with him; she couldn't live away from him either." She pressed her fist against her lips so she wouldn't cry out at the memory of Mama's death. She didn't want it tearing her apart now as it did so many times before.

The doctor cleared his throat. "It's getting late. We better continue with the consultation."

"Yes.... I don't know what made me tell you all that." The memory had been packed away for so long.

"The more I know about my patients, the better I am able to diagnose. Maybe there are other reasons for this difficulty with your healing—this blockage in your circulation." He waited a few moments as though choosing his next words with care. "I'd like to relax you. You're over-stimulated right now."

Why was there this sense of so much unspoken between them, of so much that needed to be said? Words that might lead to things she didn't want to discover. Not yet. Not now. She wasn't prepared for encounters such as these—deep stirrings of emotions that had been locked away under the tightest restrictions. She tried concentrating on the room, noticing the test tubes, vials, microscopes. "No drugs," she warned, "I don't touch morphine, arsenic, or mercury—" Why was this new panic rising?

"No drugs are used here," he said, obviously intending to soothe her fears. "Only herbs, grown in my own gardens. I relax my patients by other means." He lit the large beeswax candle in the polished brass holder and sat down, resting his clasped hands under his chin, looking straight into her eyes. "Now, concentrate on the candle."

"I can't relax, before sundown." *And certainly not here in this room with you.* She began squirming in the chair, starting to say something more.

He cut her off. "You must listen and not interrupt. Clear out all other thoughts. You are getting sleepy.... Sleepier.... You will answer all my questions truthfully. When I clap my hands you will wake up refreshed and remember nothing. Now concentrate."

She wanted to rise, flee from the room; yet, it was as if invisible bonds were holding her fast to the chair, locking her into the lambs' wool arms. "I can't do it. I just can't do it." The words flew from her mouth in a cry for help as her body lifted itself out of the chair, struggling, breaking the invisible holds.

"Please, remain seated," he ordered and then more soothing, as she sat down. "You are not even trying. You must trust me if I am to cure you."

He proceeded once more. "Your eyes are getting heavy....
Heavier...." He paused, "You are not concentrating! You must
relax."

"I told you I cannot relax in the day time."

"You are fighting me—"

"Why? Why should I fight you?"

"I don't know. You are a very independent woman."

"That may be, but I want to be cured. I will do anything to
be cured." And she meant it. Even she wondered at her
resistance.

"All right then." He heaved a sigh of surrender. "Tomorrow
night at eight o'clock, we will try again. You may be more able
to relax later in the evening. We try to accommodate the many
differences in each of our patients."

Yana took his hand in hers before he had a chance to
withdraw. "Thank you, doctor." She paused, sensing slight
tremors passing between them. "Your hands are magnetic, but I
am still not convinced about your electrical theories."

His hand withdrew; his spine straightened. "My Sanitarium
is filled with machines that expound the electrical theory.
Science proves with experiment and hypotheses," he declared as
if that were a final dictum.

"My beliefs come from within," she offered in return.
"Something connected with all of life."

"Such as—"

"When I was a little girl, I wore an amulet around my neck
to ward off evil—a spider in a nutshell wrapped in silk. And I
believed nothing would ever harm me as long as I wore it."

"Women still come in here wearing amulets. Talismans.
Some day science will do away with all superstitions." There
was no condescension in his tone, only traces of hope.

"Superstitions? Things one knows, for which there is no
explanation." She was touching her braid as she spoke—was
this a new good luck charm?

"Another time, we will discuss, or I will give you
explanatory reading material."

She could tell he was not used to women questioning his
methods. None probably ever had before.

"At treatment time today, you will use the electro-magnetic belt on your arm and leg. It will work, whether you believe in it or not. Shyam will instruct you."

Yana stood up. There was an urgency to leave. Her blood was racing.

"My heart—it beats very fast now."

He stood before her, "Do not overtax your heart, Yana. Women must learn never to overstress their hearts. Riding. Dancing. Studying. It all puts undue strain on the heart muscle. Women were created for gentler expenditures."

"You have everything figured out, don't you?"

"It is my life's study to understand the universe and how it is put together."

"And people—to you they are only chemicals and electrical currents?"

"The greater portion of their anatomy is. And to you?"

She had to express it in more than mere words, her body moving in rhythm with her speech, "Human beings are bright flurries of color that dance on the canvas of life." Her arms reached out for the sky, and the walls of the room dissolved, lifting her away into spinning forces, words flying from her soul. "Science is repeating. Art is creating, never repeating. An artist omits the detail and gives only the sprit and the splendor."

"Yes, you are an artist. And, I am a scientist," he admitted, almost sadly.

She was back in the room once more. "How did the species get so far apart?"

"I do not know."

She came toward him and then backed away. "Why are you looking at me so strangely?"

"It is nothing." Yet his puzzled expression remained.

"No—I caught something beyond your eyes just now when you gazed at me."

He hesitated and then confessed, "You reminded me of someone, the first time I saw you but I couldn't place who—"

"And now you have remembered?"

"Yes." It was as if he were looking into a long ago distance. "As a young boy, in my bedroom there was a picture on the wall above my bed. All I remember about it is the shadowy face of a woman with long flowing dark hair. She was the first thing I looked upon every morning, the last face I focused on every night. I remember her more clearly than the face of my own mother." He paused, looking at her anew. "That must be the face you resurrected when I first saw you. I have not thought about that phenomenon for years."

It rushed forward from her, a long forgotten verse:

I've seen you where you never were
And where you never will be;
And yet within that very place
You can be seen by me.
For to tell what they do not know
Is the art of Romany.

The doctor was silent. He blew out the candle, which was flickering wildly. For Yana, everything seemed to be undulating at that moment, the past, the present, the future, all swirling together in turbulent pulsating colors.

"Well, I have other patients to attend to. Please be here at eight tomorrow night. Shyam will knock on your door."

"I will be here. There is no need for anyone to knock. My time is in my head."

They stood apart, looking at one another. Something compelling was passing between them, leaving them no way to take back any of it. Yana turned and hurried out the door, away from the room, away from the magnetism that was not in the machines, not in her robes, but emanating from Dr. Zastro himself.

She did not know how to deal with such entanglements. Nothing in her heritage had prepared her for such anomalous beguilements. For once, she was not in charge. It was an aberrant feeling, almost an abandonment—the stray bird—fluttering—still lost.

CHAPTER 4

The chattering group of ladies followed Dr. Zastro like ducklings down the long white hallway to the Treatment Room later that morning. Yana was curious, yet apprehensive, about seeing the machines she would be subjected to every day for the next three weeks. Machines had not made the world a better place, despite the heralding acclaims that they would free mankind from slavery and drudgery.

Factories were dirty, noisy buildings, imprisoning laborers in grimy dingy workplaces. Workers entering their doors in the darkness of morning, leaving in the dimness of night, never even seeing daylight. Still, some people had to work in such places or starve. Had she been without her father's generous inheritance, would she be one of those who would prefer starving?

"This is the Treatment Room, ladies." Dr. Zastro opened one-half of the oversized double entrance door. "Treatment for each of you will begin this afternoon. Remember, you must never enter this room on your own. It can be a very dangerous place for those who are curious but without sufficient knowledge."

"Is too dark to see what is in there," Isobelle whispered.

"My favorite room in the whole place." Delphine never whispered.

Dr. Zastro flicked a switch, and one area was bathed in violet and blue lights that seemed to dance at first, then steadied into a humming, flickering glow.

"What is happening?" Mavis jumped back in fright. "Lightning!"

"Electric lights. Turned on by a switch." Edwina sounded impatient. "Only God makes lightning."

"These lights are even more beneficial than sun rays, specially patented," the doctor explained; it always seemed as if he were endlessly lecturing. "Someday it is hoped every household will be able to afford them. It will keep sallowness from complexions during the cloudy winter months. If healthy plants need light to survive, how much more so the lovely species of females."

"He is so right bout every thing," Delphine proclaimed.

Dr. Zastro went to the floor model music box, winding it up and soon a Strauss waltz was tinkling melodiously.

"Special harmonious music will be playing all the while you are here. What enters your body through your ears also affects your constitutions. And since these healing machines were not built for attractiveness, as you can readily see, we suggest closing your eyes during treatment."

"He can make music come out of that box?" Mavis spoke in wonderment.

"Anybody can work a music box." Edwina's impatience with Mavis was again evident. "You just have to wind it up."

Yana wasn't listening, still recalling her recent session with Dr. Zastro, when he couldn't mesmerize her, or was it because she didn't want to be mesmerized? Sometimes the body reacted in certain ways to protect itself, automatic primitive responses rising to defend, without any conscious thought.

They were now being guided to the corner of the room, where a horizontal cylindrical cage, made of heavy metal rims, was rocking back and forth. The same machine from the brochure, even more horrifying in reality. Inside on a white cushion, lay Althea, never looking more peaceful. Could this wicked looking contraption really work?

"They locked up Miss Althea." Mavis backed away muttering, "She can't get out of there."

"And this is our Rocking Machine, invented by Dr. Morgan. There are only five in use in the whole United States. They have soothed the nerves of countless women, rocking them back and forth, as if held in a mother's arms. Magnetic poles are at either end, positive and negative, running currents through the patients, restoring her nervo-electrical forces. As you can see, the machine is pleasantly soothing Miss Althea."

"Do patients have a choice of which machine they will be subjected to?" Yana asked; she would never allow herself to be caged in such an apparatus.

"I expect my patients to abide by my decisions."

"But—"

"We will save all questions until later." He walked to another area.

"Here is our galvanized bathtub for electro-chemical baths, the only apparatus you must disrobe for. Therefore, a curtain surrounds it for the genteel ladies. Shyam will assist you in getting in and out of the tub." It was then Yana noticed Shyam sitting on a high stool in the corner, observing them each in turn, but mostly watching Althea.

The doctor opened a door at the far end of the room. "This is the Dark Room, which we use as a special recovery area."

"Is nothing but blackness in there," Isobelle remarked.

"I never want to go inside that spooky place." Mavis backed further away.

The doctor closed the door and proceeded to point out three similar looking chairs. "These are patented treatment chairs. This one has an electric belt for lower intestinal ailments and lower limb areas. This one is for upper respiratory and back ailments, plus arm regions. And this high one is for disorders of the head."

Each lady seemed to be contemplating which chair she might have to sit in, which belt might encase portions of her body. Edwina's nervousness became more noticeable as she began scratching, slowly at first and then faster as her hands moved from one portion of her body to another.

"You all may have seen The Electric Belt; it is widely advertised. Thousands sold through mail orders. However, ordering these and treating yourself is not recommended. These electric belts must be used only by skilled operators, who check for the right flow of electricity." He stopped and leaned against one of the machines, taking on his lecture stance. "Even physicians of high reputation cannot distinguish between the positive and negative poles of a machine, much less explain the difference in the nature of the various currents. They apply it in haphazard fashion, and as a consequence, will sometimes be thrown into ecstasies over its beneficial effects, only to be at other times startled with its inefficiency. Such persons regard electricity as an uncertain therapeutic agent, and only employ it after every other expedient has been resorted to in vain.

"Sitting down with a gold pencil over a sheet of gilt-edged paper and writing a prescription is much more pleasant than learning the proper application of electricity." He fumbled in his vest pocket underneath his lab coat, pulling out a folded newspaper clipping. "If you ladies will bear with me, I should like to read you a portion of an article, published only this morning, in which the lazy, straight-jacketed old fogy disciples of AEsculapius were given some pretty hard raps by our largest Metropolitan Journal."

He proceeded to read the article aloud, more for his own benefit than that of the ladies, Yana concluded. They seemed restless, ready to view more items, not understanding most of the text, but politely listening.

We see daily the bitter quarrel between the old-school fashionable practitioner, who adheres to the traditions of the last century, and the man of science who brings to his aid the newest discoveries. It is the theory of your fashionable physician to keep his delicate patients in such a condition that the yearly bill will be plethoric. He attempts no new-fangled experiments; he does not rudely tell Madame that nothing really ails her, except laziness, but gives her a good deal of the latest gossip and a little harmless medication...."

"I don't understand—he talks too fast." Mavis was pulling at her ear.

Delphine was yawning through her claim that "I hardly got any sleep at all last night."

He kept droning on and on, and then at last folded up the clipping carefully. "Thank you ladies for listening to my digression. I do want to stress that physicians should not be censured because they do not all become electrical operators. It is not something one can acquire by lifelong study; it is not a secret that a mechanical electrician can impart. It is a God-given gift. It is the possession, at all times, of a good supply of animal magnetism. To be a first rate operator, a physician must be a battery in himself." He seemed almost transported into another world.

"In the treatment of many diseases, the current sent out of an instrument must be modified by individual electricity, or, as it is more commonly termed, 'animal magnetism'. There is great difference in individuals in the possession of this. While some are very positively magnetized, others are extremely negative, and cannot impart to another the first particle of this invigorating influence. Animal electricity is controlled by the mind to which it belongs, while chemical or other electricity is controlled by the operator who employs it."

"I'm never gonna learn all what he talks about." Mavis was mumbling to herself.

Delphine scolded, "Nobody ever can, cause he's the smartest man in the whole world."

Dr. Zastro looked at them and smiled in apology. "I'm sorry ladies, for sometimes giving my lectures outside the Lecture Room, but there is so much knowledge I would like to impart to each of you and so little time to do it."

"I came here to learn as much as I can from you," Edwina assured him. "Knowledge is the key to locking out ignorance."

"Yes," he said, "yes, it is." He turned his attention to the machines again. "Since this Sanitarium is for the treatment of ladies only, no male persons ever use any of these machines. There is a separate treatment room on the first floor for my daily male patients.

"In my other operating rooms, nearly fifty different appliances are employed, many of which are my own invention. The most valuable of these is my Magnetic Stool." He pointed proudly to a round metal stool with all kinds of strange extended attachments.

"The Magnetic Stool can treat diseases of both sexes without subjecting their person to indelicate exposure. A special apparatus, self-contained within the stool, stimulates the sexual organs and regenerates them"

Who among them had sexual diseases? Yana wondered. Well, such information could hardly be kept a secret since they all would be using the same room at the same rime.

"I've had thousands of offers, from both patients and doctors, to purchase, or even borrow these magnificent stools, their cures have been so miraculous. But, because of the power of the treatment on very delicate areas, only I am qualified to operate them.   With my expert touch, I can feel a woman's sexual parts during treatment to determine if the right amount of electricity is being transmitted."

He added with great seriousness, "I don't wish to contemplate what might happen if these stools fell into the wrong hands." He moved away to another area as the ladies were still mulling his last warning.

"I hope you all get a chance to try that wonderful stool," Delphine twittered. "I do recommend it highly."

"No way I sit on such a thing." Isobelle was shaking her head back and forth.

"Here, in this tank, we keep our electric eel, which we use for special shock treatment. We don't employ him as much as we used to; it seems his powers are waning. He's our only live creature, since we have never kept leeches."

One by one, the women looked into the tank, giving little shrieks of horror. The slithering form appeared more snake than fish to Yana, staring at her with pitiful eyes, as if requesting to be rescued from this woeful place.

"We've also experimented with lightning bugs, but their electrical power is very weak, and they also prefer the out-of-doors, their natural habitat. Still, a few of them did not wish to leave, and some remain, flickering their lights in our lovely roof garden. However, since you ladies will only be using that area during daytime, you will never have the opportunity to view their magical presence."

"I keep lightning bugs in a jar by my bed at night." It always sounded as if Mavis was talking to herself, as if she expected no one would listen when she did speak.

The doctor walked toward a massive metallic gray box, with a large front door that he opened. Inside were two benches. Glass tubes protruded from the walls. Who knew what this machine was supposed to do. Yana had given up any further conjectures on the purposes of these bizarre inventions. Would reading his books have prepared her for any of this? Or might they have only kept her away? The gray tubes began pulsating in bright, varied colors.

"Look at the pretty lights—Like millions of rainbows." Mavis stood with her mouth wide open.

"Never in all born days, seen such a magic machine." Isobelle stared in awe.

Delphine began pulsing along with the rhythm of the lights.

Dr. Zastro was obviously delighted by their response. "This is my Spectro-Cabinet, where different colored light rays soothe and heal various pains and maladies, each by its own generating wavelength. It was invented by the renowned Dr. Clement of the Medical Academy, and he graciously offered to let me purchase one, instructing me himself.

"Each of you will be allowed to benefit from the healing rays of this wonderful cabinet. I myself use it often—spectrums of color stimulating specific areas as they heal."

Yana was appalled. She was an artist; colors encompassed their own individual vitality, casting off various effects, all perceived through the eye, yes, but also felt through her own fingers as she applied the pigments with her brush. She loved to watch in fascination as the oils blended, mysteriously forming into their own wondrous images. To use colors in this bizarre, scientific manner, in this ugly cabinet, was more disturbing than all the other mumbo jumbo theories she had heard about electrical forces jumping around in those other machines.

How she wished she had brought along some of her own art books for the doctor to read. She would educate him on the true purpose of colors, which was not for being projected into the bodies of human beings, but sent directly to the soul via the eyes.

The doctor waved his hand toward an array of miscellaneous machines in a blocked off area. "These machines—too technical to explain," he said, as though the women were too ignorant to understand anything of a technical nature.

They did look monstrous, all those pulleys, large metal gears and other weird apparatus either attached or protruding from them.

"Sometimes I dream about those machines, that they all are coming after me—" There was real fear in Delphine's twittery voice.

"Yah, those machines get out of hand, and can do strange, strange things." Isobelle eyed the area from a distance, staying close to the doctor's side.

In the far corner, a large wooden chair with numerous leather straps and strange metal buckles was set up on a platform. "This is the Electric Shock Machine," he said. "It is not used much, because I don't believe in using shock therapy, only in very rare cases of paralysis, and then only to reactivate the nerves. All my other electro-magnetic healing devices carry much less current." There was a slight bit of humor in his voice as he added, "However, if any of you ladies would like to try it out—" He pressed a button and sparks shot out, as the women screamed and backed away.

"Ladies, ladies," he soothed them, "it takes a vast amount of electricity, even in the form of lightning to kill anyone. Electricity is a savior, not a mutilator."

This was like a circus, Yana concluded. He was running a three-ring circus with himself as the ringmaster in control of the whip, in charge of the animals and the freaks. She had to admit sideshows had always fascinated her. Gypsies were attuned to the carnivals and fringes of society. Since childhood, she had always remained at the outskirts of such performances, watching, absorbing, and sometimes later translating what she had seen into colorful paintings.

The doctor pressed the button and sparks again shot out from the chair.

Edwina broke her demeanor and began shouting, "Keep that thing harnessed, don't let it loose again in this room!"

The doctor raised his hands in a calming motion. "Ladies, there is nothing in this room to be afraid of. I know you are used to kitchens and parlors, and these strange looking machines are foreign sights to you, but let me reassure, each and every one has been tested thoroughly, with amazing results.

"I have been investigated by the authorities. And never once have they been able to prove my machines, or methods of healing, are harmful to any of my patients.

"As you know, doctors are very busy people. Everyone clamoring for a piece of the doctor's time. Books and articles to write, patients to see, volumes of mail. We do all that is humanly possible to lessen the ills of the world. Now, with these wonderful machines assisting us, we will be able to do so much more." He beamed at them with such self-satisfaction.

Yana knew enough about him and his machines for now. She was becoming more agitated, more apprehensive about what unknown treatment she might be subjected to later. She had suppressed her voice long enough.

"Doctor, you claim nothing in here is harmful to your patients; yet it seems—"

His eyes darted toward her and narrowed, his voice was angry and directed at her, as if she were the only person in the room.

"You would question my methods?" He moved closer so his voice was even more direct, his words coming in a torrent. "I have made both rheumatic and paralytic invalids run and rejoice in the restoration of limbs once painful, contracted, stiff, and withered. I have caused the haggard, downcast, nearly cadaverous face of the dyspeptic to light up under the exhilarating effects of currents of electricity sent down the pneumo-gastric nerves to the stomach. I have imparted an elastic step and glow of health to many a woman, who had for years, crept about her domicile under the debilitating effects of female weakness. I have given the neuralgic sufferer occasion to rejoice in my discoveries in electrical therapeutics. And you, you would question my methods?"

He turned away, dismissing any further exchange between them.

"It's just that—" Yana's words were interrupted by Althea crying out, "Don't touch me. Please, don't touch me."

Dr. Zastro called out to Shyam who was still seated on his high stool. "Set the switch to slow."

Shyam worked a lever and the machine began rocking even more violently.

"The other switch. The other switch!"

Althea was crying out in piteous screams, a wounded animal caught in a trap. As the machine quieted, so did her cries. Her quivering hands were covering her eyes. What was she afraid of seeing?

"Come ladies, Miss Althea is being properly treated," the doctor said, as he added in explicit reassurance, "and in no way is she being harmed. He began turning off music, lights. "It is recreation time. And then cook has a healthy lunch for all of you."

The room was left glowing in semi-darkness. Only Althea's soft moans and the steady click of the Rocking Machine resounded. A world of machines that moved and lit like they were living beings, thought Yana, but they had insides of acidic batteries and hardened steel. She would be returning here again this afternoon, and during treatment time, her arms and legs would be subjected to new, strange vibrations in one of those ugly wired chairs. Already she felt trepidation grabbing at her interiors. Why did each new aspect of this Sanitarium bring forth such forebodings of anxiety?

She strode past Dr. Zastro as he was shutting the huge Treatment Room door. She did not look at him, but she could feel the heat of his body as she passed—or was it that special electricity he said he possessed? She needed to go to her room, be alone. Maybe dance. Maybe sing. Or maybe even just cry out. So much within needed release right now.

She also needed protection from all those monstrous machines that seemed to be following her. It was as though the machines were assailing her in ways she did not understand.

"Mama, help me" she called out silently as she hurried toward her room, away from the machines, away from the doctor, knowing there was no real escape, not while she remained in this enclosure.

CHAPTER 5

Later that morning Dr. Zastro sat in his consulting room, finding it difficult to concentrate. His mind was wandering so much this week. Could it be dedication to his work was waning. Had he reached a plane of knowledge where there would be few new discoveries to pursue, so few that possibly the search might not be as frenetic as before? His carefully crafted routine, which had been perfect over so many years, was being upset by something.

Perhaps it was time to diagnose treatment for himself. He often applied treatments to his own body to test various medications or new apparatus. These were the weeks he had more time for such experiments, otherwise he was caught up in the daily rush of attending to his numerous other patients.

He must get back into focus and concentrate on his next consultation. After Yana's frustrating session of that morning, this one should be much simpler. He banished any reflection on that earlier episode. Thoughts of Yana only seemed to perturb, and that fact only perturbed him more. He rarely let things of a non-medical nature disturb him.

He looked at the file before him. A Bible verse surfaced in his mind: *Let not your heart be troubled.* These verses, learned from his mother so long ago; he thought them lost to memory, but still they emerged at various times. His mother, still seeking to comfort him with her faith as she had done in moments of childhood distress.

His father, Jacob, had been the wellspring for Phillipe's world of knowledge, but it was his mother who retained and passed on the reservoirs of wisdom. Mama—who attended church services and read the Bible daily. Mama, who suffered in silence.

His father, if he remembered correctly, was agnostic, though they never talked much about religion, God, or the hereafter. His mother didn't either. Still, it was always an energetic force within her, a constant beneath her surface.

A knock on his door brought him out of his thoughts. Shyam entered, announcing, "Isobelle Schmidt." Isobelle followed, wearing a long blue denim apron over her peony pink robe. The bulges of fat that circled her body in thick turgid clumps, were still visible beneath her garments.

"Good afternoon, Miss Schmidt." He always spoke louder to those of foreign background. Why, he didn't know, probably habit—except when he spoke to Shyam, who possessed this soft oriental quality and expressed himself in composed melodic tones.

"You may take off your apron, Miss Schmidt, when you are away from the kitchen. Cook told you what your duties are, in return for the nominal rate charged for your stay here?"

"Yah, Mr. Doctors." Always obedient, she untied and removed her apron and stood primly, clutching it in both hands, waiting for further instruction.

"We always try to accommodate one domestic each session, to help in the kitchen. Otherwise, I'm afraid most domestics could not afford to stay at my Sanitarium. My dedication is to help all women, no matter what their status. Yet, I am afraid it does take quite a sum to run this establishment. I just want to restate our position in case it wasn't quite clear when someone read it to you."

"Yah, I know. I work in kitchen here so charges don't be so much. I thankful to you."

"All right," he said, readying his plan of action. "Please, sit down in the chair—no, in the lounge right over there."

"Yah, Mr. Doctors." She sat stiff on the edge of the padded lounge, hands folded, still gripping the apron. "To sit is good for mine feets. Such swelling today. Feel like two big clubs down there."

"Just relax now and we'll get right on to taking care of all that ails you. Shyam, you are dismissed. Please take Miss Schmidt's apron and hang it on the peg in the hallway." Shyam bowed, took the garment and exited.

"Isobelle Schmidt. Age forty-five. Have you ever been married?

"Ach, no man would have me. Homely like I is."

"That is not true. All women have their own beauty because they are created by God." Isobelle put her hands over her face in embarrassment. "Now then, can you explain, in simple terms—I see you can't read or write English—what problem has brought you here?"

"Lady I work for, she writes mine letter for me. She tell you mine problem, yah?"

"Yes, but I want to hear it from you, in your own words."

"Okay." She avoided looking directly at him. "Mine back, pains me so, is gott awful."

"You find it difficult to talk to me?"

"Yah. Any persons. And specially doctors."

"I am going to relax you then, in a reliable harmless way. I want you to just lie back now on the lounge." He lowered the backrest as she adjusted her large frame into a prone position.

"Aaagh. Pains with fire." She pressed her fist against her tight grimaced lips. The bulges in her hand ballooned, highlighting cracks in the skin, the result of harsh scrub waters, hot laundry tubs and strong alkali soaps. The fingernails were broken and worn down to short stubs. It was evident she never spent time caring for her own person.

Domestics were always caring for others, and their own bodies were consistently neglected. Eating leftover food, sometimes scraps. Being called into service many times during the night. Shunted off into drafty cold rooms in attics or basements, vermin and rodents living with them, unless they had positions in wealthier homes. Even there, they were still badly treated, sometimes living in even worse conditions, given the poorest hovels in the elegant buildings. These three weeks might heal some of Isobelle's ailments, but they would also offer some respite from her days, even years, of drudgery.

"Aagh," she cried out again.

"In a few minutes, the pain will be gone." He lit the candle and proceeded to mesmerize her. This patient was very easy to relax, no resistance at all, as if she were used to giving her will to someone else, never questioning anyone of authority, letting them take over with their voice any aspect of her person.

"Now, I want to know about your pain. When it began. How?"

The words flowed out in a rush, as if she had been waiting years to tell someone.

"When I was little, I come over on big boat, with mine Mama and mine Papa. Papa, he work in mines after we get to America. He always black with the coal—like nigger—with two white holes for eyes, and—"

"The pain? Tell me about the pain."

"Yah, the pain.... Papa, he beat me. All the time, he beat me. One time, he kicked at me too. Kicked so hard with his heavy hard boots. Pain was so bad, I couldn't move. I lay there, day and night. He beat mine Mama too. Crippled her up so awful. I didn't want to get so bad like she, so, I run away."

"How old were you then?"

"Funfzehn ein—fifteen."

"Then, what happened? After you ran away?"

"Bad times. Only work I could get, housework. Cooking. And scrubbing. And washing. Last place, the man, he was dying—big tumor. I had to lift him out of his bed—to go pee pee—then lift him back. He wouldn't go in no dish. And he weighed a good ton."

Isobelle struggled and strained as if she were lifting the man, letting out a painful cry, sitting up wide awake, shaking her head, "Where is I?"

"It's all right, you were resting." That explanation seemed to suffice and she lay back down again. Since she was so relaxed, he'd try continuing without putting her under again. That sometimes worked if there were not too many interruptions.

"Can you tell me about your last work place—where you helped the large man who had a tumor?"

"You know?" There was wonderment that this doctor seemed to have knowledge of everything.

"You told me, when you were resting."

"Yah, sometimes I say things, when sleeping."

"Tell me what happened—the man with the tumor?"

"Ach, he died. Then his widow, she couldn't pay. So, I look for different work. Mine cousin, Millie, she just got job in garment factory. Is hard work. Thirteen hours a day. But when you is through, you is through. No one knocking at your door all the nights.

"Last Missus, she had one of your books. Read me bout you, and how you always cure. I begin saving mine money. Give up the bottle too. Only thing what helped mine pain. You cure me Mr. Doctors and then I go work in factory with Millie.

"Is that where you'd like to work?"

"What can women do? Typing? Ach, I'm too dumb. Too fat. The mines? Sure, they hire women, but they have to crawl in those black holes all day, naked on the top, with chains hitched between their legs. Nooo—not with mine back. I seen those women when they come out, black like hell. Cough and spit all the time. Big black plugs."

"But, you think you would be able to do factory work?"

"Yah. Millie, she just sit all day, watch the machines. Once in awhile you lift heavy barrel. Her factory, they like older women, don't spend such time googling at the men. And I can't scrub no more floors—lift no more sick peoples."

"Your back—has anything helped it before?"

"The drink. And one time, the morphine. Dr. Hegel, he give me the morphine. Och, felt so good. But then no more money for morphine. Pain worse after. I get sick. Oh mine gott, I was sick."

"Lie back down again. Carefully turn over now. I'm going to examine your back. Investigate for any visible signs."

"I try," and she strained to roll her lumpy body over, the lounge creaking under her weight.

Dr. Zastro eased away the silk gown and cotton chemise. A severely distorted back area was revealed. He began probing. "This lump, does it hurt?"

"Yah! Is where Papa kicked me." She screamed out in great agony, "No more. No more pain!"

"No more pain today. Your problem is very visible. There's quite a protrusion on your back that should be operated on, but—"

"No. No cutting. Once they cut, I'm a goner. Mine other cousin—Hilda, they used the knife on her, and—"

"Very seldom do we use the knife here. Only in very extreme cases. We will try all the other methods first."

"Doctor," Shyam called, entering without awaiting permission, "Althea—she faint once more. Miss Yana was speaking with her in Reading Room, and—" He was interrupted by Yana standing in the doorway, eyes flashing. "Is no one going to attend to Althea?"

"I go, doctor." Shyam was already putting on his white silk gloves, which he always carried in his pocket now, as he rushed down the hallway.

Phillipe could not stifle his rising anger. "Miss Kejako, I am the doctor here. Please return to the Reading Room. You are interrupting my consultation."

"Are we supposed to just leave patients lying on the floor, not knowing if they are dead or alive? Is that what you want?"

"You are to inform Shyam—"

"That is exactly what I did, doctor. I followed the rules and still you reprimand me. I informed Shyam, but he came running down here rather than first attending to Althea."

"He did what he has been instructed to do, because he must get permission from me before he performs treatment on any patient. He is only an assistant, do you understand? And you are only a patient, do you understand?"

"Yes, I understand. I am only a patient. However, I am also a human being, and I did not give away my thinking or feeling when I handed over my clothes and other belongings to store in that wicker basket. I am not one of your machines without emotions. There are no buttons to turn me on or off. I react by instinct."

"Please, return to the Reading Room," he said patiently, yet firm.

"I shall now return to the Reading Room, and I shall try my damnedest to conform to your ridiculous rules. But I will not become one of your controlled machines!" She slammed the door as she left.

It was evident Isobelle was astonished by what had taken place. He would have to remember to lock the door whenever he was in consultation. Interruptions like this must never happen again. It was disturbing—for everyone.

He found he could no longer focus on Isobelle and her ailments. The concentration had been broken. He also had to prepare himself for the next patient—Delphine, and he was not looking forward to that session.

"Miss Schmidt, please, excuse the interruption."

"Is okay, Mr. Doctors. That one is a wild person. Hard to tame someone who is like tiger." She started to lift herself off the lounge. "You is busy man. Important person. I take up no more of your times."

"You are as important to me as any of my other patients. I want you to believe that. I think I know enough about your background for the time being. I tell you what; you inform cook that I said you should be relieved from your duties for the rest of the day. I want you to go to your room and just rest. I think what your body needs most right now is rest."

"I can work, Mr. Doctors. Yah. I always work. Used to working, even when in pain. Then I don't think bout the pain so much. Work kills the pain. Sometimes gives new pains too, but what's the difference—one pain or nother?" She was huffing now as she spoke. It was evident she needed something to relax her.

He reached for a bottle of herbal relaxation elixir. "Here, take this medicine with you. It will help you relax, relieve the pain. Before you lie down, take one teaspoonful only. We will call you at supper time."

"You is a good man. So few good men in this world." She took the medicine as if he was a saint bestowing his blessings on her, hobbling out of the room with a beatific smile on her face.

Maybe he needed some medicine also, if only to relax his inner turmoil. No, he told himself; this is not the time for experimenting on himself with medicines, not today. He needed everything as clear and sharp as possible. He pressed his temples to alleviate the new pressure pounding in his head. Maybe he should go sit in the Spectro Cabinet. Let the colors work on his problems. Now might be a very good time, before his session with Delphine.

He escaped to the Treatment Room, locking the door. He didn't turn on the lights or music, but went directly to the Spectro Box. Soon, only rainbows of color were dancing about his body, through his thoughts. What a wonderful treatment. The beneficial rays reaching past the outer skin, way inside— soothing, healing, relaxing.

He must have fallen asleep in the box. When he awoke, the brilliant colors were still whirling, and he was still seeing colorful spinning Gypsy skirts, fringed flowered shawls, splashed with sparkling beads and gold bangles. Why must visions of Yana intrude continuously?

Why had the machine colors diffused his mind into these strange variations? Why the colors and visions breaking into his dreams? It had never happened before. The week had just begun and already he was inundated with so many anomalies.

The pressure in his temples was gone—a new sense of something near euphoria fluttered within. Of course, that was what the machine was supposed to do, wasn't it? Yet, never quite like this. Then again, he could not recall having fallen asleep in there before—or dreaming of Gypsies and their swirling wild colors. He left the Treatment Room revived, ready to face Delphine that afternoon.

CHAPTER 6

Dr. Zastro did not need to read Delphine's history. She had been at the Sanitarium twice before, and her symptoms were still the same, as was the diagnosis: nymphomania.

All previous treatments seemed to only subdue the problem, never cure. The one true remedy he knew of, removing the clitoris, was a procedure he would never allow himself to do. The mutilation was as cruel as the operation to make males into eunuchs by removing their testicles. Barbaric. Certainly, civilization had moved beyond such crude practices. Yet, he had to admit that in Delphine's case, he was running out of alternatives.

He had hardly opened his journal when Delphine appeared in the doorway, fanning herself as she blinked her eyes in feigned innocence. Where did she get those ostrich feather fans? She knew they were not allowed. She wasn't even in the room and already he was annoyed.

"I came early, doctor. Shyam was assisting Miss Althea." She shook her braids as if they were still curls. "I am so glad to be back, Phillipe."

"You will address me as Dr. Zastro all the while you are here, Mrs. Applewood. You have been told that before."

"I will try. But when I see you, I seem to forget all the rules, regulations. My mind just gets so distracted." She looked rouged, made up. He started to say something about that, but decided that maybe her cheeks were only flushed with excitement. Such an easily excited woman.

"Please sit down. We can make this consultation brief, since I already know your background."

"But, I have so much to tell you—"

"Mrs. Applewood, I think I also told you last season, we do not allow ostrich feather fans—only bamboo ones." Where were these women hiding these extra items?

Delphine giggled with girlish delight. "I forgot. Forgot everything you told me doctor. You'll just have to tell me all

over again. But, certain things I never forgot. Thought about so
many times." Her smile was bold and past flirtatious.

The best thing, he had learned through trial and error, was
to ignore these overtures from her. He cleared his throat and
consulted his journal. "Let's see, Delphine Applewood, age
thirty. Still married to Solomon Applewood, age sixty?"

"Still married, doctor. But sixty ain't young, and Solomon
ain't gonna be round forever you know."

"None of us are. That is why we must make the best use of
our time while we are still here on this earth. Now, what seems
to be your malady this session? Did we help you with your
ticklish problem?"

"Oh yes, doctor. Solomon can take me now, and I don't
giggle all the time, even if he still looks so funny—without his
clothes on." She went into another spasm of giggles. "I wait
until after now, and then just laugh and laugh myself sick. By
then, he's already sleeping. And he don't do it so often as he
used to." She finished with a deep sigh of relief.

"As long as he's satisfied with your cure. Now, why are
you here this season?" He preferred patients state their problems
in their own words, finding it easier to address them back in the
same words. So many were illiterate regarding simple medical
terms.

"Well, I had to come back—to see you." Her eyelids
fluttered, nostrils flared, and her wet tongue darted across her
shiny white teeth. Another man might have been tempted; he
never had been. Maybe the first time, when he was taken in by
her act of innocence. It was not a problem. He had conquered
his animal urges long ago—though yes, at times, they still
flickered. However, not now.

Sympathetic as he might be, he always needed to be stern
with Delphine. She was like a child in so many ways, yet
experienced beyond her years. "I had hesitations about taking
you back." *Why had he?* Was it because nymphomaniacs were
such rare creatures, so few admitting to the extremes of their
condition? They hid their actions in so many devious ways;
many ended up in early deaths, literally wearing their bodies out

either through promiscuous behavior or through their own repeated self-abuse.

"You will be expected to behave as every one else, otherwise I shall have to curtail your visit here." A threat of dismissal always cooled Delphine down a bit.

"I'll abide by all your rules. Anything you say."

"Well, I still would like to study your 'problem' further, for my books. Did the herbs help—the nymphomania?"

"Yes. But only when I don't think bout certain things. Lordy, I have so much time to think about things. Solomon's always working, here, there, piling up his money."

"He still travels?"

"He just struck another oil well, and he wanted to go away for three weeks to set up the well, but he was afraid to leave me alone, because, well, he knows.... So, he said I should come here to get recharged. He said he'd even pay double so I could return here."

"You know everyone pays the same. Everyone is treated the same. Wealth—or what you did in the past—makes no difference in this sanitarium."

"Well, I can't help it—my wealth. Or what I did in my past. I don't know what you expect when a person comes here—to turn into somebody else?"

"Now, Mrs. Applewood." He had to remind himself that she was as troubled as the others were.

"I get all panicky when I think of my past. I'm glad it's over, yet, I kinda miss it. When I think of my future I get panicky too. And I'm not getting any younger. Men only want younger women, who can make them babies. I can make men happy; I've sure had plenty of practice. But I can't make babies, not since that botched abortion. So you're the only doctor I trust now."

Her girlish babble had prodded his headache into returning. He began rubbing his forehead.

"Is something wrong, doctor?" she asked.

"No—it's nothing." *What was wrong?* He rarely suffered headaches.

"You all feeling all right? I mean, you just don't seem yourself. You look like you need somebody to take care of you." She got up and proceeded toward him.

"Please, stay seated. You must remember to keep your place in here." He didn't mean to sound irritated. She didn't deserve this. None of his patients deserved anything but kindness. They needed to feel they were safe here, away from all the assaults of their daily lives.

"It's been a tiring day, that's all. Now, any new medical problems we should discuss?"

"Well, I still get heart flutters, palpitations."

"I explained that's common with women your age."

"Specially when I see a certain gentleman."

"We'll try a new treatment for that this time."

"I liked the magnetic stool. Could that be my treatment again?"

"If applicable."

"Solomon says he'll buy me one of those magnetic stools, if it'll keep me happy when he's gone. He's so afraid, well, he knows—remembers where he met me."

"The stools are not for sale."

"Solomon even talked bout buying me a chastity belt." She sounded frightened. "You don't use them on women, do you doctor? I mean, he showed me once, and I said I'd die before I ever strapped one of them monsters on me. All chains, locks. Eech!"

"I don't believe in restraints for women."

"Me neither. But I still get mushy between my legs. Sometimes so terrible."

"The magnetic ointment I prescribed?"

" I used it all up, right away."

"Then you should have written for more."

"I did come in person to your office, one time last September, when Solomon was away. You were away too. I just sat on your doorstep and cried."

"You should write for appointments. September is my month for travel."

"Well, I had to do it quick, cause Solomon, he left quick. He ain't been gone since, and he won't let me go off alone, ever. And I wanted to see you—"

"Perhaps we can make up a stronger potion, to subdue those unnatural desires."

She stiffened in fear. "Not all the way, doctor. I don't ever want to lose those desires all the way. Some days those are my only comforts."

"Only an operation to remove the clitoris would do that."

"No. Never."

"I've told you before I don't perform such operations. We'll also put on cold compresses again."

"Oh lordy, I forgot bout those things. They chill me right on through. But, if you show me how again—"

"Shyam, my assistant, does the routine treatments now."

"I don't want him touching me, his dark skin—"

"Shyam is an intelligent young man, who hopes to become a doctor. You will accept his treatment, or not be allowed—"

"Oh, all right." She pouted. "I'll just close my eyes when he touches me. I used to do that before, when I had men on top of me I couldn't stand."

"And I must remind you again, not to come knocking at my room at night, if something ails you. Shyam is on night call if you need anything."

"But, what if Shyam don't answer?"

"We've been through all this before. I never open my door after retirement. And your constant knocking is always a disturbance to my rest, and that of the other patients."

"All right. But I just know I'm not gonna be able to sleep. Not with that itching going on between my legs."

"We'll give you something for that and to help you rest."

"You just seem to have something for everything, don't you doctor. When I know only one thing will cure all my ailments—" A talking machine. She was a wound-up talking machine.

"I must also remind you not to interrupt my lectures, or tell your silly stories when the ladies are reading. And, no singing."

"Is it all right if I giggle? I mean, sometimes Solomon just pops into my mind, without his clothes on—and I just have to giggle and giggle."

"As long as you do it in a quiet and a ladylike fashion. I want you to obey all the rules this time, so I can send a good report to Solomon."

"Solomon's so glad, bout my coming back. I mean, there ain't many places you can send a woman alone and know she'll be safe. 'Cept maybe a convent. And lordy, doctor, I don't think no convent would have me." Again that giggle, it always amused him somewhat before today; now, it just perturbed.

"That will be all for now. I have to prepare for another patient."

"The examination. I thought—I was waiting—"

"Tomorrow. We will examine you tomorrow. Now—"

"I got a new hobby, doctor." She was trying to prolong the dismissal.

"What is it this season?"

"I write poetry now."

"That is a good pastime for women."

She became very serious, very intense. "They're love poetry—written to you." She was waiting for his reaction, holding her breath until he spoke.

"Delphine, let me make a statement to you once and for all. I am not in love with you. I have never been in love with you, or anyone else. My practice is all that I am dedicated to in this life. It takes all my energies. It gives me all my satisfactions. Is that understood?"

"Well, I don't care if you never love me—I just can't stop feeling how I do. Nothing shuts it off. And I don't want none of your machines doing it neither. I want this feeling to stay with me all the time. It just feels good—good—good."

He had to stop this nonsense right now. "I must ask you never to speak of this again, or you will be dismissed."

She began to cry with the same up and down rhythm as her giggles.

"I can't help it, what I think about. Or how I feel. It all starts in my head and then goes down through my whole body and stops right between my legs and stays there. When I'm awake or when I'm asleep. Makes no difference." She continued crying, tears washing down her make-up in vari-colored streaks.

Women crying, they still gentled his soul. "Your feelings of love—they're just overactive glands. Those same glands that cause tears and make you hungry. That's why young girls are always in love, because their glands are more active. As you get older, they'll quiet down. I'm still doing research on the process. It's a field few have pursued, yet causes females great problems."

"I don't know what causes it, glands or that electric stuff. I just know when I'm in your presence—"

"Enough. We must end this session, now. I am asking you to leave." He reached for the bell to summon Shyam.

"I'm leaving. I'm going to go lie down on my bed and write another poem. And I don't want nobody putting any cold compresses between my legs until I'm through." She stalked out of the room.

Dr. Zastro pressed his fingers into his forehead and replayed the scene with Delphine. Females were certainly complicated persons, and yet most could be easily diagnosed as to what caused all their problems. Sometimes he had to remember this, remind himself of what caused their maladies and what would cure them. This effort troubled him. Anyone who called himself a doctor ought to be so confident of his inner knowledge he didn't even need to think about it.

So why was he uncertain about his abilities at this time? Why had Delphine affected him in such peculiar ways? Was middle age changing things about himself that he had not previously encountered? Nonsense. Doubts were the bane of clear thinking. He prided himself on clear thinking and immediately cast any thoughts of disbelief from his mind.

He closed the journal, put away Delphine's files, and stared at the walls filled with his degrees and awards. Yet, he did not see degrees and awards; all he saw was that face from his bedroom wall. There it was, staring back at him.

He needed to get away from these walls, maybe go outside to the roof garden, that special niche enmeshed in greenery where he would find seclusion in a natural habitat of fresh air and sunshine. He grabbed a book from the shelf, and hurried from his office, seeking escape.

He opened the door to the roof garden. The rush of cool fresh air revitalized his senses and cleared his head. An electric storm had passed through early that morning; the atmosphere was still activated with ozone, a natural purifier of the air. Breathing in deeply, he felt the rush of energy course through his whole body. The scent of roses engulfed him, that rich heavy aroma, sweeter than any rare perfume. The clay rose pots had just been brought out from the greenhouse and sparkled the area with bright clusters of resplendent color.

Other huge containers were filled with various flowers, trees, bushes. A lush countryside area was flourishing here in the heart of New York City. Forsythia bushes, bordering the roof edges, were just coming into bud, their sunny yellow blossoms dancing in the breeze. They served as a veil, helping hide the ugly gray buildings and the bleak rooftops of the adjacent structures. Why didn't the city outlaw such tall edifices-- piled up blocks of concrete that blocked sunlight from windows and shaded street pedestrians in perpetual gloom?

Below were greenhouses where herbs and other medicinal plants were grown, plus seedlings propagated during the winter months for this roof garden. The sun was now reflecting on the greenhouse glass, making it into patchwork squares of glistening gold and green—a jewel box of precious plants.

He had tried to encourage birds to gather in this garden, but only a few sparrows appeared thus far. One just had to be patient for the good things in life to appear. You just couldn't go out and capture everything you wished, or buy it either. Besides, it was cruel to keep birds in cages, canaries locked up for their song, nightingales tethered—so kings and princesses could be entertained. He'd rather not have any birds, than to imprison their song and beauty so unnaturally.

He relaxed on one of the bamboo lounges and looked to see what book he had taken. It was a volume by Dr. Dvorak, a colleague and pioneer in the medical world. So many acquaintances were publishing these days, so many trying to find a new approach to solving the numerous medical problems. As soon as one discovery was hailed, it was shot down and another sprang up in its place. So far, no one had disproved his electrical theories, though many had tried.

The atmosphere was peaceful, relaxing, and he dozed off with the book wide open on his lap. He drifted into a land filled with lush jungle plants, exotic fruits.

The leaves of a large palm tree parted and two huge eyes peered out at him. He froze, afraid the gorilla would jump out and attack him. The leaves parted further and another face appeared, hovering in the murky green mist. It was a woman's face—someone he knew. Who was she? A ferocious cry went through the jungle and everything started shaking violently....

He woke with a start. He wasn't in a jungle, only in his roof garden. A breeze must have come up; leaves and branches were still shaking. He felt chilled—some dream fright lingering?

Maybe it would be idyllic to live on some tropical island where one only had to pick fruits from the trees, scoop fish from the sea, and never worry about food, clothing, housing. He had been raised to believe that daily work was a necessary virtue if one wanted to make anything worthwhile of one's life. His father had impressed that on him. His father, who had a set daily routine and never let interruptions deter his resolution to make the most of any twenty-four hours.

Hearing his father admonishing his lazing in the middle of the day, Phillipe left the garden, shutting the outside door behind him. He was once more sealed inside the Sanitarium where the purified air wafted medicinal and sterile. He should consider a different method of filtering. Maybe he was shutting out too many outside things in his determination to keep the Sanitarium area secluded and uncontaminated. A better method might be to open up.

Good. Now he had some new project to pursue. Something to keep his mind occupied. New pursuits were sometimes needed as much as daily routines.

CHAPTER 7

That figure at the end of the hallway—could that be Yana?

Dr. Zastro hurried down the dim corridor, eyes still blinded from the sunlight. The women were more difficult to recognize from a distance since they wore their hair in the same manner now. Still, Yana's form, even in the shapeless robe, was recognizable: the natural majesty in her carriage, freedom in her stature, a mingling of grace and seductive charm.

What was she trying to conceal in that bulging towel she was carrying? She was hurrying away from the storage area where the wicker baskets with the women's personal belongings were stored. Had she somehow gained entry to that locked room, retrieved some of her forbidden items?

He decided to speak to her now and maybe in the process find out what was concealed in that bundle. Yet, he didn't want to confront her out here in the hallway. Whatever she had retrieved was already electro-charged, devoid of contamination. Eventually the women would be allowed to recover certain personal items anyway. Still, he would like to talk to Yana, if only a pleasant query about her treatments.

Just as he was about to call Yana's name Delphine's door opened.

"Doctor, I was looking all over for you, and I couldn't find you nowheres." Her face was flushed, eyes widened and the lower half of her thin gown crushed and wrinkled.

"Delphine," he said, trying to convey that he didn't wish to speak with her right at that moment, "you have already had your consultation, and I must hasten—" Yana was already gone, disappearing around the corner.

"But doctor—"

"I don't have time for questions." He sidestepped past her.

"But, doctor, that ointment didn't help none at all." She was following him, continuing her prattle. "When I rubbed it in, I just got more excited, an—"

"Then you must go to Shyam, tell him that I said you need cold compresses and a cold bath—"

"Oh no, lordy no." She backed away.

"Then try to control yourself until treatment time."

"I will." She retreated to her room and shut her door, the one with pink magnolias painted on it.

He detoured to the Consultation Room and seated himself behind the huge mahogany desk. His father's desk always centered his attentions properly, brought him back to his priorities. The desk had been the one ornate piece of furniture dominating his father's office at the University of Vermont, where he had been a professor of Botany. Phillipe would beg to visit him just so he could look at the interesting array of specimens scattered all about the room. All labeled in his father's precise handwriting and organized with meticulous care.

This desk and the high, carved oak bed in the next room where Phillipe slept these three weeks the Sanitarium was in session, these two pieces were the only surviving furnishings from the Zastro family home. The desk itself reminded him of his father. Robust and yet elegantly put together. Impressive size, built for hard work. Handsomely worn with use. So many hidden compartments to be discovered and searched out.

Actual memories of his father were dimming. He had been a distinguished looking man, with a trimmed beard; always dressed in a woolly-smelling tweed suit, a gold pocket watch on a long chain nested in his vest pocket ticking away in the same rhythm as his heart. A botanist, Jacob had taught and lived in the sphere of plants, any flora that graced the earth. He always had time to show his son the wonders in a tiny leaf, the spectacle in a minute seed, the marvelous miracles that could be viewed through the microscope. What patience he had, what endurance. Phillipe had always wanted to grow up to emulate him.

It came back, as it always did, in shudders of murky recall—that one crushing winter. Bitter. Turbulent. Vermont winters were ferocious, but this one was the most devastating of all. Phillipe was ten and his father was on a tramp steamer on his way to Africa, to do research on rare jungle plants. A terrible storm tore the age-weakened vessel apart, sinking the entire boat, his father with it. There wasn't even a body to bury.

His mother had carried on with stoic resolve. She changed as a person; the joy gone from her face, sobs heard nightly from her bedroom. She took in boarders. They lived frugally. Many pieces of the fine furniture were sold, one by one, but never this desk, nor the bed she and his father had shared.

One of the boarders had been a medical student. His stacks of technical books fascinated Phillipe, who would sneak into his room whenever the student was at school for the day, intrigued by the explicit medical pictures, absorbed by the scientific contents.

What an amazing world the human body was, even more so than that of plants and trees. What marvelous discoveries doctors had already uncovered. Yet, there was still so much more Phillipe wanted to know, find out for himself.

His father's inkwell was still in its cubbyhole. After his father's death, the ornate desk had been moved from the University to their home, and he remembered his mother copying all of his father's scribbled notes. Daily she sat at this desk, pen scratching on parchment paper, transferring his notebooks of research and then binding them into labeled volumes.

Phillipe went to work as soon as he was able after his father's death. Delivery boy. Store sweeper. His favorite position had been working in Dr. Foote's office. He enjoyed boiling the instruments and polishing the microscopes. Dr. Foote also let Phillipe read his medical journals—on Phillipe's own time, of course.

Nevertheless, Dr. Foote was an old fashioned doctor with old-fashioned methods, and quite soon, everything in that cramped office stank of the accumulated years of fetid sickness and acerbic medicine. All that had once fascinated Phillipe now appeared old and shoddy, belonging to another era that had not moved forward.

It was about that time his mother had become ill. She would not reveal to him what it was that caused her to lose weight and decline so in energy. Her lovely face grew sallow and gaunt. Finally, she kept to her bed, hardly speaking, barely eating.

He and a close by neighbor, Harriet, fed her and looked after her needs. Mama would only let Harriet bathe her or change her clothing.   One day, Harriet whispered, "Breast cancer," the words lacerating the air.

It wasn't long after that Phillipe himself viewed the abhorrent growth. His mother was delirious, calling out to his father, when Phillipe saw it—the swollen mass that protruded from her soiled nightgown. The tumor had ulcerated and discharges of blood and matter were oozing from the monstrous swelling, soaking through the matted bandages—a ghoulish gray and green.

He couldn't believe such an ugly thing could grow from his mother's beautiful body, even though he had seen similar drawings in the medical books. Reality was so much more gruesome than printed woodcut pictures.

He watched her die—one whole week of futility, trying to ease her pain and redo the packings on the seeping breast tissues. Harriet had stopped coming over, confiding that it was too devastating to watch her friend deteriorate so cruelly before her eyes.

Phillipe alone witnessed the profuse hemorrhaging, painful cries.   Then her death twitches, as he tried holding and comforting his mother's emaciated body while she slowly escaped from the pain of this world and eased her self into the peace of the next. It was then he made a promise to himself, and his mother, that he would work to find a cure for this horrible disease of the breast. He would try to help other women in their suffering, educate them so they would not try to keep their pain private. It was a crime that so many refused to allow doctors to view their bodies.   Even in cases where they did submit to doctors or hospitals, they still retained disbelief that the medical profession could cure them or even care to. He understood not wanting knives carving away any part of their flesh; a woman's body was the only tangible possession that truly belonged to her alone. There had to be a better way to heal diseased people. Each of the women he had cured since opening his medical practice helped diminish some of the pain his mother had suffered so shamefully.

A knock on the door interrupted his thoughts. "Yes," he responded.

Shyam opened the door, as guttural wailing filled the halls. "Lady not want to see you, doctor."

The voice continued moaning. "Nooo, nooooo."

It was Mavis Michalek, his next patient for consultation. What was causing her such agony? He went to the doorway, noting the cowering figure crouched against the wall, arms crossed over her face as if fending off some attack. "Miss Michalek, you must come in for your consultation now." Then in firmer tones: "We demand quiet in the halls."

"Don't tear it out of to me—Don't," she screamed at him.

"Please, no one is going to harm you in any way. We are here to help you." He held out his hand, grasping her trembling one.   Both he and Shyam led the grunting girl into the Consulting Room toward the patient's chair.

She lifted her face slightly, tears still streaming. A plain face, but not unfeminine. Fear, permanently etched into her features. Mavis bore the countenance of one who had never known peace. Her mother had brought her to the Sanitarium that first day, urgently asking to see the doctor, causing a commotion in the reception area. Dr. Zastro had made it a policy to speak only with the patient, never their guardians; his staff handled initial checking in procedures.

"On the lounge, I think." He motioned Shyam to help the shuddering body onto the chaise lounge. "Some vapors, Shyam."

His assistant uncorked the bottle, pouring the strong liquid onto a sponge in a circular blue dish. Dr. Zastro passed the vessel under Mavis's nose keeping his own nostrils averted. "We are going to calm all your fears, Miss Michalek. Take away all this anxiety and dread."

With the first whiff of the vapors, she let out a piercing scream that subsided into moaning whimpers.

"Now, just relax, Miss Michalek. There are no machines in this room. We do not perform operations in here. I will not even touch you during consultation."

He gave the vapor dish to his assistant, "Shyam, you are dismissed. I believe I can handle Miss Michalek from hereon," adding, "but keep within hearing."

"Yes, doctor," Shyam bowed, exited in anxiousness to get away, as though the hallway encounter had been enough dealing with such a demented person. However, Mavis was not demented, only frightened, away from her home, family, in strange surroundings. Who knows what she had been told might happen to her once she was here. Consulting his pad, Dr. Zastro proceeded as the vapors continued their effect.

"Mavis Michalek, age twenty seven, from Three Creeks. And your father is your legal guardian?"

Her voice was deep and guttural. "Pa—he made me come. Ma made me too."

"But they were willing to pay for your stay here, because they are concerned about you." He did not know her home circumstances, but the correspondence had been crude, illiterate, sent from a rural area. "They care about your health. You believe that, don't you?"

"I don know. They just made me come. I never been off the farm before."

"I see, and you've never been married, is that correct?"

She nodded, not looking up.

"Just calm down now and try to tell me, in your own words, what it is that's bothering you. Don't be afraid to talk about anything with me. Anything at all."

Her voice was a mumble. "I don know."

"Pain anywhere?" he asked. She shook her head.

"Any discharges?" Same response.

"You know the parts of the human anatomy?" No response. He pulled down the female chart. "Now, when I point to the chart, tell me where you have pain. The breast?" A head shake.

"The stomach?" The same silent *no*.

"The vagina?" A puzzled look. "Between the legs," he said, trying to clarify with terms of country simplicity. She shook her head hesitantly.

"The rectum?" Another puzzled look. "The hole in your seat?" A definite shake of the head.

Dr. Zastro proceeded lighting the candle. "I think we need to relax you a bit more." He continued his soothing repertoire of words until when he lifted her arm, it was limp and her inner sounds had ceased.

"That's a good girl. Now Mavis, tell me what is troubling you so."

"I don know...." Her voice was even deeper now, a monotone groan.

"Why were you sent here?"

"I don't have my curse—don't bleed between my legs for two months."

"Do you know why?"

"My pa, he sent me here. He says, 'Doctor will find out truth—Doctor will look inside you.' He whip me with horsewhip. I still say, 'No man touched me there.'"

"What is the truth, Mavis?" Truth was all he asked for from his patients and mesmerizing brought out the truth.

"Ma, she makes me show her the rag, every month. First month, I use chicken blood. Next month, I cut my finger for blood. Ma checks me down there, 'No blood!' she screams. 'You skipped!' Pa says I been doing it with a man. Ma says, 'no, it's something else'; her finger can tell. Pa says he'll put his own pisser in there and then he can tell too. Ma screams at him to keep it away from me." Mavis's hands clutched at her private parts in an attempt to protect herself from the memory.

"Pa, he whips me again. 'Tell me who had their pisser in you!'" Mavis began crying. "I'm bleeding all over now, my arms—my legs. Stomach is sick. And still he keeps whipping. 'Who?' he yells. No one. No one. I tell him."

"It's all right, Mavis," the doctor interrupted, "just relax for a moment. Breathe deeply and relax."

She went on. "I don't let no man get near me. Uncle Joe, one time he tried to grab me, inside my drawers, with his big hairy hand. I kicked him, hard as I could, between his legs. Ma always said to do that. I never told her about Uncle Joe."

"Mavis, do you know why you haven't menstruated—had your bleeding?" He tried to steer her back on track.

"No.... Ma says I work too hard. My brother Steve, he died of the typhoid. I do his work too. Plowing. Milking. Hauling manure. Pa says work is good for women. Gives them big tits. Ma says there's something wrong with me between the legs because I don't like boys. She wants me to get married. Tells me in secret, 'You got to move away.' Pa, he don't let me go nowhere. With Steve gone, he says I can't never leave the farm."

"He let you come here."

"Ma told him to. She can read. She read how you advertise machines to cure women. She wants me cured, so I can find a husband." She drew in a deep breath. "She's the one who brought me here, and—I don't want to be here by myself."

"You have nothing to fear here, Mavis, but you must tell me what your problem is, so that I may cure you. Remember too, there is no punishment here, for anything you say, anything you do."

The girl sat up, new agitation breaking her from her slumber state. "I don want to get married. Ma says that's how you get a baby—if you let a man's pisser get near you."

"Calm down now. Just calm down." He debated whether to put her into a deeper sleep.

"Am I going to have a baby? I don't want something that big growing inside me. Pa says it gets big, like a giant punkin, and they pull your whole insides out when it comes out."

"Let me press your stomach, very gently, see if I can feel anything growing inside there. Relax—just relax."

She cowered as he felt the pelvic area, fingers probing over her gown.

"No, there's no baby growing inside you."

"Sometimes I think a baby is growing up in there," she whimpered, "that pa put his pisser in me while I was sleeping. He used to do that, when I was little. Ma won't let him no more."

"You're sure he doesn't do that anymore?" If that were true—

"No. Ma, she locks my door at night. And I stay away from him in the barn."

"I see."

He wouldn't deal with the father-daughter problem right now, although he had encountered it numerous times before. Fathers—or a brother, mostly relatives. Even when it was the father, the girls never wanted it revealed. Many committed suicide rather than have a relative face any kind of prosecution or punishment. They believed the disgrace was of their own doing. He continued, trying to use terms she might understand.

"Sometimes women have other things growing inside that same area, that block the menses—bleeding. Tomorrow I am going to examine you. A complete examination of all your parts. Your treatment will concentrate on stimulating the pelvis, the stomach area. Massage, herbs, spices—and the magnetic stool."

He clapped his hands. "You may sit up now, Mavis. You are already feeling awake and refreshed. Every one of your secrets is safe here. These three weeks will make you into a new woman, a changed person."

The fright returned as she pleaded, "Don't make me into something else. Please. I know you do magic here, but don't change me into another person. They won't know me when I go home to the farm. They won't let me back in."

"There is nothing to worry about. You will look the same outside, but inside you will feel different," he said with as much reassurance as he could.

"I won't have big punkin growing inside me?"

"I want to convince you that you do not have a baby, and certainly not a pumpkin, growing inside you."

"No baby—how," she began wailing. "You looked inside me when I was sleeping? You poked something in me so you could see in there. Pa said you'd do that. Then, then, he said, you'd tear the monster baby out of me and I should be careful so my guts wouldn't come out too." She put her hand to her mouth. "I—I feel—I'm—going to puke—" Retching sounds overtook her words.

The doctor handed her a towel as he rang the bell. "Here, press this against your mouth."

Shyam appeared in the doorway, "Yes, doctor."

"Take Miss Michalek to the water closet. Quickly. Then give her slippery elm and peppermint tonic."

Shyam led the heaving Mavis down the hall.

Dr. Zastro sat down to compose himself. These mesmerizing sessions did drain his energies, sometimes terribly so. He must remember to take extra tonic today. Then as if in a distance, he heard faint singing.

Aye solea, solea....

It was Yana's voice. Was she in the hallway, or was he hearing it only in his head? Just as he got up to check, Shyam returned.

"Lady scream to be alone in water closet room." He shrugged his shoulders as if to absolve himself of any blame.

"All right. All right. If she doesn't come out in a few minutes, you go in and get her."

"Yes, doctor." Shyam turned to leave.

"And Shyam, remind the patients, if you should hear them, we don't allow singing in this area, only in the Recreation Room. It is unladylike and different decibels of sound might disturb some of our treatments."

"No one is singing now, doctor." Shyam appeared puzzled.

"I thought—Go, look after Mavis." Shyam left.

Then Phillipe heard it again, over and over, a siren's song calling out to him. He put his hands over his ears to quiet the melody, but it only seemed to grow louder within. He reminded himself he would be meeting with Yana tonight. He would speak to her then about her singing. He would also speak to her about...he had no idea what he would speak to her about, what might take place between them at all. He had no idea what might occur that late at night with a woman of her nature, a wild woman who did not want to be tamed.

Did he want her tamed? Had he not concluded, way back, that most animals were better left in their wild state. Domestication sometimes destroyed. But then, he was not an animal trainer; he was a doctor.

CHAPTER 8

Yana put away her *dukkering-lil,* her fortune-telling book, giving up on finding some message within. There was none, not today. Still, she felt lucky just having the treasured book back in her possession. It was a comfort to caress the old red morocco-leather volume to her heart, feeling Grandmama's presence permeating every page. It was true, the old axiom, that objects long carried or worn by someone absorbed the essence of that person's life and would give that essence back again, in another form, to those who later possessed the item.

So many times, she had seen Grandmama poring over the contents with her squinting eyes, index finger lingering along each page. Mama too had consulted the *dukkering-lil,* but not with the same sense of ritual that Grandmama had brought to her readings of the book. The book and the gold necklace were family treasures, tribal relics passed on from female to female. The tribe was still seeking the return of this special book, claiming it shouldn't remain with *pikie.* Never. Money couldn't buy such a remarkable volume nor could it buy the inherent legacies bestowed on any who rightfully possessed the book. Yana most certainly had that right.

That morning, while Isobelle was working in the kitchen, some intuition had told Yana to look in the pocket of Isobelle's extra apron, which generally hung on a hallway peg. *Bakalo!* One of the keys to the storage room was there, clearly marked. Yana had taken it and gone to the storage room to recover this book, her tambourine, and more art supplies.

While in the banned area, she had also lovingly held her Gypsy clothing—basking in their accumulated familiar scents, their comforting feel, before placing them back into the wicker basket. Her garments still awaited the fate of being sanitized. Well, she would rescue them another time, not wanting to push her luck too far today.

She had to admit that she was not uncomfortable wearing the loose silken gowns. Strangely, the material did impart a certain languidness to her whole body, soothing the skin as it skimmed along its surface. It wasn't the electrical treatments accomplishing that—or was it? She shut and locked the storage room door and hurried to return the key to Isobelle's apron.

Upon returning to her room, Yana coiled her braid atop her head, and then began poring through the treasured book, seeking buried messages. At least now she had some familiar basics to make her stay here more bearable: art supplies, this book, charms, and her tambourine to shake for special joy. Somehow, she must still retrieve her gold necklace, but that, she had been told, was secured in another area.

On hearing Shyam's bell, Yana hastily put the book up into the air vent, atop her paints and brushes. Everything about this day would be different now, with or without relevant messages from the book.

The Treatment Room was bathed in bluish light, a Strauss waltz tinkling, sounds of machines clicking and whirring, Shyam strapping the women into their chairs. Yana passed by Delphine, who was perched on the electric stool, seemingly enjoying whatever it was taking place between her and the whirring stool.

"This here stool is my favorite place to sit." Delphine was trying to convey some of her pleasure to Mavis, who was also seated on one of the three stools, but seemed to be in absolute misery.

"You are late, Miss Yana." Shyam led her to her awaiting chair, strapping the belt over her arm, clicking the ON switch. She could feel slight tremors of electricity beginning their rapid pulsing up through her arm muscles. It was not painful, but still, it was not a pleasant experience.

What if these tingling currents made the injury worse? Reversed the healing process? What if she could never paint again? The thought made her want to tear the belt from her arm, flee fast as she could. No, she decided in almost the exact same moment, marking her heart in a ritualistic gesture. *Atchava! I will make a compromise with fate. I will swear a binding promise to myself that I will try the treatments for one complete week.* If at the end of the week nothing was getting better, she'd leave. You didn't get a refund; the rules had stressed several times, if you left of your own accord. No matter, it would be worth the monetary loss to regain her freedom.

This was not a prison, she reminded herself; she could leave whenever she wished. Yet, some of the women, committed by their husbands or parents, probably had no choice but to complete the program. Of course, they were used to being ruled by someone else. She was not.

Her chair was next to Edwina, who was sitting straight and erect, a humming belt circling her head—a queen petrified in her royal throne. "Is that belt helping your head any?" Yana had a special gift for speaking to strangers. All Gypsies did. It made it easy for them to gain the trust of strangers, tell their fortunes or con them into almost anything. Yana had never used trickery but the inherent talent to reach out to others and gain their confidence was still accessible and sometimes came in handy.

"Yes, it does help," Edwina answered without turning any part of her body. Isobelle was exclaiming, to anyone around her; she was so excited about what was happening to her. "Mine back—pain is getting littler and littler. Thank Gott. Oh thank Gott."

Since Edwina was educated in correct manners, she felt obliged to return the courtesy of Yana's health inquiry. "And, are your arm and leg being cured?" she asked stiffly, as though corset stays were still in place to hold her in and up.

"Hurts even more than before," Yana admitted. "I think I'll just take this belt off for awhile."

"We were told not to remove anything." Edwina seemed a bit shocked that anyone would be that bold.

Even Mavis, who hardly said anything ever, tried to warn Yana. "Doctor says we must do as told, if we want the cure."

"Mr. Doctors, he guarantees cure." Isobelle was again spouting another unrequested testimonial about the doctor.

Yana wasn't used to being sequestered indoors with groups of women, or females with no common ground to assimilate them into any general conversation.

She remembered back, being with the tribe, and even though she and Mama were still considered outsiders, they were always welcomed around the campfire each evening, enjoying the gathered camaraderie. There was singing, dancing, someone playing the violin, tambourines jingling, dogs barking in the distance and the smoky scent of the campfire crackling into the night air.

It didn't matter what they talked about—long ago happenings, repeated folk tales. The women, generally separated from the men, had their own interlocked conversations, punctuated with gales of laughter, ringing out into the clear dark night, echoing, reverberating—even now.

Yana missed that closeness of kin. She had found nothing since that spooled those crude but strong threads of family that gave special meaning to the patterns of each day and carried their own messages along the twisting cord of life.

True, there was camaraderie among the artists, but they met only for short periods, in a salon or cafe, and then were off to somewhere else, or so busy with their artwork they couldn't take time for daily gatherings. Evenings in the Paris cafes had however come closest to the clan meetings. But once you left the gold candlelight of a bistro, it only made the your solitary room that much darker and colder. The next night might be a different mix of people, the continuity never guaranteed. Exciting, but not sustaining.

Nothing again would ever equal traveling with a Gypsy tribe, that deep feeling of belonging. No one could replace Mama's family, women who could trace their ancestry back over years and years, through many different countries, holding to this common bloodline that braided them all together. Even when they were oceans apart, the bond was still coursing.

"That Dr. Zastro, he can do whatever he likes with me." Delphine was giggling again. "I wouldn't care what it was, I would welcome every bit, even pay double for it."

"His eyes—" Edwina wasn't quite sure that it was proper to speak about any man other than her husband in a personal manner, but she did anyway. "Something so spiritual in them, that when he looks at you, you are ready to believe anything he might say or do—" She stopped as though she feared to reveal more.

"Have you ladies ever heard of mesmerizing?" Yana interrupted. "It's quite popular in France." She decided she might as well join the conversation, conceding she was going to be cloistered with this group for quite awhile; plus she was interested in their different opinions of Dr. Zastro. It was apparent he had each of them convinced of his magnificent powers.

"Mesmerizing? I've never heard of it, and I read a great deal, travel many places." Edwina seemed more intelligent than the others, and yet her practiced reserve kept her from disclosing all that she knew. Decorum also stifled many other things that seemed to be rumbling within her.

"Well, mesmerizing is when another person can take control of your mind and makes you believe whatever he wants." Yana felt obliged to inform them of what was happening to them when Dr. Zastro put them to sleep, which was not really sleep. Whether they wanted to accept what was being done to them was up to each of them, but someone needed to inform them what was taking place, since the doctor didn't always feel they needed explanations.

There was fear in Edwina's voice. "The devil—he can take control of people, if you do bad things."

"No." Yana wanted to reassure Edwina. "This has nothing to do with the devil, it has to do with a person who has a mind stronger than yours. Dr. Zastro has a very powerful mind, and when he mesmerizes you, you can be made to believe anything—even believe you're cured—whether you are or not."

"No way any one can tell me mine back won't hurt." Isobelle was staunch in her retort.

Delphine turned her attention away from the stool to join in. "I like it when Dr. Zastro mesmerizes me, or whatever it is he does to me. He can do anything he likes to me."

"It's—it's his machines. They do the curing." Mavis had a difficult time getting her words out, as if someone would strike her if she said the wrong thing. "Machines can do anything. I'm real scared of that 'lectricity stuff though."

Mavis seemed the kind of person who would jump at the sight of her own shadow. Still, she was accepting everything happening here without any protest. Sitting in her chair, scared to death, but questioning nothing. That bothered Yana most, that these ladies were ready to accept any fate any man handed them, without questioning.

"Mine lady," Isobelle interjected, "she read me letters what peoples send in—telling how Mr. Doctors, he cured them. Is truth. And some don't even see him, in the person. So how can he do that mesmerizing stuff to them then? Huh?"

"All I know is I feel good—whenever he even talks to me," Delphine giggled girlishly, "or just looks at me with those sugary brown eyes. It's his eyes do the curing. His hands move that electricity stuff all around inside my body. Mesmerizing—I call it messing with me." She giggled and squirmed around on the stool, pulling her robe close as though cocooned in joy.

"Ma says, he can cure anything." Mavis's eyes were wide and believing. "Our neighbor, Mrs. Hackbarth, she went to Dr. Zastro, with a tumor big as a pig, and he cured her. Honest. She told my ma to send me to him for whatever was wrong with me." Mavis's voice lowered into her usual muttering. "I believe Mrs. Hackbarth. I believe my ma. I believe Dr. Zastro. I don't believe nobody else."

Evidently they all had already put their trust in the good doctor, even more apparent was that none of these women had ever learned to think for herself. Yana surrendered the notion of changing their minds. At least she had tried.

Althea, who was rocking in the Rocking Machine, began moaning louder.

"There, poor Althea doesn't sound like she's getting any better," Yana said.

"Because she faints all the time," Delphine still had the giggle in her voice, "before the doctor can even tell her things— or examine her. She still won't let no man touch her. Such a pity." It seemed Delphine had a special pipeline to Sanitarium gossip, possibly because she had been here before and knew many of the assistants, probably bribed them with presents, promises. "If he once got to examine her, I bet she wouldn't need any old rocking machine. She might even want to try one of these here magnetic stools."

The women went on chattering and Yana retreated into her own thoughts. She could do that any time she wished, seclude herself from everything around her, go deep into her own mind. Yet, she could not escape the electrical vibrations channeling through her system, their constant interruption to any serious contemplation.

She felt so restless in this room. Yet, the others seemed so content, strapped in, tremored, intent and serious about accepting each of their specially prescribed treatments. Except for Althea, who kept moaning in rhythm with the machine's rocking. Shyam was at his stool station, but his gaze was mostly on Althea.

"Just sitting here, for two hours, with nothing to do," Yana expressed to no one in particular. "I don't know how I'll make it through these three weeks."

"If you had eight children," Edwina interjected, "you wouldn't feel that way."

"Eight children?"

"Yes. Rest hotels, sanitariums, these are the only places where I can truly relax. I try to go as often as Horace will allow me. It's so wonderful to have a spouse who cares for the well being of his wife."

And has the money to do it, Yana thought.

"You all have servants, don't you?" Delphine directed her remark to Edwina, trying to enter conversations whenever she could.

"Even with servants, my time is interrupted by the children. Never one moment to call my own." She added importantly, "It is a mother's duty to be responsible for the moral and spiritual upbringing of her children."

"At night, you can rest," Yana said. Nights were her private time for wandering her mind, exploring new thoughts, without leaving her pallet, yet traveling along the air waves to so many far away places, as distant as the stars. Sometimes slightly awake, sometimes near dreaming, but she reveled in letting her mind lead while she joyfully followed.

"Nights belong to my husband," Edwina stated, and then as if quoting from some biblical passage, "A wife, mother, must be giving of herself. That is her mission in life. Her rewards will be built up, given back to her in heaven."

"If that's the life you choose." Yana knew she would never choose it, be submissive to anyone nor would she take any kind of vows that said you had to promise to love, honor and obey for a lifetime. How could women make such false promises?

"God chooses our lives for us." Edwina intoned as an "amen".

"Is goot sometimes to just sit, not work. Is goot." Isobelle seemed so content in her chair, as if it were padded with clouds.

"I—I never been away from the farm before." Mavis sounded wistful. "I miss my ma—my pa too." Her mouth puckered and tremored as if she were going to cry.

"This is my favorite place to come to." Delphine squirmed with audacious pleasure on her stool. "I love talking with other ladies too. Solomon, he never says much."

"You have servants, too, don't you?" Edwina queried.

"All kinds. But, well, you can't talk to servants, not like real people."

"You should have children." Edwina sounded like a reprimanding mother. "Then there's always someone to talk to, pass on your thoughts and your philosophies. They must always listen to you because you are their guardian and teacher, here on this earth."

Delphine looked up and announced, "I can't have children."

"How—how do you know?" Mavis asked.

"I just do." Delphine finalized.

"How—how do you get so?" Mavis asked amazed. "So you won't ever have a baby?"

"I don't want to talk about it."

"I don't ever want no baby." Mavis sounded frightened even thinking of the possibility.

"That's devil talk, child." Edwina turned her head the slight distance the restraining headband allowed.

"The choice is up to Mavis." Yana felt she needed to defend the unschooled Mavis.

"If you get married, you take a vow to have children." Edwina sounded more preacher-like with each pronouncement.

"I ain't never getting married," Mavis said with fierce finality.

"You wanta stay on that farm all your life?" Delphine chided. "Lest a woman gets married, she can't hardly support herself. Men still have to pay her way. What else can you do without a man, 'cept servant work, or—" She stopped before going any further.

"Mavis," Yana said leaning toward her, "learn to read. Then you can escape, no matter where you are. Once you learn to read, life will take on new freedoms and you can never be confined to just one world again. You will be able to escape any time you wish."

"Too much studying is bad for women's constitutions." Edwina was quoting from somewhere else now. It seemed she never had an original thought, only what someone else had told her or what she had read somewhere.

"Do you believe that learning will harm a woman's brain, her reproductive organs?" Yana couldn't understand women believing such stupid concepts.

"It's a proven fact," Edwina retorted. "I read too. At every one of the sanitariums. All of their literature. They warn over and over about overusing your brain. So, I know it is a proven fact, by persons more learned than you are."

The anger was boiling again in Yana. "Proven by whom? Some man who puts a 'doctor' in front of his name, because he had money enough to spend a few months at a medical school? Or has money enough to buy a diploma? That makes him 'All knowing'?"

"Doctors *are* special people," Mavis insisted.

"Yah, and this one is a fine, fine doctors." Isobelle, too, sounded militant in her defense.

"Dr. Zastro is the finest." Edwina trumpeted.

"I'd never go to anyone else." Delphine seemed happy to find common ground with the group.

"He's—he's not like other men at all," Mavis expressed in a new awestruck tone, as though Dr. Zastro were Prince Charming coming to rescue her.

"He is special. Yah." Isobelle cheered her hero once more.

"Those eyes—they look right through me."   Delphine obviously didn't care what anyone thought of her feelings for Zastro. "His look quivers throughout my whole body. In all my life, I never met anyone like him."

"You ladies," Yana said, not quite sure how to convince them, or whether she still wanted to, "you—you are all acting like silly school girls."

"And you—you is acting like you is our boss. And you isn't. For once I don't have no boss. For once I am boss of mineself." Isobelle had such fight in her voice now. "I take orders from this doctors any time."

Luckily, the bell rang. Who knows where this beginning of a soft rebellion might have gone. Not too far, Yana reassured herself, not when they were all strapped down into their restraining machines. Yet, it was interesting to note how well they could fight with their voices, fight for their own thoughts even if those thoughts were warped by misinformation. They weren't such a bunch of subdued nonthinking females as she had originally perceived.

Women learned to fight in so many different ways. They had to in order to survive; they devised means to battle overpowering circumstances in any way they could. Gypsy women did it all the time. Maybe that was their common thread here, these background struggles that bound all women together in a unifying voice that was not always heard, but could be felt whenever they gathered. Different tones, different words, varied backgrounds, but an underlying connecting strand that interwove through each of them, transmitting their rudimentary pasts into a unified knowing.

Shyam was clapping his hands, "Ladies, treatment is over."

"Already?" Delphine seemed disappointed.

Shyam unstrapped Isobelle first. "It is time to help with the supper now."

"Yah, yah, I go." Isobelle heaved a heavy sigh and got up, leaving reluctantly.

Shyam continued unstrapping the women. Most hesitated a bit before getting up, stretching, lingering, as if to get that last particle of treatment.

As Yana began removing her belt, Shyam was at her side, his strong arm stopping her movements. "No patient allowed to remove electrical apparatus. Only Dr. Zastro and Shyam. Current must be broken in right way."

"I was only trying to help."

"Shyam need no help." There was something threatening about his tone. Something deep within him that was forbidding—or was it only the reflection of his own fright—being so far away from his homeland and having to adjust to such a strange place. She knew firsthand that feeling, and her premonitions of any threat from Shyam eased. She was also reminded that way back, both of their ancestors were from the wilds of India. They were of the same origin.

"I still feel tingly," Delphine giggled as Shyam released her. She stood shaking her arms and legs in circular jiggles.

Shyam clapped his hands again. "Ladies, doctor has asked you put urine specimen in bottle before you eat supper. Then urine specimen in bottle after you eat supper, so amount of electricity you are eating and passing through can be measured. Bottles are outside water closet room with names on. Please do not take wrong bottle. If you cannot read your name, ask. Mistakes can be disastrous." He bowed and left.

"What—what is urine specimen?" Mavis was puzzled, disturbed.

"You are a silly thing," all-knowing Delphine chimed. "It's when you make pee water. Course here you don't have to use those smelly outhouses, like you do on your farm."

"Mavis," Yana said, coming forward to reassure the girl, "if you want to know anything, just ask me."

Delphine's tone was brimming with sarcasm, "Miss Yana knows just about everything there is to know. Or else she can make it up with her Gypsy lies."

Yana gave Delphine such a penetrating stare that her giggle stopped in midair and her full pink mouth stayed open and inoperative.

"I still don't know how to work—the water closet," Mavis seemed nervous and fidgety.

"Come on, I'll show you." Yana started to lead Mavis by the arm.

"Yana, wait." Delphine grabbed Yana's hand away.

"What is it?" Yana did not like being stopped in the middle of any kind of action, especially by Delphine.

"I have a question," Delphine seemed serious, even perplexed.

"What is it? I was going to help Mavis." But Mavis had already escaped.

"This is important. It's something I need to know, but—I don't know how to say it."

"Just say it then." Yana knew it would be something trivial and not worth discussing.

"How can you tell if a person is in love with you?"

"You mean your husband?"

"No, not that kinda love. I mean the kind that flutters your heart—like Ella Wheeler Wilcox and those poet people write about." Delphine was serious and troubled.

"I don't know exactly." It was not the question for which she had an easy answer ever—but how on earth to explain love to someone like Delphine. A conundrum.

"I'll tell you a secret. Don't you tell no one," she looked about cautiously. "I'm in love with Dr. Zastro. That's why I come back here every year." She sounded so self-important, making Yana even more annoyed by the interruption, the forced hearing of her stupid confession.

"You—and the doctor?"

"I get all giggly and mushy just looking at him. When he touches me, I swoon—but," she added hastily, "not like Althea."

"He does have an effect on women." Even Yana had to admit that, but then most of these women had so little contact with men, men who cared about them as individuals and who were concerned about their well being. This Sanitarium was one place where women were given special empathy, a caring kindness they very seldom received elsewhere in their lives.

"Delphine, I don't think the doctor's in love with anyone. It all has to do with his dedication to his work as a physician. His effect on women is only his way of healing."

"You're wrong. I know he feels a special way bout me. That's why he asks me back every year, because he wants to see me again. He told me I am an unusual woman."

"That may be, but—"

"I need to know, I have to know, if he's in love with me or not. How does a woman ever know?"

"A man tells you. That's how a woman knows."

"But maybe, even if he did love me, he might not say so, I mean—he's so—professional. Unattainable."

"He seems to be a very honest and forthright man."

"Well, what if he said he didn't love me, but he really did. How would I know the truth?"

"Somehow, in your heart, you'd know."

"I would? How?" Delphine's face held puzzlement and rage.

"There's a special feeling that passes between two people in love."

Yana herself had always known that, those sparks that ignited between two individuals as if by instinct. It had happened only a few times, but she always chose not to pursue it. If she felt herself too near to giving in, she would chant her protective verse—go on to something else. Immerse herself in some new venture. She tried never looking back, never regretting any of her dismissals.

Delphine was irritated, frustration exploding, "I can't know what other people feel. I never could. I only know what they tell me."

"Then you only listen with your ears, never your heart." Yana turned to leave to see if Mavis needed rescuing. Surely, that would be a more worthwhile cause than trying to explain love to someone like Delphine.

Delphine yelled after her in tantrum-like tones. "You're no help at all, you with your smarty answers."

Yana stopped and turned around only to witness Delphine kicking viciously at the magnetic stool. "And that Solomon, he's just taking forever to die." Delphine gave the stool another angry kick. "Forever and ever!" She then limped away in obvious pain.

Yana couldn't help feeling sorry for Delphine. To be in love with Dr. Zastro would be a futile yearning for anybody. To know it could never be returned would be pure anguish.

CHAPTER 9

Dr. Zastro was in his office preparing his morning lecture. Scatters of paper were jumbled about his desk. These would soon be arranged into neat, methodical piles. His goal was to make each of his lectures fit the needs of each new group of women, seeking to introduce fresh topics rather than repeat those given the year before.

How he disliked educators who sounded as if their discourses were given by rote. His father spoke out many times against professors who rolled over the same lecture, year after year—meandering along memorized words.

"If you yourself don't have the spark, how can you pass it on?" Papa's voice echoed as memories surfaced of sitting in his father's hallowed study while his idol rehearsed his classroom discourses, speaking in clear thoughts with phrases that invigorated. Phillipe had been fascinated by every enunciated word, even if he didn't always know the meaning.

He kept trying to emulate his father's example, giving his speeches vivid freshness and inserting new discoveries as he came across them. Eventually these lectures would end up as chapters in one of his books. Voluminous sales of all his publications were testimony to his success with words, the catalyst that perpetually moved him to write new works.

He had debated about this Wednesday morning's topic. Sometimes he switched subjects around, depending on his mood and the women's interests. Generally Wednesday would be: FOOD—WHAT WE PUT INTO OUR MOUTH IS WHAT OUR BODY BECOMES. THOUGHT—WHAT WE PUT INTO OUR BRAIN IS WHAT OUR CHARACTER BECOMES. A lengthy title, but a solid subject, since women did most of the food purchasing and preparation. They were also responsible for molding their children's minds. He believed they should be aware of the consequences, the great power they did control, even if they claimed they had so little power in their daily lives.

Instead, he decided to give his lecture BRUTALITY AND INHUMANITY, a subject he was examining, wishing to share his fresh views, tabulate possible reactions. These women had so little input about so many things. Most of their news was secondhand, read to them by husbands, passed on by employers, or gossip from other women.

Tomorrow's subject would be WOMEN'S BODIES—AND THEIR VARIOUS FUNCTIONS. He preferred speaking on that topic the first week in order to prepare the women, acquainting them with certain words and the various functions about their own female bodies.

He hadn't yet decided if it was better for women to be ignorant about their bodies and what took place inside, or having them know. Some only became more distressed, wondering about all the different kinds of diseases, new problems that could happen to them. Worry warts, who took up valuable medical time.

Primitive females had no idea at all about their bodily functions, and yet, they reproduced without any difficulty. Civilization was indeed progressing, making amazing discoveries daily. This knowledge, over time, did filter down to the women, upgrading their lives in ways that even they weren't aware of.

There was so much he already knew; surely, he could share some of these discoveries with these selected women. Maybe they in turn would share with other women. Except, he knew, they would distort most of his facts, revising his lectures to fit their own knowledge. Still, he had to make the effort.

His one wish was that all women could read. Then his books would carry his messages even further, into homes where medical knowledge was so lacking. There were so many books out there, but what was written needed to be correct and much was not. He made sure all his facts were researched before being spread by the presses.

He was still ambivalent about the conclusion that too much studying atrophied women's brains. He had not found that much difference between women and men's brains when dissecting them. Yet, it was proven that men were stronger—in their muscular physiology. Might not one logically assume their brains were stronger as well, thus making men able to work harder, both physically and mentally?

Women were such fragile creatures. Swooning. Fainting. During the time of their menses and their mid-life changes, they became different creatures. Men were not subject to these bodily rhythm alterations. Throughout the ages, men had been developing their strong constitutions, perfecting their brains. Thus it was man's role to guide women, to be their—well, he never did like using the word, *masters*, rather preferring to think of men as *helpmates*. He believed no one should be master of another human being unless he could help them. That was his manifesto. Even when mesmerizing, he was helping, not mastering.

The whole country had just been torn apart regarding the question as to whether any man could be the master of another person. Even the word *slave* grated his moral conscience. Being a Northerner, it was very simple to extend his sympathies in favor of fighting for freedom, granting emancipation to the Negro.

For two dreadful years during that destructive war, he had worked at the army hospital in Boston, tending the wounded, administering medications. He had been only in his twenties, but he had gained a greater portion of his medical education in that grim makeshift hospital where he assisted in operations, working alongside experienced doctors. It was gruesome, shocking, and so very sad to administer to the bodies of these once healthy young men, many mutilated for life.

"As water spilt on the ground, which cannot be gathered up again—" The biblical verse from his mother that had echoed to him many times in that hospital, an apt summation of that terrible war, only Phillipe always substituted the word "blood" for "water". He knew he never wanted to work in such a debilitating situation again. Well, the country was safe now. Chester A. Arthur, a Republican, was president, and times were once more prosperous.

His lecture notes were now arranged in neat piles, his outlines lay in complete order. He gathered his materials and headed toward the Lecture Room.   The Sanitarium workers in their crisp white uniforms were already coming down the hallway. He opened the lecture hour to any who worked in the Sanitarium area in hopes that they would benefit from the information he bestowed, as much as his selected patients did. Most workers took advantage of this hour of non-work; Zastro's only requirement was that they stay awake and not use the period to nod off in sleep. If they did, Shyam removed them.

The section for the workers was on the far right, near the door. His select patients were relegated to the left and center. He paused, looking out over the assembled women, feeling a surge of pride and accomplishment, as though he alone were helping them to understand life and its many complexities.

"Good morning, ladies. Today our subject will be brutality and inhumanity, which many of you have never encountered, but, within your lifetime, will surely rear its ugly head. My mission during these weeks is to prepare you for all aspects of life." He cleared his throat and proceeded.

"Shocking instances of brutality and inhumanity are straining the nerves of all good people. Some people delight in whipping horses; others in kicking dogs; and there are those who cannot pass an animal of any kind without hitting it with sticks or stones.

"It is tragically enormous in men who delight in the carnage of war. Who boast how much they like to fight, and who can look with fiendish complacency upon the bleeding form of a brother slain."

Isobelle was already sleeping. Maybe she didn't want to know any more about brutality, having experienced it firsthand. Althea's head was bent downward, but at least she was in the room today.

He continued. "It is a power incomprehensible when it compels a man to murder a large family, as illustrated in the recent case of the Probst murders."

Surely, this tragedy was so prominent, that even if these women hadn't read about it in the newspapers, they must have heard the story. He didn't wish to repeat the abhorrent saga, yet he saw no signs of recognition from any of his audience. Pity they were so ignorant to the world happening around them. Delphine was listening with intense concentration, always trying to understand whatever it was he said, but words were probably as far as she got, never the meanings. He might as well skip over to the next notes.

"May it not be that the promised millennial era—*When the lion and lamb shall lie down together*—an age of peace will make its advent on earth. This will be possible as soon as man shall have subdued all his cruel passions—as soon as he shall recognize the rights of animals of every grade, to exist and enjoy life—shall love his neighbor as himself—and shall love everything that creeps upon the earth because his Father made it.

"Inhuman conduct between men produces the greatest discord in the nervous system. It not only injuriously affects the perpetrator and victim of the cruel act, but it convulses the nervous systems of those who witness it, and those in the radius of thousands of miles, who may read, or be told the affecting tale.

"*'Man's inhumanity to man, Makes countless thousands mourn.'* Our poet Burns never uttered truer words. When these cruelties culminate in murder, we witness the inhumanity of scores of people gathering in mobs to be revenged upon the unfortunate murderer.

"The law protects its victim not only from the ferocity of the mob, but with stomach-pump takes from the wretched man the poison he has swallowed, in order that it may have the satisfaction of putting out his poor life. When he has sufficiently recovered, he is conducted, trembling, to this guillotine, the garrotes, or the hangman's scaffold." This did bring about a few shudders from his delicate audience. Mavis's hands were twitching all over her chair. At least he had their attention once more.

"Does anyone consider the moral and physical injury the human family suffers from the inhuman practices of beheading, choking to death, and hanging those who, through unfortunate mental organization, or more unfortunate circumstances, commit murder or other crime?

"It is urged by many that capital punishment restrains people from committing crimes, but statistics show that more murders are committed in Massachusetts where the death penalty is rigidly administered than in Wisconsin where it has been for several years abolished. People laboring under violent passion seldom pause to consider consequences."

He went on, maybe a bit excessively, about capital punishment, a subject he was fervent about, and if he had but the time, would be out there crusading in the front lines. The ladies were again losing interest; he skipped over more notes, conceding, this was his own personal commitment, not theirs.

"Let me also add that it would be greatly conducive to health if people would suppress the morbid taste or curiosity that leads them to witness a stage, or real tragedy; that makes them attentive readers of a tragic story, accounts of actual murder; that induces them to apply to the sheriff for permission to witness the dying convulsions of a convicted murderer, or fly to the newspaper for the harrowing description of the last moments of the condemned man."

He glanced at his audience. Yana's eyes were wandering the ceiling. Edwina's attention was still focused on him, but she seemed to be more tense than usual. Even the workers were having difficulty staying awake. He ended the lecture shortly thereafter and did not linger in the room as he sometimes did; he was certain there would be few comments or questions.

At two p.m. Shyam brought Edwina Weber into the Consulting Room. This session shouldn't be too difficult. An older woman, Edwina was more intelligent than most. Sometimes years did advance their own intelligence—just passing through the living process multiplied wisdom and knowledge. Animals learned by trial and error; so did human beings. Education only helped them learn more quickly, digest more rapidly what others before them had learned, written down, passed on.

The preliminaries with Mrs. Weber were concluded with minimal effort. She didn't even need the relaxation. She was accustomed to sanitariums, spas, and doctors. She settled herself

on the lounge, reclining without waiting for Dr. Zastro's
instructions.

"You have the look of a healthy woman, one who follows
good rules of hygiene," he began.

"Yes, doctor, I do try." There was a certain cultured quality
to her voice and manner. Yet, even in this relaxing position, she
remained rigid. Her lips were pursed and tight, her eyes troubled.
Some deeper distress within her needed to be uncovered.

"Shyam, you may remain here for this consultation."

"I thought this was private," Edwina protested with some
anxiety.

"Only to observe. As a part of his training." Shyam sat in
the corner chair as Dr. Zastro consulted his pad.

"Edwina Weber, wife of Horace Weber."

"Yes, doctor."

"Age—fifty?"

"Yes. I was born April 25th, 1834."

"And, your husband, your legal guardian, sent you here?"

"Yes, doctor."

"Now, what seems to be your problem at this time? I know
we have your letter, but our consultation time is to explore all
areas of your well being."

"Well—" She seemed to have great difficulty in getting the
words out, as though they were buried too deep inside and she
wanted to keep them hidden.

"No need for holding back. I've heard everything there is to
hear." That wasn't quite true, since each session revealed new
ailments and maladies he had not encountered before. It was the
joy of research, these new discoveries. Others did exploring of
the lands; he did exploring of human bodies.

"Well—" she hesitated again.

"Surely, someone who has had eight children has little to be
embarrassed about." He pulled down the female chart. "Do you
have any pain?"

"I'm-- I'm in my changes." She sounded so guilty,
apologetic.

"I see."

"And I want you to help me, at any cost."

"My Sanitarium helps women in all stages of life, and the cost is the same for everyone."

"In my head, I—I don't want to go crazy."

"You don't have the look of a crazy woman. Your eyes appear normal. You haven't torn out your hair."

All of a sudden, it flowed forth, words tumbling one over another, as if she didn't want to stop until she was rid of the complete burden.

"Horace's mother, she went crazy when she went through her changes. Horace, he put her away. She's still in the asylum. I visited her once. She was screaming and screaming. At night, I hear myself screaming in the same way." She turned her head to look away, unsettled by what she had just revealed.

"It's all right. Just relax now. We'll help you relax."

He did not feel that he needed to mesmerize her. Sometimes the mesmerizing process was more difficult with older women; their minds were so set. She did, however, need some sort of soothing.

"I'm going to pass my hand over your forehead to relieve your tensions." He began stroking her forehead, her temples. He rubbed his hands over these areas until he could feel the relaxation taking over. "Better?"

"Yes. I think so."

"I am your confidante. You can tell me all your problems. If you feel it's too difficult, I can put you to sleep."

"No. No, I'll tell you. I have to tell someone. And I trust you. You are a man of God also."

"I believe in the Divine Providence."

She hesitated once more, her mouth quivering, eyes watering.

"Please speak freely. Whatever is troubling you? We never reveal to husbands what wives tell us here."

"Horace. He's angry my changes are coming. His mother didn't have them until later in age." She paused; her breathing became more rapid. "He wants more children. I tried. I always did my Christian duty by him. Any time he wanted, I accommodated him. No more children appeared.

"The last one, Jonathon, eight years ago—he ripped me apart so, I—I don't think my body can take another child. God knows, I never prayed to keep children away. Horace claims I did. He accuses me of not praying hard enough for a new child. He wants another heir so bad. He fills me with his seed every time he can. Then, last month, he cursed me. Screamed I was barren."

"Barren? After eight children?"

"He accused me of doing something sinful. That's why God won't give me any more children."

"Have you done anything sinful?"

There was a suppressed scream. "No."

It was so close to the surface; he sensed he must help her free it. "You are certain?"

Edwina began crying, "Yes. Yes, I did."

"Relax now. Tell me what you did."

"After my last baby, the pain was so bad, I—I prayed to God to never send me another." More crying broke through. "Now, I'm going to be punished for those prayers. I'm going to go crazy during my changes, and they'll put me away. Who will watch over my children? Who will take care of Horace?"

He passed his palms over her forehead, and then held both her hands, trying to calm her.

"Shyam, some vapors, please." He spoke soothingly as he passed the dish of vapors back and forth under her nostrils. "I'm sure the Lord has forgiven your unholy wish. The Lord knows women go through short periods of insanity every month, when their menses flow, and, sometimes after birth—"

"I wasn't insane, not then. I didn't want another baby."

"Did you do anything to prevent conception? A vinegar wash after intercourse? Wear a sponge in secret?"

"Never a sponge, Horace would know. And after, I can hardly touch myself, it hurts so. Horace takes a longer time, now that he's older."

"And does it hurt, at the beginning, when Horace puts his organ inside you?"

"Yes. Yes, it does. I'm all dried up inside, and when Horace comes near, I just tighten up even more. Each thrust is so painful, and I pray for him to spill his seed, get it over with quickly."

"Still, you don't refuse him?"

"Never. It's a wife's Christian duty. In the marriage vows."

He knew what he needed to know. She had revealed her deepest concerns.

"We'll talk more later. I think this is enough for our first session."

"But, doctor," she pleaded, "I need to know the truth. Am I going crazy or not?" She began scratching at her arms.

"No," he answered. "Your symptoms are only what women have gone through over the ages. I will give you some reading material later. Right now, I'm going to give you some special pills I've made up for women in their changes. They will curtail the hot flushes, itching skin, and the headaches. But, you can still accommodate your husband."

He went about, gathering the remedies and let her relax a bit.

"Some magnetic ointment rubbed in the vagina beforehand will lubricate the dryness, and you may find the intercourse more tolerable, even pleasant."

Her husband was an educated man, a lawyer, he would not abuse his wife. Sometimes he had to write notes to the husband about changing their sexual behavior, but so many resented outside interference in their marital rights. Most husbands refused to come in for any consultation. They never visited a doctor unless they were violently ill.

"Every day, while here, you will be put in a cold bath for one half hour in the morning and one half hour before bedtime. This will help your body cool the hot flushes and other effects, help hasten the changes. To keep the insanity away, you'll sit in the chair with the electro-magnetic head band."

Edwina was in great anxiety now, breathing in shallow gasps. "Doctor, doctor, is this an asylum?"

"No, this is a sanitarium."

Her hysteria was building as the breathing grew faster, the scratching deeper. "You're lying to me. I know you're lying."

"This is not an asylum, Mrs. Weber."

"Horace said he was going to put me away, because I was going insane, like his mother. She had twelve children. I know this is an asylum." A crazed look was overtaking her. "He said he was going to put me away and then find a younger woman who could give him more babies. He—he has all this money, all this seed. He wants it used for more children. I'm no use to him anymore. He wants me put away."

She continued even more rapidly, "Legally, if a woman is declared insane, her husband can divorce her. Horace said I'd be going to an asylum one of these days. Is this an asylum?"

"No, I assure you, this is not an asylum. Horace sent you here only because he wants you cured."

It was as if demons were possessing her, a whole new personality taking over; she sat upright, staring straight ahead, eyes bulging, saliva flowing from the corner of her mouth. "I can't be cured!" she screamed. "Women can never be cured from the curse God put upon them from the day they were born. Every month His curse descends upon us. Our vaginas flow with blood, streams of blood flowing out of us and no way to stop the constant drain. Our stomachs get cramps and our heads go dizzy, month after month, year after year!"

The crescendo continued to build. He had to let her go on, to get it all out. It proved to be the best way; it helped in the healing process.

"Then we suffer again, every night, when our husbands lie on top of us, crushing our bodies, twisting our insides. Pulling at our breasts as if we were cows. Sucking on them until they swell and hurt. A baby on one tit, a husband on another, until there's no milk left inside us. We're all dried up. How much is there inside a woman to give? How many pieces of her body must she give away to someone else? What does the Lord want of us?

"And, when we bear His children, our bodies are ripped apart again, and they keep pulling these babies out. Pieces of our flesh torn away from inside us. And they cut us with knives down there, dig deep inside with metal tools, strap us down to the operating tables—"

"Please, Mrs. Weber. Try to calm yourself"

Her voice slowed, became more ominous. "No. That's not all—There's still more. After they've used up our bodies, we still have to go through the changes. Then, either we go insane or turn into dried up withered old ladies. Hags. Witches. Men never go through these things. The monthlies, changes, giving birth. Men aren't born with the curse of Eve upon them. You can't ever stop being a woman!"

"You must get hold of yourself," he interrupted. She was going too far.

She brought her face closer, spewing accusation and pain. "There's nothing you can do for me. Nothing doctors can do. Or ministers. Or husbands. Because you're all men! Nobody ever uses your bodies. You don't know what we go through." She broke into hysterical sobbing.

"Women are doomed," she ranted through her tears, "doomed from the day they are born. And the curse is passed on from mother to daughter, generation after generation." She let out a long continuous scream that seemed to be coming from her innards, not her throat.

"Shyam," he called, "lower the couch, quickly."

Shyam proceeded to press the right levers.

"God help me! God help me!" She began tearing at the coiled braids, the graying hair springing out into tangled wild strands that shook as she continued screaming. Dr. Zastro held her down and brought out the straps hidden under the lounge.

"Now then, we are going to strap you down for a few minutes, until you calm your person. We don't want you hurting yourself."

"Keep away. Keep away from me!" she shrieked. "I don't want any more babies!" She writhed and struggled, kicking her legs.

Both he and Shyam had to hold her down, as they buckled the straps across her legs, chest, and head. They continued constraining her until her screams subsided into wracking sobs.

"We're going to help you Edwina. We are going to help you pass through these changes in your life."

He felt he could do this for her. He had done it for so many women. There was no truth in her fears that her husband wanted her in an asylum. Horace had written a sincere letter, asking only for a cure for his wife—for her problems.

Changes were just something women had to endure. Part of their nature, just as having children was—nursing them, raising them. Women were given so many wonderful, special areas of life to partake in, marvels which men could never experience. All men could do was help them.

"Shyam, stay with Edwina. When she's more in possession of her emotions, assist her with the cold bath. She will be needing many cold baths."

Dr. Zastro walked out of the room, his heart plagued by sympathetic turmoil. So attuned was he to his patients, so concerned about them, that he suffered whenever they suffered.

The Roof Garden—he needed to retreat to his own celestial city, where there was no suffering, no sickness. No inhumanity, no brutality. Yet, once alone there, his repose was needled by insecurities, the ordeals faced by his patients, and his sometimes-futile efforts in certain areas of health. *Am I making any inroads at all in easing the magnitude of suffering in the world, or am I only trying to empty the vast, vast ocean with my one tiny pail?*

CHAPTER 10

It was nearing eight that evening. Dr. Zastro and Shyam were discussing various medical practices, the conversation shifting to the patients and their progress, Shyam's observations. Phillipe couldn't quite keep his mind focused. Should he send Shyam to get Yana, or rely on her assurance that she had her own inner time clock?

"Miss Kejako should be here in a few minutes," Dr. Zastro said, consulting his vest pocket watch.

"She is very beautiful lady."

"Yes. Most women have their own special beauty."

"She remind me—of Gypsies, in northern India. They have same olive skin, flowing hair."

"Yes." He didn't want to get into a discussion regarding Yana right now, particularly not with his assistant. "You are dismissed for the evening, Shyam."

"Miss Althea—" Shyam hesitated.

"Yes, what about her?"

"She is beautiful lady too."

"She is only a child."

"Skin so white. Like ivory. Hair, like fine gold."

"Her case is very puzzling. And I appreciate the extra attention you have been giving her."

"Doctor." Again, Shyam hesitated. "Maybe Shyam not bathe Miss Althea anymore."

"Why not?"

"Shyam—get thoughts when looking at her."

"What kind of thoughts?"

"You know, man thoughts."

"I see. I could tell something was troubling you." He had come to think of Shyam as the son he would never have, someone who came to him for moral guidance and teaching. He must also remember that this ward of his was also training to become a physician. "Shyam, you must be able to look at a woman, examine her private parts, and never think of her as anything other than a patient."

"That I try, doctor, but—"

"This will be a great test for you then, a vital part of your training while assisting me here."

"I try, doctor." He still seemed fidgety.

"We can discuss this in depth another time." Again consulting his watch. "You are dismissed, Shyam."

Shyam stood and bowed, "Good night, doctor. Thank you for counsel."

Dr. Zastro went to the doorway with him. "Good night, Shyam," he said as he looked expectantly down the hallway. She wasn't there.

He lit the candle so he would be ready and stood awhile watching the flickering light, until a high, bright sound caught his ear. Was that singing he heard? Once more he looked out the open doorway, no one was around.

Concentrate on something else.

He sat down at his desk, opened his file drawer and began rummaging aimlessly. Upon looking up, he was startled to see Yana standing in the doorway. "Miss Kejako?"

"You look as if you're seeing a spirit you don't believe in." That air of mystery—always emanating from her, vibrating at her outline, accentuating her voice. Bright silver strands were threaded through her braids, now wound atop her head to form a curious halo that radiated a special aura about her whole person. Was it only the night shadows flickering in the doorway, enhancing the contrasting brilliance?

He very seldom saw his patients at night. Why had he even considered this exception? "Eight o'clock, exactly," he said, consulting his watch and then with feigned nonchalance he asked, "Was that you singing just a moment ago?"

"No, doctor. The rules. No singing in this area." She appeared in a playful mood, her hand locking her mouth and throwing away the key, then peeking at him through outspread fingers. Her mood changed to serious as she noted his perplexity. "Is something troubling you, doctor?"

"No. Nothing." He wasn't sure himself what it was that was bothering him, disrupting his usual composed procedures. "It's just been a tiring day. The first week is always somewhat draining."

"Maybe you'd prefer we wait until tomorrow?"

"No. We will proceed as scheduled. Sit down, please." He closed the door on the silent hall, sat behind his desk, pondered for a moment before beginning. "Now then, have the magnetic belts helped your arm or leg?"

"Not really. The belts are quite heavy, and—"

"You relaxed? Let the electrical forces flow?"

"I tried. They flowed."

"Tomorrow then, you must try again. Just the arm. We will concentrate on healing the arm first."

"Do you think your machines—"

"Please, Miss Kejako, you must not always question."

"How will I learn, unless I question?"

"Listening brings many answers—but only to a quiet mind."

"Very seldom is my mind quiet." Even her eyes were dancing now as she leaned forward. "I must be honest with you, doctor, I'm not very comfortable in this place. I'm used to— certain freedoms. Open spaces. It's very difficult for me to relax under these restraining circumstances. Do not be perplexed because I do not remain quiet and submissive, waiting for wisdom to descend upon me. I've always had to go after my wisdom."

"I understand. Yet, in order to obtain any benefits from your stay here, you must abide by the regulations. You do wish to be cured, don't you?"

"Of course. That is only reason I came here; the only reason that I am staying."

He took her hand, noting she was giving off a slight current of electricity. Unusual. Almost like a shock. It was the late hour, when the magnetic currents of the earth flowed along the horizontal rather than perpendicular, and circulation was not the same as during daylight hours. "Give the treatments a fair chance, before you make any conclusions," he said, still pressing her palm. "There is great tension in your hand right now."

"Tension?" There was a teasing tone in her voice now. "No, only warm compression, from your strong penetrating touch."

He released his hold. "We will continue." He commenced to roll up her sleeve and then began probing, moving his fingers gradually upward along the arm muscles. "The tension extends up—into the chest area." He stopped upon reaching the upper shoulder portion, considered the tensions for a moment and then reached for a white porcelain jar nearby on his desk and began unscrewing the cover. "I have some special magnetic ointment here that will help stir the circulation." He began rubbing the ointment into her fingers.

"It tingles," she giggled.

"That is only electricity flowing."

"Or—the touch of your hand?"

"Possibly. My hands do have special magnetic healing powers. Even as a boy, I could heal my pets just by touching them." He continued rubbing in the ointment, finger by finger. It felt soothing to him also.

"You have fulfilled your *drukkerebema* then."

He was puzzled, so she interpreted for him.

"Your prophesy, doctor. Not everyone gets to do that. You were born to be a doctor, to cure others. You could have done nothing else."

He continued focusing on her hands rather than looking into her eyes. The rubbing of the thick ointment up and down each of her fingers seemed audacious in a way it never had with any other patient. "You have unusual hands, Yana. Possibly you have fulfilled your own prophecy." He realized the intimacy and tried to steer his comments back to the clinical. "Certain bones, facial structures, physiognomy—these can depict future traits, natural talents inherent in people."

Now he was outlining the finger points. It was impossible not to respond to such beauty. "Artist's hands—these long, slender fingers."

"Magic hands." She fluttered them before him, swooping them about as weightless bird wings. "And I am in complete control of whatever they do. I can make tiny rosebuds or majestic mountains flow from these anointed fingers."

He caught her fingers midair, clasping them still. "Remember, all use of the hand is directed by the brain."

"But, doctor." Her voice held a chiding tone. "My brain is atrophying from so much overuse. Tell me, what has all this studying done to your brain?"

He let her hand drop midair and began screwing the cover onto the ointment jar. "I do not like being made fun of."

"I wasn't—"

"My profession is my life." He made his words stern. "I have sacrificed having a normal family circle—wife, children, home—in order to devote all my energies to medicine and research."

"You have never known a woman?"

"I am here to ask the questions, Miss Kejako, not answer them." His professional manner resurfaced. "Now, I am going to relax you once more. Are you receptive to relaxation at this time?" He moved the candle between them.

"Yes, doctor." There was resignation in her voice.

"Concentrate on the candle flame then, please. Turn off all other thoughts.... Empty your mind. You are getting sleepy...."

An anxious knock resounded at the doorframe. Dr. Zastro got up, calling through the closed door, "Yes, what is it?"

"I can't sleep, doctor." It was Delphine. "And I saw your light on in here, an I thought you might have something to help me sleep—"

"Mrs. Applewood, the rules explicitly read, 'you are to stay in your room at night, except for emergencies'—when you must consult Shyam, and Shyam only."

Before he could stop her, the door opened and Delphine was poking her blond head inside. "That rule don't seem to apply to all your patients, do it?" She gave him a defiant stare.

"Enough. You will return to your room." He shut the door forcibly, locking it.

There was a wailing sound, "Now I'll never be able to get to sleep." A door slammed across the hall.

Why was he continually being disturbed? He smoothed his lab coat and sat down once more. "I'm sorry for the interruption. Shall we try again?"

"Yes." Yana seemed amused by the visit but didn't comment.

"Now then, keep your eyes on the candle. You are getting sleepy, sleepier—your eyes are getting heavier and heavier.... You will relax...." He stopped, a different tone to his voice. "You are fighting me, Miss Kejako."

"Really, I'm not."

"For some reason, you won't put your trust in me."

"It's not you—"

"I'm here to help you." How could he make her understand and believe this?

"I know. But I just can't put myself into someone else's hands so easily."

"My hands do not even touch you."

"But your thoughts do. You reach into my mind where you have no right to go."

"Yes. I also go into a woman's body when I examine her, where technically I have no right to go. As a doctor, I am only concerned with cures."

"As a person, I am concerned with my free will."

"You will retain it."

"How?"

"When you sleep, do you control what you dream of?"

"No."

"When you wake, you still have your free will?"

"Yes."

"That is all I do. Put you to sleep. A special sleep. When you wake, you have lost nothing—nothing of yourself. I take nothing from you. I only give."

"Is there no other way to cure me?"

"Yes, but...." He always preferred to begin with the mesmerism, the only way he could gain that deep special truth, the only way he might extract it from Yana, if that were possible.

"I think I'd prefer—"

Before she could finish, he resignedly admitted, "It is true that the deep relaxation of mesmerized sleep is not attainable by everyone. Maybe you are one of the few who cannot be mesmerized. I've heard of such people, but I have encountered none before, not as a patient."

"Gypsies very seldom go to doctors," she said. "They prefer treating themselves. They always have, not wishing to go outside the tribe for curative measures. They are also very careful about anyone casting any kind of spell, allowing any sort of power over them, for whatever reasons."

"Surely you have been away from your people long enough to discard these antiquated beliefs, learned as a child. A woman as knowledgeable as you should form her own opinions, give shape to her own values and philosophies. A woman such as yourself need not be held prisoner to the past by burdens that were not of your making."

"All that may be true," she agreed and then deflected his argument with great seriousness. "One cannot discard Gypsy heritage as one does a piece of clothing. It is an inborn characteristic, as is the tone of one's skin, the color of one's hair, even the way one may breathe. I cannot tear it from me, nor will it ever leave me, not until my death. Even then, we Gypsies still communicate with one another from the other side. The brotherhood is eternal."

"Your father—" he needed to ask "—you inherited none of his traditions?"

"Oh, he had already discarded them by the time he moved to America. So intent was he on becoming a successful Southern gentleman. He abandoned everything of his Irish heritage that didn't fit in with his new plantation owner image."

"I see," he said. And he did see: her special charm, twinkling eyes, the teasing traits; these, he thought, must be from her Irish ancestry.

She continued. "It is well known that women are the carriers of the past. Even men must pass through women's bodies before they can be born into this world, and parts of women's bodies become components of theirs. It is also women who pass on their heritage to their children, in the flesh and in matters beyond the flesh. Teaching them words, singing them songs, telling them stories, right from the beginning—even while in the womb. It is we who are left with the care and upbringing of the family, and we nourish with more than food."

He had never considered any of these postulations before. It was never brought forth so in the medical journals—but these were written mostly by men, for male doctors. Still, whatever her reasons, her false beliefs from the past had to be eradicated, once new truths were uncovered—superior, proven truths. "And you, Yana? You will pass these Gypsy superstitions on to your own children and the cycle will be repeated over and over without anything new ever being added? Scientific refutations ignored?" Strong words, but they needed to be said.

"I do not plan to have children."

This shocked him. Very seldom did women make such blatant statements about such a natural function, the preordained function for females from the moment of their birth. "Some day, you will change your mind," he said. "It is a natural progression in a woman's life, a need that mandates fulfillment. To try to choose otherwise subverts nature's order." *Would her children be as beautiful as she?* Again, that would be predisposed by whoever the husband might be, if there ever was one. What genre of man could break through to her heart?

"And you, doctor?" She was staring at him, defiant. "You yourself said you have given up the family circle to pursue your medical profession. Is that not also stopping your progression in your mandated male cycle? Do you plan to have children? And will you too someday change your mind?"

"I think we have gotten off the track here, Miss Kejako." He stared into the candle's flame, averting her gaze. "Do you wish to continue with the mesmerizing session or not?"

"We may continue."

He tried once more, but realized it was futile; it would never take place, at least not tonight. He took a deep breath and blew out the candle. "Sometimes an individual has such a strong will, or a will of equal power, mesmerizing cannot take place," he explained. "That is why it is a man who does the mesmerizing, since he is the stronger."

Her eyes flashed with anger, which he could tell she suppressed. She rose from her chair majestically. "I think I will retire, if your session is over," she stated with strained politeness.

"Yes. Tomorrow, we will try something else."

She was already at the doorway. "Good night, doctor."

He did not want her to leave. Something was not complete about their meeting. He had failed to reach her, gain her confidence, and convince her of his abilities to cure her.

"Yana—wait. The ointment, I want to give you a fresh jar of ointment to take with you. Where did I put it—" Flustered, he rummaged around the top of his desk, afraid she would leave before he found it. "I left it here, somewhere. Oh yes, right here." It slipped from his hands, rolling onto the floor near where she stood. He knelt down to pick it up, and his fingers drew near her sandaled feet, almost touching the warm bare skin—her hem brushing against his cheek. He felt himself being mesmerized. Quickly he stood up, wiping the jar with his lab coat, he said, "Take this along with you, please."

Her flare of anger had dissipated. Yana reached out to accept the jar, gazing into it as one would a crystal ball. "What do I do with it?"

"Rub it into your arm, as I was doing before."

"I wasn't observing that closely—my thoughts were on other things." Her mind seemed to be searching—into the jar—into the room. What was she seeking with such fervor?

"Sit down then. I will demonstrate once more. Pay close attention this time."

She sat in the chair, watching him intently. "Yes, show me once more. I will try not to think of anything else."

Again, he rolled up her sleeve, rubbing in the ointment, much slower this time, as if prolonging the minutes before separation. "You must always rub it from the wrist upward. So the current flows to the heart, never from it."

"Always to the heart," she repeated.

"Always to the heart." He stopped and looked at her without speaking.

"The painting again?" she queried. "The one from your childhood."

It was the painting, but he didn't want to admit it anymore than he wanted to admit he had heard her singing earlier. "No—I—your hair, it's different, yet imparts the same remembered image. That was what I was thinking."

With deft fingers, she undid the braids atop her head and shook loose her long hair. "Better?" she asked, coming so close the silky rivulets swept teasingly against his face.

His voice softened to a whisper. "Yes. Yes, your hair needs to be as free and flowing as your are." He ran trembling fingers along the cascading tresses.

"And yet, you would control my freedom?"

"Control it? I don't know how I could control such freedom. I have never encountered it before." He wasn't making sense; all he wanted to do was smother himself in her thick blanket of soft hair and stay there forever.

She rose, her mantle of hair suddenly jerked away, disrupting his contemplation. His hands were still reaching out in a frantic grasping gesture.

"You seem distraught doctor. Maybe I should relax *you*. Show me how to use your scientific candle." She was bedeviling him with eyes, body, and hair. "Or, if you prefer, I know of other ways to relax a man."

Such boldness—he wasn't prepared. "Miss Kejako, I am a doctor. You are my patient." He had to remind himself of that very sternly right now. Something had happened in that moment when he was so close to her hair.

Her spirit radiated strongly in the flickering glow of the candlelight, as if everything else but Yana were darkness. "Do I puzzle you, doctor? I puzzle myself. But I've never probed the reasons why." She began pacing the room with a lithesome stride.

"You men of science," she derided, "you want to know the answers to everything, don't you. What causes the moon to rise, the sun to set, rivers to flow. What makes the heart beat." She pirouetted a graceful unrestrained twirl that spun her into new ethereal assertions. "We artists live by our feelings. Following them, wherever they might lead. Life is to be experienced, not constantly probed and researched and written about. It lies in waiting to unfold daily—and the reasons *why* don't matter."

She moved closer. He dared not speak. He could very easily reach out for her. He wanted to capture and tame her; instead, he folded his hands, clutching them together as she continued.

"I think you are a very special doctor. A very unusual man. But you let your head rule your heart. You are trying to harness lightning. Compress life between the pages of books, when it should be free to ride the waves of the universe. More than blood must flow through your veins, race through your heart." She leaned in, less than one breath away. "The winds of change are blowing right now, even I cannot halt them...."

Before he could stop her—too stunned to move—he watched as she removed a thin gold needle from her sandal and pricked her index finger. Tiny drops of blood flowed as she placed the bleeding finger onto the center of his head and began walking around him, chanting.

Mro rat dav piraneskye
Kasy dikhav, avava adalske.

Kissing him on the lips, finger still centered, she repeated trancelike.

I give my blood to my loved one
Whom I shall see be mine own!

He tried, but he could not move. What was she doing to him? What blood connection was she trying to make? What strange incantation was taking place that he knew nothing about?

"Good night, doctor," she said, vanishing out the door.

He looked after her. Motionless. Speechless. What sorcery had she practiced on him? She was gone, yet her presence was still there, veiling everything. Over and over her words echoed—*"I give my blood to my loved one—I give my blood to my loved one—Whom I shall see be mine own!"*

"No!" he shouted, "*No.*" As if to banish what had just taken place, reverse whatever it was he had let happen. He got up, turned off the lights and stood in the darkened room, still seeing the outline of her luminous form, her beckoning smile. It welled up from within, his own voice whispering her name over and over, "Yana—Yana—Yana!" crying out from the depths of his soul.

At that moment, he did not want to be a doctor—a scientist; he wanted to be only a man and follow whatever it was pulsing so wildly within. He wanted to rush out after Yana and— He stopped himself, or something did, years of training or simple common sense.

A nearly overwhelming sense of loss came over him, as though the universe had opened up and he had been given the rare opportunity to participate in some mystical phenomenon that might never occur again in his lifetime. It would have been kinder not to have seen it at all than to know he might never see it again. *Why had none of his learning prepared him to deal with revelations such as this?*

CHAPTER 11

Sunday morning and the beginning of a new week. Anything new invigorated Phillipe, the buoyant feeling prevailing as he strode briskly down the empty Sanitarium halls to retrieve one of his journals from his study. How he looked forward to spending the day in relaxation, catching up on his reading, going through piled up mail. No contact with patients until Monday. A needed respite. Yet, sometimes he couldn't wait until the weekend was over, leisure hours so looked forward to sometimes moved at a plodding pace.

The sound of singing flowed from the Lecture Room as he passed by. Familiar hymns, the ladies' voices rising in melodious mixed tones; the chords amplified memories of boyhood Sunday gatherings. He often wished he could join in these services, but it was better he stayed away, giving the ladies one day alone, without his ever-watchful presence.

These non-denominational Sunday services were deemed a necessary part of the women's healing process. Most were used to attending Sunday services and sometimes missing Sabbath observations could cause great guilt, which in turn impeded their healing progress. He was very aware that prayer was solace for many of his patients, and thus tried to accommodate their needs.

The service was led by a Divinity student from one of the nearby seminaries. They were always eager to begin practicing their calling, plus here they had the added incentive of being invited to stay the afternoon, which also meant Sunday evening dinner. The services included hymn singing, Bible reading, silent personal prayers and open calls for verbal petitions. Mostly, these asked for special healing. Sermons were not allowed, as he could never guarantee what the eager Divinity students might impose on these fresh souls, for their own preaching benefit.

He recalled the marriage of his agnostic father and his Christian mother. A contradictory combination, so far apart in faith and yet the two of them so close together. He couldn't remember any verbal conflicts regarding religious beliefs. Each had been respectful of the other's choice. It was his mother who had led him in prayer as he knelt with devotion at the side of her arm chair. Discussions with his father had been mainly about science, and to any questions about the Deity, the standard answers of "It is not known" or "It has not been proven."

Even now, Phillipe was certain that he believed in God. One would have to be a fool not to. He couldn't quite remember the reasons why his father didn't believe in a God. Nevertheless, his mother's beliefs had been so much stronger—*what had Yana said about the mother influencing the child more than the father?*

He still read the Bible, many times finding inspiration and answers that were not discerned in any other reading materials. He belonged to no formal religion and rarely discussed religious theories with these Divinity students, since he believed religion was a personal matter, between oneself and God.

It was evident, in Phillipe's research, various case histories, that the Almighty had given man the power to cure himself and others by bestowing upon physicians the gifted insight to seek out the right applications and illuminate these cures for the rest of mankind. There had been many times when he had to call upon the higher powers. Other times, he let the patient die peacefully. Sometimes there was no choice. Still, it was always difficult letting them go, admitting to any kind of defeat.

Today, a certain joy prevailed upon entering his study, knowing all his consultations were over. He was ready to go on to the next phase, now that he was more acquainted with each and their maladies. Human beings were made up of more than flesh, bones, blood. What they had already experienced, where they lived, what they ate, and especially their heritage—all went into their health make-up, like ingredients added to soup, each imparting its own flavor, each essential to the final outcome. Some doctors treated everyone alike, men, women, children and aged, Indians or English. Most were reputable; still, there were the quacks, snake oil men. Wrongful medical cures—so difficult to prosecute and so precarious to prove.

The women were still singing as he passed the room on his way back. They sounded happy in their communion. The entire ambiance of the building relaxed on the weekend—staff, patients, but most of all he himself, as if some heavenly joy spread from one to another.

Poor Shyam, he was by default left with the burden of attending to the necessities of these women. On call twenty-four hours, all seven days of the week. This was a part of his training to become a physician—long hours, constantly on call, interrupted sleep. Dr. Zastro had gone through it, and was a better-trained physician for the ordeal.

What the women did after these services, he was never quite sure of, since he never went into their private rooms. Many did not come here of their own accord, but were sent by guardians, husbands. In spite of this or perhaps because of it—some of the women reverted to their own methods of healing, pretending to abide by the doctor's advice while still carrying out their own cures in private. He allowed it, never calling attention to the fact that he knew, as long as it did no further harm. He would often discuss in his lectures the dangers in using wrong methods and relying on their own unscientific remedies.

He often wondered what secret rituals Yana might hold in her room, as she often left her door partially open. For circulation, she said. Sometimes he could hear muffled foreign chanting. Were they spells? Love songs? Or only verses of songs repeated from her childhood? He would hurry along to avoid hearing that which would in turn squelch his ever-present curiosity.

After that recent distressing evening when Yana did her strange chant around him, he had tried to avoid personal contact with her as much as possible. The turmoil between them, present from the very first and especially following that evening, seemed to have subsided, and by Friday she was more cooperative, now preferring to stay in the background, not questioning everything as before.

That night had been a most unusual experience. Each new encounter added to the knowledge of life and could always be utilized somewhere in his lectures or research. The morning after, he had tried to write down all his feelings but couldn't quite express what it was he had gone through—those strange stirrings. However, with the help of his staunch training, he had been able to conquer those alien feelings, sure he had them under control now.

The Sunday evening meal was served in the large dining room in his downstairs quarters. Candlelight gave a festive glow to the white linen table, set with crystal goblets, Haviland china and mirror-polished sterling silverware. Seated with him at the table were Clarence Hartford, the Divinity student, and Shyam.

Nurse Tillotson took Shyam's post in the Sanitarium during the meal, so that he might partake in this special Sunday dinner. Sometimes another medical person might be invited, a student or colleague, but not tonight. He welcomed this smaller gathering; fewer guests meant less talk, and this was one evening he preferred quiet.

"What a banquet of food," Clarence exclaimed, helping himself to another portion of the steaming breast of succulently browned chicken. Most Divinity students, as part of their training and to save expenses, were served meager meals at the seminaries, thus they tended to take advantage of the doctor's table. The two serving girls, Maria and Theona, promptly brought in another platter heaped with cut up chicken. The girls knew they would get to eat whatever was left on the platters carried away. This was followed by another bowl of mashed potatoes, rich brown gravy, more cranberry relish and candied yams.

"Is such a feast!" Shyam exclaimed. He did not eat meat—his Hindoo background still stronger than his new Christian religion, but he could find enough other food at this ample spread. Shyam took small portions, eating in slow tiny bites.

Something to note, Dr. Zastro reflected, contrasting how Americans were always gobbling their meals down in such a hurry, gorging their overworked stomachs with excess food. Excess was the root of so many health problems.

"Your women have lovely voices," Clarence commented, adding ladles of gravy to the deep lakes already pooled in the centers of his heaping mounds of mashed potatoes. "As if they were practiced in that perfect harmony. Yet, I understand this was their first time singing together."

"We try for harmonious surroundings which permeates into all of their expressions," Dr. Zastro said with sincere pride, "and it is apparent, even to outsiders. In this difficult profession, there are never any guarantees."

"This one woman in particular, with the darker skin, deep set eyes, her voice was exceptionally strong. Has she had operatic training?"

"That would be Miss Kejako." Dr. Zastro was relieved to know Yana had tried to fit herself into the service, even a bit surprised she would attend. "Everything about her is strong. She has had training in art, dance, and possibly also in singing. I'm afraid she is overtaxing her system—" he stopped himself. "We never discuss the problems of the women with anyone else."

Clarence took this as an admonishment. "I'm sorry, but— anyway, we had a very special prayer service. And I will not reveal the women's prayer requests, since we ministers must keep confidences also." He was so sure his profession was the more helpful in the lives of these women. "But, I will add each of their petitions to my own in my evening prayers tonight. And special prayers for you too, good doctor, and all your wonderful work you are doing here. Truly God's work. We each carry it out in our own appointed way."

It was evident Shyam felt ill at ease during any religious discussion, not knowing his particular place in such conversations. He was here strictly for medical knowledge, which he devoured with ardent zeal when the opportunities arose.

"Miss Althea was at service today also. Has very sweet voice," Shyam noted.

"The pale one?" Clarence nodded. "I was so afraid she might faint. It made me a bit nervous, to see her swaying so. I have seen church members go into ecstasies, and women with tight corsets faint before my eyes, but she was again—"

"We never discuss our patients," Dr. Zastro interrupted, almost severely.

"Sorry, doctor." The chastised Clarence continued eating with no more attempts at conversation. Only the sound of the cutlery clicking against the dinnerware, dishes being passed, and the slow ticking of the grandfather clock punctuated the air.

The silence was interrupted by Nurse Tillotson rushing into the dining room, "Doctor, there's an emergency upstairs. Miss Althea has fainted, and—"

Shyam was on his feet. "Do not worry, Shyam will be on duty from hereon." He left the room with eagerness for his errand.

Dr. Zastro knew there were further questions Clarence wanted to ask, but was keeping them suppressed since his admonishment. His only comments during the rest of the meal were regarding the food. His departure followed soon thereafter.

CHAPTER 12

Dr. Zastro rose early Monday morning and after a quick breakfast went to his study, eager to work on his morning lecture. The title: ELECTRICITY AND SEXUAL INTERCOURSE.

The ladies should be ready to accept this frank subject by now. They had come a long way in their openness to new ideas, innovative procedures. Still, why did he feel apprehension about giving this intimate lecture today? He had covered the subject in all its aspects many times before. This lecture was the one he always gave on the second Monday, in all the six years he had been running the Sanitarium.

Right now, he was trying to imbue it with freshness, adding any new thoughts he might have come across. As he went over his notes, Yana kept breaking into his thoughts. Why? She was an uninhibited creature, probably giving into her sexual nature whenever she desired. She was the kind of person who felt freedom was her basic right and had no compunctions in carrying out whatever sprang from her untamed nature.

She reminded him of the wild eagle that soared above everyone else—commanding the sky by virtue of its majesty. Difficult to capture, and governed only if its wings were clipped. He recalled Old Abe, the eagle mascot heralded during the Civil War. The great bird that had been so proudly carried by a Wisconsin regiment had his greatness relegated to pitiable flapping of its clipped wings while sadly tethered to a wooden perch. The sheared wings curtailed the bird's ability to sail again into the elevated skies.

The one time Dr. Zastro had viewed the bird, he had thought that he'd never gazed upon any creature so forlorn looking. No chains, no bars to hold him—only the imposed cruelty of clipped wings.

Freedom? He himself hardly knew what that meant, since he had never had the urge to cut loose and go anywhere he desired, without a known final destination. It could be a hazardous experiment. Most of his lifetime had been spent in suppressing animalistic tendencies in his nature. Still, he always knew where he was going, and all the discipline had paid off.

Freedom. Yana...He must stop thinking of Yana, but had not yet come up with the right alchemy to keep her from his thoughts. He must get to work; he had other patients who also needed his concentration. Delphine—She was not as aggressive in her advances to him as last session. He had tried to deal with her right away, so maybe that problem was under control. Still, he knew he had to keep it under surveillance.

Althea—Not healing as she should; in fact she seemed to be regressing. That concerned him. He might have to resort to other methods. Right now, it seemed Shyam was the only one who could keep her calm. Was it right, shifting such duties to someone so inexperienced? Was he overburdening Shyam with the care of one patient, when he was here to learn from all of them?

It was time. Dr. Zastro picked up his notes, straightened his attire and went to the Lecture Room. From the back doorway, he looked inside. The help, in their white attire were already in their places. His lady patients, in various shades of lavenders and purples, robe colors for the second week, were also settled in, including Althea. They resembled a lovely garden of glowing flowers, and already he could visualize how resplendent they might look outside in the glimmering sunlight with their soft gowns dancing in the fresh breezes.

He regretted secluding them from fresh air and sunshine, but they did get outside daily, in good weather, to enjoy the roof garden. Then there was always the picnic during the final week, when the women, attired in various shades of green, were taken by carriage to the countryside where they blended in so beautifully with the trees and foliage along the Hudson River.

A trained photographer went along to take group photos of the women in various poses along the river and among the trees. Dr. Zastro wished somehow that these photos might be captured in color. Better still, that there might be an artist along to paint the lovely pastoral scene and capture it forever.

This time there would be an artist—Yana. Would she still be there that last day? *Do not dwell on Yana....*

There was always one group photo with himself included. Each lady was sent a copy of their single pose in this serene setting along with one group photo, to remind them of this final healing day, a tangible reminder of the time when they felt happy despite their illnesses—many of which would have been cured or at least subdued by that day.

An album of these photos was in his study and periodically he perused them to recall former attendees. He received many follow-up letters, and it pleased him to hear how their lives had been changed due to the three weeks spent at his Sanitarium. He never answered the letters personally, not wanting the women's attachment to him to continue beyond medical attention. If they needed specific answers, his secretary always obliged with letters dictated by him.

Delphine had written to him the most and would probably continue to do so. Loneliness was one thing he could not cure. He had to admit he would be curious as to what might happen to Yana after she left the Sanitarium. Would her painting do well in the Paris Show?

Women like that—they were bright flames for a few years—then, pitiful old age. Alone. Burned out. Yet, it was hard to visualize Yana as old and withered. *Enough.*

Time to begin. He motioned to his assistant. Shyam announced, "Dr. Zastro." The doctor walked to the gleaming lectern. "Good morning ladies." He greeted the women with exuberance.

"Good morning, doctor," they answered in unison. He could sense new enthusiasm in their voices. He found patient enthusiasm inspiring, an impetus to give his best to the lecture. This morning, he knew he was going to do just that.

"We begin our second week at the Sanitarium. And since you have not been outside yet today, I am sorry to inform you, it is still raining, so you will not be having garden time today."

They gave out a united groan. They had not had garden time on either Saturday or Sunday because of the continuing rain.

"If you remember my lecture on weather and its electrical effects on humans, you will understand why you are not feeling as well as you should this morning, as there is an excess of electrical radiation—the air being denser in damp weather. We do our best to filter all the incoming air, but dampness and other elements still seep inside here too. Enough for the weather reports. Now, onto the serious subjects."

He took his lecture stance, ready to begin his performance. He never liked to term it a performance, yet, once on the platform, he had to function as an actor, doing his best to convince his audience that what he was saying was believable and from the heart.

"Now, our subject today is—" he wrote the title out on the portable blackboard, his white chalk scratching each letter more loudly than usual: ELECTRICITY AND SEXUAL INTERCOURSE.

"Electricity and sexual intercourse," he repeated again for those who couldn't read. "I assure you ladies, it will be entirely in good taste." He could always detect apprehension in their faces any time the word *sex* was uttered. "I hope by now I have relaxed you enough so you will not turn away from anything of a sexual nature. This is, after all, the nineteenth century.

"Now, electricity permeates every atom. I will try to explain how it acts upon the sexual organs and produces sensual enjoyment.

"No organs of the body, except the brain, are so extensively permeated with nerve or electrical conduction as those embraced in the sexual parts." He pulled down the male and female body charts and proceeded to point to the areas as he spoke. "Located at the inferior terminus of the spinal column, in the act of cohabitation, these sensitive nerves are exercised by electricity in three forms."

He wrote on the board: 1. INDIVIDUAL ELECTRICITY. "Individual Electricity is manifested in the sexual embrace, when the masculine and feminine forces are focalized and blended in the sensitive nerves which concentrate in the sexual organs.

"In the compatible embrace, the mind summons all the electrical powers, employing them to the fullest extent in exciting each pleasurable emotion. The greater the dissimilarity in the nature of their individual electricities, the more satisfying the effect. Some persons are so dissimilar that any contact, such as shaking hands, imparts a pleasurable magnetic effect."

Again he wrote on the board: 2. CHEMICAL ELECTRICITY. "If an acid and alkaline solution be placed so that their union is effected through any porous diaphragm, a current of electricity is evolved. Electricity is produced when tartaric acid is added to soda, an alkali, and the titillating effects of a glass of soda are produced by electricity generated by the combination of positive and negative fluid." Again he indicated with the pointer.

"Now, the vagina is superabundantly supplied in alkaline fluid. The penis of the male, except the glans-penis, exudes an acid fluid. And, in the act of copulation, the fluids are greatly augmented.

"If there are sensations produced in the mouth by drinking soda, what must be the effect on the sensitive, highly excited nerves in the sexual organs when alkalis and acids are united?" He always gave them a little time to think of that example and remember occurrences, if they had had any. Generally he could denote which women had experienced the pleasures of sexual union. Those who had painful unions—well, they could never be convinced there was any pleasure attached to it at all.

He wrote once more: 3. FRICTIONAL ELECTRICITY. "The rubbing of a piece of glass, amber, sealing wax, with a piece of flannel, silk, fur, will so charge the former with electricity, that they will be attracted and adhere to lighter bodies. I will demonstrate."

He brought out a piece of plate glass and a length of flannel from the shelf under the lectern and proceeded to rub the glass with the flannel, demonstrating how it then adhered to a piece of paper. There was believing wonder from the audience, reflected in widened eyes. Somehow, demonstrations were always more enlightening than abstract words. Maybe they had heard too many attestations without ever experiencing any real visual confirmation.

He was thankful he had inherited his father's teaching abilities, the talent to demonstrate as he talked, so the eyes, ears, and minds of his audience were digesting all of his imparted knowledge. "Slide your feet rapidly over a Brussels carpet. You can accumulate so much electricity you can light a gas chandelier by just snapping your fingers. Frictional electricity may be produced by rubbing your hands together, or by rubbing any part of the body. No part is so susceptible to this influence as the glans-penis of the male and the clitoris of the female. Nature designed it so that the generative organs should be acted upon by Individual, Chemical, and Frictional Electricity!

"Females who are apathetic sexually, find that friction of the parts without excitement, induces irritation and finally inflammation along with other uterine affections that ultimately destroy the life of the wife. Reciprocity in the sexual relation is indispensable. A cardinal law of both love and connubial bliss requires that the more tender the affection of either, the more cordially should it be reciprocated by the other...

"Coldness or squeamishness will dampen your consort's pleasure, but, if you watch the rising desire of love and bestow the welcome embrace, you crown the blessed union with the complete embodiment of all its pleasures."

Every time he related this portion of the lecture, he always thought of his one time experience of copulation. He had been so very young. While working in the Dr. Foote's office, he had gone on a first time errand to deliver some medication. This older woman opened the door wearing a silky black robe covered with bright massive orange poppies, her long hair cascading over the open front, barely covering her ample naked body. A flowery scent drifted from her, encapsulating him.

Smiling graciously, she had invited Phillipe inside. Was it her motherly warmth that ensnared him or had it been his own curiosity for anything new? Before he knew it, he was between the satiny covers of her high brass bed, smothered by her warm body, wanting to leave, yet unable to do so. Whatever was happening to him in that bed was too exciting not to pursue until the very end, which occurred so quickly, he wasn't exactly sure what had taken place.

The episode had been blissful indeed, he had to admit—his whole self transported to heights of splendor—a dizzying powerful ascent—exploding into nirvana and then gentle dreamy flotation back to reality, noting with embarrassment, he was wet and deflated. The heated woman was still moaning, thrashing about.

He escaped from her arms, dressed and left, never going back except in his thoughts, sometimes at the strangest moments. His first sexual experience—his first experience of being in someone else's power, and he knew, even at that time, he would never let it happen to him again. He must always be in charge.

Thus, he guarded against being enticed into such an episode again. Still, it had been useful—proving theories about sexual unions were as written. Whenever he remembered that coupling, it still vibrated with remembered ecstasy, and he knew he might succumb to such a temptation another time if he let his defenses down.

That night he had made up his mind: the pursuit of being a doctor was his only goal and nothing would deter his path from that fulfillment. Nothing else was worth it. He had seen too many lives led astray by debauchery and alcohol. Neither of these would be his downfall. Phillipe was certain he had made the right choice. His medical dedication now gave him his satisfactions, his human connections with others. Nothing else was needed for fulfillment.

Try as he might, however, there was nothing he could do about his night emissions that occurred while he slept. He did nothing to attract them and even waking up did not stop the continuing flow.

Among his duties as a doctor, he had to convey normalcy to the men who consulted him regarding these night dreams, fearful of losing their seed in such dreams or outside their wives' bodies. These emissions were not something they should feel guilty about nor something they could control; maybe it was not even wise to try to stifle them using mechanical means in advertised methods. Sometimes nature sought its own release.

Why then did he feel guilty about his discharge the night after Yana had kissed him, a discharge during his restless sleep that seemed to flow and flow as though floodgates had been opened? *Back to your lecture—do not even gaze at Yana right now.*

He took a deep breath and returned to his notes, not sure if he had skipped over anything or not. "Love in one and not in the other is a breach of love's cardinal requisition, and therefore can never render either happy, but must, in the very nature of things, torment both for life."

Torment for life. He paused to ponder those words. How could love cause torment? Was it love that was causing this unexplainable torment he was experiencing? Nonsense. He went onward. He wanted to finish the lecture; he must not let his mind veer off into any further distractions.

"Tomorrow's lecture will be 'PROCREATION'. I will show actual reproduction of the birth of a baby. We will use our life-size model—"

Retching sounds were heard as Mavis brought her sun-browned arm up over her mouth to stifle the flow of upheaval activity.

"Miss Michalek, you are excused," Dr. Zastro called out. "Quickly! To the water closet." Mavis rushed out, holding her robe over her mouth.

"The rest of you ladies are excused also."

None rushed out as Mavis had. It was customary that they cluster about him after his lectures, asking questions, listening intently to his answers, and simply prolonging his departure. He tried to curtail these after-sessions, but did want questions, comments. Each of these women had experienced things he never would. Some facts of life were not to be learned from books.

Yana stayed in the background, as usual. Then he saw Delphine corner her, which irritated him because he wanted to remind Yana of their evening dinner appointment. He had better do it now.

"Miss Kejako," he called out. She looked his way, and then left the room without answering, a blur of lavender silk, her filmy outline remaining in the surrounding air.

Delphine pushed forward toward him. "Doctor, could you explain some of those parts over again to me. Later perhaps?"

If some women couldn't physically experience sexual contact, just listening to a man say certain words on some sexual subject could excite them in a similar way. All the senses could excite a woman's sexuality: visual stimulation, scent, taste, even hearing. He didn't want to excite Delphine any more than needed, in any manner.

"No personal consultation today," he reminded her. "Excuse me, please." He pushed past the women. "I must go help Miss Michalek." He rushed from the room in pursuit of the float of lavender and crown of jet-black hair disappearing down the hallway. All the restraint of the past week disintegrated. He knew he had to see Yana, talk to her, and be close to her. His pulses were racing. He lacked the will to stop this unprecedented quest while acknowledging there was no desire to do so

What was happening? How was he going to get through the next two weeks with this turmoil raging within? How would he get through their evening meal tonight, being in her intimate presence? This would be another test, and he must not fail. If he did then—well, he wasn't sure what the consequences might be.

CHAPTER 13

Monday afternoon treatment time. Yana and the other women were strapped into their machines, most seeming to enjoy the soothing pulsating of the electro-vibrations. A restlessness was prevalent also. Yana attributed this to the rainy weather; they had not been allowed outdoors for the past three days.

They were less talkative than usual too, possibly still digesting the morning lecture regarding electricity and sexual intercourse. New revelations for most; though some were not sure what it all meant or even if it were true. Still, Dr. Zastro was the expert, so whatever he expounded upon must be worth knowing.

The day was already winding down. Most were looking forward to the recreation hour that would follow. Dinner after that. A new menu introduced each evening with special health-inducing ingredients, explained by Shyam, who would also read to them another chapter from Dr. Zastro's book as they ate.

After dinner—a quiet hour for reading or crafting and then bath time and into their comfy little beds, as if they lived in a fairytale land, housed in cozy little cottages in the faraway forest where they were protected from all the evils of the big bad world.

Yana wouldn't be eating with them tonight, as this was her appointed evening to dine with Dr. Zastro. A welcome reprieve. However, since she didn't know what to expect during that hour, she wasn't sure whether she was to look forward to the encounter or to be apprehensive. She had decided she would try keeping the whole evening to impersonal conversation, controlling any sudden impulses, strange desires, or other spontaneous reactions that occurred whenever she was near the doctor.

The reason he occupied so much of her thinking, she concluded, was because she had nothing else intriguing to engross her time, nowhere to go, in addition to all these constraints on her usual pursuits. Moreover, who knew what all this weird electro-charging was doing to her? No wonder her mind was wandering on aberrant pathways and imagining all kinds of erratic things. Still, even when daytime thoughts shut off, her nighttime dreams also drifted to the doctor. Well, she had made it through the first week, only two more to go.

Her legs and her arm were being vibrated at a higher rate today. She had grown used to the tremors and did not consider them intrusions on her person anymore. To Yana's amazement, the arm was getting stronger, the leg as well. She was more than ready to dance and ride again.

In some ways, she was pleased she had decided to stay. In the past week she had learned to abide by most of the rules, suppress her rage when needed, avoid unnecessary personal contact with Dr. Zastro. He made that easy. In the wake of their evening encounter, he was obviously trying to avoid her except when the few required medical inquiries made acknowledgment necessary.

Tonight would be difficult, alone with the doctor, in a different atmosphere. Try as she might, she couldn't foresee what might take place. There was never any trouble predicting for others, but it wasn't easy forecasting for oneself. Maybe that was better. She preferred the surprises in life, reacting to the moment.

Nevertheless, the great interior ache remained, with its penetrating longing for her country place on the clear winding river, looking out onto windswept hills. Another constant pang was the loss of her painting time. Painting; her inner aspirations that needed fulfillment daily as much as her innards needed food, as much as her eyes needed sleep. Sometimes even more. She had tried sketching on her sheets of drawing paper and charcoaling in her sketchbook. Now that her arm was healing she wanted to get back to the larger canvases.

Last Friday they had all been allowed to select certain personal items, taken from them that first day for sanitizing. One at a time, each was allowed to go through their possessions that had been laid out in the Lecture Room. Each made her selections—with the doctor's approval. Remaining items were locked up once more.

They still weren't allowed personal clothing or jewelry. What a disappointment. Yana had selected more books, extra art supplies and her tarot cards. Dr. Zastro looked as if he were going to disapprove the cards but said nothing.

Yana found it advantageous having Isobelle as an ally. She felt especially amiable toward Isobelle, sensing the suffering this downtrodden woman had endured. So evident, in the older woman's guarded gestures, the deep circles around her eyes and the numerous scars. So few people had shown her any real kindness that she was appreciative of even the smallest act of consideration. Yana also knew Isobelle wouldn't be taken in by insincerity.

"Yah, I speak the German. Mine mother tongue." She had smiled when Yana had asked last Tuesday, smiling even more broadly when Yana repeated a German poem she remembered from her childhood.

Gypsies picked up smatterings of languages from all the countries they traveled, sometimes finding it useful when they had to mingle among the villagers, not letting it be known they were Gypsies.

"So good to hear mine mother tongue. Mine mama, she knew such poem too." Isobelle's joy was genuine, her warmth receptive, as Yana took her rough hand, holding it tight, repeating the poem once more. The next day she read Isobelle's palm, seeing nothing but more suffering in her future, telling her only, "there would be changes."

"No good news for me. Never." Isobelle had a peculiar sense of her own future, expecting nothing but a repeat of her long afflicted past.

"I see much suffering in your past life, but there are changes coming—great changes." It was all true, laid out as a map on her palm. "You will find new work. And a cure will take place...."

"Oh thank gott, oh thank gott if that is true." Tears began streaming down Isobelle's ruddy cheeks. During the middle of last week, Isobelle readily pointed out the closets in the back storage room where all their personal belongings were stored, secretly allowing Yana to look through her cherished items, but not take any away.

"But no way you can look at the jewelry." Isobelle was strong in this answer, "Is locked up tight."

Yana also drew pictures for Isobelle, scenes she remembered from her time in Germany. In exchange, Isobelle smuggled pieces of fresh fruit to her, rescuing it before it was mashed, stewed, or electrified beyond any original shape or flavor.

Fresh grapes—Yana missed the succulent squirt of their sweet juices across her tongue. She knew it was not grape season and had to be satisfied with whole apples, stored from last fall and sometimes a pungent orange, savoring each tantalizing section, making it last as long as she could.

She would endure the remaining days; she knew that now. Those dire predictions she felt that first day had not come to pass. In fact, she would have forgotten them, had not Grandmama still visited her in the night. Yet, even *puridaia's* messages were becoming more muddled and Yana no longer woke in fright trying to decipher meanings.

Shyam was passing through on his periodic rounds. He only touched the machines, never the women as Dr. Zastro did. Would the doctor walk through this session or not? The women were always waiting for him, any time of the day, but he made it a point not to make scheduled appearances in the Treatment Room, only a casual checking in.

Shyam went behind the bath curtain where Althea was soaking in warm water. His outline was visible as he bent over the tub. The sound of him swishing water over Althea's body was in a different rhythm than the Strauss waltzes playing. Yana would never hear a Strauss waltz again without being reminded of this aberrant room.

"You shiver? Water too cool?" Shyam asked Althea when checking her and then he would sing to her, some soft Indian song, part chant, part crooning.

"Is strange words," Isobelle always commented.

"He frightens me," Mavis shivered. Her favorite phrase was "It—or he—or she—frightens me."

"Every day, he comes in, bathes her, sings to her."
Edwina's tone, judgmental as usual.

"You don't approve?" Yana queried. There was no answer.

"I don't like no darkie foreigner looking at my naked body.
When I'm in that tub, he is not allowed behind that curtain. I
scream bloody murder if he even tries. He don't do it no more."
Delphine continued babbling. "Last season, Dr. Zastro's
assistant was the handsomest Italian—Raphael—and when he
took care of me—"

"I'm going to close my eyes now and rest." This was
Edwina's signal that she would not participate in further
conversation. Most didn't care to listen to Delphine going on
and on about everything and nothing, but she continued.

"I rest now. Is big washing yet today." Isobelle too was out
of the interchange.

"Well, I'm just gonna sit here and think about the doctor's
lecture on ee—lectricity and sexual intercourse. Nobody's ever
explained it to me that way before." Delphine interwove sexual
connotations into most of her comments, feeling that was the
subject she was the most expert in.

"Sex shouldn't have to be explained," Yana said, "just done.
Naturally." Yana wasn't ready to shut off just yet. She needed
to talk, rather than think right now.

"My, my—you know just about everything, don't you?"
Delphine's saucy curls were still subdued into long braids, but
she still swished her head out of habit and rolled her eyes in
feigned innocence.

"I like listening to you, Yana." Shyness softened Mavis's
coarse voice. "You're so—smart. I—I think you're pretty too."
She rushed into her usual request. "Could you read to me
again—later?"

"Of course. Next reading time." Yana had taken to helping
Mavis learn to read, but it was a slow process. She would read
stories to Mavis from her book of Gypsy folktales. The stories
fascinated Mavis, as though she had never imagined that there
could be worlds where fairies did magical things, trees talked
and bad demons lurked. Mavis would sit spellbound, never
uttering a word. Yana was unsure of the effect these tales had on

this girl who had only known the harsh realities of life, never any of the magic. As though denied even dreaming, Mavis never had the means to transport her mind into worlds of enchantment and escape.

Every once in awhile, after a story, Mavis would relate what had happened to herself, in parallel, as if she too had been imprisoned by a bad demon at her farm and some good fairy godmother had waved her magic wand to send her here to Dr. Zastro's Sanitarium. A reward for all her hard work. Alas, after these three weeks she would have to return to the dungeon and she had concluded—there would be no happy ending.

"I'll never escape from that place again," Mavis lamented.

"But, you must remember," Yana told her, "you will not return as the same person. You will have new power. No one can imprison you again. You will have greater wisdom, so your thoughts will take on different meaning. New words to cast spells to ward off the powers of evil."

Yana was trying to teach Mavis this certain spell—to cast off evil powers, but Mavis had no ear for foreign words or the capacity for learning them.

"You will take back many gifts and you will be able to use them daily." Yana always reinforced the capacity Mavis did possess. "And the greatest of them—you will be able to read."

Yana had read in Mavis's hand that she was at a turning point in her life. She wished she could see a husband in the future somewhere, but the girl's hand was so scarred from hard work, the lines so callused over that it was difficult to make out certain areas. The death line was very sharp; Yana was not sure if it was someone close or Mavis's own death. She always skipped over death lines in any reading. It was too dire to predict that event to humans. Those revelations belonged only to the gods.

Shyam and Althea emerged from behind the curtain, Althea wrapped mummy-fashion in a huge white sheet. Shyam, wearing his white gloves, led her out the door.

"I wonder where he takes her every day after her bath?" Delphine wondered about everything aloud.

"Dark Room. Shyam puts her in Dark Room to rest."
Isobelle was the only one who had access to such places. None
of them had ever been in the Dark Room; they'd only that
glimpse when Dr. Zastro opened and closed the door so quickly
that first tour. Their imaginations invented all kinds of strange
goings-on in the Dark Room, even though Isobelle said there
was only a bed, a chair, and a huge bamboo fan.

Mystery had become an eminent part of the Sanitarium, a
world where the unusual was abundant. These women wondered
excessively about things never encountered before, mostly
because they had the time to do it.

"She looks like she never seen the sun at all," Mavis
whispered. To Mavis, this was a great pity, repeating daily how
much she missed the outdoors and its warming sunshine. She
was a true child of the earth. The only consolation she had found
in her abusive life was in nature's embrace. Because of this
affinity to earth and nature, Yana found she could best empathize
with Mavis.

Even though Mavis's mind was not educated, it was bright
and instinctive. She had a special innocence about her that Yana
admired. An innocence she herself had long passed clear of and
could barely recall.

"Thin too. No wonder she faints all the time." To Isobelle,
a person who was not fat was not healthy. Her theory was that
people needed those extra layers of flesh to store up for the lean
times when there might be no food. Therefore, she always ate as
much as possible in preparation for those hungry times, which
evidently had visited her often.

"Althea hasn't had supper with us the last few days."
Edwina was always interested in joining conversations about
Althea. She deemed it proper to discuss someone if you were
worried about his or her well-being. Edwina had repeated, so
many times, that she did not believe in idle gossiping.

"Is better she don't eat with us. Only sits and stares any
ways." Many times Yana had seen Isobelle reach over and
rescue Althea's uneaten food.

"I think it's all a put-on," Delphine interjected. "I can't stand girls who pretend to faint all the time. Swoon, just cause a man looks at them."

"Men affect women in different ways." Yana was positive about that. So far, no man had caused her to swoon, wondering what it might feel like or if she would be strong enough to forestall the final faint. It was not something she worried about much.

"They sure do." Delphine fluttered her eyelids in a knowing manner.

Shyam returned, clapping his hands for dismissal. "Ladies. Treatment time is over. You may go recreate, before supper bell is rung."

Shyam went to Isobelle first. "Miss Isobelle, you must go to the kitchen."

"Yah. Yah." Isobelle resented Shyam directing her. She was used to working in households where there was a certain descending of order, and foreigners of different skin colors were always held at the lowest rung. She wasn't about to give up the one step she had ascended while here.

Shyam busied himself unstrapping the women, turning off the lights, as the women began leaving the Treatment Room. Only Delphine and Yana were left.

"Wait. I want to talk to you," Delphine grabbed the sleeve of Yana's robe.

"What about?"

"The doctor."

"What about him?"

"I can't help noticing the way he looks at you. He used to look at me the same way."

"You're a ridiculous girl." Yana proceeded to try to leave.

"Wait." This time she grabbed onto Yana's arm. "You don't like it here, always complaining. I know a much better place. If you need money—I could help you with expenses."

"I do not intend to leave here before my three weeks are up. And I don't need your money."

"The doctor is mine, I tell you."

"Oh." *Whatever made her think that?*

"Why do you think I keep coming back here session after session? Solomon's old—and shriveling—and he'll die soon. Then the doctor and I can be married. I'll have all Solomon's money. And I plan to build Dr. Zastro a brand-new sanitarium. The finest in the country."

"Fine buildings are not what Dr. Zastro desires. He's dedicated to his work. And, I don't think he has any intentions of getting married."

"You heard his speech about love and sex—how men and women need each other to complete that magnetic circuit. He needs a woman. Someone to love him in the right way. He just gives out so much loving and caring. No one returns it to him."

She was right about that. However, Delphine was not the answer to Dr. Zastro's needs.

"I'm afraid I can't help you with your problem."

Delphine hesitated, then proceeded in a serious hushed tone. "Do you ever put curses on people—like helping them to die, a bit quicker? For a price, could you do this?"

"Curses are not done for prices. I do not do curses, I never have, even though I do believe in them and have seen them work. You may have to wait a long time for Solomon to let go of this money. So, I wouldn't plan to wait around to finish your life with Dr. Zastro."

"Maybe you want him for yourself?"

"I have no intentions of getting married either."

Delphine turned vicious. "Then, you just keep away from him, you Gypsy witch. Because I'm out to get him, somehow, some way, and I usually gets what I wants."

"You sound quite certain of yourself."

"I know how to get a man to do anything I want."

"Do you?"

"I've had lots of experience."

"I could read what you were right from the beginning. Your innocent little girl ways didn't fool me one bit, or anyone else. Especially the doctor."

"And you and your high-and-mighty ways don't cover up your dirty Gypsy bringing up!"

"I'm proud of my heritage. Both my Gypsy and Irish blood. But you—"

"I don't want to hear anymore Gypsy trash."

"I delight in my heritage, my mixed blood, swirled by a great artist's brush, this intermingling of pigments. While you—"

"Stop looking at me like that. You Gypsies think you can just look at a person and know everything bout them."

"I only need to look at your hands."

"What do they say?" Eager, Delphine spread out both palms.

Yana never turned down an opportunity to read someone's palm. It was as natural for her as an animal following scent to find prey for food, or whatever was needed for sustenance. Once the palm was sighted, she had to follow through.

"Your whole life is written here." Delphine's hands were hot and pulsing as if a tiger was raging within, waiting to pounce, tear victims apart.

"My whole life? You keep still bout whatever you see. I don't want you telling no one else. You understand?" Delphine was tensed, ready to withdraw her shaking hand, obviously afraid that Yana could see all of her past, and yet curious about her future, she let her twitching hand remain.

"Your past is not worth repeating. I'm sure you'd rather forget it." Yana hesitated, but went on, "and your future—a long tedious existence without too much excitement."

"You're lying, like you always do." Delphine withdrew both hands. "Well, I know things too. I know things between my legs that no other women know. And, I can read men between their legs too. And I know there never was a man I couldn't make want me. That's the place my hands read; there, and other parts of his body, not the palms. We both have our own talents, Miss Yana. And I think the doctor would much prefer mine to your stupid Gypsy superstitions."

"Dr. Zastro is not your ordinary man. I have read his palm also."

Delphine was not prepared to hear this. "You and your Gypsy fortune telling—Well, all the Gypsies I've known were nothing but dirty thieving lying beggars."

"I also happen to be a Southern lady—by heritage."

"You?" Delphine spat the word out.

"Yes. My father was Patrick Donnelly of Virginia—his mansion was named Emerald Shores; he built it on the banks of the Appomattox River. It still stands, destroyed only somewhat by the war."

"You're lying again. You couldn't be—A plantation owner?" Delphine shrieked with laughter.

"I'm not lying—"

It all came back, a patchwork of memories unfurling. Mama. Papa. Her earliest years at the mansion. The many ornate rooms—the bustle of servants. Somewhere in the background—always the sad singing. Mama in those strange hoop skirted dresses, staring out the windows, crying in the garden each night. Mama and Papa fighting, screaming at each other. Irish words and rapid Gypsy phrases clashing together in loud tirades.

Then one night, when she was five, she and Mama leaving, going back to Europe to rejoin Mama's family, a tribe in Roumania. Only once there, Mama still cried at night, still called out Papa's name—*Patrick*—in her sleep. Yana took to her Gypsy heritage as though she had finally come home and those first five years had only been a visit at the mansion.

Mama died when Yana was sixteen, still crying out for her Patrick. The tribe gathered at her bedside, following the genetic belief that a Gypsy must never die alone. They murmured as they waited. "Persa is dying—from a broken heart."

Yana knew it was true, and she was torn apart by the thought that love could bring such destruction to a person's soul. She had stayed for a while with a childless Gypsy couple after her mother's death, but gradually drifted off on her own, traveling at the edges of the tribe. Her father had searched all this time for her and Mama. He reached Yana by letter years later, begging her to come visit him and sending her boat fare.

She had been eighteen when she returned to Emerald Shores. The mansion—battle scarred by the war was collapsing with neglect. The slaves were gone. The fields weedy. A few animals. A few servants. Papa, when she finally saw him; the ravages of drinking and other ailments confined him mostly to his upstairs bed.

Paintings of Mama still hung everywhere. Mama—stopped in time. A life-size oil portrait over the fireplace of Mama in Gypsy garb, with her tambourine and the ancient gold coin necklace sparkling so real you could almost hear it jingle. Each time Yana gazed at it, she felt as though she were looking at herself in a mirror.

She stayed a month with her father. He was still drinking; she never got to know the real man. Yet even when intoxicated, he entertained her endlessly with Irish folktales, lore about leprechauns and ghosts, so similar to Gypsy stories, the tales capturing the mystique of the past, the magic of the present. He was an artist with his voice and words, always lamenting that he had never become a writer.

Yana begged him to write down his life, his love for Mama. If only for her.

"Alas, 'tis past. Will come no more. And writing and crying and all the drinkin in the world will not bring back my beloved Persa." Tears were brimming from his reddened eyes. "Yet, now that I have seen you, I know that she still lives."

Yana couldn't stay any longer. He made promises she knew he wouldn't keep. He played on the Gypsy guilt, continuously lamenting that he didn't want to die alone, which would come true if she left him. He maintained that she was still legally his daughter, not free to leave until age twenty-one. He was trying to own her, manipulate her. The reins were pulling in tighter and she had to break loose. She understood much better why Mama had left, why it wasn't possible for her to fight his commanding presence. In the middle of the night, Yana fled, not leaving anything behind. She met and joined up with a Gypsy tribe in Pennsylvania.

She wrote to Papa after awhile. He wrote back only one letter, but they were words to treasure. Grief, love, and beauty painted on the crumpled pages in his flourishing handwriting during a moment of sobriety. Two years later he died—alone. She always regretted that. No one should die alone. But it was too late when she heard. When she did return, it was to an empty house, all spirits departed.

Everything was willed to her. She took only the paintings of Mama, some books of her father's, selling everything but a piece of land along the river with the caretaker's house on it. This she made her home.

After, she went to Paris, now that she could afford to, and studied art there for two years. She returned to her house on the river whenever the spirit moved, or there was the need to travel across the miles, mix with different peoples, or just be alone with nature.

She had retrieved her trunk and vardo wagon from the Roumanian tribe, along with anything else she could salvage from the past. She had cut short her stay with the Pennsylvania tribe because she had been afraid they might entice her back into that carefree life. She now preferred her independent artistic lifestyle—on most days.

"Oh yes, Delphine, I did own the plantation, but after my father died, I sold it, because false Southern living never made Mama any happier, or any of us. I prefer sleeping in open fields rather than high spool beds. The sky overhead to light my day and night—not oil lamps and candles, and servants, and hoop skirts. You're welcome to it all. I've been there, and I have no desire to return."

"How come your father didn't give you his name—*Miss* Kejako? Bet you were born a bastard bitch, without any father. And that sad story is just all made up."

"Kejako is my mother's family name. She took it back. *Paraco tute.*"

"More Gypsy trash words."

"Paraco tute, means only 'thank you'." She did mean it as a thank you, for reminding her of that treasured past.

Before Delphine could retort, Shyam was back to lock up. "Ladies, out please."

"You just keep away from the doctor." Delphine threatened, eyes blazing.

"I've paid as much for his services as you have."

Yana never let anyone intimidate her and she wasn't about to begin, and not from someone as simple-minded and vicious as Delphine.

"Bitch." Delphine tromped away, fists clenched, steps stomping, her rage echoing down the hallway as she slammed the door to her room.

Yana stopped, tracing the lines on her own palm to see if anything had changed.

Mama—what can I do? It is still written....

CHAPTER 14

"Thank you, Theona, everything looks lovely." Dr. Zastro wanted to be alone for a few moments to contemplate the impending evening. Theona curtsied, excused herself and hurried off to check last minute details for this special meal and then wait in the kitchen area for the floor buzzer to summon her.

Dr. Zastro looked forward to these elegant evening meals, duplicated so many times before. Tonight, everything had to be extra special.

A small round table with a marble top and two rattan chairs were kept set up in the corner of his consulting room, behind an ornate black lacquered screen, embellished with beautiful floral designs in glistening pieces of inlaid mother-of-pearl. The table, now covered with a handmade Belgium lace cloth, was set with gold plated dinnerware and sterling flatware. The incandescent lights were lowered, a tall single candle illuminating the corner area.

It was nearly six p.m. Everything was ready. Why these tremors of anxiety?

These special evening meals with each patient during their stay gave him the opportunity to get to know each more personally in non-medical circumstances. It also enriched their Sanitarium memories. For many, a meal such as this— exclusive, grand, elegant—was a remembrance of a lifetime, compensating for all the other unaccustomed meals they were served.

He also enjoyed the novel rapport, since he most often dined alone. Oh, there were numerous dinner parties with colleagues, but they centered on medical discussions, which he, once out of his offices, was seeking to escape.

Generally, he turned down social invitations for dinner, knowing the hostess would be trying to pair him up with some eligible maiden. He just did not have the time or inclination to go through any courtship period with any young lady, should he even encounter one to his liking. No, that part of his life was already decided upon. Closed.

So, tonight was his turn to dine with Yana. Last week he had invited Edwina and then Isobelle, two women from different social strata, yet both appreciative of an evening of being made to feel special. Having money or being in high society did not always do that, especially for women.

Yana. How would she behave in this social situation? One never quite knew what to expect from her. He must make sure he maintained the doctor-patient climate.

Strange, now that he thought of it, his morning lecture regarding sex had lingered a bit more intensely than usual. Well, he had dealt with it. It had passed. The brain controlled all sexual actions, feelings, and there was no reason to dwell on such things right now.

He paused, hearing faint singing coming closer down the hallway. His heart began pounding. He took a deep breath, closed his eyes, and when he opened them, Yana was standing in the open doorway.

There was a glow about her no other woman emanated. Was it from electrical currents she absorbed so readily only to emit them back under certain circumstances? Is this what created the luminosity about her whole presence?

"So, doctor, I am here for our private meal." She walked in with grand elegance, beautiful carriage.

"Welcome," he greeted, rising.

"Welcome is indeed the feeling," she smiled, "just to know I don't have to eat that ground-up and pureed electrified food—if only for one meal." She was drawn into the candlelight as a moth to flame, closer to him.

"I promise you, tonight will be some of the most delicious cuisine you have ever consumed. But, it will all be healthful too." He held out the chair for her. "However, food is not the prime intent of this meal, as you will find out, it is the social aspect which I and my guest find the most fulfilling." He must be sure to remember all the social graces, so easy to forget if not practiced, and he was certain she would notice.

"What an elegant setting." Yana seemed impressed. Sitting so regally in her chair, he almost expected a crown to appear atop her head.

He sat too, cleared his throat, unfolded his linen napkin as he asked, "You drink wine? I always ask my ladies this question first, since some don't even know what it looks like. Many abstain for religious reasons."

"Of course I drink wine," she said, "since childhood. And in France, it is always an ample beverage at every meal. I've missed the essence of the grape since I've been here." She lifted the crystal goblet and whiffed at the edge of the rim. "Is this tokay?"

How did she know? "My own private stock. I must assure you, I only partake at mealtime. It is an aid to the digestion, and—"

"Doctor, this is not to be a health lecture, is it?"

"I'm sorry. Please, stop me anytime I forget my own rules."

"No, I too will be my most pleasant self. And we shall both enjoy this most unusual interchange." She lifted her glass and extended it toward his, proposing a toast. "To Dr. Zastro and his unique Sanitarium."

"And to all the ladies who are selected to be my very special patients."

The wine had never tasted richer; the room had never appeared lovelier. The exotic scent—her perfume? Phillipe relaxed, dismissing any inquisitive thoughts, and after pouring a second glass of wine from the crystal decanter, he began to enjoy the evening in an unforeseen way. He pressed the floor buzzer. He couldn't prolong the wine drinking with Yana any longer; he must ring for the food.

Theona appeared in short order with the first course of the meal. Tureens of mock turtle soup. Wedgwood plates piled high with fresh rolls, crisp grain crackers. Mounds of golden butter and swirls of soft creamy cheese.

Each course that followed was perfection. Roast pheasant, glazed with wild cranberries. Succulent new potatoes, flecked with dots of green parsley, doused with melted butter. Fresh asparagus spears from his own greenhouse.

For one moment, he wished he might dine like this every evening. He knew it wasn't possible, and such a rich diet was not healthy. He also knew it was not the food, but the company that made it so enjoyable. Very seldom had he dined with such an intelligent, pleasant, and beautiful dinner partner. He could imagine himself, away from the Sanitarium—dining in some faraway castle, or in an elegant 5th Avenue restaurant—a bistro in Paris, perhaps.

It had been a long time since he allowed himself to be transported into such visions. Even with all his wealth, such fripperies never appealed to him. However, sitting here with Yana—he wanted to take her to the grandest places, escort her in on his arm, show her off to everyone and then take her home— his home. Their home.

What kind of thoughts were these? What if she, with her Gypsy ways, had means to detect what was on his mind? What kind of nonsense was filtering into the evening?

"Penny for your thoughts, doctor." She smiled at him.

"I was just contemplating—the wonderful food." He was brought back into the room once more. He pressed the foot pedal to signal Theona to reappear and clear the dishes away.

"A most unusual dinner," Yana said. She was even more beautiful in the candlelight; it highlighted her tawny skin, perfect features. A rare blend of the two races, imparting the best of each. The spark of the Gypsy, the caprice of the Irish.

Sometimes the blending of races did the opposite he found, but research on that subject was inconclusive. Much had been proved with breeding of animals. There was something animalistic about Yana, wild and primitive.

His thoughts were interrupted as dessert and tea were brought in. "Let us partake of these exquisite honey and nut cakes." He offered Yana the Limoge plate, pooled with golden honey from the dripping cakes.

They would be alone now, the help dismissed for the evening. Phillipe did not want this meal to end, knowing he could not invite Yana for another dinner. One was all each patient was allowed. He could never show favoritism, even though some were more pleasant to dine with than others. The meal with Delphine was always unbearable and he couldn't wait for that evening to end.

"You are indeed a very unusual physician," Yana commented, her lips glazed with glistening honey.

"I pioneer in my own way. I always have. It is my life." Phillipe didn't want to talk about himself, his guest being the dignitary to be honored.

"I mean, what other doctor would have dinner with his patients as part of their healing." She licked the last sticky crumbs from her lips and then patted them with her napkin.

"I'll try to explain, if you have the patience to listen."

"I'll be patient as a little mouse. For once, I feel relaxed. Could it be because this food was not electrified—and I don't have a zillion bits of electricity charging about in my body," she said, laughing.

He smiled too; her laugh was infectious. "You can never be serious about my treatments, can you?"

"I try, doctor. I really try." She sounded sincere. "Now, tell me why you have these dinners."

"I tell the others, because they have difficulty comprehending many things, I dine with them to get to know them in a more relaxed atmosphere, which is true.

"But, in researching women's ailments, I have come upon a malady afflicting many females today. The term is 'sexual starvation,' a principle cause of derangement of the nervous and vascular systems." He knew he was taking on his physician role again, but couldn't stop now.

"Sexual starvation?" Her tone was between mocking and chiding.

"Now, I don't mean conjugal sex. I refer to the magnetism of sexual association between male and female persons, a natural need of the body. To keep things in balance."

"You've come upon this by research?"

"Yes. Sexual association imparts erectile power to all tissues of the body. It stimulates ambition, imparts electricity to the muscles and brilliancy to the eyes. It has been proven." He stopped, having said more than he intended.

"Tell me, doctor, do I have sexual starvation?" *Was she deriding his analysis again?*

"No," he answered, "but I have seen pitiful cases. Women denied the company of men. Spinsters. Nuns. Withered dissipated females. Magnetic equalization of both sexes takes place in great measure simply by social contact, being in the same room."

"Something takes place, even I know that," she admitted.

"There must be free interchange of sexual magnetic elements in an elevated social way to prevent those earthquakes and tornado outbreaks of passion which result in rape and sexual pollution."

"Yes, I see." She was hesitant.

Did she really? "Alas, this separation of the sexes does take place, deliberately. Our schools, even our churches are segregated by the sex." He didn't mean to go into some long discourse and spoil the relaxation of the evening. Was he rambling on just to keep her there? "Excuse me for talking of my work. This dinner is to get to know you," he said in apology.

She looked ready to go on to something else, rather than question some notion she had never even thought about and knew she would never have to worry over. It was evident she associated with whomever she wished. "What shall we converse on, to keep the sexual starvation away," she teased. There was a brief silence. "This is very fine tea." She was making an effort to restore the small talk.

"Herbal infusions. The herbs are grown in my own gardens. Comfrey and chamomile, mixed with imported jasmine and a bit of orange."

"And gold cups.'

"Gold has always been known to impart great curative powers. It is always too expensive to experiment with in great measure. Still, drinking from gold cups does impart some beneficial elements."

She was examining the delicate demitasse cup, inside and out and then peered into it. "Shall I read your tea leaves for you, doctor?" Mystery reflected in the depths of her eyes.

"I—" It was he who now hesitated. He didn't believe in her Gypsy nonsense, but his curiosity was sometimes stronger than

his logic. "You may. Be assured, however, I don't put any stock
in such oracles," he added.

"Kushti. Good, fine." She took his cup and swirled the tea
and bits of leaves left floating at the bottom. She was
concentrating deeply. "Ah, doctor, I see great things happening
to you, in the very near future. And—"

"Stop." The sound came out more abrupt than he meant it,
but he had to halt what he was permitting to happen.

"What brings this on?" She put the cup down.

"This is a haven of science." *He had given her permission,
why was he retracting now?* "Yana, I need to say this to you,
because my concern is for all my patients." Now that he had
begun, he must finish. "You must stop your Gypsy practices,
carrying them out in this place of science. You must cease using
your tarot cards and fortune telling book. Mavis, I have heard, is
frightened by all this. This is a modern medical Sanitarium. I
am trying to do away with superstitions. If I let you continue
here at this table, I would only be condoning such goings-on."

She seemed somewhat taken back. "I harm no one. The
ladies ask me to read the cards. Tell their fortunes. For them it
is only a pastime, a curiosity. I never read the bad fortunes. I
frighten no one. Why do I frighten you?"

"It does not frighten me, because I know it is not true." He
had to rekindle the friendly rapport. "Mavis needs help,
friendship, not more bewilderment. What you tell her only
disturbs her already troubled mind. Teach her to read, if you
wish to enlighten her."

"Of course, doctor, you are right," she was calmer now,
"but I am already teaching Mavis to read.*" Why was she always
two steps ahead of him?*

" I did not know."

"Now you do." He could sense things going on in her
mind, but he did not have any clue.

"Yes, doctor, I know how to read. But I do not read only
words. I read eyes, faces, and also palms." She reached over and
took his hand in hers. "Let me tell you what I read in your palm,
doctor."

"No, no, I—" He tried to withdraw his hand, but she held on with both of hers, firmly, yet such a gentle hold.

"Why must you always be so serious about everything?" she queried. "I've never heard you laugh, my doctor. Relax. Treat this only as a parlor game, not some blasphemy against your world of science. We are here to enjoy ourselves."

What would happen if he did relax, let down all guards, do as he always asked his patients to do? He would try. Just another experiment, an apology for his previous outburst. "I will indulge this one time, but only as a parlor game," he said trying for an air of lightheartedness that was difficult to foster with so much uncertainty swirling about in his emotions.

Yana began tracing the lines in his hands, soft touches that traveled throughout his body. Was it because he was relaxed, ready to accept? He wasn't sure, but he felt more pliable than he ever remembered.

"What *bak the divvus*? What luck today? I see...." The expression on her face changed from playful to serious and she let go of his hand. "Sometimes we do not reveal everything we see."

Dr. Zastro looked at his palm curiously. Why had she stopped? He was ready to hear what she would say. He was no longer relaxed; he was even a bit annoyed as he reverted to his physician role. "How can someone with so much intelligence, so much learning—"

She interrupted, "I am reading your eyes right now, doctor. Something is troubling you. Something you're afraid to express."

He didn't want her looking into his eyes, not in that way, as if she could view into his very soul. "I believe tea time is over." He moved his chair away from the table.

She folded her napkin, placing it on the lace cloth, and resumed her role as guest. "Thank you doctor for attending to my sexual starvation. But, alas, once alone in my room after this mingling meeting, it will afflict me all over again, and be that much greater to bear." The exaggerated tone was obvious.

"Why do you always make fun of my beliefs?"

"Why do *you* always make fun of *my* beliefs?"

"Only your superstitions."

"They are my beliefs."

He extended his hand politely. "Thank you for your company," he said and proceeded to assist her out of her chair.

She rose, extending him a gracious smile. "And I thank you for yours. I shall now retire to my windowless room while outside the full moon beckons, drawing all my yearnings upward and turning my sexual starvation into even greater agony. An agony I cannot cure by myself. And now that I know what brings it on, it shall be even more pitiful and lonely to go through."

He ignored her little charade. "Your room is comfortable?" Why had he even mentioned the sexual starvation theory? He never did with his other patients.

"My room? Gypsies are always restless within four walls. Every spring I take my horse and wagon, lock up my country home, and just follow the open road. This spring I came here. Something is being reversed within me; something is crying out desperately for release. All of this spring. And every day since I've been here."

She went into a slow twirl and began to chant, "*Per de, per de prajtina*—"

"Stop," he shouted. "Stop your Gypsy gibberish." He was ashamed that he lost control again; he turned away.

"Gibberish?" She walked around to face him. "It is not gibberish, it is a love chant."

"I'm sorry, but—"

"Why must you shut out, because you do not understand?"

"I-- Why did you recite a love chant?" He was bewildered.

"I don't know. I don't preplan everything I do. Words sometimes just flow forth, as mindless as breathing."

"Those foreign words—I couldn't understand; yet, my heart tells me I did." It was true; there was meaning in just the sounds, and because she had said them.

"Yes. Yes, you do understand. There is very deep understanding within you that surpasses words." She was looking at him, her eyes reflecting the light of the candle. The glow of the whole universe was reflected there. The right ignition touched to her body could discharge a whole series of magnificent chain reactions. "Even now your mind is analyzing," she said.

"There is much turmoil going on within me—for days I have been distracted, not knowing the cause." *What was he confessing and why*? "I think I do now."

"I also read hearts."

"Then you know." He took her hands in his, gazing into the dark recesses of her eyes. He had to say it; nothing could stop the force of the words, this flood of emotion. "I have fallen in love with you. I have never fallen in love before." He stared down at their joined hands; how much greater their power now? "I'm not sure about anything at this moment, except that you consume my mind, my heart—my whole being."

"The wheel spins. We have no control." It was as if she had always known and was finally admitting it too.

"I have seen hundreds of women. None of them has ever affected me as you have." He let go of her and walked away trying to gain some control; yet, he didn't want control anymore. He had found an equal, a person with whom he wanted to share everything. Could it be possible, that there even was such a thing as a conjoining of the spirits?

"Tell me more," she whispered. "Release your soul from this self-made prison. Let it soar as a bird liberated from its cage. The door has been open all the time." Yana's face clouded as though she were remembering something; then she shook her head and concluded. "It is written. We must follow the fates."

"I've written about love. Scientifically explained it," he mused, "but it is none of those things. It is as if a special chord within me was touched and now vibrates constantly. I hear it continuously. There is no way to turn it off, nor would I if I could." He felt freer than ever before, as if heavy weights were removed and he was floating above the whole earth—a bird, a song, projections of the sun's rays.

"'Tis true. You and I vibrate in a special harmony. Even apart, we are together. It is so." She pressed her warm palm over his heart that was beating wildly, as if it would leap out of his body, and if it could, attach itself to her heart.

"I've never been involved with any of my patients. Why is this happening now?" He was perplexed and couldn't summon a rationale to quell this flight into unknown sensibilities.

"Because we have never met before. Because it was destined to be." She moved closer to him.

He breathed deeply, desperately trying to regain composure. In times of crisis, he could always regain control. He had been trained to do so. He tried so hard now that tears were forming in his bewildered eyes. "Forgive me. I forgot my position. I took advantage of the hour—other things." He stepped back, "I am in control once more."

"It is not so." She shook her head knowingly.

"Please forgive me." He pleaded. "I shall never mention any of this again. You are dismissed. Our meeting is over." He stood waiting for her to leave, yet willing her to stay.

Instead, she sat down and began speaking without giving him an opportunity to interrupt. "I cannot leave without speaking also." She was serious. "I've had many men express emotions of love to me before. I am not without response to another's feelings. I decided long ago, the very first time I was in love that I would never be able to share myself with another person."

She stood up and began pacing. "I could never give up my independence to become part of someone else's life. That is where love leads, doesn't it, if it has any meaning at all? Mama tried. It didn't work. It never does. Someone always loses, and generally it is the woman. I did not work this hard to gain what I have only to lose it all because of passions I cannot rein in. We both know that we each must follow our life's work as we have set out to do." She turned away, concluding, "It would have been a wonderful experiment. Maybe I am turning down something precious that will never be offered to me again."

"We will speak of it no more then," he said.

She still was not looking at him. "I think it's best I leave."

"Yes, it is late." It was best; he could no longer bear the pain within the desire, the need to scream her name that was tearing at his throat.

"I mean, leave here, altogether. Return home. Tomorrow."

"Perhaps that would be the wise course...." A sorrow enveloped the whole room. A sadness he had not known since the death of his mother. "No!" he cried, frightening himself as well as Yana. "You mustn't leave. You still need—treatments. Your arm—your leg—"

"And do you believe you can still treat me? After these revelations between the two of us?"

"I am a doctor, Miss Kejako"

"You are also a man. You were born a man before you became a doctor."

It was his turn to disclose; he would say anything to keep her from leaving the Sanitarium. "A doctor learns to suppress many of his emotions. He sees people dying. Patients crying out in pain. And he learns not to let it tear himself apart."

He tried to express the thoughts that had become his manifesto—anything to convince both Yana and himself. "I have studied long hours without sleep. Suffered through days of poverty, without heat, food. Withstood excruciating pain in numerous experiments upon myself. I have mastered my body and emotions. I shall conquer these new feelings. It shall be one more challenge in my personal training."

"I have not learned such control." There was a softening in the whole presence of Yana, as she came toward him, bending, yielding. "Right now my body cries out for you as it has never cried out for anyone else before. I cannot control that."

"If that is true—" He couldn't stop himself, no force on earth could. They moved toward each other, propelled by the most powerful magnet at the core of the earth. Gathering her in his arms, he melded his form into hers, consuming her with a deep heated kiss, transporting them both into another realm of existence.

She broke away with sharp suddenness. "No! I cannot let this happen. I cannot." Tears streamed down her flushed cheeks.

"It already has happened," he said, giving in to this deep acknowledgment.

She faced him once more, keeping the table between them. Wiping tears, straightening her shoulders, she spoke with great determination. "I will stay. But only because I must conquer these feelings within myself also. I need to be assured that my emotions will not overwhelm me again, as they just did now, ready to succumb, give up everything."

The wonder of the kiss hovered between them. She spoke with great deliberation. "It is going to be difficult, doctor, very difficult. I don't have your years of discipline and self-denial."

Tears were forming anew, but she didn't try to stop them, letting everything flow. "I've always believed in free love. Only this time, if I give in to you, even once, I could never be free again. I would be lost to you forever."

He couldn't believe what he had just heard. "Do not decide with such haste. These are new feelings for both of us." What she had just told him—he wanted to shout with exalted joy, but he dared hardly breathe.

Yana faced him. Her voice sounded louder and harsher. "I have become an artist. Do you not understand? My art is my life. I will not give it up to become another person's wife."

Impetuously he reached out for her and she almost melted into his arms again, but in the same moment thrust herself away and toward the door.

"No. You shall never have me in your power again. Ever." She bolted from the room.

He had not audibly wept in as long as he could remember. Tears were upon him now; he sobbed in the blinding dimness. "Yana, my love, my only love. Don't leave me." He sank to his knees and let his soul pour out with the tears. To his mother, his father—to anyone who would hear. "Do not let Yana leave me. I love her more than life itself."

He knew it was true.

CHAPTER 15

Yana tossed and turned all that night, calling out in her sleep, waking up in a cold sweat. Grandmama had come to her—shouting something, but now she couldn't remember any of her words.

In the dimness, Yana perceived shadowlike figures dancing about her room, taunting, laughing. What was happening? The result of the strange food she had eaten at dinner last night or the tug-of-war with Dr. Zastro at the end of the evening?

If Grandmama was telling her to leave—

No, her mind was already made up; she was staying the rest of the two weeks, no matter what transpired within her heart. Then once away from his presence, it would be easier to dismiss him, but while here, she needed protection. Lying in her bed, eyes closed, she began chanting a seldom-used ancient protective verse until the droning words filled the room and lulled her into another fretful sleep.

When she awoke, heavy clouds were still hovering in the room and she had to fight through them to reach a wakeful state. Nevertheless, for the first time since last Friday, welcome rays of sunshine were piercing through the tinted panes of her painted window, and she escaped the room in hopes of getting into the sunlight as soon as possible.

Finally, they had fresh-air time in the roof garden. Each of them was now relaxing in one of the six wicker lounges in the lush greenery of the rooftop oasis. The sky above glowed bright blue, but if you looked down and over, the view was punctured by curls of black smoke spiraling from both nearby and distant buildings. Where did those dark smoke plumes disappear? Where did ominous thoughts dissolve? Or like the smoke, did forebodings leave a sooty residue, never to disappear completely?

Sounds from the street drifted up in a faint cacophony; otherwise, this garden might have been miles away from any busy metropolis. In spite of the city sounds, Yana savored these

outdoor sessions, short as they were. If only she could sneak out
here at night. She had already tried. The heavy door was always
double locked. Isobelle had no access to the area either, as the
gardener took care of cleaning this space.

The garden boasted an abundance of towering green plants,
fragrant flowers, climbing vines—all flourishing high above the
din of New York City. You must credit Dr. Zastro with attaining
the impossible in so many areas.

The greenhouses were below them, at ground level where
the sun now bounced off the panes in repeated golden haloes,
interiors shimmering in varied hues of tropical green. The air—
fresh, fragrant—erased those isolated hours imprisoned inside.
If she closed her eyes, Yana could even believe she heard sounds
of her river rushing by, singing to her. How she wished she
could spirit herself away, mount and ride her horse across the
rooftops, the skies, until she was back home once more.

That's what she dreamed of most—home. Sometimes Dr.
Zastro was there—in her dreams, and she kept telling him to
leave; he didn't belong there. She didn't belong here, especially
after last night.

The other ladies chattered busily. A few made sure they
stayed in the shade, as if any bit of pure sunlight might melt and
peel away their pale skins. When they were away from the
Sanitarium, their faces were no doubt shaded by bonnets,
parasols. Yana was sure Delphine never went anywhere
outdoors without her sun umbrella, treasuring her ivory pallor
that indicated that she did not perform peasant or fieldwork in
the browning sun.

"Mine favorite time of day," Isobelle exclaimed as she did
every time she came out here.

"It is lovely," Yana agreed, "Inside, it is just so—all closed
in. Cut off from everything. Not even an insect allowed in that
sterilized place. I miss the welcome chirp of the cricket."
Crickets were a good luck sound, and she hadn't heard any for
such a long time. A special yearning for that cheery chirp came
upon her, a sound that always reminded her that there were
sparks of life hidden all around, though their presence was not

always visible; their voice affected your daily life in minute ways.

"I hate those dirty little black bugs. Squash them every time I can." Delphine was always swatting at imagined insects when she was in the garden. "I hate being out here too. Can't close my eyes for fear some ugly flying thing might land on top of me."

"Nothing is dirty here. Even kitchen is clean," Isobelle commented. "Never seen such clean, clean kitchen. Eat off the floors."

Yana wondered what the kitchen did look like, as well as all the other prohibited rooms. How different were they from those of other homes, other institutions? Everything at the Sanitarium was unique, resembling no other place she had ever visited. She envied Isobelle, her liberty to wander into all the off-limit places. Still, Isobelle was not the curious kind. She was satisfied to follow orders, working within arranged boundaries. Yana thought it a wasted privilege.

"There is something about Dr. Zastro's Sanitarium, some essence I have never experienced in any other place," said Edwina, who once more appeared removed from the regular world. She claimed the pills she was taking and the Electro-belt on her head always put her into another sphere, a pure state of bliss, where there were no worries. Not even any guilt about being away from her husband and children. "If Dr. Zastro can accomplish that," Edwina said, "he is indeed a miracle worker."

"I didn't even know there was such places like this." Mavis was becoming more talkative. "I like outside here best, it's more like the farm. Only, I don't hear no cows, or pigs, or chickens. Even if I close my eyes real tight, I still can't hear their noises. Sometimes, it's like I even forgot what they sound like." She grew thoughtful. "It's going to be different—going back. My hands are getting soft too, the calluses falling off. How will I be able to plow for spring planting? I'll have to work double hard when I get back—to catch up. Pa told me I'd have to."

"Don't worry about tomorrow; it will take care of itself," Yana said. One of the many Gypsy mottoes that spoke to the uncertainties of their nomadic lives. Each day was different, so how could you prepare?

"Is good here. So good." Isobelle didn't seem to mind the hard ridges of the rattan cutting into her back; she never used the cushions. "Mine back, feels with life again."

"Because you're letting it rest properly, and not lifting three hundred pound men, and—" Yana had to stop trying to explain to these women reasons for their cures. It was a pointless exercise. At first, they had listened because she was more educated. Somehow, lately, they all had this sense of being privileged to their own special knowledge—since they were, after all, members of the "selected six".

What they thought didn't matter, did it? Yana would never see any of them again once she left. However, she possessed one talent they respected. They still believed in her psychic powers and asked, in whispers, for Yana to read their palms, tell their fortunes. Her answer from now on would have to be, "Dr. Zastro does not allow it" and explain that she would be dismissed if she ever did it again.

She was content to let her Gypsy talents rest. The only ritual she missed was her daily painting. Sneaking in short sketches did not bring the same satisfaction. If only she could set her easel out in this garden and paint the cherished setting, capture it forever—to take home with her. She also wanted to make paintings of all the areas in the Sanitarium. And the people. These women. Shyam. Dr. Zastro. Especially Dr. Zastro. What a portrait that would be, to duplicate his powerful eyes and the mystique they exuded.

As much as she was trying to ignore the memory, Phillipe's kiss, his confession from the previous night, was still embedded in her heart. He could stay there, another ghost along with all the other loves she had banished. Yet, those men had been easier to cast out. Why?

"I don't work when I'm away from here, how come I feel so good when I'm here, Miss Know-It-All?" Delphine was still referring to Yana's reasoning as to why Isobelle felt so much better at the Sanitarium.

"Naturally you feel better here, Delphine, away from all your problems and husband to cater to and servants to supervise. And Edwina does not have her eight children to tend here—"

"Another sermon from Pastor Yana," Edwina interrupted, obviously resenting any reminder of her home life. She wanted nothing to detract from this short-lived period of bliss.

Yana ignored the new title of Pastor. "All of you—you know why you feel so much better? It is not due to the treatments, but because here you don't have to worry about anything. Your whole day is scheduled for you. When to eat, what to eat. When to sleep, get up. Morning exercises—then your brain is stimulated by the doctor's words read to you during breakfast. Then the provocative morning lecture, consultation— you are so charmed by Dr. Zastro's sincere interest in you. How many other men are ever concerned about you? How many men listen to what you have to say or even care what you think? How many men, other than your husbands, even touch you?"

There was a slight silence, the women pondering what she had just challenged.

"I've had many, many other men 'concerned' bout me," Delphine interjected, "touch me too." She no longer even tried hiding her past life.

Yana continued, ignoring Delphine as she did most of the time. "Machine stimulation. Herbs. Pills. Intimate suppers with gold dinnerware. Then finally, you're all tucked into your own little magnetic bed. *Dinili!* Silly. All of this combined has made this great difference in how you feel."

"Whatever—I don't care, bout the reasons, only bout the cures. Whatever—I feel good." Isobelle looked almost serene, basking on her lounge, eyes closed, shutting out the world and all its ugliness for one short period in her life.

They didn't understand. "You've given up all your freedom, letting someone else take over your lives. Maybe you all like it. I do not." Yana got up from her lounge and went to the garden edge, looking out over the wall. Even when outside in this area, she felt caged, wishing for wings, since she couldn't have her horse, so she could fly away, in any direction from this stifling prison.

Delphine came up behind her. "Why do you stay here then, if you all hate it so? You're free to leave anytime you like." She swished her bamboo fan. Out in the sunlight, the sunken eyes, the facial lines were harder to hide and Delphine's past was manifested in its harshest reality.

"I know," Yana said, brought back to the garden again. She felt a bit of remorse for her outburst. "I've thought many times about leaving, but, strangely, my arm and leg—I think they're being cured."

"Then don't think you're so much better than we are, if the cures work the same on you as they do on us. And stop your belittling of the doctor. I'm tired of hearing it."

Maybe Delphine was right. Maybe she was always degrading Dr. Zastro only to convince herself he had no power over her. It was her problem, not theirs. Let them glory in their time here. What did it matter to her?

"Dr. Zastro knows what we need to be healed. We could never find out such cures for ourselves." Mavis had been walking the garden, stopping near them. In the sunlight her pure beauty was enhanced, as a flower that basked in the rays of the sun must search out the brightness when fortune has rooted her in the shade.

"Your life away from here is maybe more exciting, yah?" Isobelle called out. Yana found Isobelle had a natural sense of intuition about many things, made more evident daily.

"Have eight children and a demanding husband—church work—there is no freedom left for yourself." Edwina's medicine must be wearing off.

"Work for other peoples—Ach, no time is your own." It was not a complaint from Isobelle, only a fact. She had learned early on to accept life and all the hardships that came with it, as if it were her lot, part of the lower class system she was born into. No one had ever told her she could take charge of her life, not let everyone else run it for her. Even when she had run away, it was only to someone else to dominate her.

"I'd go crazy by myself. When Solomon's gone I always have my friends in. Or servants around. I have my own personal servant to talk to—rub me down, brush my hair."

Delphine always had to remind the others of all the servants she possessed as though other people's hard work put her in the upper caste.

"I—I miss the farm. Mama. The animals. Even Pa...." Mavis seemed more melancholy outside in the greenery. "But I like it here too."

"What about Althea?" Yana asked. "Has being at the Sanitarium made her any better? She still wakes up screaming at night. All they do is keep rocking her, bathing her."

"Dr. Zastro knows what he is doing." Edwina was always his greatest defender. "He has had more experience in these matters than you have."

"Course he has." Delphine's personal claim to superiority here was that she knew more about the doctor than anyone else did. "He has traveled all over the world. He even pointed out places to me on his personal map."

"He knows just about everything there is to know." To Mavis he was God, since she had never been introduced to any other deity. It seemed God never visited her ramshackle farm or appeared in the faces of any of her family. Where had she acquired her sensitive nature?

"You can't accept someone else's words so blindly." Yana knew it was useless to try to convince these women, yet, she felt compelled to try. "You must also think for yourselves."

"His lectures make perfect sense to me," Edwina said.

"And me too," Delphine chimed in, like some ding-dong that repeatedly gonged.

"Everything isn't run by electrical currents," Yana said, trying to stay on top of her mounting exasperation. "There are things going on in our minds—our spirits, that no one will ever be able to comprehend."

"Ach. Is you who don't make the sense."

Was Isobelle right? Was something happening to her also while here, so her thoughts weren't working as they generally did? She was now contemplating thoughts in a manner she never had before.

"Being an artist does not make you more superior to anyone else, especially a doctor." Edwina had joined in the rebellion.

"An artist. Lah de dah." Delphine mocked. "What do you all paint—teensy, weensy roses on giant teacups?" She giggled, delighted with her cute cruelty. "Do you paint your tea leaves inside them?"

"I paint the places I remember. People. Events." Numerous paintings flashed through her mind, a split second exhibit of colorful memories. No, her mind was still working, better than ever. She was very clear on what she was seeing, what she was saying—never clearer.

"Did you all know they invented something called a camera?" Delphine was so excited to be in possession of knowledge she thought exclusive, "and they can make an exact picture of everything, anything, much better than any old painting. Painters won't be needed anymore." She giggled again. "Unless to paint houses, or barns."

"Yah, I seen such things, done with the camera box." True wonder rang in Isobelle's voice. "Is scary, to see pictures of peoples what is dead already. Never want picture of mineself took with such a thing—dead or alive. Don't want mine homely mug to show round after I'm gone. Peoples still looking at me, and laughing."

"I know about cameras," Yana acceded, "but those brown and white daguerreotypes can never compare with colorful glorious paintings. A painting carries part of the artist's spirit. They are not mere reproductions, but reflections of life as seen through the soul of the artist." Yana had to defend her artwork. It mattered more to her than any of her views on Dr. Zastro. "A photograph can never be anything but a mechanical reproduction, a machine process without the altering human touch."

"Is magic—magic in those boxes." Isobelle and the others were interrupted by the clap of Shyam's hands.

"Ladies, outdoor time is over."

The best part of the day was already gone, and so quickly. Once inside Yana would have to go back to the determined suppression she had committed herself to, biting her lips, her tongue, anything to get through another twenty-four hours, another twenty four hours closer to getting home.

Would her resolution to last another eleven days be worth the conflicting turmoil? It was so easy for her thoughts to return to Dr. Zastro when there was so little else to fill them. She could only be distracted for so long by the idle chatter of these silly women. Phillipe Zastro was the most interesting phenomenon around here.

True, the days at the Gypsy camp had many periods of idle chatter among the women as they cooked and sewed and tended to their children. All the same, it seemed that Gypsy women's lives had deeper meaning—a knowledge embedded for generations that lent wisdom to the simplest of their conversations.

It wasn't true that she felt superior to these women; it was just that there was nothing connecting them with the exception of being women. Once more, she felt *pikie*—an outsider. The only correlating thread between the patients was Dr. Zastro and their adulation for him. Even she was part of that fabric, though she didn't want to be. She was trying to unravel the strands as fast as she was being caught up in them. For one moment last night, she had been snared into a binding knot, not wanting to remove herself, ready to become a willing victim in Dr. Zastro's soft velvet web.

Rage welled up within her, an overwhelming fury to throw, smash, something. She tore away a blossom from the nearest flower, a huge crimson hibiscus, flinging the fluttering ball of petals over the garden wall, as far, as hard as she could. A distant thud resounded as the spinning blossom landed on top of one of the greenhouse panes, splattering into blood-red sprays atop the glimmering glass.

"*Chavia. Chavia.* Stop. Stop," she sobbed, dismayed that she had made such a beautiful flower the object of her fury, destroying both its life and beauty in the process.

Shyam was at her side. "Is forbidden to pick the flowers." His voice was high-pitched and angry. "Also forbidden to throw anything over walls. You will be reported to Dr. Zastro."

She said nothing. She was ashamed of her impropriety, belittled by Shyam's tone. What kind of punishment was meted out for such digressions? It didn't matter. Her acts of rage always brought their own retribution.

The door to the outside world clanged shut once more, double locked by Shyam.

Yana rushed down the long hallway, pushing past the others. Her lungs already ached for more fresh air, her eyes still blinded from the sunlight, her heart seeking solace, and not knowing where to find it.

How comforting it would be to have a pair of waiting arms to console her, to cradle her in times of greatest need.... .

CHAPTER 16

Another restless night: Yana dreaming she was back with the tribe, dancing and telling stories. Someone was playing the violin while children giggled and dogs barked in tandem. It was a pleasant dream until Grandmama swooped in, cackling, "You don't belong here."

Where? Where didn't she belong? With the Gypsies? Where she was now? All of a sudden, the local police descended on the camp. They shouted and grabbed, rounding up the Gypsies. Wailing rose from the women and children, but the men remained quiet, stoic, not answering questions, pretending not to understand, playing dumb, when they really weren't.

While this was going on, Yana was running into the night, calling out her protection chant, but she couldn't get it right; she was trying to find Mama, trying to find Papa, and all she could find were jagged rocks looming ahead of her. Rocks that cut into her feet as she raced over them. Wolves howled all around her. Suddenly everything froze solid, her skin becoming so brittle it would shatter into a thousand pieces if she shifted but an inch.

She woke with a start, shuddering with cold. It was still the middle of the night; the troubling dream surrounding her as if it had followed her into waking to chill the whole room. She wrapped herself tight in her coverlet, needing to warm herself against this terrible cold within.

Dance—she wanted to dance, needed to dance. She had this urgency to whirl her body around and around until it dropped in final exhaustion, nothing left of her senses, having reached that other sphere of existence where mystical hallucinations took over.

Way back, her mother had told her about the Whirling Dervishes from the eastern countries, and how wild dancing was part of their religious rites. When a little girl, Yana would try to imitate the frenzied dance, pretending she was a Whirling Dervish. Her head would spin, the rhythm getting faster and faster, as if she were a top gyrating into infinity. Then always that final twirl, the drop into exhaustion, followed by beautiful visions whirling in her head, wonderful, dizzying thoughts circulating every which way.

Though she tried many times, she could never coerce this mystical ending to occur upon demand.   It only seemed obtainable when she was in the grip of a special need pulsating deep in her veins. When the mystical did overtake her, nothing could stop the momentum until it unwound itself to completion.

That was what was happening now. The imperative need to spin out all these strangling thoughts, unwind them into the night and lose them forever in hopes of replacing them with spiraling auras that would flood her mind, leaving room for nothing else.

The previous afternoon, she had gone again to her wicker basket in the storage room just to feel her garments once more. Seeing her clothing, smelling their familiar scents, induced her to gather an armful of her apparel, hiding it under her loose gown, before dashing down the hall to her room. She had shoved all of it up into the air vent, new joy prevailing over the whole room.

Was that what perpetrated those dreams last night? Her clothes hovering, hidden above her with their scent permeating the air, luring her back to the tribe. Or had she pushed so many items into the vent, air was being blocked from entering the room? The bad dreams a result of insufficient fresh air? What did it matter? Something was causing her to have a hard time breathing, some blockage in her whole system.

Yana lit a candle, stood on her chair and took the garments down from the vent, holding them to her, breathing them in, devouring their whole beloved presence.

Cautiously she removed her robe, almost as if someone were watching and would step forward to reprimand her. Had she become so programmed with rules? With swift abandon, she slid into the soft gathered blouse and the colorful billowing skirts. She was transformed back to what she once was. Yana wanted to let out a cry of joy and begin her dance unrestrained.

Her room was too tiny, too cramped for the twirling she envisioned. In this space she could never dance to completion. Where? The Treatment Room—it had a wide-open area where they did their exercises. It was, unfortunately, always locked up tight.

Too late to forestall the momentum now. She wrapped her tambourine in her skirt to keep it from jangling, and dashed, barefoot, from her room. *Please let the keys be in Isobelle's apron pocket.* It was a viable possibility; Isobelle often forgot to return keys when she was in a hurry to get to her meals. More cautious now, Yana crept down the hallway, her tambourine held tight in the folds of the skirt so that it would not betray her. If discovered, she could always say she was sleepwalking. The doctor had told of women doing this and how he cured them.

She paused outside Isobelle's partially opened door from where she could hear the woman's loud snoring, the painful grunts between short breaths. Yana felt in the pocket of Isobelle's apron hanging on the hall peg—the key ring was there. *Bakalo!* Her lucky night.

Whatever was pursuing her, she had escaped it, left it all back in her room. She was now free to go forward without restraint. If only she could dance outside in the fields under the haze of the moon, stars circling overhead in bright dizzying rings, and then sit to watch the rosy morn approach in resplendent glory as it washed away the darkness of night. That is what she would do, the first night back home—dance until dawn.

She grasped the keys and began almost floating down the hallway on her bare feet. A light glowed from under Delphine's door. She probably had trouble sleeping here too. All the women were away from their homes. Why did she feel exclusive in her longings? Was it because, for these other women, home was not the better place to be?

The Treatment Room was at the far end of the corridor. Past the doctor's office. No light. Next door was a room with a bed, wardrobe and washstand. Sometimes the doctor slept there. Other times he went to his regular bedroom in the downstairs living quarters. Next was Shyam's room, where they were told to knock during the night for emergencies. Dark in that room, too.

She was at the Treatment Room doorway. She hoped that Althea wouldn't be in the Rocking Machine tonight. Rumors were that she had been confined to her bed; the machines had only been making her worse. Of course, these were only gossipy conjectures by the ladies. Still, Althea hadn't appeared at mealtimes recently, or at the lectures. Possibly Dr. Zastro was trying some new treatment. If one thing didn't work to his satisfaction, he tried another.

Yana had to insert several keys before finding one that clicked smoothly. Again, luck was with her. The huge door squeaked open and she closed it behind her, breathing a sigh of relief that turned to exhilaration. She turned on a single light, peering behind the curtain surrounding the bathtub, just to make sure no one was in there. No one. For the first time she had the room to herself. The excitement was mounting.

Music—the music box and tambourine were all that was available. Those slow waltzes would do until she was into the rhythm, ready to spin, and by then, it wouldn't matter what she heard, the sounds would be playing in her head.

The light was soft rosy pink, casting tremoring shadows. The tinkling music, an enchanting prelude, as her body began to sway, her long hair undulating in tandem. Soon she could hear the soulful violins playing around the campfire. Picking up her tambourine she banged it against her hand, crying out, "*Avree!*" and began her dance, slowly at first and then faster and faster until her skirt was a flat circle surrounding her upper bare legs. Her whirling form, wild cries, staccato beats of the tambourine, rising above the music box sounds, filled the room with unrestrained turbulence. The floor and ceiling and walls spun in clamorous movement as if a whirlwind had entered and she was at the inert center.

Thoughts circling in beautiful shades of flashing colors, her body nearing fatigue, but she did not want to stop, not ready yet to experience the sought-after finale. Even when the music ended, her body kept moving, slowing into exotic undulations— expanding into one sensuous vibration.

She began to sing the plaintive love song, *Aye Solea*. Her heart crying out, lamenting the words over and over, tears pouring from her—all the longing, yearning, loneliness that lay deep within, rising to the surface. So immersed in this engrossing sphere of emotion, she was unaware of anything else, until she sensed something breaking into the privacy of her circle. There were two hearts beating now, where before there had been only one.

Her eyes began focusing more clearly. It was then she saw the figure, this vision in a gold robe, outlined in the doorway. At first, she thought it was an apparition, an ancient spirit she had called up during her dance. Such beings often visited her mind when she went into these other realms. She shook her head sharply, her loosened hair forming a veil over her eyes, and through that veil, she perceived him again. Even in the dimness, she knew it was Phillipe, as if the love song had conjured him from his room to here.

She wasn't prepared for this encounter. She had only wanted to dance, rid her body of pent up longings. Once in her Gypsy clothing she had reverted to the abandonment of all regulations. In one brief moment she was acutely aware she had broken rules.

"Dr. Zastro." It was an utterance of disbelief, as if expressing his name aloud might make him disappear.

He was real, moving further into the room. "What are you doing here?" he demanded, as if he too couldn't believe what he was seeing.

"I—I couldn't sleep," she answered, wrapping her arms around herself as if to hide the forbidden clothing.

"We have medicines for that. How did you get in here?"

She couldn't involve Isobelle, betray her carelessness with the keys.

"I don't know—someone must have forgotten to lock up."

"Probably Shyam. He's been so burdened of late. Still, that is no excuse for your being here in the middle of the night." He stayed at a distance. Since the night before, they'd kept an unspoken barrier between them.

"I have harmed nothing," she said. "My body needed release—extra space to dance. This was the only area. Can't you accept what I've done as a vital part of my cure?" *No, he*

would never understand why she was here, only that she wasn't
supposed to be.

"I cannot accept reverting to your ancient rituals as any part
of my cures. And tell me also, where did you get those forbidden
Gypsy gowns and that tambourine?"

"I can't answer that," she said, lifting her chin in defiance.
"They are mine and they are free of disease." She didn't care to
get into any question and answer games at this time. Nor did the
patient and doctor status apply, now that each was in different
attire. At this moment in time, Yana and Phillipe were no longer
part of the Sanitarium; the room around them dissolved. They
were transported to a communal grouping around a crackling
campfire where they might speak freely, revealing what was in
their hearts. The vision was but a brief flicker in her mind, but it
told her where she wanted to be, with whom, and why.

Reflectively, she leaned against one of the machines. Her
skin glistening from the fatiguing dance. Her hair frolicked
about her shoulders in tangled ringlets as her body began moving
in gyrations that wouldn't stop. She didn't care what he would
say, what punishment awaited. Whatever—it was worth it.
Ecstasy had been reached; revitalization was taking place.

He came closer but not too close, as if he too knew that if he
crossed over the line there could be no retreat.

"My body was restless," she repeated. "It needed release or
it would do things to my head, my muscles. It is dissipated
now."

"If your body is restless, dancing only excites it more so.
You are also breaking every one of my rules that I have set up to
heal you." He waited for her retort. There was none, so he
continued to fill the silence. "It was also reported to me that you
threw a flower onto the greenhouse roof this afternoon. Do you
realize that not only did you destroy a beautiful flower, but you
could have shattered the precious glass also?" His tone changed.
"Do you ever stop to think of the consequences of your
impulsive actions?"

She was ashamed to be reminded of the flower incident.
Would he make her leave? As much as she had wanted to be
back home, she realized now she no longer wanted to leave. All

that longing had just been released and she was ready to return to her room, the comfort of routine, and the assuring daily presence of Dr. Zastro.

"I am truly sorry," she said, "I shall try harder. But it is so difficult—"

"You are disturbing all of my treatments. Everything—"

"No," she protested, "My limbs are healed." She lifted her skirt. "See, I twist my leg, there is no more pain. I stretch my arm, and the soreness is gone. I had to celebrate this cure, rejoice in my newfound healthiness, and I had to let my body be part of the celebration."

"If you feel the treatments have worked, helped you, then I am pleased for you, but—"

"And you thought I might be one of the few women you were unable to cure." She was smiling at him now, not hiding her joy that he had not banished her back to her room. She sensed the tension easing in him as well. "Come, rest with me." Together they walked over to benches where they sat facing each other, but not touching.

"There still could be problems," Phillipe said.

Why did he always have to revert to his doctor role, couldn't he react as an ordinary man ever? "Problems?"

"Your—situation—presents unusual aspects." His face tightened as though he was rehearsing what he would say next. "If you will allow me, I'd like to write up your case history, include it in my new book, *The Study of Women: A Scientific Survey.*"

"Always the doctor. Even now, sitting here, you are studying me aren't you?" She could read the deep concentration that was taking place beyond his eyes.

"Observing," he said, "because you see, right now, you are flashing bright sparks off your person."

"Sparks?" She laughed. "I certainly feel something hot and warm discharging from me. Is that what flashing sparks feel like?"

"I don't know," he said, "I've never had them myself. You do radiate a great deal of magnetism. Most people absorb. I can feel them drawing energy away from me. You—you give out energy, in a very unique way."

She had always known she had some force, some special emanation at certain times, but no one had ever commented on it nor explained it in this revealing way. As though powered by this emanation, she got up and began to twirl again.

"The wheel spins, the forces flow," she sang. He watched her, but did not stop her.

She danced about, singing a ribald Spanish-Gypsy love song and focusing on him, touching his shoulders on passing, swirling her skirts in wanton rhythm, using her fingers as clicking castanets, and then raising her hands together, resounding them in sharp ringing handclaps. As she ended the flamenco inspired dance she threw her head back in the traditional gesture of hauteur. Smiling, radiant, she bowed before him, as if she had intended the performance only for him.

"Come, sit for a minute," he said, pointing to the space beside him. "Turn off your energies and relax."

"I have no switches I can turn off and on like your controlled machines," she said, sitting next to him, inner movement continuing, feet shuffling, neck pulsing.

"We do have switches, in our brain," he said, "yet, sometimes those switches are not strong enough, or we do not know how to control them."

What was troubling him so? "Then what do you do?" Something was warning her, now was the time to leave, before it was too late.

"I do not know."

"You've tried?"

"Yes, I've tried." He was struggling for words. "I have tried with all the powers of my being to turn off thoughts about you, but—"

She recognized the yearning expression in his eyes and turned her head away, trying to ignore the pounding in her heart, "Please, Phillipe—I've asked you—"

"It is no use," he whispered, "No matter how I try, you're still there. In my head, my heart, my soul—repeating over and over, until I hear nothing else. Yana—Yana. You have possessed me. I don't know what to do about it. It disturbs my work, my thoughts—"

Yana got up and walked away, "I'm not going to listen."

He followed her, pleading in a louder voice. "I've hardly slept since you've been here. I have not been able to concentrate on my work—my patients. 'Physician, heal thyself.' I cannot. I am powerless to do anything about this—spell—love, whatever it is you cast over me."

"It is not my doing."

He stopped, his voice filling with new wonder. "It is as if my heart were lifted out of me, suspended on butterfly wings— and I don't know how to bring it back to where it once was."

"You speak now as a poet, not a scientist."

"When I am with you, I am not who I usually am."

"Nor I, but—"

"Does it never go away?"

"No, not if the souls have been touched."

"Tell me," he reached for her hand, "has your soul been touched?"

She did not want to reply, trying to suppress the inner answer pulsing through her heart—*"Yes! Yes!"* Instead, she pulled her fingers away from his warm hold, verbalizing, "No."

"It's there," he continued, as if not hearing her denial. "It passes continuously between us, this attraction we have for each other. So strong, so melding, nothing else can come between."

"I know," she admitted, struggling to remember her promise of never letting anyone control any part of her. "It consumes me daily too. But, it is not possible...." Her words broke into soft sobs.

He put his arms around her, and she surrendered to letting him hold her.

"Do not cry, Yana. Please. I do not ever want to be the cause of your tears."

"They flow from the heart, not from my eyes." She pulled away while still able. "I cannot stay here any longer."

"Don't leave. What will I do without you?"

"Whatever you have done before." She was calmer now, away from him.

"No. It will never be the same." He moved closer, locking his fingers into hers. She felt as if held in a vise, her mind searching for escapes.

"We both have work, important work. We can lose ourselves in that," she offered.

"I have tried that solution. It is no answer."

He brought her closer to him and she yielded into his arms, submitting to his long passionate kiss, their lips burning into each other's flesh. She couldn't breathe—all the air sucked out of her. She could expire now and it wouldn't matter.

She broke away. *"Tatcho.* It is true."

"See, I am trembling." The doctor stood to show her; the hem of his gold robe quivered as a leaf caught in the wind. "What you just said—"

"It is true. But I also know I cannot give up everything."

"I would never ask you to give up anything," the quivering was in his voice now.

"I could never live in this brownstone prison." Even the thought stifled her. "I would be as a caged bird, always yearning to be somewhere else."

"I have never caged anyone, human or otherwise. I would never want you living here as a restrained woman. Your unique spirit is what sets you apart."

"You say this tonight, but—"

"You would be free to come and go, I promise. Pursue whatever goals you desired. I would grant you anything possible."

"Mama, she had the same freedom from someone she loved so deeply, who loved her also. It didn't work. It wasn't possible for her to live with another and still be in charge of her own life. I remember it all too well. Her restless nights, tormented wanderings through the mansion, agonies released in the moonlight." The tears were flowing fast now, remembrances of the past, fear of the future, intermingling in tangled emotions.

"And, was she happy—away from him?"

"No," Yana admitted, "the years after leaving him—she cried nightly to be at his side."

"This will never happen with us. We are two different people."

"I am my mother's child." Yet, in so many ways she was not like her mother.

"Live where you wish then. Do as you must. I ask only for what you *can* give me; I need only the hope that we will be together whenever possible. Once a month. One week a year."

"And the days between?"

"I will immerse myself in other things, always living for our future liaison, whenever possible."

"I am not sure—I would still be torn two ways. Wanting to be with you—suffering while apart."

"I would write to you. Daily words of love. I'd learn a whole new vocabulary just to express all I feel."

"And I would be reliving Mama's torment. Yearning to be with you, yet knowing I could never live your kind of life. No," she said. "A clean break is the best break."

He took her hands in his, their pulses beating counterpoint rhythms. "Yana, tell me you love me."

The words came without restraint. "I love you as I have never loved any man before."

"Then nothing else matters."

"Not at this moment."

"Come with me then, now, to my room."

Go to his room? That was a proposition she hadn't even considered. Nevertheless, the idea of breaking all rules, running off with him, aroused new expectations, obliterating her resolves of a few moments ago. "I—I don't have the power to resist you anymore," she said. It was true; all resistance was gone. Her whole being was pliant, ready to be formed into a new person, a person who was loved, who gave back this love, whose every day would be filled with love.

"You must come of your own free will."

"I must come, because—I want to, I need to...."

Willingly she grasped his extended hand, looking up at him, "And you will not use our love as a case study?" She smiled, happy for the first time in so many days.

"Never. I promise. Our times together will be much too private to share with anyone. The experience will be only for you and me. Finally, I have something of my own, that I do not wish to share with the world—with no one, but you."

Yana stood mutely gazing at him. He had never looked more captivating—never seeing him in anything but street or lab clothes before. Now, he appeared strong and Gypsy-like, his naked form outlined under his silk covering.

She was ready to go wherever he took her. But she wanted it to happen in its own time, their coming together must be long and drawn out, their acknowledgement of the time it took to find each other. She never preferred short bursts of passion— incomplete fulfillment. Tonight must obliterate whatever she had known about love. They must forge new pathways. Two human beings—destined to fulfill their mating since the world began—would acquiesce.

It would be her *drukkerebama*, to guide him through territory he had never explored before. "Before I enter your world, Phillipe, you must enter mine." She went to the music box and began winding it. "Come, dance with me." She extended her arm, her whole being. He hesitated. Was it possible he was resistant because of his natural reluctance to venture into areas out of his realm of experience?

"I have never danced." Panic appeared to overtake him. It was evident he had not expected dancing as a prelude to lovemaking.

"Tonight you are going to. A whirlwind Gypsy dance that will exhilarate your whole body. Touch the very core of your being. And we will be one." She beckoned him to join her. "Come, it will prepare us."

He could not resist her capricious summoning gesture. He moved into her arms, his feet taking little steps at first. Soon the expanding release took over them both and he began following her movements as if he had been born with the ability to dance. The pace got faster. He relaxed even further, crying out along with her, imitating her sounds, letting out loud shrieks of his own.

He was laughing, crying. "Look at me," he called out in exhilaration, "I'm dancing—my whole body is dancing."

She twirled him faster and faster, until he let out a freeing shout that echoed off all the machines, the walls, the building—the world.

Within those final swirling movements, piece by piece, they removed each other's clothing and flung it aside. They were now fused together in a naked primitive dance that had slowed into a subtle oscillation of bodies and whispering kisses.

"I'm ready," she said in breathless surrender.

He swept her toward the doorway, never letting her out of his encircling arm. She gathered their clothing as she went. With one hand he turned off the light, closed the door, and whispered, "You will never regret anything that ever happens between us."

There were no regrets, not now, not at this moment, only expectation and wanton yearning. She heard only the echoing beats of his heart calling her to follow, and her own heart answering with only one word—*Yes!*

CHAPTER 17

Clothing clutched against their bare bodies, Yana and Phillipe crept along the dark hallway, afraid someone might see them, yet willing to risk that possibility. Fingers interlaced, they said nothing. A moan from Shyam's room startled them both and then sent them into muffled giggles, two children daring some mischievous deed, fearful of being caught.

Phillipe opened the door to his room, pulling Yana inside with such force she was lifted off her feet and into his arms. Phillipe's new passion had transformed him into another being— from her past, her future—she wasn't sure. Did it matter? *Was she fantasizing what was happening? Had the dancing so transported her that a final visionary episode was now taking place?*

It was deep dark here; she could see nothing, only feel this strong firm body pressing so fiercely against hers that she could scarcely breathe.

"Wait," he said, gathering his own breath as he pulled away. *Don't stop; don't go into some medical reason for not going any further.* She didn't know if she could postpone this raging desire building within.

"I must lock the door and give us a small light." She heard him bolt the door. "This rug against the door bottom will conceal any light or sound." *What other cautions must you take? Why are you extending this separation in the dark?*

He struck a match, and his face glowed in the expanding circle of flame as if illuminated by some magical phosphorescence. His was a face Yana had envisioned before, that had dominated her dreams for so many nights. Now it was as if his skin was translucent and she was seeing beyond the outer covering into mysterious inner workings of his soul.

He put the candle on a shelf high in the corner where it cast moving shadows over everything, merging real with unreal. He tossed his gold robe aside and then took Yana's clothing from her arms. He buried his face into the fabric, as if a mock prelude to his gathering all of her unto himself. The tambourine made slight jingles as he set the clothing aside, causing them to laugh in kindred merriment.

He grabbed the tambourine, lifting it high. He called out in a muffled shout, "*Ole!*" as he banged the drum skin in a staccato beat.

Yana answered with another "*Ole!*" and set to twirling before him. He grabbed her waist and swirled her around in a dance that wasn't expected, no knowledge of where it would take them, or how it would end. He bent her in ways she did not know were possible. No arms, legs, body—just guided currents circulating them about in the small candlelit cave of his room.

Her bare feet pivoted on the polished wood floor. Her nipples were hard and erect, her private parts so moist—she was ready, more than ready to know this man in all his entirety. *Let him take me now, in any manner he wishes.*

Phillipe stopped the dancing, put down the tambourine, and lifted Yana up onto his bed, atop the lambs' wool coverlet. She felt as if as she were laid out on a soft cloud, floating into the universe, no human control over her fate anymore.

He lay down beside her, a hairsbreadth apart, his fingers outlining all the areas of her body, as if a woman's form were something new to him. She lay there, accepting, letting him explore, anticipating the next locale he might arouse.

There was no need to guide him. Men instinctively knew what to do with women—each in his own way. It was born into their maleness. All along she had sensed that whatever Phillipe did, he would never do it the same as other men.

"Yours is the most beautiful body I have ever seen. The most sensitive skin I have ever touched." He moved closer, whispering in her ear, "And you are the most arousing individual I have ever been near."

"And you—" she whispered, yielding, awaiting, "I want you so very much, to consume every part of me so there is nothing left of my solitary being and we are melded into one." She reached for his hardness as he let loose with an inward gasp. Then she began outlining his trembling form with both hands, letting her passion guide her fingers as if they were searching for hidden treasure in the folds of his skin.

Another gasp and he turned her over on her back. Gentleness was gone as he became another creature, an untamed primitive, moving on top of her, thrusting inside her with such strength, her interiors burst with new pleasure.

He took her breasts in his hands, massaging them while his lower body propelled up and down—inside her in circular movements that brought her to the heights of arousal as she let out wanton sounds, welcoming, waiting for the next thrust to drive her further into the realms of ecstasy. He was a zestful stallion astride her, riding her—using her long strands of hair as reins, thrashing his legs against her answering thighs.

He quieted for a moment, still caressing her breasts, running his tongue over her cheeks, eyes, lips, kissing her deeply, his tongue probing into her mouth as if exploring some wondrous new cavern. She responded— both tongues curling with impassioned hunger.

They rolled around on the bed in savage recklessness. Then he lay her down once more, spreading her hair across the coverlet, cupping her breasts and then drove with unrestrained momentum deep inside her, each penetration expanding new areas, her interiors breaking apart, primal sensations exploding within.

One giant freeing cry and he shuddered in continuous eruption, flowing into her, filling her with moans of pleasure as he overflowed her emptiness with his expanding warmth. She wanted it to continue, never before feeling such extensions of human pleasure. From now on, she belonged to him. Whatever the consequences—she belonged to him, if only in gratitude for the euphoria just experienced. His world of electricity, her world of magic—had just melded in an incredible fusion.

Both were still floating on elated sensations. He gazed at her in the flickering candlelight, their eyes meeting in a knowing that penetrated all barriers. He outlined her lips, her eyelids, with moist fingers. She massaged him between his legs, probing his damp hair there with sensitive touches, gentle kneading. They answered each other in satisfied moans. If she had ever known complete contentment, it was now.

"I want to celebrate this momentous occasion." His voice was that of a new being—no authority, no commanding, only a natural stream of words, deepened with newfound awe. "I want to drink a toast, to both of us. Seal this wonderful event into our hearts forever."

She was hearing him through a haze of reveries. He could have asked anything of her and she would have answered "yes."

He rose from the bed, his form outlined in the dim candlelight. She wanted to reach out for him and begin all over again, but her body was too exhausted, too content and satiated. She lay there watching his movements and reveling in the memory of his vitality flowing through her.

He opened a cabinet up high and took down a wine bottle and one gold goblet. "I rarely have guests in this room," he said, referring to the one goblet. "In fact, you are the very first one."

"And I hope the last." She was sincere in that. He uncorked the glowing green bottle and poured a deep ruby port wine into the goblet. A new heady scent perfumed the room. Both sat cross-legged on the rumpled bedding. They intertwined arms as he raised the cup, offering her the first sip, toasting, "To my new love, as sweet as rare wine, more intoxicating than any potion."

She drank from the offered cup, letting the liquid mingle with the other erogenous tastes in her mouth—a wonderful combination. "I drink the nectar of the gods tonight," she whispered. "To my magnificent lover."

They continued drinking, with numerous toasts that got giddier and giddier, as they continued exchanging the cup until the bottle was drained. Still they put their lips to the empty goblet, murmuring yet another toast, and another, until they crumpled into each other's arms, falling into deep sleep, bodies entwined.

Yana dreamed beautiful dreams, her whole body involved. Anytime Grandmama came into the dream, she shouted her away; no intruders allowed.

Yana was on a mountaintop, soaring above the whole earth, flying across deserts, valleys, plains. Her arm extended out at one side, holding onto another—only she could never entirely see this other person, never catch onto him completely, as if he were flying beside her, but something was keeping their forms apart. All she could see was blank air between them. *What was it keeping them separated?*

Phillipe woke with a start, calling gently, "Yana." She stirred dreamily. "Yana," he called again. It was a voice that had never before summoned her out of a dream. She opened one eye and saw his smiling face gazing at her, and she remembered everything in one quick flash and closed her eyes again. She wanted to relive it while it was still so close to the surface and embed it in her memory.

"Yana, it is four a.m. You must leave, before the others are up and about." It was not a dismissal; he meant it for her sake. His yearning for her to stay was inherent in his warning. She turned over and gathered him into her arms. It was a mutual coming together; the passions of the night before rose once more as if the rhythms were imprinted on their bodies forever to be recalled any time they wished to summon them.

Exhausted once more, he repeated, "Yana, you must leave."

"Never," she murmured.

"You must. I only ask you to come to me every night while you are here. I will not be able to exist unless I know this is true."

"I will. I will," she answered. "My torture will be not coming to you in the daytime, staying away from touching your magnificent body. I will listen to your words as you lecture but will only be hearing your tender passion in my ears. How will I be able to pass through these remaining days here in your Sanitarium, wanting you beside me every minute?"

He got up and put on his robe, as if the sheer material might protect him from another encounter. "We will speak of this further—later. Make all our plans for our future," he promised, "but not now. Now, I can only think of last night, our beautiful coming together. I did not know human beings could experience such rapture. Now I know it is possible, but only with someone you love—and only with you." He stood there observing her, not moving.

She got up and kissed him with impetuous ardor. "I love you so." She moved away with swift resolve before the chain reaction started again. She put on her clothes—slowly, knowing he was watching, wanting him to carry her form on his mind for the rest of the day. No longer would she be just a reminder of the portrait above his boyhood bed, the woman with the long flowing hair. From now on, she would be a complete entity, imbued with intimate new memories.

The candle was sputtering out in its pool of melted wax. It was time to leave. He walked her to the door, looking out to make sure no one was outside, no doors open. None must know she had come to his room. There were still rules to abide by. This was still a Sanitarium. What happened between them had not changed the surrounding enclosure.

She crossed the hallway to her room on the other side, each step putting miles between them. Yet, she still felt his vibrant flesh, breathed his arousing scent, and knew with resigned finality, she had crossed the line into another person's life and there was no return.

CHAPTER 18

How was he going to be able to give his lecture this morning, do anything, with last night still thundering in his head? He had no regrets, yet, his professional training kept coming up with reasons why such a union wouldn't work. He reasoned back that such a union *could* succeed, affirming that he would do everything in his power to make sure that it did.

The ladies were entering the Lecture Room as he waited in the back doorway. Fortunately, it was to be a lecture he had given many times before: ANIMAL MAGNETISM. With little time to prepare anything new since last night's events, he was using his old notes. Right now, he was double-checking through them. No sexual connotations. That was probably best, not knowing how he himself might react to such references today. Then he saw her, looking up as she entered as though he had felt her presence preceding her, Yana sweeping into the room, more radiant than ever. He wanted to rush forward, gather her in his arms and take her to his room, bypassing everything else scheduled for the day. His body remained motionless, while his blood raced.

He tried thinking of Bible verses. Only one came to mind: *The morning stars sang together and all the sons of God shouted for joy!*

Taking a deep breath, he took his spot at the lectern. "Good morning, ladies."

"Good morning, Dr. Zastro," they answered in unison.

As usual, Yana sat in the back row. If he kept his eyes focused to the front, he might keep thoughts of her from intruding. Might. "Today is Wednesday, and the weather outside is balmy—beautiful. You shall enjoy a very beneficial garden time."

All the women looked radiant this morning, even Delphine had a special glow. Was it the result of the healthful treatment they had been receiving here, or was he seeing women from a different perspective today? He cleared his throat and straightened his tie, hoping he could focus properly. He was embarrassed for the flush he felt filling his face, the throbbing in his body.

"Animal Magnetism," he said, pointing to the chart. "If you will recall, in previous lectures we sometimes referred to this as Individual Electricity. Many others will call it a humbug, but I will prove why it is useful in matters of health.

"Examples are abundant. Let us say the other day you came in collision with a chair and bruised your skin. Instinctively you bent over and rubbed the contused limb with your hand. The baby fell from your lap; you pick it up and rub its little head until it stops crying. One night you are attacked with cramps in the stomach and your hand goes there pressing immediately, pressing, manipulating the region until you are relieved.

"Now, these are all instinctive and involuntary applications of the hand, and you yourself use animal magnetism whether you believe in it or not."

He paused for their acknowledgment, giving them time to contemplate what he had just related, but not pausing too long so his own thoughts wouldn't sidetrack.

"Now, Dr. Frederic Anthony Mesmer was the first, I believe, in the Christian world, to recognize the effects of animal magnetism and employ this agent in the cure of disease. He presented his theory in Paris in 1778 and was denounced, as a matter of course, by the medical faculty. In less than ten years one of his pupils discovered that some people could be put into unconscious sleep by the power of animal magnetism, and this condition was called mesmeric sleep.

"Many have attempted to utilize this mesmerization in the cure of disease, but with no marked success, as few have learned the proper techniques. I am one of those few. However, thousands of others have professed the ability to cure suffering humanity by the laying on of hands. A large number of these are impostors, who prejudice the public mind against a valuable agent for relieving physical infirmities.

"While disciples of Mesmer have been laboring to make some headway in our Christian civilization, in Japan, the beneficial effects of animal magnetism are so common as to employ manipulators whenever anybody feels a little unwell.

"The manipulators are blind men, who go about the streets with long wands in their hands and reed whistles in their mouths. The whistles are used to acquaint the residents of their presence as they pass by.

"In the actual operation of their manipulation, the patients are entirely nude, which may be one of the reasons why only blind men are employed as manipulators, though women of Japan take no pains for concealment of their bodies when taking their daily baths." *There was no concealment of body in the bed last night—*

"These blind manipulators work over their patient about thirty minutes, rubbing, kneading, and gently pinching them from head to foot, without missing a part, with remarkable benefit.

"In our own country, people are often relieved of pain by animal magnetism without knowing the active agent employed. Recall how many advertisements have directions—'Rub in briskly with a warm hand for several minutes. 'The effectiveness of the relief from these remedies in many times is due to the touch of the hand."

The touch of the hand—the touch of— He had lost his place. He looked out, briefly glancing at Yana, then returned to his lecture notes, speaking faster than usual, hurrying to get through this section of time, make the whole day speed up, make night arrive faster. "In the religious world we find people employ animal magnetism combined with religious faith in curing of disease. A prominent case was a lawsuit in Switzerland, where private circles were aware of the wondrous cures effected by Pastor Blumhard, merely by the efficacy of believing in prayer.

"In a village near the Lake of Zurich, similar cures were effected by similar means. Dorothea Trudel headed an establishment where persons afflicted with bodily or mental diseases flocked in great numbers. She prayed over them, and laid her hands upon them, in the name of the Lord, and they were healed. Dorothea, her family and assistants, worked night and day attending to patients without remuneration, out of love to God.

"Her history came out at the trial. Her story. After a long-continued endurance of sickness of her own, she had developed the spiritual life in her soul and close communion with God. Thereafter, she experienced many answers to her prayers. On one occasion, when five laborers fell suddenly sick, she came to the sick chamber, prayed over the patients and laid her hands upon them in the name of the Lord. The sickness left all of them.

"Extraordinary cures followed, in many cases suddenly. Contrary to her wish, sick people were brought to her house and soon she had a little hospital. The medical men interfered, to prevent her practicing the healing art without a license. She was fined, ordered to desist. Still the people came to her, begging her to pray with them, as she used no other remedy than prayer.

"Then, two deaths occurred at her home and she was once more investigated by the medical board and ordered to desist. She appealed to a higher court. Hundreds of testimonials from the most eminent men of Switzerland and Germany bore witness to her self-denying zeal and proved she made use of no other means but prayer. This was the high court's ruling.

"'Miss Trudel's whole influence was brought to bear on the soul, and the healing of the body was a mere accidental circumstance. She promises no one a cure, nor declares any sickness incurable, but declares to each patient, 'if you only believe, you may be healed by prayer.'

'The medical laws are designed to prevent quackery, not to prevent the physical benefits which flow from prayer. The charge that she prevents patients from applying to a regular physician must fall to the ground, for there is no law to fix the time when any one must send for a physician or to prescribe that every patient must submit to be treated according to the prescriptions of a college of surgeons. She never forbade anyone to use licensed physicians'

"The counsels for the plaintiff granted that the medical men had no right to prohibit prayer, or the laying on of hands. She was acquitted of every charge. This was a rebuke to those doctors who play upon the popular prejudice in suppressing anything which is irregular for the cure of disease.

"There can be no doubt in any rational mind that animal magnetism is the agent employed by this woman. Good men and women always make the best magnopaths. Bad people cannot attain any marked success in applying animal magnetism. It is not necessary that they be a professed Christian or member of any religious sect, but they must possess a Christian spirit, the desire to do good and sympathy for the sufferings of mankind-- to achieve any great success in administering animal magnetism.

"The blind Japanese manipulators may possess these qualities, notwithstanding they may never have heard of the Christian religion...."

He continued on, almost rote, to the conclusion of the discourse. His thoughts had taken off on their own course, ruminating the implications of what he was saying. *Animal magnetism—kneading of bodies, manipulation of skin—was that what had been put into practice last night? What kind of healing had it brought about? Or had it only transposed into frictional electricity?*

Yana and he had employed it all, throughout the night— Individual, Frictional and Animal Electricity. The results had been spectacular, unusual; yet, he had no desire to pursue the reasons why. A completely new part of his life, he wished to keep separate and guarded as treasure.

Back to the lecture. Fixate on the immediate. "Thank you ladies for your presence this morning, and as usual, your wholehearted attention. Tomorrow's lecture will be: WATER— ITS BENEFITS AS A REMEDIAL AGENT. Go now, and continue to be healed."

He avoided questions, hurrying to catch Yana to see if she had found the note he had slipped under her door earlier. The note asked her to meet him again that night at ten in the Treatment Room. He did not want to risk speaking to her alone, concerned the others might overhear, the attention they might both attract. He worried most over the impulses he would have to suppress just being near her.

"Yana," he called, seeing the back of her slender neck crowned with the coil of black braids. *Last night her hair had been shimmering in loose glory.*

She turned, giving only a brief glimpse. No smile, no recognition, just a knowing, instantaneous remembering, all within that single second.

"Miss Kejako—I just want to remind you of your next appointment," he said in his most professional manner, forcing his arms to stay at his side.

"Yes. I will prepare and I will be there at the appointed time," she said, walking away as if she too were afraid of being too near him.

The day was endless. He had consultations with Edwina and could hardly concentrate on listening to her words. He felt guilty that his wholehearted attention was not devoted to her. Still, she did not need in-depth listening today as her schedule of cures was working very well. All she needed was an ear to speak to, someone to care how she was progressing. Caring for his patients would never change. His new love for Yana could only enhance his compassion for humankind, plus foster new insight into the wonders of the female species.

Supper—he hardly ate any. After, in his office, he fell into a slight doze while preparing the next day's lecture. He rarely remembered his dreams, but this time he woke with a start— recalling Yana screaming at him to get off her, to keep away from her. What was the meaning? A dream that had begun with such bliss, to end in such a distraught manner? He tried to dismiss it. Dreams were only the nervous forces of the brain ridding themselves of excess accumulations—weren't they?

Don't ponder that for which there is no solution.

He went to the Treatment Room early, to prepare. First, a stop at his sleeping room for the soft lambs' wool coverlet, still crumpled, still infused with last night's interlude. In the Treatment Room exercise area, carefully, as if preparing for royalty, he spread the coverlet out on the polished wood floor. The lights were lowered, music playing. The bath was ready. Why was he trembling? Why was he so afraid she might not appear?

The hall clock struck ten, and the door opened. Yana. He went to her, locking the door with one hand, and circling her silk robed body with the other. Her hair—loosed and flowing. An exotic perfume surrounded her.

"Let us take our time tonight," he said, pulling away from the intensity that was already drawing them together.

"Whatever you have planned. I am here for your bidding."

They interlocked arms, and she moved with him, her body so yielding that he felt he could mold her into anything he wished. But he wanted to change nothing, not anymore. He dare not disturb any of the alchemy. Perfect, as she was.

"I have a special bath prepared, with oils and perfumes that have been steeping, awaiting for you—anticipating your arrival," he said, leading her to the galvanized tub filled with scented blue-tinted water. He slid the robe from her shoulders, pausing to gaze at the beauty of her naked form before helping her into the tub.

"Relax and enjoy," he said, bowing ceremoniously. "Tonight I am your humble servant."

"Tonight, you are my *chavo*—my boy, and I am your *chavi*—your girl."

He began by sponging her back, gently going over each section, the water gliding through his hand in silk-soft motions, a thin sheen of moisture the only layer separating them.

"Lie back now, relax," he said, placing a rubber pillow on the tub ledge to support her head. Submissive, she lay back, resting her tresses on the pillow as he, in languid strokes, sponged the front of her. He was not used to being in the servant role, maybe that was the reason—or was it the unwanted separation—but impulsively he pulled off his robe and climbed into the tub. Something he hadn't planned, yet once done, seemed so natural. They belonged together, whatever the place.

They washed each other's bodies in playful delight as though they were children frolicking in a pond, scooping measures full of water, emptying them from on high, letting the streams flow over their heads, down over their torsos— splashing, laughing, converging.

Then he broke out with a proverb—*"Many waters cannot quench love, neither can the floods drown it."*

"You amaze me, with all your different knowledge," she said. "Yet, it's all confined within your head. My knowledge—flows from the air, the whole universe being my storehouse. And yet we still have this interlinked knowing." She was now lying against him.

"You are getting chilled," he said after awhile, noting her slight shivers and the tiny goose bumps prickling her skin.

"It cannot be—I swim when the rivers are ice."

"No," he said, as he separated from her embrace. "We must warm you."

"Your bidding." She stood up, water glossing down her satiny form.

He helped her out of the tub and then rubbed her velvety skin with a large white Turkish towel, until the friction aroused her. She took the towel from him and wrapped it mummy fashion around them both, binding their bodies together. They stood embraced by the towel, their wetness soaking through the fabric until heavy, the towel slid to the floor.

"Come," he said, taking her hand while leading her to the Spectro Cabinet. "Sit in here and let me watch the colored lights dance across your body."

They sat on benches across from each other, watching the lights flicker over their moist bodies, wanting to touch the other but holding back, each seeking to stretch the night out for as long as possible.

"I wish I could paint your form right now," she said, "capture each of these vibrating color that mixes with your own brilliant rays. You are indeed worthy of a special painting—for the benefit of mankind. And, a naked one, for the benefit of myself."

He was not used to being the one who was studied. "Would you like to sit on the magnetic stools?" A spur of the moment question intended to move himself away from her intent gaze.

"No," she answered, "I need no stimulation from machines. Right now I have more than enough electro-atoms or whatever they are surging through me. When I am with you—everything lights up of its own accord."

"We create our own electricity, don't we?" He hadn't thought about it, but it was true. "Things have happened to my body that I have never even considered, yet I have no desire to write about these happenings, research them. For once I only wish to experience." With what he hoped was a gallant gesture, he offered his arm and led her from the Spectro Machine. He had Yana wait while he rewound the music box, turned off the lights. The only illumination now was from the open Spectro Cabinet, casting unreal patterns over the vast darkness. He returned to her side, extending his arm in an invitation. They danced, their naked bodies moving as one, closer and closer.

The music slowed into halting notes and then stopped. "Come," he said and pulled her toward the coverlet. Gently, he lay her down, drying her further with a lambs' wool towel, the friction warming and expanding into the space between them.

It was time. He took her with such fierceness her breath was sucked from her lungs and she could only gasp. He manipulated her body into malleable yearnings, her flesh responding in cycles of grasp and yield. The floor was not as soft as the bed, but it didn't matter, she was welcoming the deeper penetrations, until they both reached the final crescendo that discharged simultaneously, shaking them in unison.

They lay exhausted. He spread another towel over them and they relaxed, looking up into the darkness, talking in soft whispers. "I could not wait for this evening," he said.

"Nor I."

"Today was the longest day of my life."

"Tonight—if this were all there were of life, it would be enough," she said, murmuring. "All that was before, doesn't matter, all that follows will only have meaning because of this."

They rested, holding onto each other, afraid to let go, as if the other would vanish into the wavering darkness and they might never find each other again.

"Yana, my love, I shall dedicate the rest of my life to making you happy."

"You have already made me the happiest woman alive."

He kissed her. *Was that true—the happiest woman alive belonged to him? What a magnificent thought.* They melded once more, with less passion, but more tenderness, moving slow, suspending themselves in time before the inevitable sorrowful farewell.

"Tomorrow night we shall meet in the garden," he said. "I will bring a special bottle of wine and soft bedding for the stones."

"Anywhere, Phillipe. I would go anywhere you ask," she said. "I am willing to lay in a field of thistles, atop a bed of brambles—as long as I would be with you."

He knew she meant it. Was this the power love could hold over another—making one willing to do anything for the other, no matter the consequences? Neither must ever abuse this power, but treat it as a rare gift. He had not guessed she could be as yielding as she was. He rather missed the challenge of her defiance, but did prefer this mutual love. That he had captured Yana, in all her glory; that she was his—the thought amazed him. Yet, she had captured him also. Were both imprisoned now?

All too soon she was robed and going out the door—no time to linger over parting. The separation already aching throughout him, Phillipe watched her disappear down the hallway.

Dr. Zastro drained the water from the tub. He needed to keep moving. He folded the towels as he watched the water's swirling circles sucking away particles of himself and Yana they had washed from each other. He didn't want to lose any of it—not one tiny speck, but already it was vanishing into the depths of the earth.

The coverlet was barren now, as he watched their fading forms dissolving into nothingness. He lay himself down on it, spreading his legs, burying his face into the warm softness that stifled his cries, soaked up his tears. Was this happiness, or was this sadness? Were all his emotions so muddled right now he was unable to differentiate? *Was love the peak of all emotion, never to be reached by any other means? Was it ever possible to control?*

CHAPTER 19

Yana stirred dreamily. The bell was ringing up and down the hallway, a distant chime resonating between sleep and reality. She didn't want to get up, not yet, make that decisive separation from last night. She was reluctant to allow the episode in the Treatment Room escape so soon—recede into memories without holding onto it awhile longer.

Feeling the laggard, she sat up, reaching for her chemise, wishing she could stay naked all day, which she sometimes did at home, mostly when painting. No greater freedom of movement was possible or abiding awareness of her own sensuality than moving naked through the world.

How could she perform all the expected routines this morning? Go to the Treatment Room, sit there calmly, all the while besieged by fervent memories from last night? What about when she next encountered Phillipe—how would she restrain herself? The yearning for him so strong right now she wanted to leap from her bed and go find him. Instead, she stretched leisurely, then rolled from the bed. She put on her chemise and grabbed her toiletries and went down the hallway toward the lavatory.

Sunlight was streaming through the stained glass ceiling windows, as though the light was speaking to her: *I have given you another new day. I have taken away yesterday. Even if it is secured in your memories, still, it is gone. Nothing is guaranteed forever. A new morning wipes the slate clean, leaving you free to begin over once more. Fill it as you wish.*

She did not want it wiped away and she did not have the freedom to do as she wished. Not here. Not until tonight anyway.

She found an empty cubicle, rinsed her mouth, and then began sponging herself off, reminded that her hands were not Phillipe's—his fingers had throbbed with such penetrating power.

Delphine was in the next cubicle, and Yana could hear her singing. She did have a rather nice voice—was it operatic or dance hall? So hard to tell, since Delphine was such an imitator. What was Delphine's true self? Had she ever uncovered it, or was it so deleterious she didn't want to bring it forth? To go through a lifetime and never find out who you were, so many layers, just piled one on top the other, submerging everything deeper and deeper. What a difficult burden to carry.

Yana had never let pretenses accumulate, always knowing the path of her being, also sensing when she strayed. It was then Mama or Grandmama's voices admonished her: Remove the mask! Banish the fakery!

"Beautiful dreamer, come unto me..." Delphine sang out. Yana knew the song, joining in on the chorus.

"Twilight and moonlight...."

Delphine giggled, poking her head out from behind her curtain. "My, my, we make a good duet together, don't we? Like two songbirds singing an splashing in the morning sun."

"Just trilling out their song of praise for this glorious new day." Yana gave out with the warble of the wood thrush. She sometimes did this in the mornings, down at the river when she was especially happy, answering the bird calls and harmonizing along with them.

"I never heard you sing in here before, or do those trembling bird chirps. Something special going on today, something I don't know about?"

"Yes, yes, there is." Yana said no more for fear that she might, in her exuberance, shout everything to Delphine, to the whole world, that she was in love, that this Sanitarium was a joy to be in and Phillipe Zastro was the most wonderful man she had ever met.

"See you all at the breakfast table," Delphine giggled. Even her giggle sounded melodious, not simple-minded as usual. "Make sure you all get there early for your morning birdseed, or fresh worms, if you all like them fresh." Delphine's sense of humor was in fine form, or was it because the day had not yet worn her down, and Yana began singing once more.

Kayo Kam, avriavel, Kiya mange lele beshel!
Kayo kam tel avel, Kuja lelakri me beshav.

When the sun goes up,   Shall my love be by me!
When the sun goes down,   There by him I'll be.

Whatever had brought forth that song from her memories? Phillipe, of course. How long since she had sung it? You were supposed to put a blade of grass in your mouth and turn East and West while singing it, but there were no blades of grass here. It didn't matter; she wasn't following the old rules anymore. With a new air of defiance, she smothered her body in forbidden perfume oils. Let herself steep in them all day long, until tonight.

She began warbling again as a wood thrush, knowing instinctively how birds must feel—singing joyously from their heart, not needing words.

She thought of Chillico, her parrot, back home alone. Her neighbor Jeremy would be coming in daily while she was away to check the horses, her garden, and Chillico.

"Jeremy! Jeremy! Here comes Jeremy!" the bird would squawk from his perch at the window. Chillico was not tethered. He was free to leave his stand, but he never did, as if this were his chosen station in life. He would sit for days in this same worn spot. An old bird, Yana had inherited him from the childless Gypsy couple. Who knows how long they had had him before that? Parrots lived to be over one hundred. What stories this one could tell if he were a storyteller instead of a mimic? Even thinking about home did not summon the usual yearnings. Yana skipped out of the lavatory and down the hall to breakfast—her morning birdseed.

Then exercises. Then lecture time.

Yana took her usual seat in the back row; anticipation and apprehension intermixed in her heart. She would be seeing Phillipe from a distance, listen to him speak, but the words would need to be shared with others, not spoken for her alone. Was this jealousy? She didn't recall ever feeling emotions of this type before.

The subject was spelled out on the easel chart: WATER— ITS BENEFITS AS A REMEDIAL AGENT.

Water; last night's memories surged forth, splashing through her mind in waves of remembrance, and she was once more immersed in the depths of the galvanized tub.

Phillipe's voice broke through her reverie. "Good morning, ladies."

"Good morning, Dr. Zastro." *Good morning, my love.*

He began to lecture, but the words meant nothing, said nothing she wanted to hear. He was talking about how all the nations, distinguished philosophers, physicians and theologians extolled the virtues of water. "Yet, the establishment of the school of hydropathy was an error," he emphasized.

"Water is not an infallible remedy, and less so in the hands of the disciples of Priessnitz than in those of the great founder himself. The latter was so naturally gifted with peculiar skill in the application of water. Had he explored the green fields and forests of nature as well as waters, Priessnitz would have had a choice of remedies and been more successful.

"While I do not deny the contracting and relaxing influences of water, according to its temperature and the beneficial effects of each in appropriate cases, I maintain that the real philosophy of the 'water cure' is based on electrical principles.

"I will explain. Water possesses a great amount of electricity. If the blood of an individual contains its natural supply of iron, it attracts the electricity from the water, thereby rendering the body of the invalid in an electrically positive condition compared with the atmosphere. As soon as the application has been made, an active radiation of electricity from the system takes place, which accelerates the escape of effete matter, and renders the pores, skin, and other organs more active."

He stroked his beard, which he rarely did. It did seem he was a bit distracted in his presentation this morning. "It is therefore diametrically wrong to resort to water in the treatment of invalids with thin blood. In bloodless patients, tepid and hot baths are injurious because the blood does not possess the attractive property of iron to draw in the electricity of the water;

all the while the increased temperature relaxes the tissues and leaves the system open to the ingress and progress of disease."

Whatever was he talking about? How could someone who whispered such meaningful words last night be going on and on about something so boring now.

"Ladies, did hydropathists generally understand this philosophy, *water-cure* would not prove so often *water-kill*." He wrote both words on the board.

"The great amount of electricity possessed by water has been demonstrated by Professor Faraday, showing that the quantity of electricity set free by decomposition of ten drops of water is actually greater than exists in the most vivid flash of lighting."

He proceeded to pour water from a porcelain pitcher into a washbasin, pouring it slowly, so the sound resonated. "Even the sound of water can be soothing, to both eyes and ear, as evidenced by the fashion for fountains in our own public parks.

"In my practice I have resorted to the virtues of water as an auxiliary agent with uniform success." His stance became more serious. "Hydropathy is not as popular today as it was twenty years ago, because many a good man and woman has unwittingly committed suicide with water. It is a great pity that mankind is disposed to abuse and misuse almost every good thing." He gave them a moment to contemplate this.

"In union there is strength. This is a political proverb of universal application. The Botanics, Hydropaths, Electropaths, and Magnopaths should coalesce, under the name of Utilitarian practice. Such a coalition could not fail to defeat disease in every aspect in which it presents itself.

"I have assiduously pursued all these systems in my practice, and would rather abandon my profession than to discontinue any one of them. Although I must confess that I would rather give up hydropathy than vegetable medication and therapeutic electricity, were I obliged to remove one plank from my medical platform. If forced to drop one, the choice would rest between water and electricity, and I am convinced that the latter can be made far more conducive to the requirements of the invalid than the former."

He began pouring the water back and forth without any real purpose this time. *Get on with your speech!*

"In my treatment of chronic diseases, my experience demonstrates that electricity can be made more available. In the treatment of acute disease, particularly fevers, water may be, and without doubt is, preferable."

Would he never finish? She was drowning in his talk of water. Yet, the others were intrigued by every word, probably understanding very little, but water was something familiar to each of them.

She too was now one of the doctor's great admirers, but that did not mean she had to convert to all his scientific verbiage. The last few nights had only heightened her own beliefs. Also the knowledge that her body was being used as it was meant to be, created for—and that her fate could not be deterred any longer, but must be played out to the end.

Hurry with this speech. Hurry until it is night again.

As he spoke, her mind went wandering. An old Gypsy adage surfaced from the dim past: *What divides is evil, and what joins, relates, flows, is good. Life is a flow, a dialogue, and death is an isolation.* Whatever had brought these words to mind? Water—flow—?

May angle sar te merel kadi yag—Before this fire burns out.

Why were all these strange old words breaking into her thoughts? Was it because she no longer let Grandmama dominate her dreams and now *Puridaia* was coming to her in daytime thoughts? Warnings?

Finally, he concluded. Waves of applause. Yana left the room, not wanting to face Phillipe, get too near, knowing she would have to feign disinterest through the rest of the day, carry on as normally as possible. Then tonight.... Easier somehow, to just following the rules, all the directives. Had she too become one of those mindless children, content to be told what to do and have everything laid out for her?

Her defiance was gone. She had been so afraid to lose the protective resistance. It had proved unnecessary, an armor she didn't need that had only weighted her down and kept her from participating.

Fresh-air time, at last. They were outside in the sunny roof garden, always a welcome escape from the confines of the building. It was indeed a beautiful, balmy day. An atmosphere so lovely that she wanted to share it, run and search for Phillipe, skip over time to bring him here right this minute. Her body cried out for him. Her soul was searching to connect with his and nature was amplifying this uplifting euphoria.

"Something ailing you?" Delphine asked, concerned when she didn't get Yana's usual retorts to her biting quips. "I don't hear no bird sounds neither—or do you only chirp in washrooms when your feathers are all wet and ruffled?"

"I'm singing in a pitch so high right now that human beings can't even hear it." Yana looked upward. "But the birds, the bees, all of nature is attuned to my special aria of joy." She felt as if she possessed soaring wings without any desire to fly away.

"Well, not me." Delphine pouted. "I may have been singing this morning, but not now. I'm just getting worse and worse, and Dr. Zastro's not helping me none. An I hate using that old magnetic stool in there all the time. Machines can never take the place of a good man."

"That is so true, so true," Yana agreed.

"And I feel so horrible looking when I can't wear my curls, and my rouges, and powders—"

"I think you look much better without all that frippery."

"No I don't. And neither do you without your Gypsy bangles and beads. We both need those traipsings to advertise who we are."

"Sometimes we need to strip ourselves of all those added traipsings, begin all over again, maybe even in different attire and try new directions." She didn't even know if Delphine was listening anymore, but she was listening to herself.

"You always look beautiful, Yana," Mavis said, leaning towards her, "but never like now, as if you were someone who was not real—some magic person, brought up from some faraway enchanted land."

"Because right now I am in a special enchanted place, where magical things can happen," Yana answered with a mysterious smile.

"You mean this garden?" Mavis was so eager to learn. She questioned and discerned information, whenever she could get up the courage to get past the impediments seeded within her personality since childhood.

"No, in my mind."

"How do you make fairylands in your mind? With pictures or what?"

"Your mind can take you many places, Mavis." Yana took Mavis's scarred hand in hers. "You can direct your mind to go anywhere you wish. Fairylands. Farms. You never have to stay locked into where you are, at any time. You can wander the whole earth. It's all in your power. You are in charge of your mind."

"If that's true, then I'm going to try right now, to take my mind, my whole self, back to the farm. I'm going to will it like I never willed anything before." Mavis closed her eyes tight, breathing deeply, her mouth breaking into a slow smile. "It's happening. I'm moving away from here. So fast…. I'm there! I'm really there. I made it happen—because I thought strong. I'm there, without being there. And it's not like just thoughts, my whole self is there. Why, I can even smell things, hear sounds. New pictures—not remembrances."

"Keep your eyes closed then Mavis, and stay there as long as you wish."

Yana went back to her own daydreams. The jasmine and roses never smelled sweeter, nor the air more buoyant. Even Shyam's manner did not irritate her, though he seemed preoccupied, as if in a hurry to be done with the ladies, so he could attend Miss Althea. He had brought her out earlier, sitting her in a white wicker lounge in a protected corner, as if a strong breeze might knock her over, or the bright sun wilt her. The minute she looked as if she were going to faint, he led her away, back inside. Absent for a while, he was now back and standing at the ledge, looking into the horizon.

He kept a professional distance from the rest of the women these days, doing his duties, sometimes seemingly annoyed at them, sometimes not understanding all of their accented words. He seemed so uncomfortable in his position. It can be difficult, Yana thought, being away from your homeland, partaking in strange customs, forced into a subordinate status. The only time his eyes lit up was when he was talking to Dr. Zastro, whom he seemed to revere, or when he was attending to Althea. It was as if he had made himself available to her as her personal servant— maybe even her special savior. Being Hindoo, Althea might be his way to enlightenment. Whatever, they both needed each other at this particular time in their lives.

Maybe that was what Althea had needed all along—a man to care for her. Maybe that was what Yana herself had been missing, what this eternal yearning within comprised—to have someone care about her, love her, without any demands in return. She had that now in Dr. Zastro. There was a serene feeling of arms continuously wrapped around her.

Yet. Yet, she warned herself, the rapture would mellow as the days went on. Right now everything was so new, untried; she didn't even want to foresee the future. That's why she sought to block Grandmama from her dreams, from her daytime thoughts. Grandmama had always been the purveyor of doom.

Shyam rang his bell. Yana left the garden area in reluctance. She shut herself out of the sun, while at the same time, she visualized with growing anticipation being there again that evening. Night changed every area of the earth, cloaking it in its dusky mantle of mystery. That was the time when potents worked best, especially the potency of love.

Ten p.m., the clock barely finished striking and Yana was already out of her room. She wore only her thin chemise, her hair tied back loosely, perfume surrounding her hastening form.

Ah, what luck— a bright moon tonight; the soft light gleamed through the skylight ceiling, spreading stained glass colors across the hallway floor, spattering bits of color on her hurrying bare feet. She did not need any light to guide her; she had bat instincts at night and could perceive walls and nearby bodies. Many times the Gypsies had to travel in the night, through deep forests, running from their enemies. All their instincts were keenly developed, heightened in times of danger. Also in times of love.

She opened the heavy garden door, feeling the rush of fresh cool air sweep over her. Out of the dim greenness, strong arms reached for her, lifting her gown off her as if a gust of wind had swept through, rising it from her.

"This day has been unbearably long," Phillipe murmured in her ear. "The wait has been torture."

"For me also." Yana kissed him tenderly, suppressing the surging hunger.

He led her to the large square of bedding he had spread out on the flat stones. The stars were out, the moon overhead. That would have been fulfillment enough—to be with the moon and stars once more at night. Life at this moment had already satisfied her deepest longings.

"I have prepared an exclusive nighttime picnic for us," he announced. "Special delights to go with a precious bottle of new May wine will make this an unrepeatable event." On a small low table he had placed a porcelain dish overflowing with succulent grapes, a crystal goblet filled with bright red strawberries that had been dipped in dark chocolate, and on a Dresden plate, segments of aromatic oranges had been laid out.

"Here, rest your head on this," he said, placing two large pillows at the end of the bedding, "and I shall feed you until all your hungers are satisfied."

Again she did not know what to expect, but was eager to find out. Lying back on the pillow, mouth opened as a bird, Phillipe dangled clusters of grapes above her and then placed them, one at a time, into her mouth. His fingers lingered as Yana sucked the juices from the pods, taking the skin, pulp and seeds in slow gratifying swallows.

Next, he rubbed a segment of the orange across her lips, the sweet juices spreading over her mouth. Phillipe brought his own lips to hers, licking the droplets away. Her mouth opened, drawing in the fleshy part of the orange and they passed the segments of the fruit between them, consuming the pieces together.

"Now it is my turn," she whispered, taking one of the chocolate strawberries, rubbing it along his body, her tongue following after to lick off the melting sticky residue. She then put the choice berry into his mouth following it with her tongue until they both tasted mingling strawberry and chocolate. They repeated the gourmet sampling until the dish was empty.

"And now, we have the special wine to finish this marvelous feast and tantalize our thinking." The cork was already off the bottle—but there were no glasses.

"We shall drink from the bottle in proper picnic procedure," he said, lifting the green bottle to her lips and then to his. They passed it between them, sometimes both drinking at the same time, lips forming half-moons around the opening. They said nothing, sitting next to each other, shoulders touching, mouths meeting, bending their necks further back each time, until catching the last drops on their outstretched tongues.

"There's always an ending to everything." She sighed.

"And always another beginning," he countered.

One by one, bright little sparks of light began blinking among the foliage. "Look, fireflies!" Phillipe whispered, excited, "flickering their search light beacons for their mates."

"My lights are flashing for my mate too." Yana beckoned, the wine circulating in her blood at a turbulent pace, her hands tracing Phillipe's body in lazy finger patterns.

Lovingly, he lay her down on the soft bedding, in the shadow of the trees and flowers. He was now lying at her side, her head in his arms, only their lower bodies interlocked. They moved in perfect rhythm, the stars circling in the heavens, the entire universe whirling within, faster and faster—then the freeing release that transported them both far into the dark, spiraling them across time and space.

She wanted to stay the night, begged him to let her. "Tell the others it is a special cure I needed," she pleaded. It was true; she needed to be with him as naturally as she needed to breathe.

"Would that it were possible," he said, "but we cannot. I need rest, and when I am near you I can never rest." Even as he spoke, he was running his hands along her hair, coiling silken strands around his fingers.

"Someday that will be changed," she promised, "and we will be together, whenever we wish. And I shall be your comfort and joy." She rested her head on his chest.

He didn't answer, but she could feel his chest quivering. She then watched as droplets of tears moved down his cheeks— diamonds glistening in the moonlight. If ever she painted his countenance, she wanted to capture this exact expression, these same tears, reflecting longing, manifesting love, with her face mirrored in each teardrop.

"Tomorrow night, I want you to come to my room," she said, rising, putting on her chemise.

"Your room?" He grew concerned. "I never go to any patient's room, day or night. It is one of my rules."

"We have broken all of your rules."

"I know," he admitted, putting on his robe that shimmered both gold and silver in the moonlight.

"I have entered your world so freely; come, try entering a bit of mine. If we are to be equal, there must remain no barriers between us."

He took her hands, holding them firmly. "I will be there. I will be anywhere you wish me to be." He followed his words with a gentle kiss and then walked over to the ledge. "Come, stand here with me."

They stood in silence, his arms around her in a loving embrace. Phillipe reached beyond her and picked a large red rose from a nearby bush. "Here, this rose is for remembrance." He wrapped a hibiscus leaf around the stem and placed it in her hair.

"I shall keep this rose," she said, "press it in my book and always remember this night each time I touch the delicate petals, breathe in the lingering scent."

The words from an old poem came to her lips, *"When all the stars were burning flowers that we might pluck and wear as crowns."*

He answered, *"Let us crown ourselves with rosebuds before they be withers.* Proverbs."

One final kiss and then the night demanded their parting. Yana left the garden before he did, so no one would see them together at these late night hours. He would also have to put things back in order, remove all traces of their being there—if that were possible.

How wonderful it would be to live with Phillipe, be open about their love. She never liked subterfuge and knew he didn't either. They were both honest people. For all their numerous differences, they had so many similar principles. Could they have been made for each other, fashioned by heaven so that each completed what the other lacked.

She took the rose from her hair and pressed the soft petals against her cheek only to feel the sharp thorns piercing through the hibiscus leaf and cutting into her hand. *How could pain and pleasure mingle so closely in the same expression of beauty?*

CHAPTER 20

The week had passed quickly, recent nights' memories burning in his mind, flickering intrusively into every minute of Dr. Zastro's day. It was morning again. Once more, he told himself—*As a doctor you must separate your yearnings for Yana from your work as a physician.*

He tried concentrating on his profession during the day; his patients demanded it; his strong code of ethics mandated it. Still, he was tired from lack of sleep, his brain muddled with these new intrusions. Never encountering such complications before, he wasn't sure how to solve these perplexities. It was always so much easier working with other people's problems.

Was it true, as he had written in his books, as he had researched previously, that "unleashed passions" had dire effects on the brain, the whole constitution? He had written those theories in the abstract, having never experienced real love or its consuming fires in actuality before.

As a young boy, he had been drawn to reading romantic novels passed about by his friends. A symptom of his fermenting curiosity about everything at that time. His father, upon finding those cheap novels under his mattress, burned them all, disdaining each as "putrid trash." Phillipe watched as volume after volume burst into bright flame, linger for one brief moment before settling into piles of dirty gray ash.

Even at this great remove, he could remember some of the more vivid passages, describing the feelings of love with words he didn't understand at the time, but did now. Love; it was a total consummation and vibration of his whole being. That's how it was whenever he was with Yana, even away from her.

He reviewed his schedule, and made up his mind that he would not see Yana during this weekend. Otherwise, their nights might extend into their free daytime hours and somehow they would be found out. Domino effects could be pushed into unwanted motion.

Phillipe's habit was to spend Saturday and Sunday in other pursuits, a recuperative period. Sometimes he made short trips to nearby medical establishments; other times he concentrated on his inventions in his basement workshop. That's what he would do, go away this weekend, miles away from the Sanitarium, and then he wouldn't even be tempted to come near Yana. She would have no possibility of seeking him out either.

He had to resolve now where he would be tomorrow, not leave such decisions for tonight when she would be in his arms, and might persuade him otherwise. He would travel to the Surgical Institute in Philadelphia over the weekend, visit with his old colleague, Dr. Pierce, and talk medicine.

He would tell Yana at the very end tonight, when he was leaving, so she could not protest. Why was he still so afraid he might offend her in some way, anxious that some unintended breach of her ethics would lead to losing her, without him ever knowing the reasons why.

That must never happen. Rather, he would lose his own life. *No, don't even think such thoughts.* To a physician, the gift of life was the most precious quintessence there was. His sworn mission was to preserve even the tiniest spark of life, keeping it alive at any cost. Nothing could swerve him from that cardinal vow.

Distressed by contradictory thoughts, he paged through his lecture notes. Earlier he had been in the Spectro Cabinet for revitalization, making up for lack of sleep—soothe his mind with the vari-colored rays. Yet, during previous years of training, he had gone without sleep, food, and it had only made his mind stronger. Was he depleting his body these days, arousing his passions so many times each night? Was it possible that because he had stored his manhood up over the years, there was excess to give?

One more week and then Yana would be gone to Paris. This forethought was already torturing him. Miles of separation, oceans apart. Only after long months would they be able to start the true beginning of their lifetime together.

Still, the knowledge that she had said she would marry him, the incredible awareness that he had even dared to ask her, was overwhelming. Marriage had never seemed even a remote possibility and he had dismissed many an attractive female, knowing there was no future for them together.

Yana had told him, *there is only one true soul mate in a lifetime.* Was this so? Were there other beliefs embedded in her background also true? Perhaps ephemeral laws of life he was not aware of, that could not be dissected, studied under the microscope, ever truly proven?

Maybe these were new areas he could investigate. Yana would be the person to help him. She was not the standard female; some vital force in her core made her distinctive, as if the species had produced one person that did not match any other, a personality that could not be categorized.

He no longer wanted to analyze her. He had gained a new unfathomed freedom from the medical world. When he was with Yana, being alive took on a different perspective, as if he were looking at creation with fresh wonder and nothing worked as he had previously supposed.

Back to his notes. *Force yourself to concentrate on your lecture.*

FEMALE ATTIRE AND FEMALE HEALTH. That should be an easy subject on which to elaborate. Few sexual references. He must remember to collect all of his illustrations to show the ladies. Drawings always held their interest so much more than words.

Some of the women did not always know exactly what he was referring to in his allusions to today's clothing, especially those who did not subscribe to Godey's Lady's Book, the Bible of the fashion world. Its contents had led so many women astray in health habits of attire.

Thank heavens Yana didn't follow outlandish fashions and was instead a devotee of fresh air and nourishing foods. Why was he always bringing her into his thoughts, even such mundane ones as fashion? It was true; he could not compartmentalize her, try to keep her in one section of his thinking. She intruded in every area now.

He went to the Lecture Room ahead of time, grateful they had not yet used the Lecture Room for their trysts; no leftover memories would surface during the midst of his speech. He attached the drawings to the easel. As a rule, Shyam was there ahead of time, getting the room in order, setting up the drawings, making sure the glass of fresh water was on the lectern.

However, on Wednesday, he had given Shyam the authorization to spend whatever time was needed to care for Althea. It seemed Shyam was the only one who could soothe her during her periods of greatest stress. He had also been giving Althea extra sleeping potions to help her get through the unsettled nights.

Dr. Zastro thought that he must note on his schedule to spend extra time with Althea next week, see if there were not some other methods to initiate that might ameliorate her increasing distress. The time for her cure was shortening.

Normally he did not take patients so young, but the aunt's letter had been so desperate, and he felt so sure the cure he had in mind would be simple and effective. Right now, he was not sure of anything. All that had appeared so well structured before was gaping with holes in places he had never even suspected.

He put his notes on the lectern, briefly going over them once more. Before he had time to back out and await his formal entrance, Shyam was opening the door and the ladies were beginning to drift in.

As usual, Isobelle was the first. Was it because she was in a hurry to get away from her kitchen duties, or was it because she wanted to make sure she got that one double chair that fit her body so comfortably?

Delphine too was always one of his early audience. He had to admit, looking at her now, she was an attractive woman, and he could see why men were tantalized by her, but her intelligence was so underdeveloped. Of course, certain men did not care about a woman's intelligence. What a rare jewel Yana was.

Delphine smiled at him in her expected attempt at enticement. She was on her way up front to talk to him, but he waved her away pleasantly, "Later Mrs. Applewood; we have consultation time later."

Now that his sexual passions were so aroused, would it make a difference during his private meetings with Delphine?

Would he treat her malady differently? Would he be more sympathetic to her nymphomaniac nature, more attuned to a person who could not control passions? That was how his and Yana's encounters were different; they had love with their passion. Without love, it would have been only animalistic mating.

Mavis appeared and then Edwina. Edwina was coming along nicely. He had convinced her she was not in an asylum, that she was not going insane, and the machines had been able to help her, plus the various herbal medicines. If she could only go calmly into old age accepting that her childbearing days were over and that her body would gradually decline in accords with the dictates of life itself. Fighting it would only lead to more distress.

How marvelous that he would not pass into old age and never know the wonders of true love. Would that he and Yana could spend their final years together? *And they lived happily ever after....* Yet, he couldn't visualize Yana as ever being old, as if she were crystallized in her present form forever, her beauty never fading, her spirits never waning. Still, if he was sure of one thing—no one had yet discovered a Fountain of Youth.

They must not waste any of their days together, treasure every precious moment.

Where was Yana? He grew panicky, wanting to see her lovely form; it had been an eternity since last night. He kept staring at the doorway, waiting for her to appear. Maybe she had overslept.

His other fear was that this sharing of her self might still be too much, that she would slip away in secret. Such an unpredictable person and he was not acquainted with all the intricacies of her culture, what things set her off, what was good luck, bad luck. She had left other men before, she had told him that. Yet, she had also told him there had never been another such as he, that he was her "one true love." She did not lie. She teased, she said wild things, but she never lied.

And then, there she was, filling the room with her presence, lighting up the whole area surrounding her. The thin lilac robe filming over her chemise, but all Zastro saw was her naked body glowing underneath, as if his eyes had special vision and could view through her clothing.

Her hair was braided—yet to him, it was still thrashing across the garden bed, as remembered scents of the garden flowers excited his nostrils, the taste of sweet fruit moistened his tongue. He closed his eyes to erase the memory of the previous night. When he opened them, Yana was staring at him with those molten eyes. He answered with a knowing all-encompassing gaze, and then, in an instant, they both resumed their proper roles: he the doctor and she the patient.

"Good morning, ladies."

"Good morning, doctor." The joy in their voices was always heartwarming. He looked forward to it. He did care about these women. Now he had an even more compelling reason for treasuring all the female race. He wanted to go down there, embrace each one of them but restrained himself from doing so. Why had he never felt this way before? Had he always put up an invisible wall between himself and his audience—a curtain that never parted until this morning?

He wanted to shout to them the joys in the world, if only they would open up their inner spirits and partake in the gifts God had given to those who occupied His earth.

The greatest of these of course was love. Love never harmed anyone. Love was the greatest cure in all the world. He had never felt healthier, stronger, even with his lack of sleep. He could go out and conquer armies, slay dragons, leap from mountains, now that Yana was here.

He kept his voice steady, however, as he announced, "Our topic today is: FEMALE ATTIRE AND FEMALE HEALTH." He wrote the words on the chalkboard. *Gather your thoughts, you only have five more lectures to give. These ladies have paid special sums of money to hear your words. You must give them their full due.*

"Now then, as you ladies know, you and every other human being have come into this world unattired. Mother Nature, in her sense of humor does not even attire the newborn in a fig leaf. However, most mothers can hardly wait to wash the newborn and wrap it in layers and layers of clothing. Those of the feminine gender are wrapped differently right from birth on, already the waist is pinned to conform to the female figure.

"I'm sure you ladies are familiar with the ancient Chinese custom of binding women's feet as a mark of beauty." He flipped to a drawing of a pitiful Chinese lady with bound feet, and there were gasps that such a practice could be done in the name of beauty, when it was so painfully ugly.

"Here in our own country, we bind the women's waist so tightly it is equally unhealthy and deforming. Young girls are ever laced so they can be fashionably dressed. By the time they reach maidenhood, they are not even aware anymore that these lacings are tight, since they have already had years of dressing that way.

"As for husbands who demand their wives dress in the latest fashion, I say he should be sentenced to wear for one week his waistcoat as closely fitted to his body as his wife must wear the waist of her dresses. Tight nightdresses, tight stockings, tight garters, tight boots, close fitting vests and waists, tight caps and hats, all tend to obstruct the circulation of the blood, and also the electrical radiation which carries off the impurities of the system."

He showed more illustrations, always aware of Yana's amused attention to the drawings. He had never noted the humor in his lectures before and today the realization descended as an enlightenment.

"The most injurious of all is tight lacing. Now, here we have the outline of the normal diaphragm and the abdominal muscles during expansion and contraction of air. The diaphragm rises and falls to aid the lungs in inhaling vital air, and exhaling that which has been deprived of its electric property and loaded with animal effluvia. How common it is now for women to have shortness of breath."

Yana's arduous breaths—exploding in shrieking gasps, culminating their mating, that first time—he, so afraid she might expire. Now, he awaited those shrieks.

"The disturbance of the functions of the diaphragm is by no means the only evil of tight lacing. The circulation of the blood and the electrical radiations are impeded thereby. A more alarming evil is the pressure thrown upon the bowels, and from the bowels upon the womb. The shocking prevalence of 'prolapsus uerti', commonly termed 'falling of the womb', is greatly owing to the pernicious practice of tight lacing.

"It is a known fact that the fashionable woman's corset exerts an average of twenty-one pounds of pressure on her internal organs, and extremes of up to eighty-eight pounds. Some of the short-term results of tight lacing are shortness of breath, constipation, weakness, and a tendency to violent indigestions. Long-term effects can be fractured ribs, displacement of the liver and uterine prolapse, in some cases even, the uterus is gradually forced, by the pressure of the corset, out through the vagina."

Again, the ladies gasped when illustrations of the forced-out inner organs were pointed to.

"Ridiculous tight lacing is even maintained during pregnancy, injurious to both the mother and child, frequently the cause of miscarriage.

"And now, the latest repulsion to the female figure is the bustle that weights down the back of her body and distorts the female anatomy so there is no real semblance of the beautiful female form that was meant to flourish."

The beautiful female form—is the most beautiful when naked, unadorned—Keep to the lecture, keep thoughts of Yana away.

"We laugh at the idea of women in barbarism wearing rings in their noses, pendulums from their ear lobes, and Kren women wearing fancifully constructed bags, enclosing their hair, suspended from the backs of their heads. Yet, our own women have adapted this heathenish custom of wearing 'The Waterfall' hairstyle.

"Our aristocratic ladies think the Indian squaw acts absurdly when she tattoos her skin to gratify rude tastes of her warrior lover, but these same ladies do not hesitate to use paint and powder on their own face."

Would Yana ever tattoo her body for him?

"The use of lead in cosmetics has been proven to cause physical and moral dangers. Instead of making the women more beauteous, destroys that which is already beautiful. Some women are even addicted to arsenic eating for improvement of the complexion, and the obliteration of the marks of age. What vanity causes such poisonous pursuits?

"Hindoo women paint their eyelids and cuticle around the eyes with lampblack, and you often see in Central Park, fashionable women with penciled eyebrows, blackened eyelashes.

"What you wear does impart good health and bad health. Another example—which will impress this on you ladies. Did you know certain colors are harmful? For awhile, green ball dresses were the fashion for fair complexioned females. Dressmakers, and the ladies who wore these green gowns, suffer from the effects of arsenate of copper used to dye these gowns. There is vivid proof that one seamstress was made ill by the poison, manifesting itself by sores about the mouth, because she bit the threads while sewing this green silk.

"The most poisonous dyes are red and yellow aniline, and cases of poisoning have been documented from women wearing red stockings." The illustrations were shocking—one leg clad in a red stocking, and the other bare leg, with garish ulcerous lesions.

"Another area of reform needed in women's dress is the long skirt. They interfere with the free motion of the limbs, and make the exercise of walking exhaustive. Nervous force is wasted in the effort, and weakly or sickly women are thereby discouraged from attempting to move about to any extent, or sufficiently preserve what little muscular strength they still possess. Long skirts hang too heavy from the waist and generally have no support from the shoulders. And while the lower body is covered, the top is scantily clad, making circulation into a great disadvantage.

"It is a great pity that we go to Paris for our fashions."

Paris—that's where Yana would be in a few weeks....

"Better for the health of women if we imported fashions from China, where celestial women wear trousers and dressing gowns and sandals; or from Japan where they put on only silk or woolen coats and sandals; or from Persia, where they wear an open muslin chemise, over trousers, having the amplitude of a petticoat. The women of the village of Seroda, East Indies, are remarkable for their physical beauty and fine complexion—*Were there any Gypsies in that country?*—dress with only a flowing robe, confined around the waist with a simple zone, and looped up on the side, so as to expose the leg a little above the knee."

He looked at Yana, who was now twitching her nose at him, now opening her mouth and extending her tongue in a fake yawn, her real meaning was telegraphed quite graphically. *Where was he? Oh yes, the pores—*

"There are said to be nearly three thousand pores in every square inch of the human body. Think of the effects from plastering up twenty to thirty thousand of those useful little orifices through which the electrical radiations of the system carry off the noxious and waste matter of the blood. That is why I warn invalids against the use of plasters stuck to their bodies in promoting their cures."

What happens when another body is sealed against another?—

"Also, for this reason, India rubber and patent-leather boots and shoes are objectionable because their texture prevents escape of the insensible perspiration. Rubber, patent-leather, close fitting and insufficient dressings for the feet, are in many instances the causes of colds, paralytic affections, and of the extremities, corns, bunions and other infirmities."

Bare feet are also best for dancing....

"One final warning, persons should never wear deceased relative's clothing, since if the person is diseased, his garment is also diseased. The electrical radiation of the impurities of the system, known as insensible perspiration, enters the minutest threads of the cloth. Bring these in contact with the absorbing pores of another and the person is at once inoculated with noxious matter remaining in the clothing. Syphilitic and other venereal diseases are frequently transmitted in this way."

It was true about the essence of clothing being inoculated by another person—his bed sheets transmitted Yana again and again each night as he lay in them.

He continued; the material could go on forever it seemed—this subject so fascinating to the women. Why were females so interested in clothing, their own appearances? Was it all done for the enticement of the male? Yana, with her colorful Gypsy clothing, the bangles and beads, surely was a more vivid person. Still he considered all the artifice as gilding the lily.

Designing special robes for his Sanitarium ladies solved many problems, especially doing away with class distinctions, since most of the wealthy chose to display their riches on their bodies, the highest fashions being the costliest. *What you wore was not what you were.* Dr. Zastro wished to emphasize this by his issuing the same robes for every woman patient. He always hoped the ladies would go back to their homes after wearing his garments and design similar robes for their own use, wearing them the greater part of the day. But few attributed their well being at the Sanitarium to what they had been wearing during their stay.

"Thank you ladies for your kind attention once more. I wish you all a restful and healing weekend. I shall see you all in this same room once more on Monday, when the subject will be: THE EFFECT THE MOTHER HAS ON THE UNBORN CHILD."

They applauded. He didn't know if he should discourage this adulation or not, but then he had never encouraged it. Many times previously, the women he had selected went through the complete three weeks and never once applauded. Surely, this was an exceptional group.

Yana gave him a brief smile and disappeared through the door. Delphine was approaching him; he decided he would linger and speak with her, as he had no desire to leave just yet, wanting to fill in the hours before the awaited rendezvous tonight.

"Doctor, I have special questions to ask about clothing." She was hesitant as though she expected him to dismiss her as he usually did. When he didn't, she gave a sigh of relief and went on hurriedly. "Well, Solomon expects me, likes me to—well, dress up in certain garments. I have a whole wardrobe he has bought me—from different countries, different places."

"What kind of garments?" Delphine had never broached this subject before.

"Things that women wear in those harem places, veils and such—And he likes me to dance with those veils, just veils sometimes. And sometimes he wants me to put on this grass skirt and ropes of flowers round my neck and just stand there and swish back and forth, and those stiff grasses just scratch and itch, making me jiggle faster. But his favorites are the dance hall outfits, with those tight lacings up the front, so my tits spill out an over, cause there ain't no room for them any place else. And then he wants me to smoke this thin cigar, and feed him drinks...."

Her chattering list of trivia interested him today. He wanted to hear more, but this was not the time. "Mrs. Applewood, we have consultation time this afternoon, why don't you bring all your concerns regarding this clothing problem to me then, and we can discuss it in privacy."

"I know about our consultation time, but I was afraid I would forget by then—and I have so many things to tell you all the time, but then I forget them, can't remember when I see you."

"Why don't you write them down? Keep a pad and pencil in your room, and when you think of these things, write them down. Then bring the pad with you when we have consultation time. However, I must remind you, we can only discuss medical situations and what concerns your health."

"My pad is all filled up with poems to you, and—"

"Then you must start a new pad, and—"

"I gotta tell you, before I forget, right now, Solomon, he dresses up in these same clothes sometimes too, and I have to sit there and watch him perform, and clap and hoot, and he puts on this old wig, with long hair, and—"

"What are you wearing while watching him?" This all seemed so very ridiculous; yet it was something new to add to his journals, men's dress deviations. He stayed to hear more.

"One of his old bathrobes, and my hair is stuffed under a man's cap, and sometimes he puts a false mustache on me, and—" she was distressed, tears forming in her green-blue eyes.

Delphine had always been so audacious, so flirtatious, he had never seen such disturbed emotions surface so nakedly in her. The impulse to take her in his arms and comfort her surprised him. He stood there, afraid to move.

"Does this disturb you when you have to dress as a man?"

"Yes it does. I don't like looking like no man, binding my titties, strapping on that long thing—I'm proud of being a woman, and proud of my figure. He wanted me cause I was such a fine figure of a woman. Why does he want me to look like a man on those crazy days?"

"He may have certain problems that I may have to discuss with him privately. There have been cases—" This was a side of Solomon he hadn't heard about before. Had he failed to find out all the reasons for Delphine's nymphomaniac distress? Had he dismissed her too easily as a shallow and wanton person?

Delphine prattled on, "He won't come to see you. I said it wasn't right to act like that, and he said he had enough money so he could act any way he wanted. He owned me, and so he could make me do anything he wanted—that I was his slave, even if he didn't have no papers. He said the marriage papers was the same as owning me. Didn't that Abraham Lincoln free the slaves? Solomon can't have me as a slave, can he?"

"No, I think Solomon plays games with you; perhaps because he's bored—"

"Bored? How can he be bored with me? I entertain him all I can, in every way I know. What more kin a person do?'

"He can have anything he wants, buy everything he wants. Such men, they always want more. Greed is a never-ending funnel needing to be filled."

"I don't know bout that, but let me tell you, quick, and then I will never say it again, but I think about it sometimes, even plan it...." She brought her face close to his and whispered, "I think about how I can kill him. Especially those crazy days." She herself had a crazed look right now. "I don't know how else to solve my problems."

He took her hands, grasping them hard. She must be in great desperation to be thinking such thoughts. He couldn't advise her to leave Solomon, yet he knew Delphine had a violent temper, was given to doing rash things. He was used to treating troublesome health problems, not great moral ones. He didn't even know what Delphine's moral upbringing was. Surely if she had broken so many commandments for such a long time, she might not even think twice about such a monstrous deed as murder.

"You must not even think such thoughts," he commanded. "As you must already know, what we think becomes our actions."

"I know, I know. When I think of doing away with Solomon, I cover up those thoughts with thoughts of you, doctor, and how much I love you. No matter how much I think those love thoughts, I know they can never come to be real. That drives me deeper and deeper into anger and—"

"Delphine, you must find some other thoughts then to drown out those horrible ones about Solomon. We will discuss this also at consultation time. I think I must dismiss you for now, I have things I must attend to." He didn't want to linger any longer, not while she was in this state. He wanted time alone to ponder just how to advise her.

"You know who else I think about killing?" This time she was looking at him with eyes that were cold and hard. "I think about killing Yana."

"What?"

"Because ever since she's been here, you ain't been the same. Your attention is always on her."

"That is not true—"

"I seen her sneak out of your room one morning, and—"

"Enough. I will not have you making false accusations. I will not have you singling out one of my patients for your jealous wrath. If you wish to stay here for the rest of your term, you will say no more regarding any of this."

What was happening to distort minds into thinking of killing?

"I love you so much, I don't want no other woman to even look at you." She reached out for him. He pushed her away.

"Enough." Just the thought of Delphine wanting to harm Yana brought cold fear into his being. Love? Delphine said love could make her want to do this. *Love never destroyed, love only nurtured and built up. Yet, love made emotions run mad, compelled persons to do things beyond their nature.*

She was waiting for his next move, next words.

"Delphine, we will discuss all this later. Meanwhile I want you to take a double dose of your medicine." The medicine he prescribed for her was a calming potion meant to subdue her nymphomaniac tendencies, help her sleep. More of it could help control her rages also, keep her from having thoughts of wanting to harm Yana.

"That medicine cools my body, but it don't stop my mind." Her feisty spirit was back. "And you ain't never learned how to know what I'm thinking bout in my head. And you can't put me out of this place, cause I'll tell everything I know."

What was she talking about? There was nothing—and who would believe her? Still, he never allowed anyone to threaten him, about anything. "I will not listen to any more such talk. I will put this hysteria aside as a symptom of the distress you are suffering. But if you ever make such threats again, you can be committed to—" He stopped himself; how could he counter her threats with one of his own? He knew he had the power to have Delphine committed to an asylum. A doctor's word was inviolate, but he would never abuse his privileges in such a way. He also knew Solomon would never consent to putting Delphine away; he liked having his pretty pet around.

"Committed? Where will you commit me to, doctor? To where?" she screamed at him.

"I will commit to your leaving here and going home," he said calmly.

"We'll see. We'll just see." She flounced away; anger manifested in her every step.

All this unsettled him. He had witnessed an aspect of Delphine's personality never revealed before. Her emotions were festering, and there were cases of nymphomaniacs going mad and doing insane acts. What was he willing to do to protect

Yana?   He couldn't wait for the next week to be over, his
patients gone home and all these new dilemmas dissolved.

Maybe he should warn Yana about Delphine's threats. No,
thinking back, they probably were only threats to stir him. No
need to worry his love. Had Delphine seen Yana coming out of
his room? Delphine was forever making up stories, anything to
keep her illusion alive that she could still attain his love.

He made his way down the hallway, out the double doors
and down the winding staircase until safely in his downstairs
office, cut off from the Sanitarium area. He shut the door but
knew he couldn't shut out the problems that followed him.
There were always solutions. Answers somewhere; he had only
to persist in unearthing them. Problems had always been a
welcome challenge before. Today they were only disquieting.

CHAPTER 21

At fresh-air time that afternoon, Yana pretended to be asleep in her lounge, all the while reliving what had taken place in this garden the night before. As the others were leaving, she lingered a bit to gather rose petals and jasmine blossoms into the flounce of her chemise. These were to play a special role in the ritual she had planned for Phillipe when she had him alone in her room later that night.

Early evening was spent in preparation. First, she anointed her body with the olive oil Isobelle had secured for her, in which sticks of cloves had been steeping. The oil's spicy aroma was pungent. With artistic flair, she spread the flower petals across her bed. The whole room was perfumed with exotic scents, effacing all the sanitized odors.

She had cut candles into small pieces, placing them in miniature saucers that she used for her oil paints; the saucers still held bright splatters of colors. Near ten p.m., she lit the candles, unlocked her door and lay on her bed, scattering moist petals lightly across her naked torso.

The door opened quietly. There he stood, in his golden robe, enshrined in the shimmering candlelight. He closed and locked the door, and then just stood there, gazing at her as she lay in a yearning state, each petal inciting new arousal as they brushed across her skin in featherlike touches.

"You are more beautiful than ever, if that be possible," he said, kneeling beside her bed, burying his head in her flower-covered breasts. He looked up at her, gazing at her whole body. "You surpass even the beauty of the rose."

Lamentations of affection, not heard before, washed over her. Cherish.... Adore.... Idolize.... She closed her eyes, breathing in the vapors of love as they fell upon her heart, floating through the entire room.

Something cool and heavy was laid upon her neckline. She opened her eyes. Her longed-for keepsake. "Oh Phillipe—"

"I have brought you your necklace," he said.

She gathered the treasured chain to her mouth, kissing it repeatedly, wanting to devour every coin, every link so she would never be without it again. "Thank you, thank you," she cried. "Now I am complete."

"Your body needs no adornment," he said. "You have told me, I remember, that this piece of jewelry holds parts of your past, and so it is more than decorative metal. It has added preciousness because it was once wedded to your flesh." He lifted the necklace from her hands and placed the chain across her waistline, the long center bangles brushing against her lower pubic hair. Gently he moved the chain back and forth, the tingling coins excited her in a new way, even more so when he pressed the warming gold circles into the soft mounds of her privates.

"My necklace will be invested now with new memories," she whispered, as she took the beloved ornament and placed it on the nightstand. "But for tonight, we will only let it watch, not participate."

He took off his robe and lay down beside her. The bed was narrow, but there was such a feeling of closeness tonight, they would not need extra room. Their passion began slowly, as if the softness of the flowers had gentled the evening, quieted their animal appetites into more delicate probing, the fragrant perfumes directing all sensations into floating rivers of exploration that traveled leisurely into new areas of love.

She rubbed scented oil over his body, glazing every portion. The spicy aroma changed him into a glistening prince in the Arabian Nights, and she became the teller of a thousand stories that would keep him captured and enchanted all night.

And so Yana spoke; beginning with simple folktales, she went on to more exotic escapades, letting her imagination run wild, spinning fables that grew stronger in passion, more stimulating in action until the gentleness of the flowers vanished and the power of the spices dictated the enactment of the last fantasy she described in erotic detail.

She was his princess. He was her prince. They were alone in a tent on the hot desert sands and they had to perform fantastic feats of love to free themselves from the spell that had been cast

over them by the wicked genie. Their task was to release from
their bodies the passions imprisoned there for so many years—
let them out in whatever way possible—only then could new
marvels be allowed in to take their place.

The resulting exhaustion was wonderful. Yana lay there,
mingling thoughts and feelings, scents and sensations,
circulating perceptions that would not cease.

"You keep surprising me," he said, holding her, calming her
quaking. "Just when I think we have surpassed experiencing
anything new—up from the depths of your being, unprecedented
delights spring forth. What a wonderful creature you are."

"Maybe tonight, the necklace has also enhanced this
gathering, adding its own magic," she murmured. "The room,
the flowers—"

Each night it had been a different setting. With a quizzical
smile she asked, "How many rooms do you have in your
building?"

His answer, in serious jesting and mock theatrical voice, "I
have a deep, dark, dungeon hidden in my basement."

She laughed. "Even there, our meetings could be exciting."

He shook his head, and with some apology, "No my love,
my basement is filled only with old and new inventions. Bits
and pieces of wire and machinery that would make sense to no
one, but me.

"I consider myself an eminent inventor, but I could never
invent our times together. They are unique in every aspect.
They cannot be predicted, duplicated, and of course could never
be patented. If such a thing were possible, the world would be
lining up at my door. Yet, I would be no wealthier than I am
now, in this precious moment in time."

He is loosening his inner bonds, Yana thought. He was
opening himself to areas of his own persona that he hadn't yet
explored, learning to express his heart more freely, without
weighing each word and action. An added gift: he was revealing
a fine sense of humor.

The rest of the evening was as enchanting as the beginning,
this fairytale she didn't want to end. She kept entertaining him
with more Gypsy tales, stories of her own life embellished with

made-up impressions. Many of these stories had happened so long ago, already long forgotten in their truths. She didn't want to hold anything back, wanting him to know her in her entirety, whatever she remembered—whatever she imagined.

His gentle fingers rubbed flower petals over her breasts as she continued her narrations. He glided the petals across her legs and then placed the wilted membranes into the folds of her private parts, rubbing the soft interior of her sex with the extracts from the roses and jasmine.

When she finished her story, he let his tongue taste the inserted petals. A continuous arousal permeated her bringing, a heightened stimulation that vibrated with deepening momentum. His mouth continued searching the sensitive, pulsating area. His beard bristled into her tender secret places.

As his tongue probed deeper, she moaned as sensations burst forth within in rocketing spasms. She caressed his head between her throbbing thighs. His mouth moved to hers, as he filled her below with his erection, petals and juices swirling together, his hands holding the lower half of her so tightly against his groin they moved in unison and the eruption that followed was a dual crescendo, his nails cutting deeply into her buttocks, inflicting both pleasure and pain.

After their energy was spent once more, she nestled close to his side, leisurely telling him more stories—Gypsy lore, Irish tales her father had told her, and things made up during the moment, all to enchant and keep him in her beguilement. The candles were sputtering out one by one, as they lay in the tiny room, the deepening darkness expanding the walls further and further into the never-ending night.

"We must plan our future," he said, holding her hand, outlining her fingers. "I ponder it daily—anticipate the months, years ahead."

"Not now, not tonight," she murmured, "maybe never."

"Not plan our future?"

"I mean, let us make no specific plans," she said. "Plans can change so easily, with the slightest shift of the wind. We must let our love guide us, take us wherever it will." She wished it were so, that nothing ever had to be preplanned. Even she knew one must at least try to control the course of life. Existence flowed as a river on a predetermined course, through swirling rapids, across dangerous rocks and over hazardous waterfalls, and sometimes planning could circumvent disasters, if one could view them far enough ahead. Sometimes, even planning was not enough.

"Our plans to marry?" he asked with some anxiety.

"They have not changed." She reassured him with a kiss. "I know in your society it is imperative to announce to the world our commitment of love in a certain prescribed manner. A tradition that has been in all cultures since time began—to publicly proclaim exclusive love between a man and a woman. Our tribes too have always celebrated the sanctity of marriage with special rites."

"When? When will this take place?"

"After I return from Paris. Then we will make all of our plans for our future together."

"I don't know if I can wait—"

"For what? Consummation of love? We have gone far past that. I am yours, whether we are married or not. Marriage will only be a signed parchment—an announcement in the newspaper, proclaiming us husband and wife. I'm not sure about the 'Mr. and Mrs.' though. None of that will change what we are now, intimate lovers."

That is what they were—*intimate lovers*, married or not—*until death do us part*. It was a commitment she was finally willing to make.

"To wake up each morning, knowing you are beside me," he said thoughtfully.

"Where? Where will beside you be? I have not yet committed to living here. You will certainly not want to come and live with me. So—"

"We will wait then—to make our plans...." His voice trailed off sleepily as he escaped into dreams. His breathing took on the steady pattern of sleep.

It was comforting to feel the pulse of his heart beating so close to hers. At that moment she wanted to move in with him completely, without reservations, just to be with him daily, nightly. Never any separation. *Do not disturb this evening with thoughts of the future*, she reminded herself. That had been her maxim—letting tomorrow take care of itself. The Gypsy maxim. The arrival of visitors, strangers, set new chains of events into motion. Births—deaths—never predictable. All plans for tomorrow were tentative. It was easier to go with the flow, than trying to harness the direction of the wind.

This time she was the one who woke him, kissing him on his eyes, ears, mouth. "Phillipe," she called softly, "Phillipe, it is time. The sky is brightening into daylight."

He stirred. "Hmmm."

"You must leave. We will have all day Saturday and Sunday together."

"Saturday and Sunday?" He sat up and rubbed at his eyes, adjusting to where he was, reacting to her words. "The weekend—I—I decided—we would not see each other this weekend."

"You decided—You? Without even consulting me?" She was more disappointed than angered.

"I must go to Philadelphia," he said, not facing her as he got up and put on his robe. "I thought if we had unprecedented time together—for two days and nights, there's no telling what might occur."

"Nothing," she assured him, "but wonderful things."

"I know." There was new distress in his voice. "But we must still abide by Sanitarium decorum, at least until next week. I thought it best, for you—for me."

"You cannot do my thinking for me."

"I did not consult you because I didn't want you to persuade me otherwise, and I'm in a very persuadable state whenever I'm with you."

"Do you regret—being persuaded?"

"Not one solitary second."

"Then let me persuade you again, about this Saturday and Sunday." She was reaching for him, but he moved away.

"I thought it could be a practice prelude to when you are in Paris," he said, "when I already know I won't be able to bear being without you."

"I do not want you to do my thinking for me—ever." She felt contrite upon seeing the hurt in his eyes.

"I'm sorry. You must be patient, this is all so new to me," he apologized. "It's like I'm having to start all over, adjusting to another person. Not thinking for you—I have always done it for so many."

"There'll be many adjustments, for both of us. My temperament is not always so patient either."

"Of that, my love, I am already aware," he said, reaching for her.

She turned away, not wanting to initiate another session of lovemaking. Let him start missing her right now. She continued dressing. Then she saw the necklace on the nightstand, grabbed it up and fastened it around her neck. The metallic jangling caught Phillipe's attention.

"The rules still hold, Yana. You may not wear the necklace outside your room." The doctor's voice again. Why was he always reverting to his rules? Would he never change?

"Is this going to be a challenge of wills again?"

"No. But I cannot favor you over my other patients."

"You already have."

"Privately."

"But—" she started to protest.

"I would do anything I could for you," he said. "Though lovers may live in their own little world, the planet also has other inhabitants we need to consider. The Sanitarium encompasses more than the two of us. Please, help me in remembering this. The next week will have difficulties enough."

She didn't need a sermon right now. Her defiance, erased for so many days, rushed forth. "And if I refuse to take off the necklace, you will send me away?"

"If you refuse, it is because you do not want to stay."

She did want to stay, and she did not want to cause him any further distress, so attuned to his feelings, she now suffered when he did. She unclasped the necklace. "After I leave this place, I am never removing it again—for anyone."

"Thank you, Yana," he said, a smile of relief lightening everything.

"For you, I will try as I never have before. But you must also try to understand my needs, they are not the same as other women."

"Yes," he said, holding her tighter. "I know all about different women, but you, I will never know you completely. And that will be the wonderment of our union—living our lives together, getting to know each other, yet knowing we will never completely discover what is buried in the depths of each of us."

"Tatcho—It is so."

"It will work, because—I am learning that love works many unpredictable miracles. The greatest miracle will be our love combining into a creation of new life. Our children." His voice grew soft with awe.

She put fingers to his lips, "I must confess I never wanted children, and—"

"Not now, we will talk this out later," he cut her off as if afraid to hear what she might say.

"No, I must tell you, and I have thought of it many times this week, how wonderful it would be to have a child by you." She couldn't believe she was speaking this aloud. When any thoughts of curtailing birth had niggled, the anticipation of a child being created by their love was more powerful. It was the same feeling that overcame her whenever she was contemplating a painting, the visualization forming in her mind, the expectancy of the final creation.

"Yana, I was always so afraid—I did not want conception, not without marriage. But, during our passions—"

"Enough." She pressed his lips together. "If one is destined to be with child, then let it be so. Do not try to outsmart the fates."

"That is not possible, is it?" he said, and then added with some hesitancy, "Our religious beliefs—they might cause some differences."

"Not for me." She meant it. "You can believe in whatever you wish, and I will do the same. What difference in the privacy of our souls?"

"It worked for my mother and father," Phillipe said. "He was agnostic, she a devout Christian, but when it came to the children—Well, my father let my mother do the greater part of the rearing."

"And you are afraid to let the children follow my thinking?"

"I don't know. I haven't thought that far ahead."

"Then do not perplex yourself about it right now. I do have some religious heritage, you know. I'm not a heathen. Both my mother and father had traces of Catholicism in their backgrounds. But traveling Gypsies belong to no congregations and devise their own religious beliefs, picking others up along the way, from various tribes, different countries."

"It's not important." He was trying to dismiss the subject, which meant it was something he felt deeply about.

"I'm not an agnostic," she said continuing the discussion in spite of his protests, "but my beliefs are mixed up into many things. I have never sorted them all out. Never any need to, since I was the only one who used them. Maybe, once I had children, I would reassess my religious beliefs, choosing what was important to pass on, or maybe letting the child choose. Right now, that is the farthest subject from my thoughts. Children.... Religion...."

"Mine too," he said, "and I don't even know how the subject broke into this special morning interlude."

"Oh, I'm sure there will be many more contentions to discuss. Not today, however. We will have a lifetime to do that."

"A lifetime together." He made it sound as if he had been granted the Holy Grail.

"'Tis getting brighter," she warned. "You don't want anyone seeing you leave."

This was Saturday, he had nothing scheduled, she thought to herself, *he could have stayed in her room all day long if he wanted to. But then, when would be the best time for him to leave? When would no one see him? He would need to stay until night again. No, now was the time for separation.*

Already the room was changing in texture and mood, as the daylight seeped in, outlining the contents. The flowers were withered. The candles were flattened, clouding the paint on the saucers. Their night of wonderment was diminishing and

Arabian princes and their hot desert tents had already vanished. The shadowy ending of something wonderful was dissolving into the past.

Let it go—shift into place with the other treasured memories.

Phillipe was standing at the window, looking out into the minimal distance that could be viewed through the tinted glass.

Without turning around, "Yana," he said, "Delphine—" then stopped.

"What about Delphine?" she asked.

"She is a troubled woman," he spoke rapidly, "just be careful when you're around her. She has professed her love to me, and her jealousy of you. I have given her no cause—"

"Do not fret about Delphine," she said, "I know how to deal with women like her."

"Please, no trouble."

"No trouble," she agreed, "Delphine is not worth troubling about."

"I wouldn't want anything to happen to you."

"Phillipe, I can take care of myself. That is one thing I have always been able to do." *Sometimes, with special help*, she recalled. Maybe she'd have to go back to her Gypsy chants. She hadn't used them since their nights together, feeling so complete; she hadn't felt the need to call on any outside forces.

"I better leave then," he said, moving to the door.

She opened it slightly. All was clear.

"Thank you for coming to my room."

"The pleasure was mine." He took a last look around the room, now burnished by the morning sun. "I had only thought of these rooms as antiseptic, electro-charged places for my women patients to be alone. You have changed that perception, in one night, making this into a space of untold paradise."

"And you," she beamed, "you have transformed me into an enchanted being residing in this paradise. Not through your machines, not through your potions, but by sharing what is in the depths of you."

They kissed and he was gone. She closed the door to find that loneliness loomed more thickly than ever before.

She gathered the remaining flower petals and wrapped them in a square of silk, knowing she would sleep with the packet under her pillow the remaining nights she was here. She would anoint her lips with clove oil also, reliving, tasting again this night when sleeping alone tonight.

Alone. Such a sad thought. She went to her empty bed and lay there, tears dampening her cheeks, arms reaching out. The bed that had held their bodies only a short while ago was agonizingly barren without Phillipe there beside her.

She knew right away that she wouldn't be able to sleep on the bed. Yana put the coverlet on the floor as she had done the first night here, pressing the square of silk against her mouth to suppress the sounds fighting to escape.

Phillipe, oh Phillipe, how can I ever exist without you?

Exhausted, she fell asleep and dreamt that she was a nymph in the woods. Flowers were falling all around her, covering her in soft mounds, so voluminous she couldn't get up from under them. When she did break through, it was winter and the ground was buried in drifts of snow—all the flowers vanished, and everything had turned to brittle ice.

CHAPTER 22

Dr. Zastro went from Yana's room to his office without even attempting more sleep. The night had already passed and he must catch the early morning train, remove himself as far as possible, as soon as possible, before he had a chance to change his mind.

Already his thoughts were wandering. *Maybe he should stay here the weekend? When would such an opportunity arise again? What was he running away from?*

He left abruptly, going to his assistant's door, knocking softly. "Shyam, you must come to my office, immediately. There are things we need to discuss."

Soon thereafter, Shyam was sitting across from him, not very awake and looking fatigued. Maybe it wasn't right, leaving Shyam in charge the whole weekend.

"You not be here for two days?" Shyam appeared alarmed at the prospect.

"Something calls me away—And being in complete supervision, that too is a part of your training. I feel you are ready and capable to handle this important responsibility."

Shyam sat up straighter upon realizing this was a bestowal of trust.

"I foresee no problems with any of the ladies," the doctor continued, "except for Althea. Since she is already under your care and responds to you so well, I feel very confident in your supervising her alone."

"But, doctor," Shyam paused as if searching for words.

"It is a favor I offer you, my young friend. I have overburdened you with Althea's care; thus you have not had adequate opportunity to pursue your own medical studies."

"Is no burden, Doctor—"

Looking at this frail foreigner, Dr. Zastro realized with new guilt how his concentration on Yana had led him to abandon Althea's care to Shyam—not to mention his neglect of other responsibilities. "On Monday, you will be relieved of taking care of Althea, and Nurse Tillotson will be in charge of her

physical needs.   I will take over all of Althea's medical
supervision. You have devoted enough time to her. And for that
I am grateful."

"No doctor," Shyam protested.

"It is settled. You should be learning from all the women,
widening your experience.   I'm sure you will encounter few
females in your native India with Althea's malady."

"Has not curtailed any of my learning—"

"No, next week you will have special freedom, time to
pursue any interests you wish. Use other areas of my building.
Visit with colleagues.   Write in your journal what you have
already learned.   And the week after the ladies are gone...."
Yana would be gone then too. "You will assist me in my regular
practice before returning to your homeland. You must already
be homesick for the land of your birth."

"No, Dr. Zastro. If possible, if the law would allow me, I
would be so grateful to be able to stay in your country forever."

"I'm afraid immigration could not allow that, and the needs
of your people are so monumental—you are indeed needed back
in India, to put into practice what you have learned here."

"Is true then, doctor; I am in charge of Sanitarium, today
and Sunday?"

"That is correct."

"And on Monday, I will no longer be caring for Miss
Althea?"

"Yes. On Monday, I will sedate her with a new remedy.
Let her mind and nerves rest a bit. No more Rocking Machine.
A period of peace and quiet. Nurse Tillotson will be fanning her,
singing to her—"

"Shyam always sing to her—"

"I know. I think it best if Althea has a female caretaker for
awhile.   Having a male attendant has not worked out as we
hoped. We still have not been able to cure her of this strange
affliction, fainting when a male's bare hands touch her."

"But Doctor—"

Why was Shyam so disturbed about these new directives?
He never questioned orders.   Both were tired and the doctor

didn't wish to go into any further discussion. He needed to pack and be on his way.

"You are dismissed, Shyam. I will leave a telephone number where I can be reached." He got up, moving toward the door, a final signal the conversation was over, though he knew there was more Shyam wanted to say.

The train rumbled under Phillip, around him, cradling his body in a trembling cocoon. The motion made his upright sleep even more fitful, as thoughts and dreams intermingled. Murmurs of conversation from the other passengers filtered into his own cognizance—muffled voices entangling with his own jumbled thoughts and restless semi-sleep.

The countryside flashed by in a panorama of mottled landscapes, a thick green ribbon unraveling, separating him further and further from Yana.

"Philadelphia!" the conductor called, as the train screeched to a halt. For one short moment Phillipe wanted to rush off the train, turn around and board the next coach going back to New York.

Instead, he hailed a carriage, and was on his way to the Invalid's Hotel and Surgical Institute, a facility headed by his good friend and one-time mentor, Dr. Edward Pierce. Dr. Pierce did not know of Phillipe's arrival, but there were always rooms available at the Hotel, for both invalids and visitors. Even if Edward was not there, Phillipe knew many of the other staff and he was always welcomed at the medical facility.

The Institute was far enough away from New York, so they were not rivals for patients. Not all healing methods were shared, since sometimes people did travel great distances for certain types of cures.

The entry sign noted Dr. Pierce had Saturday morning office hours. To accommodate his working patients, Phillipe remembered. He announced himself to the reception nurse, and almost immediately, Edward came into the patient-filled area and greeted him heartily.

"Phillipe! What brings you here? You have an ailment you wish to be cured?" he laughed boisterously and extended his hand. He was robust, balding, and short of breath, but still retained his jovial disposition.

Usually there was great pleasure in visiting here, but today disquietude overrode the joy. "No, I'm perfectly well. But I needed a change of pace. If you recall, these are the three weeks I devote to my Ladies' Sanitarium, and—"

"And you were tired of talking to genteel ladies every minute of the day."

"That has never happened," he was sincere in his reply, "but there is a situation right now, which I will not go into, so I felt it best to get away for this weekend. My assistant trainee is in charge, and he has this telephone number. I plan to spend today and tomorrow in your hotel."

"You will do no such thing. You will come home with me when I am through at noontime. Anna will be more than pleased to have you. She complains that our guest room gathers dust daily."

Phillipe spent the rest of the morning browsing the Institute's vast overstocked library, an overwhelming area. Walls and walls of books on medicine, cures, case studies. One could never digest it all, not even in a lifetime. He paged through various books, but could not concentrate. Normally his mind was hungry to devour new bits of information, assimilate it into his own practice. Strange—he felt as if he were sealed in a prison of books, walled in from all sides, and his only escape was to rise through the top of the ceiling and float into the sky to soar back to his Yana.

Yana—she had once told him how she would let her mind rise into the universe, soar across the land, and visit with other people. Was she doing that now—trying to reach him—battling through all these books?

He soon fell asleep, a book open on his lap. He was climbing over mountains of books to reach his destination—a distant haze-surrounded peak. Along the way, surgical needles, operating knives, scalpels, protruded from between the volumes and he had to claw his way over them to reach the summit. Just as he was nearing the top, a bolt of lightning hit, and he fell endlessly—everything tumbling down, books, knives, scalpels—

surging past, around him. Startled, he awoke to someone calling his name.

"Phillipe? Are my books that mindless that they put to sleep?" Edward was towering over him, laughing. "Borrow any you wish. I can recommend several new ones—"

"Not this time, thank you."

"Then, let's be on our way." Edward clapped his hands and Phillipe was grateful to be led out of the labyrinth.

Anna greeted them in the reception hall of the opulent, recently built mansion. The house boasted electricity, indoor plumbing—all the newest modern conveniences. Anna was still an attractive woman, dressed in a corseted blue gown with heavy bustle and pinched pointed shoes. How Phillipe wished he might tell her what harm she was doing to her body. Instead he said, "You look lovely as usual, Anna."

"Thank you." Her aging face, surrounded by upswept rolls of blonde hair, broke into a rosy flush. Women had such difficulty in trying to conceal their inner feelings when their countenances became a public thermometer for whatever true feelings they wished to suppress.

After a light lunch in the breakfast nook, the afternoon was spent in the study in deep medical discussions. Edward drank brandy and smoked fat cigars. Phillipe had a glass of port wine, relaxing him somewhat and soon he was immersed in the medical world. His thoughts honed more centrally into the discussion, further stimulated by theories and arguments as to why this suposition would not work and this one might.

Their approaches were different— Dr. Pierce believed primarily in using the knife. He had given up bloodletting. Both were dedicated to curing their patients. "The patient must feel secure that the illness has been cut out of their body, or else they believe nothing has changed," Edward said.

"There are other ways of curing which must be tried first," Phillipe argued.

"None that I have discovered. And, with this wonderful array of new anesthetics, the patients feel they have lived through a miracle—without pain." Edward took another long drink, contemplating what he had just said.

"Still, many deaths occur with your methods."

"Many also occur *without* the knife."

Even though Edward was wealthy from his practice, Phillipe knew it was not the foremost purpose of his dedication; he zealously cared about his patients and was known to have a special part of his Institute set aside for indigents.

"All must be cured, by whatever method that works," Edward expounded, "and the spread of germs must be stopped once and for all. What a wonderful world this will be then— after we wipe out every single disease carrying germ."

"Is that even possible?"

"It is up to us, as doctors, to try the impossible."

"That we do. And many times we succeed."

"Vaccination for smallpox is already eradicating that dreadful disease. Soon we will have vaccinations for all the scourges of humankind. What a wonderful era of medical discoveries we are living through. Forging ahead, pioneering for future generations."

"I agree," Phillipe assured his mentor. "As you know, my prime dedication is finding medical cures through the uses of electricity and electromagnetic discoveries—practices not researched before."

"I know, I know. I tried tinkering with some of that stuff at various times, but my patients, they still consider it all hocus-pocus."

"Because they do not understand it."

"Well, frankly, neither do I. Germs I can see, under the microscope. Ugly little monsters. But, well, after the last experiment with electrical contraptions and getting walloped with a giant shock—no more for me, or my patients."

It was a pleasant afternoon. The debate on medicine had taken his mind off Yana. *Was it only this morning they lay together?* The scent of flowers was becoming more evident as the clearing air from Edward's last cigar settled away. A crystal vase of fresh flowers, set atop the magenta fringed velvet scarf on the library table, ensnared his focus. Soft yielding petals...captivating colors... fluttering leaves.... The fringed scarf began dancing, his body started swaying with it. Last night surfaced so strongly he was no longer in the room.

"Faraway dreams, Phillipe?" Edward chided.

"No—" *Was his face flushing?* "—Just thinking of my patients, as usual."

"Ah, you were always the dreamer. That's why you can invent. I am the practical one; I want to see and feel my cures, watch the diseased parts being cut away, discarded with finality. I've never had the time or the inclination to dream."

Was he a dreamer? Was he chasing a new ethereal cloud in the sky, and upon reaching it, would it only disintegrate into greater nothingness?

The servant came in, announcing, "Supper is served."

"It's about time," Edward chortled. "My stomach is grumbling horribly. And you, Phillipe? You must be starving. I shall reward you at my bounteous dinner table for sharing your medical secrets with me." He guffawed at that remark.

"Except for my special inventions, my medical discoveries are never secret," Phillipe said, "and if you ever wish—"

"No, no," Edward cut him off, looking him over anew. "I must say you look well. A special glow about you today. That may well be because you do not partake of the cigar and heavy liquor. Abstain from women too, I presume. You practice what you preach." Edward downed the last bit of brandy. "Me—well, life is short—and I have worked too hard not to enjoy the fruits of my labor."

The supper was a sumptuous banquet midst lavish settings. Edward's two daughters demurely joined them at the long dining table under the gleaming chandelier. Agatha was in her mid-twenties, shy, withdrawn, and uneasy with men, especially strangers. Somehow, she reminded Phillipe of Althea. Was there something in the female psyche that caused so many to withdraw into themselves, to stay there and never come out? Was it more comfortable remaining locked-up in their emotions than stepping out to face the realities of life? He must stop making a medical case study of everyone he met.

The other daughter, Julia, was in her early thirties, very attractive. She had been married quite young—her husband had abandoned her. Phillipe never knew the whole story; it was never spoken of. Julia's countenance was fixed with a continuous anger—tightened lips, pinched eyes, a total attitude of defiance, most evident when she greeted Dr. Zastro. It was not, however, the same defiance possessed by Yana, which broke out freely. Julia's was a bitterness that wound itself inward, coiling into a tight ball that could someday spring forth, unwind in all directions, and Julia might not be able to control what might happen when that eruption took place.

Edward treated only the body, feeling the mind had nothing to do with disease or its cure. Phillipe believed all of life was interconnected—mind, body and soul, just as people were connected in indiscernible ways and somewhere there was a master design to it all. This design was knowable if one learned to intuit the distinct invisible patterns, through precise mathematical fields, as evidenced in the areas of electricity and magnetic powers. Clearly, everything was locked into a prearranged framework.

Some great mind planned and directed the universe. The key to it all was so near to being discovered. Mankind was getting closer and closer to answers, as if God wanted these revelations disclosed now, this period in history. It was an era specially selected for the secrets of the universe to be unlocked. An exciting time to live.

The conversation at the table was pleasant. Edward kept draining goblets of wine at his end of the table. Anna was directing the servants from her end. The two girls, across from Phillipe, spoke little, eyes on their food, eating daintily and chewing quietly. Comparing Yana with these two, he again realized what a rare creature she was. What a jewel in the world of women he had discovered, knowing her in the most intimate ways possible. *Why was he not with her now?*

Concentration diverted, his fork came down so forcefully on his plate, peas splattered across the spotless damask cloth. The two girls could not suppress their outburst of giggles, erasing everything suppressed, great beauty breaking forth from their faces, a joy to behold, the mirth contagious. The room glowed with shared merriment.

Maybe laughter could be a new kind of cure. He had never researched that possibility. Did melancholy cause disease, or did disease cause its own melancholy? Conundrums.

"I've begged Edward to come to New York with me, when I go to buy my seasonal clothes," Anna, as hostess, did not want to dwell on the splattered peas incident, "so he can visit with you at your Sanitarium. But, he feels his Institute cannot be run without him."

"Oh no, that is not the reason," Edward said in mock solemnity. "I am afraid Phillipe here might electrocute me in one of his marvelous new curing machines." He broke into his familiar chortle.

Anna countered, "I have heard wonderful things about your machines, Phillipe. I should like to see them demonstrated sometime." She had hinted before at becoming a patient of his, but Phillipe knew Edward would not allow it. Anna was his possession, as a person and as a patient. Would Yana ever want to be treated by another physician? Would he ever want her to be cared for by someone else? *Why wasn't he with her now?*

"He has a magic stool you could try." Edward was laughing so hard he almost choked on his raspberry tart.

"Really. Might I just sit on it?" Anna asked.

Edward was in hysterics by then. "Conversation closed. No more about the magic stools. We men are moving into the library."

"Julia has consented to entertain our guest for a bit, at the piano," Anna interrupted, "so let us retire to the parlor first."

They sat on armless velvet parlor chairs near the rosewood grand piano, showered with fringed scarves—ornate framed photos mapping the top. As soon as she sat at the piano, Julia transformed into another being. She let her fingers fly across the keyboard, soothing away her interior rage. Melodious sounds transported each into a world of special harmonies, euphonious language understood by all.

To think these fleeting sounds could now be recorded, forever, thanks to that genius Alva Edison. The voices of people long dead would continue to be heard for years thereafter. The world was full of amazing wonders, and Phillipe found himself enjoying this melodious interlude, watching Julia's spirit blossom as a flower unfolding in a warm spring breeze. Sound waves—light waves—electrical—and human waves, they circulated in the air continuously, invisibly, yet their power was immense.

Julia stood, bowed, and smiled graciously. The applause was sincere. Edward was a proud father, but still eager to get on to the cigars and liquor. The tightened mask returned to Julia's face once she closed the piano lid.

The girls excused themselves, obviously relieved that the intrusion of a stranger into their family circle was no longer their concern and disappearaed up the staircase. Phillipe wished he could retire also, but knew he was in for a long evening with Edward. But then, that would lessen the anxious time he would have to spend alone in his bed in this unfamiliar place.

"I will say good night then, Phillipe," Anna extended her warm hand, "your bed is ready for you. And don't let Edward keep you up all night."

Her farewell bore a sadness, as if she wished to stay and discuss the things of the world with them instead of being confined to her limited world of fashion, society and servants. After-dinner in the library was reserved for men only.

As Phillipe watched Anna disappear down the lined wallpapered hallway, the song, "A Bird in a Gilded Cage" began threading through his mind.

The library discussion turned to politics, which had never interested Phillipe much. Some men ran the country; others ran medical institutions. Each pursued their own particular talent, and some were better at their chosen field than others. In America, they had the right to vote in leaders of their choice, and vote the scoundrels out. He let Edward ramble on about the sorry state of the country without much interruption, clouds of smoke diffusing the room into another realm, some distant place into which Phillipe was drifting. The words were boring.

Why wasn't Yana telling him her wonderful tales as she had done only last night, each word so enchanting. Why was he numbing his brain with these pontifical ramblings?

Finally, he excused himself with a covered yawn.

"Still keeping to your schedule of moderation," Edward chided. "You need a good woman to go to bed with sometime— while your equipment's still working. You need a family, someone to make all your hard work worth the striving."

Phillipe smiled, "Yes, I have often thought of such things." *But never more than now.*

"Julia needs a good man too. I can't say she's a bitter old maid, since she was once married, but she should have had children. He didn't even leave her that. Women need children to carry out their prime mission in life. What else do they have otherwise?"

Phillipe might discuss many things with Edward but never women. Especially tonight. Edward believed men had a right to their enjoyments—cigars, liquor, and women, especially if they had money enough.

"I must retire," Phillipe said again, as Edward sat morose and sleepy, his head bobbing.

"Anna's a good woman. Why do I even think of those others?" His head nodded downward in a final snap, and Phillipe left the room without Edward's noticing.

The night was restless. At home, when he couldn't sleep, he could get up and do numerous things—read, go into his basement, relax in the Spectro Cabinet. He didn't want to roam the halls here. Edward and Anna's bedroom was right next-door and though the house was substantially built, he could still hear Edward's rising and falling snores.

If a train were still running this late, he would have snuck out, leaving a note.

His heart was aching, his body yearning, and his mind would not stop thinking of Yana, reliving each night of the past week, and instead of soothing his turmoil, the memories only entrenched him into deeper misery. Was this the supposed joy of love? Or did true love only take place when one was with the loved one, making all absence painful? He had no guidelines.

All the flowery poetry about love—he had so easily dismissed it. Poets had their heads in the clouds. Those romance novels that his father had denounced? Phillipe had concluded long ago, as his father had—they were only pages of cheap trash.

The love between he and Yana was distinct, special, as each love must be, dependent on the two people who were in love. A Doctor and a Gypsy—what an unusual combination. What a rare fusion—Inventor and Artist—Scientist and Dancer. There were so many combinations; it was hard to define which of them was the strongest.

Man and Woman. That was it. Since time began. Man and Woman. It was spelled out in the Bible *that God had created Woman so Man would not be lonely.*

Had he been lonely all these years and not known it, pursuing medicine as his surrogate love? Yana had pursued all her other interests while still searching for love, and discarding it each time she thought she had found it. Yet, she explained repeatedly, that there was none like Phillipe. "There is only one perfect match in a lifetime," she whispered. "The gods have brought us together. We will never be apart."

The Bible condemned fornication before marriage. It had been so easy to bypass that guilt—once they planned to be married. In God's eyes, they were already united. That pleasant thought settled him into a deep sleep, riding rhythmically on the crests of Edward's snores still sounding through the wall next door.

After a grand breakfast the next morning, at which the girls were not present, with no reasons given, Phillipe was invited to go along to the Episcopal Church with Anna and Edward. Anna was already in her special "go to church" finery, and Edward had stuffed himself into a vest with gold watch bob, tight suit coat, top hat, and gold-topped cane.

"I do not wish to offend you by turning down your gracious invitation," Phillipe said, "but I think I would rather take a walk to the nearby park. Fresh air would bless me more than the confines of the church this morning."

"As you wish." Edward never questioned Phillipe's decisions. He himself only went to services to please his wife.

She was possibly disappointed that Phillipe was not going to accompany them, deterring her visualization of gliding grandly down the aisle with a male companion on each arm, her world aglow in the radiance of the stained glass windows.

"You will return for lunch, won't you?" Anna asked.

He had thought of taking the morning train, but no, he came to stay the weekend—Shyam was in charge.

"Yes, yes I will. But then I must take the afternoon train."

"Not stay for supper?" There was great disappointment in her voice, "Sunday supper is the grandest meal of the week. We have special guests, a small concert after. The girls have their friends over—"

It did sound tempting, very seldom was he present at such gala affairs, but as usual he was adept at turning down enticing invitations. "You have been most gracious and hospitable these two days, but I'm afraid I must be on my way before supper."

"Phillipe has his own institution to run, and some patients still get sick on Sundays," Edward offered as explanation to his wife.

"Well, we better be on our way, so we're not late for services." Anna adjusted her feathered hat and began putting on her white gloves, reminiscent of Shyam gloving his hands. How he wished he was back at his Sanitarium, where he always longed to be whenever he was away, and now the attraction was even more compelling.

"I will return at lunch time, but after such an abundant breakfast shall decline any more food," he said and then added, not knowing why, "but, if there is the opportunity—Pray for me."

"Anything special?" Anna queried.

"Don't always pry, Anna," Edward remonstrated.

"No, nothing special—maybe just for my patients." *And Yana especially, he wanted to add. Pray that she still loves me, aches for me as much as I do for her. Remembers these past nights and yearns for the time we can be together again....*

"A beautiful day for a walk, Phillipe," Edward winked, "but watch out for the maidens in the park. On Sunday they flirt audaciously from behind those floppy hats and fake fans."

Edward proved right. The park was indeed filled with fancily dressed young ladies bedecked in their sweeping white lace dresses, beribboned bonnets, and fancy parasols. They tittered and gazed at him, in coyness or brazen interest, as he briskly strolled the promenade in the park, which was dotted with huge metal statues, meticulously laid out flower gardens and meandering paths.

He escaped down a branch path, finding a secluded bench and sat there for at least an hour, looking up past the green leaves, sunlight filtering through in golden shafts—Yana reflected in each of them.

His departure later was hasty. It had been a pleasant interlude, but he was eager to leave. On his next visit, Phillipe hoped he would be bringing along his new wife. How surprised they would all be.

"Please do not wait so long, before you call on us again," Anna pleaded, "and don't even think of staying at the hotel."

"Thank you both for your gracious hospitality," and he was out the door into his awaiting carriage.

"Make hay while the sun shines," Edward called out after. "It sets sooner than you think."

The ride back was much faster than going, the skyline dimming with each mile. "New York!" sounded more like "Welcome Home." He had a light meal near the depot, prolonging his final return. He would stay in the downstairs bedroom for the night, not even go into the Sanitarium area until morning. However, once inside the building, his medical concerns superseded his need for rest, and he decided he must check with Shyam.

It was after nine, the place was quiet and most lights were out. He hurried past Yana's room, to Shyam's door where a light was still shining beneath. Phillipe knocked.

"Yes? Who's there?"

"Dr. Zastro," he called softly. "May I come in?"

The door opened and a weary Shyam stood there. "Doctor, you are back already?"

"Just arrived, and thought I would check in as to the condition of the ladies. I received no messages, so I presumed there were no problems."

"No problems. Everything well." Shyam seemed evasive, disturbed, but let him into his room.

"Althea—is she any better?" Phillipe asked.

Shyam looked away and then in a trembling voice, "Aiiiee doctor, she not any better, maybe even worse. I try, try everything…." He broke into tears. "You give me permission to take care of her, best I could—" new tears "—but today, all day, she just lay there, breathing, but not moving."

This alarmed the doctor. "I will check on her right now. You have done all you could. Do not feel any failure on your part."

"But, but, Dr. Zastro," and he broke into new sobs.

It had not been right, leaving Shyam in charge; the young man was not ready. The burden of responsibility had been too great, shaken his whole confidence.

"You need a good night's sleep now. I will alert Nurse Tillotson to answer any of the women's calls tonight." Shyam was still lamenting when he left.

Althea's room was at the end of the hall. He went in and lit the candle. She lay on her bed, motionless, as if in a coma. So still, seemingly peaceful, this angel of pale beauty. Dr. Zastro took her fragile hand; it felt cold, as if her life were draining away. He began rubbing her fingers, her whole body, to stimulate the blood circulation. Then he took the vapors from the table and held a whiff up to her nose. Her head began to move and she began crying out, "No—No! Don't touch me. Keep away from me." The peacefulness was converted into trembling fear.

He stayed with her for a long time, soothing her, singing to her, holding her hand, rubbing her forehead, putting compresses on her, anything to relax her and bring her out of this strange stupor. He could not fathom what had brought it on.

Tomorrow he would concentrate on stabilizing her, just talking to her in a mesmerizing tone, steeping the room in herbal vapors. A cure for her malady wasn't primary right now; only that he bring her back to a normal state of existence, if that were possible. Otherwise, she might have to be committed to an institution and he knew from experience that someone of such a delicate nature could not survive there among the other vicious inmates and stern attendants.

Even if her husband Arthur protested her being committed, the State always had priority. Phillipe had only one week left to treat Althea, feeling he might have already wasted the past two weeks.

He must have dozed off holding her hand; he was awakened when he felt movement. Her eyes were open and she was looking up at the ceiling, smiling. She didn't try to remove her hand from his.

"He was laying with me," she whispered, "he was in my bed, next to me...." Even if she was only telling him her dreams, it was a good sign, at least she was communicating.

"Althea, listen to me. Tomorrow I will be taking care of you and we will try new treatments. Nurse Tillotson will be with you—"

"I will not be here tomorrow, I will be home—with Mama," she said, closing her eyes, turning her face away.

He must let her rest now. He needed rest too. Her circulation was moving again and tomorrow he would concentrate on her care even if it meant not seeing Yana. He blew out the candle and left Althea's room, feeling a great sadness for this beleaguered child. Anyone who could not experience the world in a normal manner—was it living at all?

Delphine was coming around the corner from the lavatory just as he was exiting. He hurried down the hall to his room, not sure if she had seen him in the dim light or not. If she had seen him, he did not wish to speak with her. Right now, he didn't want to talk to anyone, not even Yana. He wanted only to escape to his room.

Exhausted, he sank onto his bed fully clothed. Soon a new restlessness took over, almost as if from the bed itself. Yana's scent still discernable, the bedding carried her imprint, her voice echoed above in the darkness, calling to him—*take me*. His tired body began to writhe and turn, reaching out for her elusive form.

Grasping onto the thick roll of bedding, caressing it tightly to him, he began thrusting into the softness without restraint, relieving the tensions held back these past two days. The wetness spread down his legs as he fell into a deep and troubled sleep.

CHAPTER 23

Monday morning and still no word from Dr. Zastro. The weekend had stretched into an endless eternity. Yana's arm ached, leg hurt, her whole body throbbed with distress as she rose from her bed upon hearing the morning bell.

She wasn't sure if it was more anger or anticipation that she felt at the prospect of seeing Phillipe again. How could he set the rules to be away from her for so long? Would he always set the rules? Maybe it was a mistake, thinking such a union might work—their vast differences and polarized dispositions.

The silk square of flower petals had fallen to the floor during the night. She picked it up, pressing it close to her warm cheeks. The fragrance of that night in her room and all the nights before flooded back in vibrant repeats. All was forgiven, only the yearning remained.

She pulled the chemise over her naked body. The emerald green gown went on next, the color for their third and final week at the Sanitarium. She felt at ease in the garments now. Maybe she would even sew some for herself, or ask Phillipe to have a few made for her in his workrooms.

She still hadn't settled on where she would live. Maybe she could do that while in Paris, away from here when her mind would be clearer. Would the separating weeks in Paris bring as much loneliness and misery as this past weekend had?

Breakfast and then morning exercise, and still no sight of Dr. Zastro. *What if he hadn't come back?* Ominous dreams had disturbed Yana's sleep during the night, but the meaning was elusive—although it suggested a terrible tragedy. Sometimes she had prophetic dreams before a great natural disaster, such as earthquakes or hurricanes, took place. The meaning of these calamitous dreams was not always clear until after the event occurred, and then it was too late for any warnings.

Shyam led the exercises but not with his usual vigor. At the breakfast table gossip, Yana had heard that Shyam would not be caring for Althea any longer, as Dr. Zastro had decided to resume that duty. *When had he decided?*

"One—Two—Three— One—Two—Three—" Shyam lifted his arms up and down with the ladies and then stopped earlier than usual. "You may rest now. Remember, Dr. Zastro ask all of you to continue these very same exercises when you return to your homes. Helps circulate blood, oxygen and electrical currents." He clapped his hands with finality. "Ladies, you are dismissed."

"Mine back, ach, I can even bend over now," Isobelle exclaimed. She had indeed become more agile. "But, I must go now, help in kitchen today. Bridget, she got fever, and doctor order her to rest. He say I can miss lecture today. Be on, 'Mother and Unborn Child'. Cause I nefer going to have no childrens, no need to know bout such things."

He had spoken with Isobelle, why not her? Was he avoiding her? Lecture Time was next, and she would be seeing Phillipe then—but not alone.

"I—I used to hate getting up in the morning, when I first came here." Mavis was blossoming in both speech and comeliness. "But now, I look forward to the morning. When I return home—what will mornings be like there again? What will happen to me—away from here?"

Edwina was standing, looking up. "I thank God every sunrise for sending me here. I thank God every sunrise that there are men like Dr. Zastro, men who devote their lives to helping women. So few are as giving as he is."

"Hold on there." Delphine grabbed Yana's arm before they left the Treatment Room. Each time she did this, it annoyed Yana. Always some far-fetched question, or theory about the doctor. Delphine's viciousness had toned down, since realizing she couldn't disturb Yana in the ways she wished. Today Yana didn't wish to speak to anyone, except Phillipe. *Where was he?*

"I don't have time to tarry this morning," Yana said, trying to get past Delphine in hopes to catch the doctor in the hallway or somewhere.

"Well you just wait one little minute, cause I have something we need to discuss, and since you won't talk to me privately—"

"Later." Yana tried dismissing her once more.

"No. Now." Delphine stood her ground.

"What is it then?" Yana's frustration with everything in the world broke forth. "I don't have time for silly talk."

"Silly or not, I want to know what's going on. I've seen you come out of the doctor's room at night." Delphine made the accusation with a superior tone.

"Really?" Yana dismissed the woman's disclosure. "You must be having your own special dreams, wishing it were you."

"They are not dreams," Delphine countered. "I've seen you with my own eyes, sneaking out of the doctor's room, and—"

"I don't care to discuss this with you, now or ever." Yana turned away.

"I seen him come out of your room too."

"Your nighttime vision is as bad as your daytime babbling."

"Well, Miss-Know-It-All, you're just as weak as the rest of us. Your high-and-mighty speeches those first days—bout how the doctor was using his power over all of us. Well, now he uses his power over you."

"No one uses their power over me."

"How do you think he got you into his bed then? Men are always stronger, and women are always weaker, and—"

"You don't know anything about men, or women."

"I sure do, in ways you never even thought of." She smiled. "Is he giving you late night treatments, like he did me?" Delphine's smug attitude disturbed Yana, as well as her dubious revelations.

"I will not listen to any more of your stupid made-up stories." Yana turned to leave.

Delphine blocked the doorway with both arms. "Well, you're gonna." Narrowing her eyes, she said, "He was in Miss Althea's room all last night too."

"Your mind is so mixed up—"

"And, he came to my room last year, every night for a whole week."

"I don't believe you." Yana broke through Delphine's outstretched arms with such force Delphine staggered, but still kept shouting at her.

"Ask him then. If the man don't lie, he'll tell you the truth.
And I bet it's my turn this week—after he's finished with you."
The scornful giggle was high-pitched and piercing.

Yana couldn't help it; she had to shut Delphine up once and
for all. "It won't happen for you, Delphine. Because you see,
the doctor and I are planning to be married." With that, Yana
stalked away, already feeling remorse for the reckless disclosure.

Delphine yelled after Yana, "Liar. Dirty Gypsy witch.
Liar."

The commotion brought Shyam rushing back to the area.
"Is disturbing the Sanitarium with such shouting." His voice had
turned into a bellow. "Enough! Enough disturbance in this
place."

Yana expected Dr. Zastro to appear after these outbursts,
but he never materialized.

It was a small group that waited in the Lecture Room;
Althea and Isobelle were absent, and most of the help busy
elsewhere. Yana took her usual seat in the back of the room,
Delphine's words still echoing. When at last Phillipe entered,
just as the first time, his presence sent ripples throughout her
body, his smile lighting up the whole room as if a comet had
reappeared. She hung onto the rungs of her chair to keep herself
from rushing up to him and taking him in her arms to devour him
with kisses.

He looked out over the room, and for one moment his gaze
rested on her with such deep longing, she knew he suffered as
much as she did.

Tonight, tonight would be so wonderful. Even if they did
nothing, just the rich sensation of being close to him once more
would be fulfillment enough. That's all she wanted from now
on, just to be with him. She even thought of canceling the Paris
trip…. Dr. Zastro cleared his throat, smiling broadly—that
wonderful, contagious smile. It was still magic, whatever it was
he possessed, whatever it was that he could spread throughout a
room to enter into the hearts of each lady present. He possessed
a special vitality few men were born with, and he knew innately
what to do with it.

"Good morning, ladies. I am so pleased to see you all looking so well, in your olive and emerald green gowns. This last week of our session. Miss Isobelle is excused for this lecture and Miss Althea is resting comfortably.

"I am happy to inform you, the sun is shining brightly today. Therefore, I am going to break with tradition and take you ladies outside of these walls. As a special surprise, we will go on our anticipated third week picnic this afternoon."

A picnic—where? To have to share him with others. Picnic—nothing could surpass that first nighttime picnic together in the Roof Garden....

"We will spend those golden hours on the banks of the Hudson River, arriving by carriage. As usual, I will be observing what healing effects the fresh air and sunshine will have upon your physique. I do not stop being a doctor just because I am outside of this building. I have tried, but it is not possible."

Always the doctor. Always. Would that forever dominate his life, his thinking, even his love?

"Let us hope that Miss Althea will be well enough to join our picnic. Miss Isobelle is already helping with the picnic lunch right now, putting together special delectable surprises—not our usual daily fare."

Thank heavens for that.

"We will also have a professional photographer along to take photos of each of you, and all of us together in the lovely pastoral setting. Thus, each of you will have a tangible memory of your days spent with this group. And you will note in the photographs, how especially well you looked this one memorable day in your recovery sojourn."

I need no photographs to refresh my memories. I don't want any photographs of you with anyone else either. I only want one photograph—our wedding. Me in Mama's traditional wedding gown, and you—if you consent—in the Gypsy folk wedding attire. What a great celebration that will be. What a festive striking picture. If only cameras took in the color with the image. I shall paint such an eminent portrait, you and I together, a piece of artwork that will endure forever locked into that one moment in time, the day we proclaim to each other, to the world, that our love will endure and that we shall remain faithful, keeping only unto each other—until death do us part.

Phillipe was at the blackboard, writing broadly as he spoke. "Our subject for today is: THE EFFECT THE MOTHER HAS ON THE UNBORN CHILD."

What about the father? What was his effect on the unborn child? Or did his influence only take effect after the birth? What effects from my father are still manifesting in me? My mother's turmoil during her pregnancy—had that been imprinted?

"Conception should not be allowed to take place without a preparatory season of abstinence from sexual indulgence in order that the procreative systems of both parties may be free from morbid excitability and exhaustion."

Morbid excitability? Excitability was never morbid.

"It should not occur when the muscular system is exhausted by overwork or exercise or for some time after eating, when the nervous forces are being largely employed by the digestive organs and consequently refuse to be sufficiently engrossed to perform the function of reproduction. The procreative organs are capable of best performing when the stomach is at rest and can lend its energies to the cause."

Did he still believe all this verbiage, or were they just memorized words he repeated year after year? Didn't the past week teach him that real passion was difficult to control as to time?

She believed in conception taking place whenever the heavens deemed it so—and the mates were right. No preparation, no prevention. When the time was appropriate, nature took over, planted the seed.

How would the two of them prepare to conceive their children? By reading a book beforehand? Listening to Phillipe discourse on scientific studies? Men were not equipped to deal with any of the aspects of childbirth. Women had inherited all of the necessary knowledge, imprinted in their bodies, and nature's wisdom superseded books.

"During the period of pregnancy, excessive sexual indulgence unduly develops, in the unborn child, the passion which leads so many young people to a destructive vice. Even amative excitement on the part of the mother, without indulgence, has a tendency to do this. She should avoid such food and drink that stimulate the amative impulse. When the impulse becomes strong—when the desire is so great as to take possession of the mind, it is then better that it should be gratified, lest the foetus be marked by this unsatisfied appetite, thereby producing the very evil sought to be avoided."

Had her mother not satisfied these urges while pregnant with her? Had this left Yana with this insatiable sexual appetite? However, she had also known women, whom after birthing children had no further sexual desires. What he was espousing made no sense. How could he dispense such unproven nonsense?

"Sleeping in separate beds may be advisable in some cases, to prevent the tendency to excitement by contact."

Delphine turned her head sharply, giving Yana a slow simpering smile and then began darting her tongue in and out of her mouth salaciously. At that moment Yana wanted to go forward and yank Delphine's braid so hard that her tongue would come out the back of her head along with the braid.

"Association with deformed people, or those having birthmarks, or diseases which cause unnatural manifestations and expressions, should be avoided as far as practical to avert the danger of marking the unborn child with any of these peculiarities."

She recalled hearing this before. Gypsies had so many admonitions for a woman with child, and even though far-fetched, most were still followed because there might be some bit of truth in each. That's how superstitions continued for so many generations, not because they were truth, but because there might be some bit of truth in them, and no one wanted to take the chance of testing the fates. Surely, their forebears knew something they didn't.

"Why are the effects of fright, or sudden emotions of the mind of the mother, thought to be daguerreotyped upon the body or mind of the unborn child? I must illustrate my theory again with the electro-magnetic telegraph, as with this instrument, almost everyone is familiar." He began sketching on the board as he spoke, his deft fingers moving across the paper, but alas for all his other talents, he was not very artistic. Still, the message was conveyed.

"Continuous currents of electricity along the telegraph wire are sometimes interfered with by the approach of a cloud charged with atmospheric electricity. When it comes in contact with the wire, it being a higher degree positive, its electricity darts both ways, effecting a break, driving the telegraphic current in opposite directions.

"As the cloud recedes from the wire, the telegraphic current resumes its path as if nothing had happened. But the strips of paper, on which the registers impress the messages, give evident marks of the shock. And instances have occurred in which telegraphic instruments were twisted in all manner of shapes."

He moved away from the board. Whatever he said always sounded so very convincing; he always provided understandable proof. It was true; he could make anyone believe whatever he wanted.

"Now, fright may make its impression on the growing foetus in obedience to the same electrical law. Sudden accumulation of the electrical forces of the nervous system in the brain, and a sudden propulsion to all parts of the system, including the uterus, cause a daguerreotype picture of the object that originated the fright or annoyance.

"A documented story— A countrywoman was watching a cow in an open field, when a violent storm arose. She took refuge under a tree, which, at that instant, was struck by lightning. The cow was killed and the woman felled to the ground, where she was soon found. Upon removing her clothing, they found the exact image of the cow killed by her side, distinctly impressed upon her bosom...."

There was the usual reaction from the women, many claiming they had also heard the story.

Just because a story was repeated again and again, did not make it more true.

"The mind of the mother should be kept tranquil and happy, free from sudden and disagreeable emotions of any kind—"

Screams from Isobelle shattered the rest of the sentence. She rushed into the room howling and sobbing. "Mine Gott— she is dead! She is dead!" Isobelle stood there stiff and unmoving.

Dr. Zastro rushed to her side, trying to shake her back to her senses. "Who? Who is dead?"

"Miss Althea! Oh mine Gott. Is blood all over—blood pushing out all over!"

"I must go to her." Dr. Zastro dashed out, leaving behind him a plethora of panicked confusion. The women grouped around Isobelle, who was still in shock.

"What happened?" Yana demanded, "Isobelle, tell us what happened."

"Scissors—was still in her stomach—Oh mine Gott. Blood—pushing out all over—like river of red."

"Althea—dead?" Delphine stood with her mouth open, repeating the words in disbelief.

"No. No." Mavis wailed in her former guttural timbre.

"God's laws have been violated," Edwina intoned. "May He have mercy on this place." She clasped her hands upward in supposition.

Delphine broke out into pathetic sobs, "Poor, poor child. Poor Althea." She ran from the room, her face buried in her hands.

"I must go lie down. I must go pray." Edwina left too.

"Mama, Mama—what is happening here?" Mavis circled as if not knowing which way to turn and then rotated out the door.

"Was anyone with her?" Yana demanded from Isobelle.

"No one. I went to take her tray with the food—Oh mine Gott." Isobelle broke down again.

Yana took her in her arms, holding Isobelle's huge moaning body, rocking her like a child. "It's all right. Dr. Zastro's with her now."

"Is too late. There she lay—gown—white sheets—soaked with blood. One hand on the scissors—other hand holding the note."

"Note? What note? Where is it? What does it say?"

" Don't know. Can't read. Here. I bring it for doctor. He leave too soon. You give him." She handed the bloodstained piece of paper from her apron pocket to Yana, anxious to rid herself of it. "I go—I go now." Isobelle bawled strange lamenting cries as she exited. The whole room was shocked into turmoil that bounced against the walls, floors, ceiling—a whirlpool of devastation that sucked everything up into it and then spat it out in scattered broken pieces.

Yana took the note and read it. The revealing words caused her to give out an anguished cry as she fell to the floor, chanting.

"Matin, chagrin, Soir, espok.... Matin, chagrin Soir, espok...."

She was kneeling now with her arms upraised.

"I am not from these parts;
I was not born here.
The wheel of fortune, spinning, spinning
Has brought me here...."

She crossed her arms over her head and collapsed in cataclysmic sobs.

CHAPTER 24

Yana locked the door of her room and wouldn't open it the rest of the day, no matter how hard anyone pounded or called. Throughout the morning and afternoon, excitement and turmoil filled the hallway—voices, continuous movement. Her body remained motionless, while within constant churning and clawing tore away at her insides until everything internal felt raw and bleeding.

Several times, she heard the doctor's pleading voice outside her door, "Yana, let me talk to you. Please, you must let me speak with you."

She couldn't answer him. Couldn't face him. If what Althea had written in her note was true, if what Delphine had said— She didn't want to believe any of it. Yet, if there was even a hint of truth...

Exhausted, she fell into a deep and numbing sleep. When she awoke, darkness covered her window; the hallway was quiet. An escalating urge to do something was surging within, an impetus to carry out some extraordinary act. She needed an expression of vast momentum, not to just lay inert.

What? What would obliterate this deepening anguish? This was one occasion she couldn't dance her pain away. Even screaming, letting everything rise up from her depths would not suffice, not this time. She remained stiff and silent.

Looking at the dimly outlined moon and stars she had painted on her window that first night seeking some illusion of escape—now it was flat and uninspiring, holding her into the room, rather than letting her out.

Painting—only that could exorcise this whole episode out of her system, rid her of this creeping repulsion before it ate everything away.

Hurriedly, she pulled down her paints from the vent. She needed a larger canvas, some greater area on which to discharge all this mayhem—space to work with expanding rage and momentum. She looked around—the linen sheet. She tore the covering from her bed, grabbed the paints and brushes, and clad only in her white chemise she hastened down the hallway. She paused only long enough to take the keys from Isobelle's apron pocket, hurried to unlock the Treatment Room door and closed it hard behind her.

Refuge. Solitude. Anywhere alone. When she turned on the pulsing lights, the first thing she saw—the Rocking Machine. Moving. Mocking. Gently swaying back and forth, as if Althea was still lying in it. She was positive she could see Althea's vapid form, or was it only her dead spirit hovering?

Don't look, don't dwell, do what you came to do.

She stretched the white linen sheet over the door of the Spectro Cabinet, catching the edges onto the frame. It made for a crude but workable canvas.

First, she sketched the outline of Althea's body in tremulous charcoal lines, a lifeless form stretched out on a single bed. Then, as if inspired, she took the jar of crimson paint and began to sketch a stream of blood flowing from Althea's middle that kept running, circling, moving in mazelike pathways across and around the whole sheet, flooding it with bizarre red arteries. As she painted, she felt her own blood draining away with the outflow of the paint.

Don't faint. Don't become weak. Now is the time when you must remain the strongest you have ever been. Her arm continued its movement, blindly sheathing everything in a coating of blood, layering it over and over, so the pure truth would be covered up, never seen—she didn't want the truth revealed—bury it deep into this river of red.

She was opening a drain hole to funnel everything into, and if it had been large enough, she would have crawled into it herself, followed it all the way down into the deepest bowels of the earth. The demons she would encounter there could not be any more tormenting than what she was going through right now.

Then she heard it, through the haze that surrounded her, his voice, softly calling, "Yana." She dismissed it as a voice in her head. She painted more furiously to drown out the call of her name.

"Yana—" He was there, or was it his spirit?

"Stay away from me!" she screamed to the specter in front of her. "Don't come near me."

As he materialized, she knew he was not the same man as this morning. He resembled those paintings of saintly martyrs, who after days of torture, appeared sallow and afflicted, yet bore a halo of beatific expression about them. It was as if they still were seeking some end to their affliction of continous pain, were still seeking relief that could come only from sanctification outside this world.

"Why won't you speak to me?" he asked in anguish.

She didn't answer. She couldn't. Her body might explode from the ferocity within.

"I need to speak with you." Tears brimmed from his reddened eyes. "My world has fallen apart—"

"You destroyed your own world," she accused, continuing painting.

He grabbed her wrist, halting the flow of crimson onto the sheet, making it trickle down her arm. She twisted out of his hold spewing, "Don't touch me."

"Why, why have you turned against me?"

"Because you took advantage of a helpless child."

"Althea? Never. I tried to cure her. I had no idea she would take her own life. I didn't know she even had such thoughts. This has never happened here before."

"And it will never happen again—with Althea—Delphine— Or with me."

"I have done nothing but try to help. All of you."

"Help? You destroyed Althea with all of your help."

"No."

She began slashing more red paint across the canvas.

"Look. Look." she spit the words out. "The red blood, draining her life away. That's what you did to her."

"Yana, stop."

"You almost had me believing that the two of us—" the agony was so great; she couldn't even continue the thought.

"I still love—"

"Love?" she cut him off. "It wasn't love. You, with your eyes, your words, your body. You were consuming me bit by bit until there would be nothing left of me."

"Never."

"You have to use every one of your patients for your own satisfaction, don't you? You couldn't even let her alone."

"You don't believe—" he reached out for her.

"Chavaia. Stop!" The words roared from her. "Keep away from me. I don't want you sucking the lifeblood out of me as you did her." With great violence, she began brushing red paint across his white lab coat. "What color does blood-red cure? What disease is healed by having blood splattered all over you? Does it kill the contagious malady of love?"

"Yana—"

"You mesmerized Althea, like you did every one of us, and then, when she couldn't help herself, you used her—"

"Oh God, you do not believe—"

"I—I can't even bear to look at you."

"But, I never—"

"You thought no one would find out, didn't you? You have such control over everything. But I know what took place." She took the note from her bosom. "It's all here, in her own handwriting."

"What are you talking—"

"Althea left a note. A blood covered note."

"Please, let me see it."

"No. I want you to hear it, so the words will be imprinted on your mind forever, as they have been carved into mine."

She had to sit down; she was feeling faint. Wavering, she sat in one of the nearby treatment chairs. Gathering her strength, she read the words, intending him pain and recrimination. It was as if she was reading a condemned man's indictment:

Dear Mama,

This is my last letter to you. It happened Mama. I know it happened. Doctor's medicine put me to sleep. When I woke up, a man's body was next to mine. I don't want an imbecile baby, Mama. It happens this way. I cannot go back to Arthur now.

Your gold scissors—they will kill the baby—kill myself.
Nowhere to go Mama, only to be with you.
  Althea

Phillipe reached for the note. Yana let it go, relieved to be rid of the soiled piece of paper. He read it again to himself, shaking his head in disbelief. "She could never sleep. Insanity often results from lack of sleep."

"So, you took advantage of her confused mind."

"Never."

"Who else then?" Yana accused.

"You don't believe—You can't—I never touched Althea. Not in any carnal manner."

"Someone did."

"Maybe no one. She had nightmares—dreams. She must have dreamed all this in her troubled mind." He was crying audibly now. It was heartbreaking to see this man weep. "But this I do admit, I did neglect her care—mostly because of my commitment to you."

"I don't want to hear any more. Excuses—"

"I never meant to neglect her. If only I had not gone away this weekend."

She had to ask, needed to know, even if she never saw him again. "Do you also deny sexual relations with Delphine too?"

"Delphine?"

"Yes."

"Delphine—she makes up stories, you know that. She always has. I treated her problems. Yes, sexual problems. Nothing more."

"You went to her room last session. She told me."

"Yes, I went to her room. She was disturbing the other patients at night. Calling out for Raphael all the time. I couldn't send him to her anymore. He refused to go. So, each night I went to her room and stayed with her until she calmed down and went to sleep."

"One whole week?"

"Yes, one whole week. That is what I promised her. I sat by her bed but never touched her. She begged me to—to alleviate her problem. I never did. Anything I may have done for her, was part of her treatment. Never anything else."

"And—those nights with me, were part of my treatment also? Part of your experimentation to see what electrical currents could be ignited between a scientist and an artist? Were you doing research for your new book about women and their sexual problems and decided to investigate unexplored areas, personally experience sexual practices so you could write about them more clearly, not allude to them secondhand?"

"How could you think—"

"Was Althea one of your firsthand case histories also? What a marvelous book this will be. Personal testimonies by the famous Dr. Zastro—the various ways different women react to his sexual stimulation."

"Stop, Yana, before you—"

Shyam's stricken voice interrupted their altercation. "Doctor? Doctor?"

"I must leave." She didn't wish to be there with the two of them, to hear any more heartache, or participate in any further discussion with Dr. Zastro or anyone else at this time.

"No. Go behind the screen," Phillipe pleaded. "I will send him away."

Confused, Yana slipped behind the gauze bath curtains, wishing she could disappear from this monstrous place forever.

"Doctor?" Shyam entered, frenzied and bewildered. "I could not find you. I could not sleep. I—you must help me."

"Shyam, I have told you, you must rest. You may have to help me tomorrow. I don't know what my strength will be by then. It is ebbing away." Phillipe stood near the doorway, trying to keep Shyam from entering further. "Go—take some asafetida pills. They will help you sleep."

Shyam did not move. "She is gone master. The fair one is gone." He wailed as a wounded animal.

"Yes, she is gone. Nothing will bring her back. Her mind was gone too. I should have tried some other treatment. I accept responsibility."

"Master, do not blame yourself."

"Who else? A doctor is responsible for each of his patients."

"Shyam is the guilty one."

"You showed her nothing but kindness. She left this note. It shows definite signs of mental derangement." Yana watched Shyam read it; his whole body trembled.

Shyam crushed the paper to his heart and began wailing anew. "Aiiee—Aiiee—it was aiiee—master," and he fell to the floor at Dr. Zastro's feet.

"You must get hold of yourself. Patients die. Sometimes there is nothing we can do."

"Aiiee—aiiee—I am the one who lay beside her." He banged his head against the floor.

"You?" Phillipe sputtered, first uncomprehending and then angry. He pulled Shyam to his feet. "You? You have betrayed everything you were ever taught."

"Demons overtook me, master. Alone with her, all that day, in her room, just she and I. Never had I gazed upon such beauty. Felt such soft skin—Aiiee—I could not restrain my love any longer."

"Love? You call that love. You are not fit to be in my company." He shoved Shyam away. His frail body fell across the painted sheet, flailing against it as he tried to regain his balance. He could not and dropped to his knees.

"I only lay beside her, nothing else." Shyam sobbed into the splattered cloth.

Phillipe pulled him away. "Pack your things. You will leave here, first thing in the morning."

"Where shall I go, master?"

"Away from here, because I never want to see your face again. Do you understand?"

Shyam continued his unearthly wailing as he stumbled out of the room, his anguished cries tearing away at the protecting walls Yana had built around her heart. Numbly, she emerged from behind the curtain.

"Shyam," she said softly. "Why didn't I realize—I am so sorry."

"I cannot comprehend. I am too stunned. I could not believe—Two blows in one day." Phillipe was not even looking at her, just staring straight ahead.

"He loved her," she said with deep conviction.

"That was no reason—"

"Did you expect him to react only as one of your machines—a robot, without feelings of his own?"

"If one is to be a good doctor, passions must be controlled."

"And could you control yours when you were with me?"

"No," he admitted, turning away. "I am no longer able to call myself a good doctor."

"This place," she said, gazing at all the curious machines, "it does strange things to people. It even made me believe that you might—that you and Althea—"

"Nothing can undo what has already happened. The burden of blame rests upon me." He was walking about the room now. "I prescribed the pills for Althea, every night this past week. It was the quickest method, to make sure she would be quiet throughout the night. Then I could be with you, undisturbed. They helped confuse her mind.

"I left Shyam in charge this weekend, so I could selfishly get away, to avoid temptation. Shyam was not capable, not trained sufficiently, to take on such responsibility, weakened by the burden." He paused, looking up, "I put my personal pleasures ahead of my doctor's duties. I have defiled my sacred oath." Eyes brimming, he reached out his trembling hand to hers, "I would still do it all over again. For you—I would do anything."

She didn't know how to react. A terrible struggle was battling within.

"Please, let me hold you," he begged. "That is all I ask. Nothing more."

She almost yielded, needing his comforting arms about her. Something resolute within kept her unpliable. Backing away as she spoke, "No. Then I'd be back in your power again. I have loosed all such connections, cut away the linking heartstrings."

"Power? I no longer have any power left within me. Everything is dissipated."

"That may be true," she said, "but tomorrow it will be back. And when that happens, I know nothing can, nothing must, return to as it was before."

"Whether my power returns or not, I can do nothing about it. I was born this way. Even as a child, I had this special gift. I don't know how I got it. I don't know how to get rid of it. All I have ever done was try to use it the best way I can." He faced her, beseeching, "Yana, do not ever come to me because of my power—come to me, only because you love me."

She did love him. She wanted to wrap her arms around his suffering body, absorb his burdens, his anguish, and crush them all to her in a punishing cloak of piercing nettles. Instead, she began tearing down the sheet, any movement to keep herself away from him.

"I can no longer remain in your presence and think rationally. I must escape, before it is too late."

"Do not leave—"

"This magnet, this drawing power you have, even as weak as you are now, I still find it hard to resist. I don't want to be held captive anymore, by anyone, willingly or unknowingly." She picked up the sheet, art supplies and rushed from the room.

He ran after her, calling, "Yana!" reaching for her, but only grabbing onto the painted red sheet, pulling it from her, muffling his face into it with sobs.

Yana ran as if wild dogs were pursuing her. She sought refuge, safety in her room—slamming the door, locking it behind her. She was gasping for breath, leaning against the door with all her strength, trying to keep out everything that was pushing in from the other side, whatever it was, from attacking her.

The room was dim, still she saw it lying on the floor where she had thrown it in anger that morning, gleaming like a twisting snake, her mother's golden necklace.

She gathered the shimmering keepsake from the floor, needing to connect physically with its comforting presence. Something permanent, tangible, a golden anchor in this frightful storm, a connecting link welded across generations, forever binding her to Mama and Grandmama in a mystical chain that time could never unloose.

Yana pressed the cherished heirloom close to her heart, crushing it deeper into her bosom with all the strength that was left in her. The metal was cold, sharp, cutting painfully into her flesh. Still she kept pressing, asking herself over and over, *"Why must everything I love cause such suffering?"*

CHAPTER 25

Shyam did not wake them the next morning. It was Nurse Tillotson who knocked on Yana's door.

Had it all been a bad dream? Had the whole episode really taken place?

Inside Yana's head, a leaden crystal ball was rolling back and forth, but she was never able to stop it long enough to capture what it was trying to reveal. By sheer force of will she got out of bed. *How would they be able to go through any kind of routine today?*

Once she opened her door, she realized the normal day was already altered. Lined up in front of each room were the wicker baskets with their names on them. Their sight brought flickering memories of the first day.

Nurse Tillotson was standing in the hallway, arms folded, telling each as they came out, "Please, put on your original clothing from your basket, before you meet for breakfast. There will be no morning exercises. Please, meet in the Lecture Room following breakfast."

Yana went to the washroom without speaking to anyone. Everything was being carried out in great haste and immense silence. On returning to her room, Yana took her wicker basket and dumped all her clothing along with her other belongings onto the bed. There was little joy in seeing them this time. The flowered fringed shawl that had been her partner in so many wild dances—now limp and wilted. Framed pictures of Mama and Grandmama with mocking smiles. *I told you so,* echoing from each. Then in an overlapping of their voices: *Love brings its own burdens, its own downfall. Once a fragile treasure is broken, you cannot piece it together again, the cracks will still show.*

Layer by layer, Yana put on the clothing she came here with—leather sandals, jewelry. Everything felt heavier. Or was it her heart that was weighted?

Breakfast was silent, solemn. The missing voice of Shyam reading from the doctor's book was an audible reminder of how much their safe little world had changed. Most ate very little. Even Isobelle sat mutely, looking down, not touching her food. Clad in their original street clothes, the women had regained their different positions in the strata of society. They acted once more as strangers.

"Why do you think they gave us our own clothes back?" Mavis whispered, sounding afraid to know the answer.

"Well, we're not going on any picnic today," Delphine simpered, "nor any other day." Her braid was gone, but no curls replaced it, just limp rope-like locks.

"The doctor will announce his plans," Edwina advised, speaking to them as children, "when he meets with us."

"They don't even want me in kitchen today," Isobelle lamented, as if abandoned by everyone. "Nowheres to go."

One by one, they got up from the table and went to the Lecture Room. They sat restlessly, awaiting Dr. Zastro. Had it been only a little over two weeks since they congregated the very first time in this same room, in these same clothes? Even as downcast as they all appeared, there was still a certain healthy glow about them. Their eyes appeared more alert. Better posture. Yes, good things had been happening to them, and now it was all going to be taken away, before the completion, that final absolution.

It was disconcerting to see Shyam's stool vacant. Althea's chair never appeared emptier. Again, Yana saw Althea's entity hovering above, and the words from the note floated out once more. All night long, those words had sounded through Yana's head until she put her hands over her ears, repeating, one after another, litanies of protecting chants.

Finally, Dr. Zastro entered. Even in his dissipated state, Yana sensed the electricity still sparked within. The ladies alerted themselves, so sure he had some answer for each of them. The doctor was always the rescuer, helper in their distress.

Yana wasn't clear about her own feelings this morning. She was still trying to sort them out, without much luck yet in finding clarity. She didn't hate Phillipe, but she wasn't sure about her sentiments of love. She was certain only that there was a great void within her, waiting to be filled, knowing she could not do it herself.

The doctor was not wearing his usual lab coat; instead, he was dressed in a dark suit, white shirt and black tie. The power was still there, only, it wasn't turned on.

"Good morning, ladies," he tried a half smile. "You all appear so different this morning." Forcing a broader smile. "I hardly recognize you. I don't know if you welcome your old clothes back or not," he cleared his throat, "but, we are not here this morning to talk about clothes or health." He looked out over them.

"A great tragedy has taken place in our Sanitarium. We will try not to dwell on it, as we are still trying to sort out the reasons. However, I have come to the conclusion, and not without a great deal of soul-searching, that because of all that has happened, I can no longer carry out my medical duties. I no longer have the reserve strength needed to effect cures for each of you."

Small cries of "Oh no." emitted in sporadic despair from the women. Their wonderful doctor—not able to cure. It was as if their worlds, all they had come to believe in, had just collapsed, leaving no hope for them whatsoever.

"So, you are all being dismissed several days early, as we are closing down the Sanitarium." More protesting cries sounded from the ladies.

"Refunds will be sent to your homes. Most of you are already cured, or in the late stages of healing. I will try to send medications along with you, also instructions, later, in the mails." He took a long deep breath. "I don't know when my Sanitarium will open again, if ever."

"No. Is not true!" Isobelle cried out.

"You can't close the Sanitarium," Delphine objected.

"I cannot explain my reasons for this action. I'm not sure of all of them myself. This I know to be true, above all else: a doctor must use all his energies to effect cures. I can no longer do this. At this point, I do not know whether my private practice will resume either."

He walked about a bit without speaking, and then composed himself at the lectern. "Now, I want to take a few moments for us to remember our sister, Althea. Her family has requested that her body be returned to her home for the funeral services, and asked that she not be displayed here. Nurse Tillotson has the family address, should any of you wish to send condolence cards."

He struggled to forestall his own emotions. "I will inform you as best I can. I want to dispel rumors that have been circulating with what I know to be true. This frail young woman suffered from a very special disease, one of the mind, which are always the hardest to diagnose and the most difficult to cure. She could not bear for a man to touch her. She believed one did and could not live with that knowledge. Instead, she chose to die."

He was near the breaking point, Yana could tell by the quivering in his words, the deep breaths he was taking.

"Maybe someday there will be ways of reaching inside people's minds, helping them overcome these abnormal fears. I tried. I failed in the short time she was here." He paused, searching for words.

"Life is the most precious gift we have. Sharing life is the greatest sacrifice we can give. Althea could not do that. Althea could not even share another's touch. So, she isolated herself into her own little world, withdrawing tighter and tighter into the protecting cocoon she was spinning about herself, until neither I, nor any of my treatment could reach her." He looked at them, beseeching. "If any among you are withdrawing from human life, human contact, cease spinning those life threatening cocoons about yourselves. If you keep going within, never reaching out, you can only arrive at a dead end, with nowhere else to go."

Then a slight spark of hope arose in his voice. "But, if you reach out, in some way, there is the whole world, the universe you can touch, if you will only but try." He extended his hands. "Please come forward now. We will form a circle."

He came down to meet the group in front of the platform, reaching out for Yana's hand. "Let us join hands." His touch was soothing. Delphine took his other hand. "Let us bow our heads in silence for a few moments and remember our dear departed sister, Althea."

The sense of being as one was immediate and intense. They were more united in pain than they had been in their collective search for Dr. Zastro's cures. Pain was traveling between them, among them, a deep, deep sorrow, that circled and recircled, filling the room with grief, sobs spreading from one to another, echoing the pain.

It was Delphine who began singing, in a pure and lovely voice.

Soft as the voice of an angel—
Breathing a lesson unheard.

Edwina joined in loud church choir resonance.

Hope, with her gentle persuasion
Whispers a comforting word.

Soon all were singing, one strong voice asking for hope and guidance from beyond this earth. The voice of an angel—the voice of Althea herself.

Whispering Hope, Oh how welcome thy voice,
Making my heart—in its sorrow rejoice.

A long moment of silence followed. They still held hands as if the circle had become a welded chain.

Dr. Zastro, his voice quaking, said, "Go now; return to your homes. The staff will help you with your arrangements. May God's peace be with you. With all of us."

He broke the circle and turned away to hide his tears, stifle his sobs. They knew not to disturb him, dispersing slowly.

"He is crying. Such a good man. Such a good, good man." Isobelle was wiping her wet eyes with her thick clean shawl.

Delphine began lamenting protests as she turned to leave. "He can't— he can't close down this Sanitarium. Where will I go? How will I see him again?"

Mavis, still bewildered by everything, said forlornly, as if speaking for all, "What is going to happen to us, what will we do—without doctor's help?"

Edwina echoed their thoughts, "He reached every one of us, didn't he?"

Yana stood motionless, watching them exit. She was not ready to leave the room yet. She didn't know why she was staying, only that she must.

After a while, Phillipe lifted his head, surprised to see her still there.

"Don't close the Sanitarium." The words were chosen for her.

"I am no longer capable of running it," he answered.

At that moment, she cared more about this man—more than she cared about her own self. What would happen to him if he gave all this up? His pain engulfed her. Medicine was his life. "You are more capable, than anyone I know, to continue in the medical profession. You have this rare genius for healing people. I didn't believe it at first. I do now. It is one of life's truths."

"I no longer have whatever I once possessed," he said.

"I have seen women come here, frightened, suffering. You cared about them, were concerned for them, their whole being. You and your strange machines—you helped these women, when no one else was willing. Your Sanitarium is one of the few places women can go to for comfort and help."

"Thank you for telling me this. It makes all the years worthwhile. But, it is too late. I cannot continue." Agony blanketed his face.

"You are overwrought. We all are. Do not make such a major decision so hastily. Take your time—days, maybe weeks."

"It has already been decided."

"What will you do then, with all your skills and wonderful knowledge? You cannot waste such talents."

"I do not know...." There was great sadness, almost despair, welling in his voice. "For the first time, I do not know what I will be doing tomorrow, or the next day. My life stretches out into a vast unknown."

She looked at him. She needed to guide his thinking back toward hope. "If you do not know what tomorrow will bring, then possibly for the first time, you are truly free."

"Free?" It was both a laugh and a cry. "I am not an artist who can live with such freedom. I am no longer a doctor who is restricted by schedules. I am—nothing."

"You are you. A very special human being. That's all you need to be." She might decide to leave him but she couldn't leave him in the state he was in now. She had to give him some sense of a future. His life had to have some meaning, some purpose, to keep him from even deeper despair. Words were all she could offer right now.

"Dr. Phillipe Zastro, that's who I am," he said, "a human being who existed on the planet earth for a short span of time— who dedicated his life to the problems of women and pioneered in the use of electrical healing. Thought he had found answers, but was only left with more questions."

"But you existed. That in itself is a miracle. Do you know how very few souls are chosen to live a life on this earth?"

"No, the greatest miracle was loving you," he said. "Now, I don't even have that."

"That is not true."

"You are leaving me."

"For the moment. I feel it is best. I have made no final decisions." She knew she couldn't resolve anything, not at this time, not here. "This I have decided—I will go into the city today, find a quiet spot, somewhere in Central Park, perhaps, among the trees and birds, and search for an answer. It must be an answer I hear within myself, away from you, away from this place. I have not been outside these walls since I met you. I need to do this, but it does not mean I have abandoned you."

Why was she having such a difficult time telling him what she had already rehearsed in her mind, when all she wanted to do was throw her arms around him and cover him with consoling kisses, gather up all his pain and launch it to the winds.

"And I will have no say in your decision making?" he asked.

"No, because I do not want your influence. I already know what you might say."

"How can you, when I don't even know myself. I only know I want to convince you, in any way I can, that I still need you. And that I only want you to stay, because you love me. I have nothing else to offer you now, but love."

"I have never stopped loving you."

"Then why? Why?" He reached out for her. She got up and walked away from him.

"Strange things have happened to me in this Santarium," she said. "I have fallen in love. My body's been cured. My mind turned on to new paths. That is why I must get away, see if all this still holds true, once I am not within these confines."

"I cannot bear any more pain," he pleaded. "To know I might lose you forever is the most unbearable thought."

"What we had together will never be lost."

"Without you, I shall be a withered man, a ghost of the past living in the present."

"*Mandi kom*, my love, listen to me. Love must be like the blowing wind, fresh and invigorating. Capture the wind within the walls and it becomes stale. Open tents. Open hearts. Let the wind blow free. Let our love be unfettered and take us wherever it will." She had always believed this; she must continue believing it.

Nurse Tillotson came into the room, "I'm sorry to disturb you, Dr. Zastro, but Althea's family is here."

His face became ashen pale. Yana knew he dreaded facing the assemblage in the downstairs reception room.

"Do you want me to go with you?" she asked.

Gratitude for this gesture brought back some color. "Thank you, but this is something I must do on my own."

"I will leave then," she said, "and return this evening. By then—I don't know." She turned to depart.

He grabbed her arm. She pulled away, "Don't."

"Please," he said, "I only want to say this, if you return, come in by the main entrance. The Sanitarium outside entrance door will be locked." He straightened his shoulders and walked past her to meet Althea's family.

Yana looked about the Lecture Room. Would this be the last time she would be here? She didn't know that answer. She gathered it all in, then walked through the other rooms that were still open. The special rooms that held memories of her and

Phillipe, the recall in each, so vivid, so graphic, it glossed everything else away. *Leave them here,* she cried inwardly. *Don't take anything with you to subjugate your decision this afternoon. Leave, now, immediately!*

To insure her return, she left her packed valises with all she held dear on her bed.

Nurse Tillotson let her out.

"I will be back this evening to pick up my things," Yana said.

"But—" Nurse Tillotson started to argue.

"It's all right. The doctor has asked me to return." She went down the winding stairway, past the admissions desk, and out the same door that she had entered only fifteen days earlier.

The world outside was altered. Her spirit inside so disarranged it might never come together again.

CHAPTER 26

Yana took the streetcar to Central Park. The noisy congested city was disconcerting. So many unknowns surrounding her, closing in on her. The thought of going to Paris must also be part of her considerations.

Paris-- it was also a bustling metropolis, but the bohemian atmosphere gave it a certain *joi de vivre*. Parisian buildings and environment were artistic and historic. Also, she knew her way around, having strolled the banks of the Seine daily. She'd spent time among the artists and writers, conversing at their bookstalls or sitting in the sidewalk cafes, evoking creativity just being in their presence.

Here, everyone seemed a stranger. Most people on the streetcar were speaking in foreign tongues, making her feel stranded midst aliens. She was also aware some were pointing to her, the word "Gypsy" murmured. Mothers pulled their children closer, and men gave her bold penetrating stares.

She averted their looks, gazing out the window. All she could view were tall buildings, some being newly constructed, filling in huge empty holes, others being torn down. How could people live so high up, so far from the earth, suspended in boxes in the sky, removed from grass and greenery? Many of the towering structures blocked out the sun completely. How could sunlight or fresh breezes even reach inside those brick prisons?

The aromas from restaurants, windows open to cool off kitchens, wafted past her in strangely mixed smells. The streetcar was crowded, those hanging onto the straps crushing into her with each stop. All she wanted was to get away from people and be by herself.

Finally, the conductor called, "Fifty Sixth Street!" This was where Nurse Tillotson had said she should get off. She pushed her way to the exit door, so afraid she might be trapped inside this car past her destination, sentenced to ride on it forever as a punishment for all her sins.

Back on solid ground once more. Yana watched as the shuddering streetcar clanged into the distance. People bustled past her, all in a great hurry to get somewhere. Where? What was so important when they got there?

Then she saw it, looming before her, in all its green majesty—Central Park. An emerald oasis of vegetation and quiet in the midst of all the drab turmoil.

People were scurrying on ahead to reach the entrance. Once there, they rushed along the pathways inside. Some sped by on those peculiar looking bicycles, with one huge gigantic wheel and one tiny one, looking as if nothing but faith was holding them up. Did you have to believe, in order to make those vehicles stay upright? She was convinced horses were the only way to travel. The spirit of the horse was attuned over the ages to inner human commands.

Once in the park, she followed the path leisurely, strolling, not knowing where it would take her, not caring, as long as it kept her within this uplifting acreage. Gypsies mostly roamed, without any specific destination. If they felt the place was right, they stopped. Maybe for a day, maybe for the season. The only time they had a definite destination was when they were being chased, and then their only directives were to get away.

There were also certain times the tribes congregated at mandated places, for traditional festivals, or when one of their own was dying. Gypsies must not die alone, the worst of fates, and kinfolk came from near and far to gather at the bedside for the sometimes long death watch. Would she die alone, no one to mourn her? It didn't matter, all those old customs, she didn't belong to the tribe anymore—her harbored fears of dying alone should have been banished from her thoughts long ago.

It was so refreshing, invigorating to be in the midst of this wonderfully carved out cache of nature, this beautiful woodland flourishing in the heart of New York City. A pristine expanse of land that belonged to all the people. Anyone could claim a space, as compared with those opulent gardens reserved only for the rich—fenced and hoarded. Gypsies believed all land under their feet was their own. They loved the world and all nature was their fatherland. They also believed fields and forests had their own spirits, and when one was in their midst these spirits communicated with your own.

Gratefully she gathered it all in, through eyes, breath, scent, even the pores of her skin. Still, a saddened thought crept in beside the joy: how long would this area be preserved in this natural state?   Probably not too long, remembering all the structures being erected nearby.   Someday, would this too vanish—would tall buildings bleakly shade, where breathing trees once stood?   What would New York do without such a blessed sanctuary for its common people?   How would they survive without some touchstone to nature?

There were benches scattered along the pathway. Lovers, sitting close, holding hands. She hurried by, not wanting to intrude on their privacy, or be reminded she was alone. Near the lagoon, she found a spot, as if she had been directed there. Settling on the thick soft grass, her hands reached down to feel the velvety texture between her fingers, probing deeper, making closer contact with the rich living earth. All of a sudden, there was connection again, and this feeling of being tossed about evaporated.

The bright sun mirrored on the shining blueness of the peaceful lagoon. Beautiful white swans were gliding by, and in the distance, canoes floated serenely with parasoled occupants. Near the shore, small boys were launching assorted sailboats, their playful laughter ringing out. White-uniformed nursemaids cautioned them in accented voices. The exuberance of youth reined in by the caution of age.

Had she lost that, her exuberance, her cavalier attitude toward daily life, allowing existence to happen without the worry of plans—tomorrow.

Had she changed that much in these few weeks that she needed the days laid out, scheduled?   Had she really been looking ahead to some happy ending, that was only true in fairy tales?

Gypsies lived from day-to-day, welcoming uncertainty. Sudden changes from comfort to discomfort were essential for a healthy life. It resulted in a deep sense of self-reliance. But now that she had sampled euphoria, she didn't know if she could let it go that easily, wanting to hold onto it for as long as possible.

Release it; Yana, told herself. *Let it all remain here in this congested city filled with so many tangled emotions. Do not take it away with you, where it will age and fray and shred. Tell Phillipe good-bye and be on your way to Paris and then back to your land. Your life is not empty without him. You have your painting, your freedom, and you will always have your memories. Do you still need more?*

Whatever she would do, wherever she would go, she knew she could never recapture life as she had lived it before she came to the Sanitarium. That kind of existence would never satisfy anymore, not in the same way. She had reveled in knowing another human being, sharing that person's body, spirit, and loving him with all her heart. Only a fool would discard such a valuable gift so readily.

She lay on the grass, immersing her whole body into the earth, hearing the rhythms of the ground moving beneath. As children, they would take off their clothes and roll themselves around in the grass, feel its feathery coolness against their naked skin. Sometimes she did this at home. As much as she wanted to now, surely, she could not indulge herself in this public park.

Birds were chirping everywhere, squirrels scampering, children calling. The soft steady lapping of the water, where it met the land and receded again, was playing an endless game with the pond, harmonizing with the rustling leaves. All of these sounds, and still Phillipe's voice kept intruding. *Stay with me, Yana. Marry me, Yana. We will be together Yana, for all time.*

She drifted into semi-sleep. Unguarded, Grandmama was soon beside her, towering above her. This time there were no threats, no proclamations of doom. All she said was, *"What will be, will be"* as if neither of them had control over what would take place. Then she heard Grandmama repeat, as she had so many times before, *Death is the worst of fates, a senseless unnatural occurrence. Life is the only worthwhile tribulation. Do not worry about anything but death.*

She didn't know how long she slept, but a sharp crack of thunder startled her awake. What had once been a sunny blue sky was now crowded with dark rolling clouds, punctuated by brilliant flashes of lightning, opening vast caverns of illumination into the churning heavens above.

Would she ever see lightning again and not be reminded of Phillipe and his expounding on electricity? That was what made him so intriguing, his unique interest in the unknown. That soared him away from the ordinary, making her want to know the depths of his persona, the secrets within his unusual inquiring mind.

Rain soon began falling in heavy pellet-like drops. Children and nursemaids ran scurrying and screaming in all directions. Yana found a bench under a large sheltering tree and sat there absorbed in watching the battles of nature play themselves out.

Tree branches were swaying in gigantic turbulent dances. Streaks of jagged lightning rocketed across the sky. Thunderbolts exploded, shaking her body, rattling the whole earth. Storms captivated but never frightened her. These outbursts from the heavens were only a swifter pace of nature, showcased in the grand theatre of the sky. The vast power of the universe revealed in dynamic displays of forceful glory.

She arched her head, welcoming the rain as it washed across her face, cleansing her skin, purging her thoughts. Soon her garments were soaked, her hair dripping, and she had this radical impulse to get up and join in the melee, swirl about in this special cascading gift from nature.

Anyone watching would think she was a madwoman, if she danced about in this massive storm. Looking around, Yana realized she was alone; the whole area had emptied out. First, she discarded her sandals and went forth into the open space and spun about on the wet grass, rain showering all around her, lightning and thunder accompanying her speeding movements.

Grandmama, I am living. I am participating in all events in this magnificent world.

She twirled and twirled, near the lagoon and away from it, laughing, shouting, a child delighting in its first rain; she was a Whirling Dervish spinning for answers; finally, she sank into a sitting position, lifting her face to the skies, tongue extended to catch the refreshing droplets, letting her entire body partake in this bestowal from the cosmos.

Grandmama, I am not running away from what is greater than I am. I've come to meet it, revel in whatever turbulence this day brings.

Impetuously, she took off her blouse, throwing it aside. Extending her arms outward, she let the rain fall in staccato beats against her bare breasts, drip from their aroused points, and wash across the rest of her naked torso, seeping downward between her legs in rivulets of cold moisture.

Her hair became a special waterfall splashing onto Mama's necklace, washing over her breasts. Wild ecstasy prevailed within and around her, and oh, how she wished Phillipe might be there to share it with her, make passionate love in this woodland setting, midst the violence of untamed nature.

She rose, cupping her wet breasts, offering them up to the rain gods, letting out a boisterous cry, "Phillipe! Phillipe!" she echoed across the lagoon. "I love you. I love life. I love the challenges. I love the pain. I love—Existing!" She was calling out to him as if he could hear her clear across New York City.

Suddenly he was there beside her.

The yearning within rose up so strongly, there wasn't time to halt. Lifting her skirts, she ardently wrapped her arms around a slender nearby tree trunk, and with wanton abandon, began rubbing her damp undergarments, yielding thighs, against the slippery rough bark, faster and faster. The rustling leaves forming a protective umbrella above as her nails dug into the pulpy wet tree skin below—searching, frantic with passion for some trace of Phillipe's answering ardor. With a loud cry of release, as lightning flashed and thunder roared, the tumult within her exploded, shaking her violently as she collapsed into a moaning heap at the foot of the tree, her body still pulsating and her arms still clinging to the unyielding trunk.

"Phillipe—Phillipe," she moaned. But he was no longer there.

The storm was slowing, quieting, moving into the distance as the rain receded into pittering drops. Languid, she arose, wringing her hair dry, swooshing her blouse around in the air to release some of the water, all in slow motion.

She was fulfilled. Drunk with the power of the day. The answer had come to her—*Run away from nothing. Welcome each tribulation, each day, with great anticipation, no matter what it brings.*

Then she heard it, the distant howling of a dog; it grew louder, closer. An old fear resurrected, bringing shivers to her wet skin. The howling of the dog—it was a sign of death. Whose death? Althea's? Who?

She gathered up her blouse and sandals, yanking them on, her skirt still dripping. She must hurry back to the Sanitarium.

Yana stood on the crowded streetcar, clinging to the swaying strap, clothes damp and heavy, hair wet and matted. She felt drowned, clutching for air, oblivious to those around her this time, only this strong sense of urgency to get back to Phillipe before it was too late.

The sun never reappeared and evening dusk was taking over when she reached the Sanitarium. Out of breath, she rang the bell at the front entrance. Miss Davidson answered the door. "I'm sorry, the doctor's offices are closed for the day," she said, trying to shut the huge door.

Yana kept her foot in the doorway. "I am a patient in the Sanitarium for women," she said loudly.

"The Sanitarium is closed also."

"But, Dr. Zastro asked that I return—"

Nurse Tillotson soon appeared, seemingly disturbed, but let Yana into the reception area.

"Miss Kejako, your bags are down here," she said, pointing to the valises in a corner. "There is no need for you to go upstairs."

"But, I must see Dr. Zastro," Yana protested.

"That is not possible, he wishes to see no one."

With all her remaining strength, Yana pushed past Nurse Tillotson, running up the winding stairway, stopping at the door: SANITARIUM FOR WOMEN —DO NOT ENTER!

Yana pushed the door open forcefully, closing and locking it behind her so that Nurse Tillotson could not follow. Already she was pounding on the door. "Miss Kejako. Unlock this door."

She must hurry and find Phillipe. She went to his office first—empty. His bedroom—empty. Maybe he wasn't even up here. Maybe he was downstairs somewhere—hiding in his basement.

She ran down the hallway toward the Treatment Room and heard harsh clanging sounds coming from within. With a new burst of energy, she threw open the door. There he was, an ax in his hand, viciously destroying his machines, which were all turned on, moving, sounding in a thunderous din of discord. So intent was he on his mission of destruction, he did not even notice Yana enter.

"What are you doing?" she screamed.

Then he turned and looked at her. His face was ashen, his spirit destroyed, a rampant viciousness about his person as if he were being consumed by madness. He continued his fierce destructive strokes.

"What are you doing?" she repeated.

"Destroying them." His voice was lifeless.

"Why?" She went about turning off the machines. Many were already broken, lying in shattered pieces on the floor. He continued bashing even the broken ones.

"Why are you destroying your machines?"

"Because they have turned on me," he said. The multiple noises began stopping. He stood staring vacantly ahead.

She went to him, gently taking the ax away. There was no resistance, as if he were grateful to be saved from any further destruction. She reached out for him, gathering him to her. He broke down in great heaving sobs against her damp shoulder.

She guided his pain-wracked body to the bench and sat holding him, as he continued his convulsive sobs. Then in broken words, he told her.

"Shyam—I found him—this afternoon. In the Electric Shock Machine."

"Oh no."

"It was still sparking. Safety release off. He—he was still twitching. His strapped-in body, still thrashing about. It was the most horrible sight I have seen in my life."

"Shyam?"

"Yes, he's dead. Electrocuted. In one of my machines. It's as if I killed him myself."

"He did this, because of his guilt."

"No—because of what I did to him. I sent him away, with nowhere to go. I treated him like an animal. What other choice did he have?"

"You did not know."

"I showed no compassion for his dilemma. I am as cold as these machines, without feeling for my fellow human being. I have taken on their nature."

"That is not true."

"I do not want these machines destroying anyone else. Even if I leave here—they must not remain."

"Phillipe, listen to me. I want to stay here with you. I've come to that decision." She wasn't sure if he was comprehending or not, but she had to tell him now, in his time of greatest need. "I love you, no matter what happens. And I will always be with you."

"You can't—You can't stay," he said.

"You cannot face this alone."

"I've called the authorities, they will be here soon. I don't want you present, involved in any of the questioning."

"Why? Why the authorities?"

"There have been two deaths here, in two days. All deaths must be reported to the authorities. Unorthodox deaths are investigated. Althea's death has already been ruled a suicide by the examiners. Shyam's electric death is sure to be investigated more thoroughly. He left no note. I may even be charged with murder."

"Murder? You?"

"Yes, me. And I could very well be guilty."

"Then you cannot face them alone." Never before had she felt more empathy for another. It was welling up so strongly, overtaking her. She wanted to endure for herself any sufferings

Phillipe was going through right now, or in the future, serve his years in prison if need be. She had the stamina for such things. He didn't.

"Yana, listen to me, and do not interrupt, there isn't time— Once they arrive, I may be arraigned and taken away. I must tell you all this, now."

"Tell me then. But first, let me tell you, once and for all," she spoke the words as never before, "I love you Phillipe, and I will do anything you ask of me."

"Then you must do this, without question. You must go to Paris. You must never contact me, or write me. I need to go through this alone. That will be the only way to cleanse myself of the guilt." He looked at her tenderly. "My love for you is so strong, nothing will ever destroy it. It will survive any ordeal."

"You can't do this," she began crying, when she wanted so desperately to remain the strong one. "You can't close me out now, not when we both need one another more than we ever have before. Love is not only for the wonderful times, it is for better or for worse, until—"

"Stop," he shouted and then more composed, "whatever they decide—I must accept. I promise you that I will do everything within my power, do whatever needs to be done in order that I may see you again. That is the only thing that will give me hope, keep me surviving."

"Don't banish me too."

"After it is all over—whenever that is, then I will write to you, but not until then, and make preparations to come to you, if you will still have me."

"No," she wailed. "You cannot do this."

"I promise you, someday, I will find you, come to you."

"You cannot send me away."

"If I should be locked up, I do not want you visiting me. Each of us trying to reach through the bars, seeing the agony in your face, knowing you suffer every pain as I do."

"Don't make me serve a prison term too. That is what you are sentencing me to, if I am to be without you." Her cries were uncontrollable.

Then she heard it, the pounding on the Treatment Room door.

"Go out the back entrance," he said. "I left it open to the outside."

"Authorities! Open up, Dr. Dr. Zastro!"

She took his hands, pleading with all her heart. "Come with me, Phillipe. Come. We can escape together. Now. Go to Europe—anywhere. They'll never find us. We can be together, anywhere on this earth, never apart again."

He tore his hands away. "No. I must face this—Now. Alone."

The pounding grew fiercer.

She threw her arms around him. "Phillipe, *mandi kom*—my love."

"Yana, Yana." He held her so very close, she thought he might relent, but instead he pushed her toward the back door.

She began resisting, fighting him. "Do not push me out of your life," she pleaded.

He continued his propelling force, but not as strongly, as if he wanted to prolong the moment. "I promise—I will see your face the first thing every morning, the last thought every night, wherever I am."

"Nooo—"

"Wait—for my letter, no matter how long."

She heard them crashing through the other door, as Phillipe shoved her into the hallway, forcefully shutting and locking the door behind her, and she knew it was no use trying to get back in.

She crumpled to the floor. Numb. Hearing harsh muffled voices on the other side of the wall. And then everything was silent.

Time evaporated, sucking her into the void behind it only to spit her out on the other side of this moment, twisted her into a writhing mass. Somehow, she made her way down the darkened stairway and found herself outside in the damp cold night air. The police wagon was leaving, the steady clop of the horses' hooves fading into the vague distance. Phillipe was gone. She did not know if she would ever see him again or not.

Mama—She screamed inwardly—*Death is not the worst of fates!*

CHAPTER 27

Yana did not go to Paris. She returned home, and once there had no desire to go anywhere, least of all festive Paris.

Time travel swiftly. Devour these days, minutes, seconds, until I might be with Phillipe once more.

That flickering hope was the only thing that kept her breathing, somehow living, which wasn't really living, only inhalation and exhalation of unceasing pain. She was more alone now than ever. Grandmama and Mama had abandoned her. Silent days. Silent nights. Chillico, her parrot, silent too, or maybe she didn't hear him anymore. All the voices were within, roaring so loudly and shutting off everything else in the chaotic hazy world surrounding her.

Jeremy, her older neighbor, still stopped by daily to do the farm type chores, as he had done while she was gone, but there were no further words between them, after she silenced his first brief attempt. The *drukkerebama* was abandoned. No reason to try to forecast days ahead when she already knew what they would be—empty. She put the worn red leather book, along with her gold coin necklace and Gypsy garments, into the old family trunk. She wished there might be some trunk into which she could escape, lock herself away.

Daily living was an arduous effort. Her breasts were tender, swelling, yearning for another's touch. Her body was numb at times and then bouts of continuous arousal. What kind of metamorphosis had taken place during her stay at the Sanitarium? What had the electricity, Phillipe, and everything else done to change her so?

This new illness or whatever it was overtaking her whole body seemed to be twisting around her already altered personality. Throughout these days of turmoil, there flickered this underlying knowing, a faint whisper, even in her sleep, that somewhere in her pain-wracked body a part of Phillipe still pulsed. Not in her heart, not in her mind, but somewhere deeper within. A nest had been secretly built; it became more apparent each day that his child was now suspended inside her, serving its time, waiting to be freed, not knowing what welcome lay outside the safety of Yana's protective womb.

Daily she fought the evident awareness that she was sharing her body, letting Phillipe remain within her when he wasn't anywhere near. It was his physical touch she wanted and not this growing speck secreted within her. It ate away at her, using up her energies. A constant clawing at her innards that would not be quieted.

At times she contemplated doing away with the intruder she could not see. A few times, she took herbs, potions, but with the constant nausea, nothing stayed down. Even though she had given up the fight, this tiny soul would not surrender so easily.

One thundering night, as she lay writhing on her pallet, Grandmama materialized at her side, shouting: *Run away from nothing! Welcome each tribulation, each day, no matter what it brings.*

Yana covered her eyes, ears. Still the voice continued.

Wasn't it you, Yana, crying out in Central Park? 'Grandmama, I'm not running away from what is greater than I am. I've come to meet it, revel in whatever turbulence this day brings.'

The apparition vanished, but the words reverberated with such force they broke apart the shell that had encased Yana all these days. A sharp crack of realization spread throughout her body. The pain had broken through. The light could enter once more. She jumped up from her pallet. For the first time since coming home, she felt ready to dance, launching herself into a free form dance about the room. Life was within reach once more. Yes. She was prepared to face whatever turbulence life would bring.

The next morning she could see and feel the sun engulf her, and she was ready to participate in the world around her once more. She was also resigned to do whatever was needed to be done to protect this child waiting within. She began to will her body to new strength, forcing herself to take extra nourishment.

Yana had not touched her paintbrushes since the first halfhearted attempt the day she returned home when she tried pushing herself to finish the Paris painting. It was useless; her mind and arms couldn't connect. The myriad of eyes in the Gypsy campfire scene that had once glowed with a combination of perceived merriment and mysticism now reflected only sadness. No amount of retouching could change that impression. So, she abandoned the piece that had propelled her aberrant journey, turning it to the wall.

Today there was this urgency to paint. What would make a worthwhile subject? What was there left to inspire her? She knew the answer even as she demanded it. Only one inspiration existed for her—Phillipe.

She would work on a life-size portrait, capturing his magnificent physique, gathering his remembered radiance onto canvas, impregnate the bare cloth with his image. Then, whether he returned or not, she would always have his visible form to be with her, and their child would know some likeness of him also.

Within a few days of beginning to paint, she heard Chillico calling out louder than usual. "Here comes Jeremy! Here comes Jeremy!" Jeremy was marching up the walk with more purpose than he generally displayed. Today his weathered hand was holding onto the skinny arm of a frightened young black girl wearing a skimpy tattered dress.

"I find her—hiding in your shed, down by the river, Miss Yana," Jeremy said triumphantly, as though maybe he expected some kind of reward. However, the days of turning in runaway slaves was long past.

"I didn't steal nothing. Just looking for a place to sleep," the girl muttered, her body trembling. There were long deep scars on the child's scrawny arms and legs. Her large eyes were flickering, and her whole body cowering, as if preparing for another whipping, knowing nothing she could say would stop the inevitable.

"Where are you from?" Yana asked, as kindly as possible in an attempt to quell the terror in this pitiful creature shivering before her.

"Nowheres. And nowheres more to go." Tears of despair began rolling down her hazelnut colored cheeks.

"I can take her into town," Jeremy offered, "and they can lock her up. I know, not as a slave, but mebbe as a vagrant, mebbe even for thievery."

Mournful whimpers cut the still air.

"It's all right, Jeremy, I'll take care of this myself."

"But, Miss Yana, I'm goin into town anyways today."

"No," Yana said. "This child is not going anywhere. First thing, she's going to eat a nice breakfast. Looks like she hasn't had any food in a good while."

Jeremy knew it was useless arguing with Yana, he had learned that long ago. He turned and left, not hiding how perturbed he was, not even to be thanked for his extra diligence.

The girl gazed awestruck, as if she couldn't believe what Yana had just said. She spoke up quickly before this benefactor might change her mind. "I am awfully hungry, ma'm. But I can work for my food. I know how to work, hard."

Her speech—somewhat educated. Her manners—not lower class at all. She had a certain intelligence about her, and Yana took an instant liking to this frail child.

What was it Phillipe had said at Althea's memorial? *If you keep going within, never reaching out, you only arrive at a dead end, with nowhere else to go.*

"What is your name, child?" Yana asked.

"Lulah. That's what I've always been called. I never had two names.'

"Well Lulah, my name is Yana," she took both of Lulah's scarred hands, "and you may call me by one name too, Yana, not 'Miss Yana'."

"Yes, Miss—" Lulah cut the word "—Yana."

"First, you are going to have a fine breakfast. Then a bath, and we'll find you some different clothes too." She could easily cut down one of her new robes, her mind already racing ahead with various ways to help Lulah. A far cry from Phillipe's dictum, but here was someone to care about again.

Throughout the day, between eating and clearing out the storeroom as a place for Lulah to stay, Yana found out about Lulah's past life. She had no need to pry into anyone's history, but it was as if Lulah wanted to talk about her past, as if telling might release some of the burden from her memory.

"My Mama and Papa were slaves, so they could not be married. Soon as they were freed, they ran away. I was born soon after. They were so poor they couldn't keep me, but," she hastened to add, "they still wanted me."

More working in silence followed by more revealing.

"They sold me to this rich man and woman, as an indentured servant, but Mama and Papa, they thought life in that big mansion would be better for me. Food. Clothes.

"Fine at first, long as I did what I was told, worked hard and didn't sass back. The mistress, Miss Sally, she was born in England and she was strict about me learning proper English. Didn't want me reverting to any darkie talk, especially in front of her high-class friends. I had to dress up in this fancy uniform, serve tea and cakes. Smile lots, even though my heart wasn't smiling."

When they stopped to eat lunch, Lulah devoured everything on her plate, and continued to confide in Yana. "All I got to eat was leftovers," she recalled in a soft voice. "Miss Sally, she wouldn't teach me to read either, afraid I might leave, once I learned. But, she did read to me from the Bible, every day, and see that I went to a Negro church on the other side of town, every Sunday." Lulah stopped talking for quite awhile after that.

That night, when Lulah was reassured she could stay, she clapped her hands, shouting, "Hallelujah! I just know the Lord brought me here, because I prayed so hard to Him to help me, when I was hiding in that shed."

"He brought you to the right place. And you can stay here as long as you wish." Yana gave her a tight hug.

Lulah was already up, sweeping the floor the next morning when Yana began retching into the tin pan, unable to stop. Lulah observed for awhile before speaking. "Lordy, Miss Yana, you must be going to have a baby." Then interjected, "But maybe it's false, because you don't have a man, do you?" Lulah was afraid she had overstepped with her words.

"I do have a man, Lulah. Only I don't know where he is right now." Yana didn't want to discuss Phillipe with Lulah or anyone else, not until he became a reality again. That possibility seemed more remote than ever.

See? Grandmama kept repeating. *We have no control. What will be, will be.*

Lulah was a great help during the pregnant months. Yana found herself filled with mothering instincts she never thought she possessed. She began teaching Lulah to read. Yana's spirit was uplifted by the eagerness with which the child devoured the written word; Lulah so pleased that she could now read her Bible. It was her one and only possession—a used Bible given to her at church—the only item she had carried away from the mansion.

During the winter months, they sat before the fire sewing clothing and blankets for the baby. Lulah was an artist with her fingers, embroidering bright flowers and dainty butterflies on everything. They talked, read, cooked. The wind howled down the chimney causing strange apparitions to dance in the fire, sing with the blaze. They were cozy and protected from the outside elements, and Yana realized how lonely she must have been all those years before.

"Lulah, I feel the baby moving!" she exclaimed one evening. What an enthralling sensation, as if someone were dancing within her, to its own separate rhythm.

Lulah broke into unexpected sobs. "I can't never know that feeling, Yana. Never again." She began rocking her convulsing body, clutching at her stomach.

"What is it, Lulah?" Only more sobs. "What is causing such anguish for you?"

It took awhile for the whole story to come out, like a long ugly corkscrew that twisted its way out of Lulah's throat and body. "The master, Mr. Jake—a big strong man, he started coming into my bed at night. He said, if I told, he would say I was lying and Miss Sally would beat me and he would beat me himself. He did all kinds of sinful things to me, but, I didn't have nowheres else to go." Piercing sobs soon filled the room.

"It's over, Lulah," Yana consoled. "You're here now, and you don't ever have to return to that kind of place again."

"That's not the end. One day I became with child, and Miss Sally, she accused me of being sinful, beat me every day; I know she was hoping maybe both the baby and I would die. When the birth time came—"

Lulah was silent for a moment, a look of horror overtaking her whole being before continuing. "Miss Sally, she would allow no one near during the birthing, yelling when the baby came out, 'It's black; the baby is black! Your sin cannot remain living in this house.'"

"She took my babe and was gone for a while. Then—no more tiny cries. She came back with a kitchen knife in her hand. 'I'm going to fix it so you never have any more bastard children.' That's what she says. And then her knife cut away at my insides, fainting me."

Guttural sounds rose from Lulah's throat, a wailing cry of loss that gathered all the broken voices of women before her. This child, who was hardly more than seventeen, had already suffered the worst of all cruelties. Yana held her tighter, choking back her own rage and tears.

"I know I was a bad girl for letting Mr. Jake do those things to me," Lulah said between wailing sounds. "You can't never wash away sins like that."

"You listen to me, Lulah," Yana interrupted angrily, "you are not a bad girl. It was a bad man who did those things to you. He was bigger, stronger. He's the sinful one. Not you."

They sat huddled together in the rocking chair, the pain passing back and forth between them. The fire died, darkness crept in to cover them, absorbing their shared grief.

"What happened in the past, to both of us, is over," Yana murmured sleepily. "We do not live there anymore. We need never go back. We can only go forward." By morning, there was new bonding between them.

Jeremy still went into town each week for supplies and to pick up the mail. Each return he brought back the same disappointment—no letter from Phillipe. She had written to him about the baby. It was returned, as were the other letters: "Moved—No forwarding address." Why was he not receiving her letters? Where had he gone?

Daily, Yana stood before Phillipe's painting, silently speaking to his image, past his image, into the ether, wherever he was. Their nights together were fading, making it difficult to grasp those times with the same wondrous intensity she thought she'd never lose.

Phillipe's life-sized portrait now covered most of one wall of her cabin. Older paintings of Mama and Grandmama occupied other walls. Surrounded by those she loved brought a certain comfort, also a knowing loss, because they were not real. Only now, there was someone real, presiding right within her, someone never seen, yet already loved, stirring emotions she had never experienced before.

The small cabin was beginning to feel crowded, as crib and baby things were readied. They would need another room for the baby. But right now Yana couldn't wait for the child to be next to her, in her bedroom, for as long as possible.

In the spring, she would build an addition to the cabin. Jeremy knew people desperate for work, good honest carpenters. Planning ahead was a nice diversion. She could project any kind of future she wished. What if airy dreams didn't turn out as perceived? It was still better anticipating, giving some vague hope to the future. The child had brought this about.

Jeremy, after getting past his initial dislike of Lulah, and Yana's having made it clear Lulah was not to be treated with any deference, he and Lulah took to being friends. They'd have long talks whenever both were outside, almost a daily ritual; Lulah would invent some excuse to go outdoors whenever she saw Jeremy approaching.

The need for interaction between the sexes, not conjugal sex, but the magnetism of sexual association between male and female persons.... Phillipe's words again, his sexual starvation theory that he had expounded upon during their first private supper.

Is that what she had now, sexual starvation? No, she had something even better. She was being divided into two, no longer a solitary person. What a wonderful way to conquer loneliness. Duplicate yourself. Replicate your love.

How she wished she had stored more in her memory during those long talks around the Gypsy campfires, when the women discussed pregnancies, childbearing, child raising. Would those words of passed-on wisdom still hold true today? This was a different time. Another place. Still, some things remained constant, as did the stars in the heavens, and time and place didn't alter their course.

She also hoped that some basics of motherhood were passed on inherently, as they were in animals, on how to care for their young. Secret ciphers nature hid within the female, instinctual guidelines set into motion once the offspring was born. Many times she yearned for tribal sisters to chatter with, relatives, anyone. She even missed the combative discourses with Delphine. Lulah was company, but she was from a different culture, a culture that others had tried to suppress, stamp out, but still survived somehow; and Yana was aware of certain rituals that had never been completely stifled.

Sometimes she found Lulah mindlessly engaging in strange songs, curious actions, which may have been voluntary or involuntary. Passed on from her parents? Remembered from babyhood? Every person contained these curiosities from the past, mostly forgotten after childhood; they could never understand the reasons when they reverted to these strange acts, weird words. Wherever did they come from? Yana always knew—her culture was reinforced so strongly, verbally and ritually, from birth on, never stopped, never forgotten.

With the help of books—many times wishing she had some of the medical books written by Phillipe—Yana instructed Lulah on what to do when the baby's time came. The mantle clock ticked off the minutes. *One minute closer.... One minute closer...*

"Yana, you're going to have a big, big child," Lulah often commented. "Your belly's big like a cow."

Yana was getting large fast and movement becoming more difficult. Her breasts were swollen; her legs ached. No more dancing or horse riding for awhile. She walked the fields, searching for plants and herbs—burdock, goldenseal, boneset, snake root—gathering those she remembered as curing children's illnesses. These she hung from the cabin ceiling, filling the area with long forgotten scents.

Christmas came and went without much observation by Yana. Living alone, who was there to celebrate with? But for Lulah, Christmas was the most celebratingest day of the whole year. As the great day approached, the girl joyfully decorated the cabin with mountain laurel, crowfoot and mistletoe. Every nook and angle draped evergreens and red berries. A spindly pine tree, she cut down and dragged into the house, was transformed into a gala speckled pyramid. Working feverishly at the decorating, Lulah sang Christmas carols, her exuberant voice echoing from the log rafters far into the still countryside. The whole place was filled with expectation—the awaiting of a birth.

On Christmas Eve, before going to her church, Lulah presented Yana with a beautiful filmy shawl, made from curtains she had fringed and embroidered. No one ever gave Yana presents anymore and she was touched at the generosity, being the receiver instead of the giver.

Lulah went to Christmas Eve services at her church, taking the horse Drom. Yana, alone for a few hours, went to her trunk. Way at the bottom, she found an old doll, one that her father had given her. It was a beautiful cloth doll with fancy silk clothing. The doll was a possession she held dear. That made it a true gift. She wrapped it in one of her mother's embroidered blouses and set it under the tree.

Lulah was overwhelmed with joy on finding it. "Now I'll never be alone, Yana," she said, cradling the doll in her arms. "Her name is Glorie, my Mama's name, the name I was going to give my own baby."

Tears transformed to giggles as Lulah tried on the blouse. "Yana, I don't know how Gypsies feel, but I sure feel like one now. Colorful—and maybe kind of wild?"

Yana decided that night that she would begin celebrating the Christmas season too, once her child was born. Families needed to establish holidays of their own, commemorate special times together, traditions that could be passed on.

She had always been intrigued by the bright spirit that seemed to exude everywhere at Christmastime, wanting to linger longer in the decorated European towns during those bleak December days. Even Gypsies were wished well during that season, everyone smiling, and sometimes ladies would come to their camp, baskets laden with food and presents. All done to celebrate the birth of a child....

January. It had been about nine months since that final parting with Phillipe. Snowing heavily, unusual for Virginia. Yana and Lulah were watching the fluffy white dots fluttering outside the window and exclaiming at the beauty of the world being frosted with fresh fallen snow.

"Some new bright gift coming down to earth from heaven," Lulah exclaimed, "just like your new baby will be something brand-new coming down from heaven too."

Yana had tried explaining sexual relations and childbirth, but Lulah still believed the baby seed was planted by God, not brought by the stork, as she had been first taught. Even with her sad experience of the world, Lulah put no store in any other explanations, especially ones that involved the man's part.

So engrossed were they in watching the snow, Yana wasn't aware of the first pain. Then they became sharper and closer. "It's time, Lulah," she said, in quiet amazement.

Events unfolded at high speed. Lulah never panicked, but Yana did. Once into her bed, she yelped with each pain, crying out to God, Mama, Grandmama, but mostly to Phillipe. Why wasn't he here? Why wasn't he present at the miracle of his child being born? An entire person created by their love; love materializing in a new form; their love entering the world as if for the first time—and Phillipe wasn't there.

"It's a boy, Yana!" Lulah exclaimed. Yana quieted her screaming. A lusty wail sounding from far away, moved closer and louder. A boy—the tears were flowing freely now. A dear baby boy. She would name him Phillipe.

The pressure in her stomach was still there, birth spasms continuing. Was that supposed to be? Maybe just the afterbirth.

"Yana? Yana?" Lulah was yelling. "There's something more coming through, another baby. You're getting two babies. Two!"

Two—why hadn't she realized. Twins. That's why she was so big. Way back, in her mother's family, there had been many twins; oh, the fun they had fooling everyone about which one was which.

"A girl, Yana. It's a tiny baby girl. Oh, thank the Lord. He's blessed you twice." Lulah's stamina broke down as she got on her knees crying, praying, wailing.

"Your name will be Persa." Yana held the newborn girl in one arm, the squalling boy in the other, "after my mother." At this moment in her life, she was truly blessed. Two children— rare gifts from God, love gifts from Phillipe. He was here with her after all, doubly so.

Every hour from that day forward was busy, but satisfying in so many ways. Never had she dreamed all this might flow through her life. She nursed Phillipe and Persa, sometimes both at the same time. What fulfillment—food and nourishment flowing from her body into another. Two lives, depending on her.

Already they were taking on their own personalities. Phillipe was lusty, robust, dark curly hair and those same penetrating eyes as Phillipe. Babies' eyes were as large at birth as they would be when adults. Would he have healing hands also? Were such gifts inherited? His grasp was tight, his fingers exploring.

Persa was such a gentle baby, what an endearing smile, yet, temper tantrums occasionally surfaced, loud and long. Good. You couldn't live without occasionally letting out what was corked up inside.

One day Yana took Mama's necklace from the trunk and placed it around Persa's tiny pink neck. "Someday it will be yours," she cooed to her daughter. "Now, I have family to pass this heirloom on to. The succession of women will not be broken."

Only Persa did not welcome the feel of cold metal and scratching coins, screaming vociferously, trying to push the necklace away from her skin. A mind of her own. *Mush.* Good. Yana hung the necklace on her mirror, and there it would wait until Persa was ready for the bestowal, it was her *drukkerebama.*

Should she begin teaching Persa Gypsy words or not, or might it be too confusing for someone so young? *Chavi*—girl. *Chavo*—boy. It would be a shame to lose that part of her heritage. Sometimes, her language said things that could not be expressed in any other way. The old chants and folk songs were still part of her ancestry. Words must be passed on, the same as the treasures in the trunk.

Soon both babies were sitting up. Then eating coarse food. Crawling. What a joy children were; even the endless work of caring for them was a pleasure. A pleasure she had previously decided to exclude from her life. Maybe it was best that one wasn't always given complete charge of one's destiny, letting other powers take over. Maybe the philosophy of accepting whatever fate brings was still the wisest.

The month of May once more. Apple blossoms perfumed the gentle breezes with their fluttering petals of pink velvet. Only a year ago she was preparing for New York, not wanting to depart from this same lovely scene. Never could she have predicted the year that followed. Even Grandmama could not have foretold—or could she?

The annual spring urge to get on her horse and ride and ride did not take hold this year; stronger urges had taken its place. With children, the desire to leave was always overbalanced by the anxiety of being away from them. Whenever she was away from her babies, the urgency to return and be at their side always intruded. They needed her to watch over them. She was their caretaker—for life. What other bequeathal carried such preponderance?

Workmen were busy about the place, pounding, sawing, and hammering. It was gratifying to watch the new rooms taking shape, as wooden outlines of the rooms arose in the air, similar to paintings being etched in space. Where there had been nothing, new shapes were materializing for each special room.

Her old bedroom had fabric tacked onto the walls and ceilings to give it the billowing air of a tent interior. Her new bedroom was plain pine board, with a large circular window centered in the ceiling so she could sleep under the moon and stars.

The freshly cut wood retained the smell of the pine trees. How could she keep it from dissipating with time? How could she keep anything from fading away from the senses?

The workmen were strong; they worked hard sunrise to set, their hearty voices ringing out to one another. Sometimes, as Yana watched them working without their shirts, muscles moving and glistening in the sunlight, their maleness reminded her of Phillipe. That was all, just a twinge of remembrance. There was not one of them she even contemplated desiring. No one else even tempted her, and she dismissed the men's interested glances. She had no sexual starvation, not for their company.

Yana went into town each week now herself, needing supplies for the babies, for Lulah, for the new rooms. Each trip included stopping at the post office, quickly flipping through her meager packet of mail. Always the monthly check from the bank, really still from her father. Never the one envelope she was looking for.

Each day she saw Phillipe repeated in her son. In addition, traces of her own father appeared: a quirky smile, a hint of red in his dark curly hair.

Riding the fields, looking out across the land, her father came closer in spirit these days than ever before. Was that what happened after having children, you looked further back into our own past, trying to seek connections with various family members, links that hadn't mattered so much before.

She began looking for correlation in the babies that might bear semblances to other relatives, strong bloodlines that had fought for continuance, as if civilization might die out if they didn't pursue their relentless tactics for survival. She began to appreciate what had gone on before her own birth, the ceaseless battling efforts, so she and her offspring might inherit an improved niche in a once barbaric world. Each generation needed to contribute to this reservoir of civilization by passing on their best and mitigating their worst.

Persa reminded her so much of her own mother rather than herself. She had a mysterious air, and even as young as she was, often gazed into the far distance, pointing so many times, into the air, the sky.   Always examining Yana's hands, outlining Yana's face, with discerning fingers. Exclaiming in her own baby language, as if she had an inner knowing about things out there that she could not yet express.

Each day the children changed, growing more into themselves, endearing those selves to her, their mother. Love for her children overfilled Yana's heart and soul, lessening the other void.   Lulah was blossoming too, eager to learn, reading more challenging books each week and finding new stories to read to the babies.

Another Christmas.   Another May. The children were already over a year and a half....

Was it useless to make the weekly pilgrimage to the post office? The spark of hope was no longer there and she had given up trying to revive it. Yet, last night Phillipe was in her dreams, the same as similar ones, behind bars, in dragging chains. Then all of a sudden he wasn't there; the cell was empty. Was he gone only from the cell, or had he left the earth completely? *Will I ever know what has happened to my love?   Or has the end already taken place?*

There was a heavy spring rain the next day as she rode Drom to the post office. She wore no protective cloak, welcoming the cooling drench. Weary and dripping wet she forced herself to ask for her mail at the desk in the same tedious monotone. "Mail for Yana Kejako, please." The usual pile of envelopes. Wait; there was one that—one that had a special handwriting. Could it be? It was! It was a letter from Phillipe! With trembling fingers, she tore open the envelope on the spot.

My Dearest Yana,

I am a free man, June 1, 1886.   By then, I will have completed my two-year sentence in this place.   The details are not important, only that I was never charged with murder, and my medical license was revoked. It is over, behind me. The guilt dissolved.

I have not forgotten you, my love, and long for you even more than before. There has not been one day that I did not see your face, each morning when I woke, at night before I slept, even during my sleep.

The medical practice has been sold. The money is in the bank. Other things in a warehouse.

I will come to your farm on or about June 3, if arrangements work out. If you are away traveling, I will await there for your return. Forever.

I do not know what else to put in this letter, except that I still love you. As changed as I am, my love is only deeper.

Affectionately yours,

Phillipe.

She held the letter close to her pounding heart. Two years—a lifetime, they had been apart.

Then, all of a sudden, the realization hit—Phillipe was returning into her life.

Yana ran from the post office, across the street to the Town Square, and twirled and twirled on the soft springy wet grass, crying out, "Phillipe is coming. Phillipe is coming, " not caring who saw her, who heard her. She wanted the whole world to know. Her whirling joy transported her off the grass onto another plane; she was back once more in Central Park, almost expecting thunder and lightning to perform along with her.

CHAPTER 28

There was so much to be done. Yana's protracted inertia of maternal contentedness transformed into whirlwinds of activity. First, she had the carpenter build a huge double bed. She drew up the design herself, memorized from that indelible first night with Phillipe—the scrolling patterns carved into the headboard of his father's ornate mahogany bed that had shadowed them throughout that night.

No more sleeping on her pallet on the floor, not while Phillipe was here. Had he kept any of his family furniture? Would he even want to live here?

Worry about such things later. Focus only on that first meeting. Run it through your mind over and over until the day becomes an actual reality.

The babies were just beginning to walk, exploring their new world with expectant wonder. In a few weeks, they would be embracing their father—the bearded man in the big picture on the wall. Yana and Lulah made new sets of clothing for the children to wear for the homecoming, with a patch of "red for good luck" sewn into each hem.

Food was prepared ahead of time as if for a banquet. Lulah scrubbed and cleaned the whole house, caught up in the mounting excitement. Yet, Yana noticed her countenance was becoming increasingly serious, also a new reticence about her. Yana finally had to ask, "What is troubling you so, Lulah?"

"If your man is coming here," Lulah said hesitantly, "maybe you won't need me, want me here anymore."

Yana gave the girl a reassuring hug and said, "Lulah, I'll need you even more than ever, because 'my man' and I have a lot of catching up to do. I don't know how I would manage with these two lively children if you weren't here. Did I ever tell you Lulah, how much I love you?"

"No, Yana, no one has ever told me that."

"Well, I do. My heart is so overflowing with love, I'm about to burst."

"Don't do that Yana, and mess up this whole clean place," and Lulah was her old self again, giggling and laughing; the babies were giggling and laughing too, the whole house filled with mirth. Yana was sure she saw Phillipe, from his portrait, giggling and laughing with them too.

Monday, June 3—Bright and sunny, a glorious golden day. Anticipation permeated every corner of the house, rose from the earth, descended from the heavens. Yana sang as she bathed. Had her body changed since the children's birth? She had no mirror that reflected her whole self, just a tiny square above her dresser. Before it had not mattered, today, everything mattered.

She and Lulah dressed little Phillipe and Persa in their crisp new clothes, primped their hair, put on their new soft leather shoes. They were not sure what was happening. Even Lulah had tied a colorful sash around her dress, gathered a ribbon in her hair.

Yana wore a new hollyhock-rose gown.

She had been teaching the children to say *dadus*, for father, pointing to Phillipe's painting. "Dadus is coming," they repeated eagerly all day long and then grew tired of saying it. Their clothes became wrinkled and soiled. Anticipation was sinking with the lowering sun.

"Maybe he'll come tomorrow," Lulah consoled at the supper table. Neither ate very much; Yana kept an anxious eye on the pathway.

After, they sat outside, watching the fading light. The children frolicked in the grass, barefoot, having long discarded their new shoes. All day Yana had kept willing Phillipe to come; she was giving up. Once it became dark, few coaches would hire to come out this far. There was only one small, ramshackle hotel in the nearest town. She should have gone into town to wait for him, but he had told her that he must come to her.

"I think we should prepare the children for bed, Lulah," Yana said, rising from the bench.

"Dadus coming, Dadus coming," they repeated like parrots, Chillico chanting along.

"No, not today," Yana said, "maybe tomorrow."

Then, in the distance, a hazy form, with the sun glowing behind it, appeared as a specter in the twilight. The form gradually got closer and larger. Yana dared not hope, let alone celebrate until she was sure who it was. The figure moved like an old man, and then the approaching outline waved.

It was him. *Phillipe!*

"Watch the twins," Yana yelled, springing forward, running down the road toward her beloved, shining golden in the last of the sun. Her feet took wing as her heart raced ahead of her. "Phillipe!" she called.

"Yana!" she heard faintly.

Within minutes they were in each other's arms, crying, laughing, kissing. The ecstasy was explosive—the love, the passion, magnetism for each other, cycloned around them, twirling them away and then setting them back down on earth again.

Yana stepped aside to look at Phillipe. His beard was missing. He was thin, tired looking. Dusty. Pale. The sparks still radiated in his eyes, dimmer, but still unequaled.

"I was so afraid the day would be over and you would not be here," she said. They held hands as they walked not daring to part touch.

"I could not get a stage," he said, reliving the frustration. "I did not want to wait the night, away, yet so close to you. I asked for directions—everyone knows Yana, 'the Gypsy artist', and I started walking, leaving my bags at the station. I did get a few wagon rides along the way."

"I should have met you—wherever, whenever."

"No matter, I'm here. We're together."

They were getting closer to the yard. All of a sudden, two tiny figures were running toward them. "Dadus! Dadus!" Persa and little Phillipe were calling.

Phillipe looked at Yana, with strange frightened curiosity.

"Yana—you didn't—marry someone else?" His hand separated from hers. "I didn't know."

"*Diniolo*—silly fool. I haven't even thought of anyone else. These are your children, Phillipe—ours. Twins. Persa after my mother, and Phillipe, after you."

As soon as the children reached them, Phillipe knelt down and gathered them both in his arms, hugging, kissing them, tears streaming his face. "I didn't know—I never realized."

"Dadus, Dadus," they repeated.

"My dearest children, my dear, dear children." He grasped their tiny hands. "Two whole years," he said, "I missed your first two years on this earth." He rose, and turned to Yana. "You should not have gone through this alone. Had I known, I would have fought—I gave up so easily."

"Enough," Yana said, pressing her fingers against his lips. "This is a night for celebrating. Nothing else."

The children ran to Lulah, yelling, "Dadus is here, Dadus is here!"

"Phillipe, this is Lulah, who is my dearest friend, my greatest help. The children and I love her as our own."

"Then I shall love her too," and Phillipe extended his hand to Lulah, who was honored by his words, obviously taken in by his charm.

"I'm pleased to meet you, Mr. Phillipe," she said and then giggled, "Yana's been like a grasshopper with ten legs since she got your letter."

They all went inside and Yana showed Phillipe around while Lulah laid out another meal. The bedroom would wait until later.

"I did look like that once, didn't I?" Phillipe said, standing before his portrait. "How could you capture me so perfectly, without my being here?"

"You were always here," she answered.

"Then I know, when I spoke to you—"

"I heard, with my heart, my soul. But it was never loud enough or close enough."

They stayed near to each other, resisting the inevitable mating.

The meal was a chatter of voices. A reunion that was not really a reunion, but a gathering to celebrate a new beginning, the ending of things best left in the past.

There was special wine, rousing toasts. Then one by one, Yana saw them enter, the extra guests—Mama, Grandmama.

Next, the women from the Sanitarium appeared, smiling, all going toward Phillipe. Only two shadows stayed in the background—Althea and Shyam. Still, it was a wonderful gathering, and she let the apparitions fade as she shifted to the present.

The children were tired; it had been a long day. Phillipe insisted he tell them a bedtime story. He sat in the large armchair, one child on each knee, arms around both. Yana and Lulah sat at his feet. The fire was dying embers.

"Once upon a time," he began and then proceeded to tell one of the folktales Yana had told him the night she entertained with her thousand and one stories, repeating it word for word. His voice still entranced her; he'd lost time and strength, but he'd lost none of his magic. The children's eyes kept blinking and then shut. How she wished she had one of those new cameras to capture this scene in all its glowing perfection. No, she would remember, paint it.

Phillipe took his son, Yana took her daughter, and they put them into their beds. Phillipe kissed each and stood by their wooden cribs for a few moments.

"To be blessed with such an abundance of gifts—when I was ready to accept—" he reached out for her, "that there might be nothing. Not even you."

"Come," Yana said, "we're both tired, let's go to bed now too." She paused, calling at Lulah's door, "We are retiring, Lulah, can you listen for the babies? And thank you for helping prepare this day." At that moment, she was grateful to everyone who had ever lived.

They went into the bedroom, carrying a lit candle that illuminated the room in a phosphorescent glow—the moon casting a shimmering spotlight on the waiting bed.

"Yana? My father's bed—how did it get here?"

"Through memory. It is only a replica. Many things can be recreated from memory, or new ones conceived."

He took her in his arms and then backed away, hesitating, "I have no other clothing," he apologized, "it is all at the station."

"We do not need clothing," she began unbuttoning his shirt, "the eiderdown quilt will be our apparel for the night."

Within seconds, they were undressed and under the downy covering, holding onto each other, so tight, so close, their pulse was one.

She waited. Nothing more was happening. Where was the passion that had always kindled so quick between the two of them? Lost? Gone? Could it still be resurrected in the same way, or had time and distance dissipated its energy.

Phillipe turned his head aside, "I'm sorry, Yana, I am so tired, and—"

Before he had time to say more, she hushed him. "Do not worry so Phillipe, we have a lifetime to catch up—on everything. We do not need to do it all the first night. You are here. That is all that matters." And it was enough.

Soon he was asleep, his arms locked around her, as if she might escape from his hold. The candle sputtered out, and Yana lay there, gazing at the moon showering them with a silvery glow. She observed the outline of Phillipe's face, the steady rhythm of his chest rising and falling, the comforting sound of his breathing, his heart beating, and his whole body next to her. She wasn't dreaming, this time it was real.

He came back to me, Mama, he came back.

And now the world could begin turning once more, spinning on its correct path, whereas before, for two years it had been off track, wobbling on the wrong orbit.

From somewhere, the last lines of a poem surfaced. *God's in His heaven—All's right with the world.* She fell asleep in Phillipe's arms.

The next morning Yana woke with a start. Someone was in bed with her.

Stifling a gasp, she remembered, and a wonderful tranquility settled over everything, veiling the room in a gauzelike web of dreamy bliss. Happy, she nestled into the curve of Phillipe's back, feeling his warmth, his muscles moving as he began to stir.

In a moment, he was turning over, reaching for her, exploring her body with both hands, slowly at first and then more ardently as his passions gained momentum, sweeping through both in magnificent torrents. Passions held back, locked away those two long years. Within moments, everything was unleashed and they were once more first time lovers.

Her body moved and yielded, wanting to receive it all—joy, pain, whatever he had to give that would quench this eternal longing, saturate her emptiness. He buried himself deep within her.

Everything stopped. It was a moment in time when nothing else in the world moved, except her interiors, which began weeping with joy. When the final freeing scream rose from her depths, she stuffed her hand into her mouth so she would not disturb Lulah or the children, who might think she was in pain. This was the furthest thing from pain she had ever experienced, the nearest she had ever come to glimpsing the bright radiance of heaven.   Flashes of brilliant light—catapulting her far into space—whirling her across the universe, culminating in that freeing second of time that was not time.

It was Phillipe who cried out, over and over, as his body rode the crest of crashing waves. "Oh my God. Oh my God!" Animal sounds roared out of him, across the jungle; he was staking out his territory, claiming his mate as his own.

Time had not diminished their affinity for each other, only deepened it, sealing their reunion with the knowledge that they must never part from one another again. They were each other's lifeblood. She realized now, home was the perfect place for love to reach the apex of completion. The Sanitarium trysts had only been an introduction; those times could never equal what had happened here, this brightest morning of her lifetime.

After, they lay quietly, touching, memorizing each other's flesh anew, fingers moving as if delicate paintbrushes, searching and filling in untouched areas.

"This body, which gives me such ecstasy," Phillipe's fingers were zigzagging across Yana's stomach, "has also given me the most wondrous reward—my own children."

"The children belong to both of us," she countered dreamily.

"Yes, and we belong to each other."   He kissed her abdomen , smothering his face into her soft folds.

"We belong to each other," she repeated, pressing him closer to her body, the whole performance repeated once more, encompassing everything they might have left out the session before.

Exhausted, they moved apart, knowing they had to shift to the next portion of their day and proceed on to other segments of their life. They were no longer alone, there were children who needed attention now, daily, and never again would they have the freedom to think only of themselves.

The days following took on new patterns, but not regulated ones. They would evolve in time. Of course, they had to make some plans. Phillipe could not exist without plans, an organizing purpose. Yana had known that from the day she first met him. It was now up to her to help him get back on some kind of track after those debilitating years in prison.

Her life was more than fulfilled in caring for the children and Phillipe. What could Phillipe do to attain some daily sense of achievement? She didn't want him leaving the farm, working elsewhere. Besides, between them they had ample reserves of money.

Phillipe wanted nothing more to do with medicine, wouldn't even discuss the subject. "I have no desire to resurrect any of my former life. I've had two years to place it all behind me. The door is clanged shut," and he was resolute in his decision. The only thing that mattered to him now was Yana and his children.

So he spent his days doing various chores around the farm, helping Jeremy in mundane tasks, inventing work saving devices, claiming this was fulfillment enough, providing for his family. They bought extra goats, chickens, planted more crops.

Nevertheless, Yana was so aware Phillipe needed to work with his mind, not just his hands. To waste all his knowledge would be a desecration. Writing did not interest him anymore either, claiming the only things he knew how to write were all medically related and the words were no longer there.

"The answer will come," he said. "Give it time. First, we must be married. Our children need legitimate parents."

That was their first bristle.

"And what do you think they have been these past two years, fatherless and motherless bastards," she retorted.

She was ecstatic to have Phillipe back, but in no way would their relationship revert to the man being the head of the household and the woman subject to his commands and whims.

"I'm sorry, Yana," Phillipe apologized, "that is not what I meant."

"Our children are the fruit of our love, and that is the most legitimate claim they can ever have." Yana did not stifle her anger, never realizing how powerful the mother's protective instincts could be, even against the children's own father.

There were other tiffs, mostly about raising the children. She believed in letting them grow naturally, as flowers in the field. They needed to carve out their own niches in life. She guided them only when needed. They were already thriving on that methodology. Phillipe believed in a much stricter upbringing; claiming it took rigid training to develop strong character. That might have to wait, as he could never find it in his heart to even shout at them, much less lay a hand or stick to them. And so the twins continued growing and flourishing as they had begun before his arrival.

Even if she and Phillipe quarreled in the daytime, which was inevitable, as they were so unlike in temperaments, once they were in bed at night, nestled in each other's arms, all was forgiven, forgotten. Neither wanted to go back to those nights of being apart, they could abide no separation of any kind. Nighttime was their reward for whatever they had gone through during the day, the balm for wounds they had suffered over the past two years.

They spoke to each other in a language both understood because their hearts were attuned, even when their minds weren't. In the quiet of the night, they settled many matters, arms encircling one another. Phillipe conceded Yana could have charge of raising the children while they were young, but once they were of school age, he would take over. She yielded readily, thinking those years were too far away to worry about now.

Their wedding was planned under the eiderdown quilt, where plans were usually conceived following their sexual union, which was almost nightly. If it didn't take place, touching expressed its own culmination, with promise of fulfillment the next time.

"We must be married by a preacher," Phillipe insisted. "For the children's sake."

"I will not be married in a church," Yana argued. "I do not belong to any church, and I will not stand up as a hypocrite on the most important day of my life."

"What do you want, a Gypsy celebration in the fields? Wild dancing and feasting?" He was not making fun, but asking seriously.

"I have no desire for any kind of Gypsy celebration," she said, remembering the carousing that sometimes went on for days. "That could only take place with friends and relatives and I no longer have any of them left to celebrate with," and she felt pangs of loss about that, but it was only fleeting. "And the townspeople, they look upon me as a pariah, living here alone, an artist, Gypsy, raising two wild children without a husband. Even worse, treating a Negro as an equal. No, I don't think they are the guests I want to gather on my wedding day either."

The discussion went on for days, and she thought they might never get married, which was all right with her, but not with Phillipe. What harm to give in to make him happy? What was one day out of her whole life? If he desired a church ceremony—

The solution was so simple. They would be married by Lulah's preacher. Yana had gone to this humble church once, taking Lulah when she wasn't feeling too well. It had been the most joyous ceremony she had ever witnessed. A spiritual experience that reached deep inside—soul expanding. She had stood in the back of that plain wooden building as the rafters burst with song and prayer. The rough interior of the building glowed with its own celestial beauty.

The preacher, Reverend Moses, agreed to marry them, "Outside, in the churchyard, since you are not congregation," he said, never mentioning any other reasons. "But," he added, "you will get the whole, complete ceremony, the same I would bestow on any of my flock."

"Then you may announce to all your Church of Jesus congregation, that they are all invited to a very special wedding," Yana told him, "and they will be honored guests. There are to be no gifts, only their presence, their blessings, their singing and music."

"Praise the Lord! And you will have a whole choir of angels there too," Pastor Moses beamed, "because they love that stand of pines, and I see them flitting over those treetops on special occasions. On quiet nights you can even hear the rustle of their wings, and their singing, accompanied by the dancing needles of the towering pines."

Jeremy was invited too. "Miss Yana, I don't know who will be happier on the day you marry; you or me." He was still uneasy about unmarried women who had children.

Yana gave him the task of fixing up the old vardo, the Gypsy caravan wagon, which had been saved, kept at the edge of the farmland, but neglected for years. Now it was being repaired, repainted in bright colors, and decorated with colorful banners and ribbons. They would ride in it to the churchyard on their wedding day. The wagon that had sheltered family along so many roadways, had been her home for so many years, now would take her on one of the most important journeys of her life.

It was a memorable day. Bright. Glorious. As if the heavens had been invited too. Or was it only Mama, Grandmama, and even Papa, showering their blessings down from above, partaking in the long awaited festivity. Yana had decided she would wear her Gypsy garments, as they were the most colorful gowns she owned, plus they bespoke "celebration", and she wanted the children to remember her in this festive array, if only for one day.

Anticipation and joy surrounded her as she put on the colorful apparel and the gold necklace. She was wearing these clothes when Phillipe had first seen her. Immediately she felt like dancing. These skirts were made for movement, the bangles and beads made to jingle tinkling accompaniments. Her long loose hair furled and swung as she danced about the bedroom.

One last maidenly fling, and then her girlhood would have to be packed away. She couldn't keep forever foraging it up, trying to skip backward instead of moving forward.

But then, whose rules were those anyway? That women must continuously grow old, without any turning back, without trying to recapture any part of their youth? She made a vow to herself that morning: whenever she felt the need, she would take out these adornments, put on any freeing attire she wished and go forth with whatever sensations they brought out in her for as long as they lasted.

One could return to days of past joy, you didn't need to follow a straight laid out tract in life. You were the maker of your own rules and need follow no one. You could cut your own pathways through all the un-walked wilderness because you were not like anyone else ever born before you, or after. Life was to be lived anew for each individual, and life gave you the freedom to make your own choices, chart your own destinations.

She also decided to wear Mama's embroidered wedding vest. The threads were now frayed, but still rich, still elegant. All the jewelry—earrings, bracelets, extra necklaces, embellished the vivid costume. Only her fingers were left bare, waiting for that one ring Phillipe would place on her finger, his mother's wide golden wedding band, thus joining their families, circling their souls.

The lovely shawl Lulah had given her that first Christmas made a perfect wedding veil. She decided not to wear the bandanna over her hair as Gypsies did on their wedding day. Phillipe preferred her hair loose and flowing. Maybe she would never cut it as some women did upon marrying—let it grow for as many years as she wished into cascades of gray. Who dictated that flowing gray hair couldn't be beautiful too?

The children had been made special Gypsy garb. And oh, they looked so colorful—and were so noisy. Each was given a celebrating instrument. Persa—Yana's yellowed tambourine and little Phillipe—a sheep's horn to blow as loud as he wished. They had been practicing for days, not understanding that Phillipe, who was already their dadus, would now be made their dadus again.

It was a boisterous, merry group riding in the decorated wagon to the church grounds. Yana kept the veil over her face, laughing as the children kept trying to peek. Phillipe appeared solemn, as focused in concentration as she had ever seen him. He had insisted they abstain from any sexual union the whole previous week so that their wedding night might be even more special.

The games we make up for ourselves, the prizes we select for winning....

They passed the red banners she had put up along the roadway, an old Gypsy custom to help travelers find their way to the marriage celebration. Then the red silk scarf suspended on a pole to mark the actual spot where the wedding would take place.

The church members were already there, mingling quietly, dressed up in their Sunday best, on this first Saturday in August, 1886. The church benches had been moved outside, under the arches of the majestic pines, which formed their own green gothic ceiling. An altar was set up and buckets of flowers were everywhere, bright wild flowers mixed with luscious green ferns. The birds were already tuning up, singing lustily.

It was a hot day, with periodic breezes for respite. The choir sang of mournful hopes and transcendent joy; the pines whispered along in chorus—*that from this day forward, they would love, honor, and obey each other.* Yana had required that both the man and woman's vows be the same.

Phillipe solemnly placed his mother's ring on Yana's finger, his hand trembling. They kissed, and everyone clapped as the children jumped up and down. She did feel different; she did feel she and Phillipe were more completely joined. There were so many witnesses, reverberating the union, one to another, making it a public commitment. That fact could never be private again.

She would not take his name though, nor would she be called "Mrs."—an argument she had finally won. Still, when she was congratulated as "Mrs. Zastro," it didn't matter, not one wit, not at this turning point in her journey.

Makeshift tables had been set up in the shady grove—planks and boards with bed sheets as tablecloths. Yana had ordered all kinds of food from the grocer in town, who came out with all the fixed dishes. The grocer had been happy for the extra cash, but he was not willing to stay and serve this odd mixture of people. So the guests pitched in and helped serve, partaking of the food as if attending a banquet for royalty. Yana felt that she and Phillipe had just been crowned king and queen.

When the wine bottle was offered, the church members politely refused, so Yana and Phillipe recorked the bottle. They would have their private toast tonight, alone.

After the food, out came the instruments, many of these had never been allowed inside the church—banjos, violins, drums, washboards and clacking bones. Soon everyone was dancing. This was one of the churches that allowed dancing, allowed joy in their congregation.

The grounds bounced with exhilaration. Yana sang an old Gypsy tune that sparked everyone into joining in the repetitive chorus—Mama and Grandmama joining too. The children had more fun than anyone. Persa and little Phillipe playing with congregation children, running wild through the fields and trees. These staid, hardworking people, who rarely spoke to strangers, opened their hearts full wide that day, pouring out enough merriment to overflow the whole countryside.

The clouds became dark, as thunder rumbled in the distance and then closer.

"If it pleases you," the pastor announced, "you may continue your celebration inside. The Lord don't mind celebrating with 'married' people in His church. Those are His favorite celebrations, as weddings honor His laws on earth."

Everyone scurried, packing things up. Yana had told them to take the leftover food home with them, all except the mountainous cake, which hadn't yet been cut.

"Hurry, take it all into the church now," Yana said, as she and Phillipe carried the cake in together. Aware of the approaching storm, trying to balance the large cake, vague remembrances fluttered—"*A storm on your wedding day*—" but she was too engrossed to try recalling further.

Soon, adults and children, all the food, were crowded into the tiny wooden church. It didn't feel crowded, only cozy.

The musicians moved into the choir space, using only the approved instruments up there. Candles were lit, and while the storm shook the world outside, the interior of the shadowy church glowed with warm moving spirits. They ate wedding cake, sang, even danced, more slowly than before, while rain pattered on the roof and lightning shot across the floor in erratic zigzag dances of its own.

"Phillipe, you always get your way, don't you," Yana smiled, dancing as closely as they dared. "You had your wedding celebration in a church anyway."

"I don't care where it would have been held," he beamed, "I am now the most happy man there ever was."

There was even a glowing rainbow following the storm. A perfect ending to the whole unconventional event.

As Yana and her new family rode away, watching the waving church members, receding sunset, fading rainbow, the whole enchanting day-- vanish into the distance, she felt herself part of a storybook ending.

But this was not the end. It was a beginning. "Once upon a time there was a man named Phillipe and a woman named Yana..." And then what happened?

CHAPTER 29

The next morning Yana packed away her Gypsy clothing in the family trunk. Now it was all carried out according to the laws of man, the laws of God. The legal certificate—Phillipe's name, her name—wedded on a piece of parchment, was placed in the trunk tray, for whomever might wish to refer to it at some future date.

She had done it, committed herself to another of her own free will. True, some of her freedom would be curtailed, but she would always retain that inner circle of independence, liberty granted her the day she was born.

Daily, Yana observed how Lulah revered Phillipe, the uplifting effect he had on her. He had never lost the ambiance that reached out to women, his healing touch, soothing words.

Again, she was thankful each had ample money; neither had to work for wages. Now the generous side of her nature was peaking and she had this bursting desire to expand her benevolence. Being a mother, wife, Lulah's caretaker, all of this new giving had brought such unforeseen satisfaction, even more rewarding than painting. Or was it just loving and being loved formed its own circle of fulfillment?

It came to her one night, lying in Phillipe's arms, looking through her ceiling window into the distant heavens, as she did when seeking answers.

"Phillipe," she said, "we must build a haven here, for women."

"Hmmm," he mumbled sleepily. "What women?"

"Any woman. All women. Whatever women need refuge, a place to rest. A retreat—for troubled women."

"I told you, I no longer wish to practice medicine."

"No, no medicine. Only healthy food, herbs, fresh air, sunshine. A month in the country, a month of freedom for impoverished women—impoverished in spirit, impoverished in hope, life. Where else is there such a place for these women to go to?"

"I don't know," he answered, but she knew he was thinking, could feel thoughts racing through his half-sleeping mind.

"Those near three weeks at the Sanitarium," she continued, "not only healed each of those women physically, but individually gave them an entirely different outlook—on so many things. The benefit of just being with other women, learning from each other, exchanging ideas. I know it changed my life."

"Because you fell in love."

"No, because I was made to think about myself in various new ways."

"We'll talk about it. Tomorrow."

And they did talk about it. All week long, they discussed the novel idea. While it was still only an idea, it gave them a new diversion to pursue, the ability to make plans they need not carry out. They conceived extreme approaches, untried concepts. Every day Yana grew more certain this was what she wanted to do, a mission she was obliged to accomplish. The zeal to carry it out manifested itself in unusual ways.

"Women need to be sick or dying, before they can be given any kind of rest, which is not really rest, only care for their ailing bodies," she argued. "The wealthy can go to spas or rest homes, but for those who truly need it, there is no place, anywhere, for them."

"And, what will I do about women falling in love with me?" Phillipe teased. She knew it could be a problem, for the women, but not for her.

"You will have me around to fend them off," she growled, "you know I can be a terror if need be."

"Yes, I know," he said, feigning fear.

Yana did have days when she was beastly, especially before her monthly. She would scream at the children, a shrill string of half-forgotten Gypsy words. Tell Phillipe to keep away from her. Lulah avoided her too. The next week, the beastliness would be dissipated. Her benevolent temperament took over again. But repentance didn't erase the previous ugliness. Yana knew their uneasiness around her was of her own making. Words—actions could never be annulled.

Luckily, Phillipe, with all his previous medical knowledge, was understanding, claiming it was common for women to undergo such mood changes at certain times of the month. "That is not your true nature," he assured her each time she fell into a rage or tears of remorse.

What if it were her true nature, what if she had only been suppressing her authentic self and when unable to do so, displayed her true persona in all its disrupting tempestuousness? How could that be, when she was uncomfortable acting so intolerably, wishing she could take back each screaming word as soon as they flew out of her mouth. She truly wished to comfort Phillipe instead of pushing him away.

Before, it hadn't mattered so much how she acted, because she had been by herself or else stayed by herself those few days. Now, she was among family and it did matter how they treated one another. It would matter, perhaps more, when she was providing shelter for women whose troubles were far more debilitating than monthly spates of bad temper.

"I've thought of a name for our new place," Yana announced excitedly one day to Phillipe. "Sanctuary Juvli."

"Juvli?"

"Gypsy word—for women. A sanctuary in the country for women. A refuge for those who have no refuge. A harbor for those most in need of help."

Once she convinced Phillipe that she was serious about the whole project, ideas kept tumbling from both their heads. His excitement and verve returned, spilling over into everything else. He was back on track, outlining plans for new cottages, maybe tents—a main dining and meeting hall, possibly even installing electricity.

They would be open from May through September, starting out with ten women, preparing for maybe fifty or more later on. The women would be charged no fee. They would share cottages, moving from one to another during their stay, getting different roommates. They would sign up for certain chores— kitchen, laundry, cleaning, garden, tending the animals. None of this would be overburdening, working mostly in groups, so they'd always have companionship.

The contributions of work had to be voluntary so that the women would be relieved of pressure. If someone just wanted to stay in her bed all day, she would be allowed to do so.

Yana also wanted to pattern it somewhat after tribal living, which had so many built-in benefits. A campfire each night—singing, dancing, storytelling. Revealing their pasts to each other. Sharing their problems. Sharing a kettle of food.

Phillipe was infusing the aspects of health—baths, food, herbs, rest, sunshine and exercise—into the plans.

"We'll design new robes, in rainbows of colors, and let the women choose their own shades, depending on how they feel," Yana suggested, remembering how fond she had grown of her garments at the Sanitarium.

Phillipe even conceded to doing massage, using his hands to soothe tired and abused bodies. He taught Yana how to do it also. They would teach the women these same techniques, so they could help one another, take home and continue what they had learned. There would be books, and crafts, and other things to take home too. Her hope was that what the women had been given so generously at the Sanctuary would be examples to continue and pass on too.

Of course Phillipe wrote up a list of rules. No alcohol, drugs, or bad language. There would be no threat of punishment, only termination—being sent home. Maybe even a chapel in the woods could be built in the future....

"And now it's time to start looking for these women." Yana wanted everything to happen so quickly, already anxious to bring it all to fruition.

"Wait a bit, and then we'll put a small ad in the paper. I'm sure we'll be inundated," Phillipe said. "And we will pick them by their letters. No time for personal interviews."

"What about women who do not read, or can't afford to buy papers?" She wanted to be sure no one was left out.

"Then we will have to inquire of the churches, social workers—those who are in touch with women of need."

It was a great diversion, planning everything, working, building. They would also used the refurbished Gypsy wagon, for excursions into the woods, maybe even overnight trips.

She could hardly wait, as the days grew colder, next June seemed so far away.

Come quickly June....

They were busy, but there were also relaxing interludes. Phillipe had been so enamored with the simple music played at their wedding that he purchased an accordion and proceeded to teach himself to play. Many evenings, melodic strains of the accordion echoed across their changing landscape.

The children loved to sit at Phillipe's feet, watching his fingers fly across the ivory keys. Sometimes they sang, sometimes they got up and danced in the grass. As winter approached, they would sit around the fireplace, singing, listening. All those she loved, gathered in one warming place. Happiness.

Yana was painting a huge arched sign Phillipe built— SANCTUARY JUVLI—with a rainbow arching across the top, as a special entrance greeting.

November, and still so much to do. They decided to maybe wait until July to open rather than force for May. They still had not put out the call for applicants. Lulah asked if colored women would be allowed, because she knew many who would benefit, but might be too afraid to inquire.

"Any woman of need will be welcome," Yana said. "And they must be welcomed by everyone else too. It will be a classless grouping."

The children were included in the plans also, helping daily. Now they would have all the aunts they might ever want.

That first Christmas together, the family went to Lulah's church for evening service. Back into this tiny wooden structure that held such precious memories of their joyous wedding, now awaiting the holy birth. The congregation sang out its praise and wonder: Go tell it on the mountain!

Yana and Phillipe had put together packages for each family, things they bought, made, and of course, food— gathering nuts from their trees, dried berries, cheese from their goats. They did not stay long, going home for their own celebration. The snow fell gently as they headed there. It had almost obliterated the lettering of the SANCTUARY JUVLI sign by the time they arrived.

They had a simple tree, exchanged gifts, telling the children it was the spirit of Christmas that had brought them their treats. Phillipe read to them from the Bible, the story of the first Christmas.

Yana gave Phillipe miniature paintings of each child, and he gave her a stained glass window he had made in secret. The pane held a large glittering star in the center with rainbow sprays of color exploding from it.

"You do have the artistic gift," Yana said with admiration, immediately going to hang the luminous work of art in the main room window. Their own special Christmas star for that night. *And for every Christmas thereafter*, she promised herself.

Spring arrived, at long last. The cottages were built, but they needed to be furnished—bedding, supplies, food. Yana spent the days painting scenes on the cottage walls, their doors. Phillipe kept busy cutting wood, stockpiling it for the campfires. Little Phillipe followed him around like a miniature shadow.

Persa stuck equally loyal to Yana and Lulah, always questioning, always wanting to know "why." She was not happy to learn that sometimes there were no answers to the "whys," other than "that is the way things are."

When the pressure and busyness got too great, Yana went to one of the cottages and just stayed there awhile, gathering herself in. She needed time alone, just as these women would. The cottages were soothing surroundings, as they would be for the new inhabitants. Love and care embellished each building—her artwork, Phillipe's special designs, reflecting the generous spirit of their enterprise.

There were setbacks, of course, frustrating days when Yana's temper flared, sometimes at the workmen, sometimes at Phillipe, and once in awhile with the children. She worked at harnessing her words, but flashes of temperament were part of her, just as passion at nighttime was innate in her nature. She was a volatile personality, Phillipe a soothing one. They balanced each other.

He was speaking out with more ease; he found he could yell back at her. Yet, by nighttime, the fuss was talked out and mostly settled. They were united by so much sharing now—words, emotions—nothing could tear them apart. Nothing.

Letters were already coming in, and it was difficult picking ten women from the hundreds that applied. Therefore, they decided to take fifteen their first session. Many might not even stay through the first month. It would all be experimental for awhile, and everything would keep evolving until they got it right. Maybe they never would. It was the same with painting—you just started over each time, utilizing what you had learned along the way, culling from your past experiences.

They offered Lulah a cottage of her own, also raising her wages. "Yana," Lulah looked uneasy, hands twitching, "I am so grateful for all you have done for me. But, you know, Ben, the young man from the church I been seeing?"

"A wonderful young man. He could come and visit you any time, in your own place now."

"No, you see, he is going to be a missionary, and we plan to being married—in September."

"Married? I had no idea." Yana hadn't even considered such a possibility. Had she been so busy with her own affairs?

"I would stay on here, until your first Sanctuary season is over. Then, I'm afraid I must be moving on, traveling—as a missionary's wife."

Yana gave her a big hug. "I'm so happy for you, Lulah. As much as I'm going to miss you, being with someone you love, is always the better choice."

"And he doesn't care that I can't have children, because he says—missionaries are always so poor, it's better not to have children. But, I'll come back and visit you, and Phillipe, and my dear sweet babies."

"You better, because no matter where you live, you're always going to be family."

Yana felt a great loss, knowing Lulah would be leaving. She had come to love, depend on her so much. Of all the losses in life, people were the only ones that truly mattered, could never be replaced. You couldn't just go to the store and pick out new ones.

Life was moving, everything changing at such breakneck speed, Yana decided they all needed a day off. A special celebrating picnic, on June third, the anniversary of Phillipe's return.

They would take the Gypsy wagon, and go on a first time journey, up along the river, stopping at a special secluded area, trees and wilderness all around. Maybe even camping overnight.

Lulah declined Yana's invitation to join them. "You and your family celebrate this special day alone. Ben and I—we have things we need to do."

Once they heard the plans, the children were jumping with excitement. They packed the night before, wrapping up little treasures to take along. Surely, they had inherited vagabond tendencies; the song of the open road was already calling to them.

Just as the sun was rising, they were all in the wagon, ready to depart. It was a merry group—Phillipe playing his accordion, Persa her tambourine, and little Phillipe fingering his new reed flute. A raggle-taggle float of music filled the air, drifting along behind them, trailing discordant notes as they meandered through the quiet countryside.

Yana was singing in her heart, racing ahead of the moment with plans to repeat the same journey every year, on this same date.

Do not make plans— Grandmama warned, shutting out the warbling of the birds. *Live only for today!*

The apparition was gone even before Yana had a chance to answer. Grandmama came to her so seldom these days.

Why was that old woman breaking into this glorious morn with nothing new, only her same old warnings of disaster?

CHAPTER 30

One year…. One year was all they had together.

Had she known—had she foreseen—Yet, what would she have done differently? Dreaming. Loving. Planning. Moving on as if their lives together would continue forever. *Foolish child,* Mama's words echoed, *grab all you want for the brass ring, but even if you catch it, you cannot hold on to it forever….*

It all happened so fast, as if the heavens decided in one moment to reach down and take away what it had so graciously bestowed. Never cautioning, never alerting them, that the dream was not permanent, not theirs to keep forever.

None of Yana's other instincts warned either or else she had been so enraptured in those blissful days that she shut out any messages with hints of foreboding.

Each time thereafter, whenever she recalled that day, no matter where she was, life stopped and dropped her into a whirlpool of thick circling time, never going forward, no way to go back, only swirling suction spinning her deeper into a dark hole with no way to climb out, nothing to hang onto, flailing helplessly into engulfing emptiness.

It had happened near the river—replaying over and over in her head, in slow motion, jumbled with the music, singing, dancing—soft ripples of June breezes.

Persa. Running toward a section of grass, finger pointing at the ground…. Phillipe darting toward her, swooping her up, crying out in sharp piercing pain that reverberated across the water, the grass, the whole earth….

Yana—running toward them….

Watching the long brown outline of the water moccasin snake, slithering back into the water. *"Drabaneysapa! Drabaneysapa!"* she screams in horror—Poisonous snake! Poisonous snake!

"Quick, tie something above the bite," Phillipe yelling, pointing to the red fang marks on the bulging vein on his bare ankle. Yana—kneeling to suck out the venom. Phillipe pushing her away. "No! Any skin opening—you will be poisoned too."

Trembling hands—Yana tying a strip of cloth, torn from her skirt, tight above the reddening puncture wound. Phillipe—screaming in agony, vomiting, swelling up. Purple blotches—erupting all over his body as blood vessels began bursting inside his skin.

The children—wild with fright, shrieking, babbling—"Dadus! Dadus!"

The ride home, or wherever it was she was speeding to, or away from, with demonic haste, went on forever. Phillipe—retching, screaming, crying out—to her—to his God—to anyone—to save him—"Stop the pain!" Yana yelling at Drom—"Faster! Faster!"—knowing there would be no salvation no matter what destination they reached.

It had already happened, no way to go back, turn around, erase this one shattering patch of time. No control of anything at this point in eternity.

Lulah and Ben ran out to greet them as they neared the yard. Yana knew—without even looking back at him—Phillipe was no longer alive. An unearthly silence shrouded the wagon—the entire world.

She felt her heart being torn from her as she turned and beheld Phillipe, his swollen distorted body—twisted face. This beautiful man, who had given her so much love. She cried out, asking to be removed from this nightmare—seeking some way to be awakened—so she wouldn't have to suffer any further dementia, wanting to go with him, wherever he had vanished to.

"I cannot live without you, Phillipe!" She screamed and howled, convulsing with grief as she held onto him so hard that they had to pry her body apart from his.

Ben was invoking prayers over Phillipe's dead form, still in the wagon—each word piercing her heart in sharp jagged syllables.

Wailing uncontrollably, Yana began to dance across the yard, across the fields, with great abandon—the same dance bereaved Gypsies did throughout the ages, upon the death of a loved one.

Weeping in despair, screaming out from the center of her soul, twirling in all directions, trying to lift herself off from the face of the earth, escape from the demons of death. Exhausting herself into insensibility—collapsing in a throbbing heap of human agony.

All the days that followed were only continuations of that initial nightmare, going in and out of periods of lucidity. Somewhere in the vagueness, she knew she had to make plans, somebody had to—final plans for her Phillipe—because he could no longer make plans for himself. Search as she might, he was nowhere to be found. How could someone just evaporate from reality—in one brief second?

She remembered deciding—Phillipe's body would be buried on their land, in a grove of sycamore trees. Reverend Moses would read the ceremony. Phillipe would have wanted some religious closure.

She had Jeremy fashion a coffin from the specially carved bed she had made for Phillipe—no longer needed. She wrapped him in the eiderdown quilt that had cocooned them together for so many memorable nights.

The day of the burial, Yana took the large shears, and cut off all her hair, leaving only a fringed black halo crowning her tortured head. She took the long quivering tresses, placing them in Phillipe's arms, folding his hands over the still shining locks. Only days ago, he had caressed them so lovingly. Now, he would have some part of her with him always.

She placed his accordion at his feet in the coffin, never wanting to hear that plaintive sound again.

At the service, as Reverend Moses thrust the first shovel full of dirt into the yawning dark hole, Yana felt her whole self dissolve away, as if she was no longer a person, but part of the whole ether surrounding her—removed completely from any sense of feeling.

"Phillipe!" she screamed, falling to the ground, wanting to plummet into the hole after him. Strong arms held her up, forced her away.

The days after were complete blurs—bobbing up to reality then sinking back into the depths of despair—as if she were riding the crest of waves that crashed her to shore and then back out again. This futile reaching, grasping to touch some dry land, while being sentenced to wash back and forth, day and night, a piece of shipwrecked driftwood, torn away from the rudder of the only trustworthy vessel she had ever known.

As she lay alone at night on her pallet, gazing up through her ceiling window, tears obliterating seeing any further—viewing past the window, into the heavens as she used to—she realized she could no longer even find her guiding North point star. Her sextant for direction had been taken away.

Vaguely she remembered telling Lulah—"Yes, we must still open the Sanctuary. Phillipe would have wanted us to."

And some distant voice—telling her, that what she did for herself didn't matter any more. Her only salvation would be in helping others, devoting her time to those in need, drowning out her own desires, which she knew would never again be fulfilled.

Her children, these needy women, they would be her only consolation, if there were any such solace left in the world.

Then within the hazy blur, something broke through, a bit of flash, a tiny spark—What? Where? The glittering star in the stained glass window, the one Phillipe had made for her—a ray of brightness reaching out to her—from him.

At that same moment, the message she had been trying to suppress rose to the surface, the picture of Persa and Phillipe in the field, so sharp and clear, Phillipe's voice telling her—*"I gave my life so Persa might live."*

By morning, she was also ready to acknowledge that her pain-wracked body was forming a new child. Phillipe's last gift to her....

Days later, as she was having the vardo wagon burned, a Gypsy custom upon death, she watched the bright floating colors heat into dancing flames, memories being charred.

Suddenly, fighting through her fog of grief, she cried out, "*Chivia!* Stop!" Some things had to be saved. Not everything needed to be destroyed. It could be repainted. The women, they might need this colorful wagon. They might need some brightness in their dim days.

But her Gypsy garb—she knew she would never wear it again. There would never be any future celebration warranting such attire. Thinking ahead, she resolved she would make one last request—that she be buried in her Gypsy gown. Then, when she and Phillipe met again, she would be dressed as the first time.

And oh, what a wonderful reunion that would be....

"Matin, chagrin, soir espok....
I am not from these parts;
I wasn't born here.
The wheel of fortune, spinning, spinning
Has brought me here...."